The Sky Below

Books by Stacey D'Erasmo

TEA

A SEAHORSE YEAR

THE SKY BELOW

The
Sky Below

Stacey
D'Erasmo

Houghton Mifflin Harcourt

BOSTON   NEW YORK

2009

www.hmhbooks.com

Library of Congress Cataloging-in-Publication Data
D'Erasmo, Stacey.
The sky below / Stacey D'Erasmo.
p. cm.
ISBN 978-0-618-43925-6
1. Life change events — Fiction. 2. Gay men — Fiction.
3. Manhattan (New York, N.Y.) — Fiction. 4. Mexico — Fiction.
5. Psychological fiction. I. Title.
PS3554.E666S59 2009
813'.54 — dc22   2008025673

Design by Melissa Lotfy

Printed in the United States of America

DOC 10 9 8 7 6 5 4 3 2 1

The author is grateful for permission to quote from "Knockin' on
Heaven's Door" by Bob Dylan. Copyright © 1973 Ram's Horn Music. All rights reserved. International copyright secured. Reprinted by
permission.

FOR BETH

Heaven was no safer.

OVID
Metamorphoses

ACKNOWLEDGMENTS

For their incomparable help and support in the writing of this book, I am extraordinarily grateful to Andrea Barrett, Jennifer Carlson, Jeanne Carstensen, Maud Casey, Laurence Cooper, Michael Cunningham, Alice Elliott Dark, James Lecesne, Elaine Pfefferblit, Peter Rock, Jane Rosenman, Anjali Singh, Chuck Strum, Patti Sullivan, and the Twenty-sixth Street salon of Michael Warner and Sean Belman.

I would also like to thank the MacDowell Colony, Casa Brava, and the Hald Hovedgaard Manor House for vital time, space, and inspiration. Thanks as well to Heide Fasnacht for the story of the starfish.

And for everything, through all the changes, I thank Elizabeth Povinelli.

The Sky Below

Prologue

YOU'VE SEEN ME. I'm the guy opposite you on the subway or the bus, I've passed you on the street a million times, I've stood behind you or in front of you in line. I look familiar, though you can't quite place me—I look like a lot of people you know, or used to know. Average height, average weight, wavy red hair cut close, khakis, intelligent expression, but something—there's something about me. Slyness, maybe, or sadness; hard to say which. An indeterminacy just beneath my ordinariness. Lines at my eyes: forty, forty-two? Graying temples. I carry a surprisingly nice briefcase, leather, initialed *G.J.C.* When I put on my glasses and open the briefcase on the subway, you see that there are lists of names inside, highlighted in different colors. Who are those people? You try not to be obvious, not to stare. Next to each name, a date, most of them recent, though as I page through the list, the dates recede, back into the last century, the 1930s, the 1920s, even.

I close the briefcase. Probably, I smile at you in a distracted way. My eyes behind my glasses look large. I hold the briefcase on my knees awkwardly, possessively. Tattooed in the triangle of skin between my left thumb and index finger there is a small, dark blue bird in flight. It heads toward my pinky and, presumably, away, off my hand. Though, of course, it doesn't fly off; it is fixed there, wings open. You notice that I am looking at myself in the dark subway window, watching my face change from invisible to visible, dark to light, younger to older, and back again, as the train moves and stops and moves again. Like an image on a loop of film, or in water, I hold, blur, hold, blur, over and over, swaying slightly with the motion of the train. You look at yourself, then at me. Our eyes meet in the window, hold for a moment, before we look away. Later, you can't quite remember my face. You remember instead the bird, fixed, flying.

1

The House

WHEN DID I FIRST stumble into the wrong grove?

My mother's house was beautiful.

I mean before. We lived on a cul-de-sac called Tinker's Way, in Bishop, Massachusetts, and behind our house were woods that were wet, or dry, or icy, or soft, depending on the season. I was a small, dreamy, very nervous boy. From the outside, our house looked as if it had been pinched out of clay. The roof tilted. The windows sat uneasily in their frames. The brick walkway to our house curved, sort of unnecessarily. It would have been easier, and a shorter walk for the walkway to have been laid straight. It was missing a brick here and there in a pattern that looked as if a tune was being picked out. At the back of the house, another brick walkway curved in the opposite direction, leading into the woods until it dissolved in leaves and dirt. There was a gate, standing on its own, connected to nothing but the ground, at the very end of that walkway. My mother put the gate there; she trained a vine with blue flowers on it to grow around the gate. One of my earliest memories is of sitting at that gate, staring steadfastly at the woods, where I was not allowed to play alone, with a tremendous sense of anticipation. I was waiting for something or someone to materialize, a monster or a ghost or a wild boar or a band of dirty, magical children who would spirit me away. I was sure that they were coming. I listened hard for them.

Inside, the bare wood floors continually rang with the sound of the three of us—my mother; my older sister, Caroline; and me—running over them, being kings and queens and tarantulas and creatures from outer space and nameless beings with one or two or three cardboard horns. We spun around the living room, knocking things over. The furniture was draped in different, lush fabrics, the endless beginnings of projects to make it all over. Paisleys, brocades, and brilliant colors of velvet. Ghostly muslin at the windows. Shells and important rocks and leaves of particular specialness in the corners of the room. Everything could be moved in an instant for a game or a show or a pageant. My mother flitted between us, her long, loose, wavy red hair like a flag we followed. Both of her parents, my grandparents, had been high school teachers; she had wanted to be a modern dancer. She had spent some time in Boston after college going on auditions, but it was our house that became her stage.

I had a sad brown bear of a father who ran a small contracting business. In Bishop, the contracting work to be had was building additions on the backs of houses, maybe an extra bathroom. I never saw my father in a suit; there was often dust in his eyebrows. He had a beard like a man from the Civil War; his jeans sagged. His hands were big. In the evenings, particularly in the winter when contracting was slow, he'd go out to the garage where he was teaching himself to make guitars. He stayed there for hours, in silence except for the barely audible, scratchy sound of his transistor radio. We didn't include him in our games, and on the rare occasion when he joined in, he was awkward; he broke things with his big hands. He couldn't thread a needle, couldn't manage yarn, couldn't glue. Eggshells were a catastrophe for him. He brought me a football, a set of little green soldiers, a magnifying glass. I put them all on my bookshelf and left them there. I did, though, like the shape of the magnifying glass, and the way it made the book spines behind it look strange and dreamy if you propped it on its side.

I didn't like war or footballs or magnifying glasses or the half-built additions he took me in the drafty truck to see. I liked to make beautiful things with my mother. When I was very small, my mother would fill the sink with ice and then, together, we'd pour food coloring onto the ice, and the blue and red and yellow would swirl, making purple and green in some places, while in other places the blue or the red tendriled down on its own, cutting a long blue path, a river or a ribbon, over the frozen hummocks heaped up in our ordinary sink. I thought it was a miracle. It seemed that she did, too, leaning on her elbows on the counter. We could do that for hours, not getting hungry or tired, staring at the treasure in the kitchen sink, pouring in the red, pouring in the blue. "Gabriel," she said, "be a maestro," and I was a maestro with my bottles of food coloring, conducting our symphony in the kitchen sink.

Gabriel, my mother used to say. *My angel.* When she said it, I really thought it was true. That's the kind of kid I was. I believed everything. In Massachusetts, Caroline was always outside, running around the yard finding things or digging holes for archaeological digs or, later, making up songs on the back porch with those two weird guys, the two Davids—we never knew which one was her boyfriend, and they looked just the same, anyway. My mother and I would be inside making things, or using little paintbrushes to paint the things we had made. She could make four dots of paint look exactly like a dog, or a dragonfly, or a bunch of grapes. I was desperate to know how she did that. I gripped my little paintbrush in my sweaty hand, trying to make my dots look like hers.

My mother draped raspberry-colored silk over my bed like a

tent, and on the wall next to my bed she nailed up a secret shelf where I could put my flashlight and a water glass and whatever treasure I was hoarding at the moment. You had to tie back the entrance to the tent with string. From inside the tent, the silk walls glowed purple-red from the lamp on my dresser. That was the sun over the desert. When I was sick, which I often was—I had strange fevers, palpitations, and buzzings in my ears; I was underweight—she would coat my chest with Vapo-Rub, turn on the lamp, close the walls of my silk tent, and read to me from a thick, navy-blue book with a crumbling spine. Her face, through the lighted silk, was even more dear to me for being muzzy; her voice was steady and low.

In that book she read from, ancient people were always getting into huge amounts of trouble with the gods and ending up being turned into trees or lizards or statues. There were line drawings in the book, illustrations of centaurs clopping through glades, nymphs fleeing bulls. A boy a little older than me took his father's chariot and burnt the earth: in the picture, he was falling from the sky with flames trailing from his feet like ribbons. Another boy fell into the sea: his hair was the waves. Gods disguised themselves as hunters and dolphins; a young woman's upraised arms were branches at the ends, birds already nesting on the branches. One of her sandals was untied.

I didn't understand a lot of it, except for the fact that so much of what happened to ordinary people seemed so random. Mortals would stumble into the wrong grove, get into trouble with Diana or Zeus, and then at the end of the story be transformed. In the drawing that most fascinated and terrified me, a young man named Tereus was midway between warrior and bird, his hair a bird's crest, his nose a beak, but his hands and body still mostly human. In one hand he clutched a sword. From the other, feathers sprouted. Peeking out of my tent flaps at the book on my mother's lap, I looked at those feathers and felt a strange thrill, as pleasant as it was unpleasant.

When my mother thought I had fallen asleep and she left the room, taking the book with her, I would stealthily touch my ribs, wondering how they could extend into wings. If my feet could fuse, my nose grow and curve into a hard, clacking bill. I was half alarmed, half enchanted by the possibility. What if I were a bird? Forever. Actually, I think that was what she wanted me to feel, then. She believed in other realms, a reality beyond this one. For her, this world was nowhere near enough. She would have loved to wake up one day and find herself a big white swan, paddling down a winding blue stream. She would have loved for me and Caroline to be birds with her, honking as we flew away together.

I seem to remember that sometimes at night my father sat outside my silk tent, too, but in the dark, late, after he came home from work. I would hear the clunky, phlegmatic sound of his truck turning off, then his foot on the stair. He just sat outside my tent for a while. I could hear his breath. He sat there, and then he got up and left, carefully closing my door, because he didn't know that the right way was to leave the door a little open so the light from the hall could shine in and keep all the dark things away. I think he sat there the night before he left. He was one of those guys you hear about but never actually know: the ones who pick up their suitcases and walk out one day. He left my mother a note: *Have to go. You keep Gabriel and Caroline. Will send checks.* He never sent any checks. Maybe one. Then my mother got papers in a big envelope postmarked from San Diego, and that was that. It was just after Christmas and we were on our own in Bishop, Massachusetts, like a boat locked in the ice. Eating Cheerios in the drafty kitchen, Caroline said, *You don't get it, Gabriel. We can't stay here.*

I said, *You're wrong*, and ran into my tent and pulled the strings in after me. I heard Caroline, in her snowboots, thump down the stairs and out the front door. She was going to go sledding on cardboard boxes down the hill at school with her big, smart friends, her black hair flying out behind her. I walked my bare feet on the raspberry silk wall first one way, then the other. I wasn't leaving that house, not ever. Then I jumped up, out of the tent, and ran downstairs. I stood at the foot of the stairs, looking at the City that all but covered the living room floor. I needed to know that it was still there.

The City was our masterpiece. We waited all year to build it every Christmas, my mother and my sister and I, out of the opened Christmas boxes and torn wrapping paper and empty paper towel tubes that my mother had saved up for the construction, plus my Legos and the murals Caroline drew of thriving citizens with lots of black hair on long rolls of butcher paper, and we had little wooden trees and rectangular colored blocks stacked like logs to make buildings or enclosures or the tracks of city trains. We began the City next to the Christmas tree, still in our pajamas, excitedly clearing a space on the floor. My mother moved the armchair out of the way. My father, in the years that he was there, usually watched for a while, then went out to the garage. Caroline would stand with her hands on her hips, surveying the bare plain of wood where the City was going to go.

"Don't start yet, Gabe. We have to make a plan."

But my mother was usually already cutting the scalloped circles out of wrapping paper that would become the shimmering cartoon forms of trees pasted onto bits of cardboard, or folding the rough origami birds of construction paper that would perch, taped, on the wrapping paper and cardboard treetops. She was small and quite thin, like the dancer she had wanted to be; she liked to go barefoot, even in the Massachusetts house in the winter. While Caroline and I argued about where the first building was going to go, my mother, in her nightgown, would be curled up with her little white feet in that chair draped in emerald-green velvet, cutting out trees and birds and lions for the zoo. She walked barefoot into the growing City, towering over all the buildings and streets, a shiny wrapping-paper lion in her fingers. I remember the hem of her nightgown brushing City Hall, which was made out of a box that said *Jupiter Telescope*. Caroline and I always built the City, but our mother populated it and made everything that grew in it. She affixed each origami bird to its treetop with great concentration and a light, sure touch.

Once the City was built, it often stayed up, winding into the dining room and bordering the kitchen, for months. Caroline and I stepped gingerly around it, not tumbling any of its buildings or houses. My mother seemed not to notice anything out of the ordinary about it, as if everyone had one in the living room: Turkish families would have minarets in theirs, Japanese families would make theirs with footbridges. Our City was American, civic-minded, happily functional. We spent one entire winter on an elaborate outdoor elevator system, with real pulleys. When the three of us packed up that house, we kept finding stray rectangular blocks and old wrapping-paper dogs and horses and hedges fluttering, half torn, in the corners of rooms and under the furniture.

Caroline said, "We should have built a City and left it here. For the new people to see."

"No," I said. I was so sure we would be back.

On that winter morning, after I sprang downstairs to make sure the City was still there, I ran, the cold burning my bare feet, out to the garage, as if my father might still be there, too, hiding. He wasn't. Instead, the unfinished bodies of his guitars hung from a length of clothesline in the gloom: tawny, curvilinear, hollow. I put my toe on an oil stain on the concrete where the truck had been before, but my toe remained unmarked, only cold. Why hadn't he taken the guitars with him? Were there already unfinished guitars hanging from the ceiling where he was going? I walked underneath the row of guitars with my arms raised overhead, just barely able to brush the lower wooden curves with my fingertips. They swayed, clicked together with a hollow sound, but didn't fall. He had left his transistor radio on his worktable. I turned it on. Scratchy, incomprehensible noise came out—a sports channel? I held it to my ear. Men shouted excitedly from what seemed like a great distance. I studied the other things he had left behind—rags, nails, the knee-high machine I wasn't allowed to touch that turned flat planks into elegant spirals of wood. I touched the machine now. It was cold and completely still, as if it had been petrified. I clambered into his workbench chair, my bare feet dangling. The toolboard was empty, dotted with a few hooks.

A bit of glossy paper protruded from the space between the empty toolboard and the garage wall. I pulled it; a creased *Penthouse* slid out. I spread it open on the workbench and slowly turned the slick, colorful pages. I knew what women and men looked like, but I had never seen women who looked like this. Smiling, they held their large breasts in their hands. They held their legs open. They licked their own big, round nipples. What were they trying to turn into? Where were the centaurs, the delicate nymphs? These women looked to me as if they wanted to eat themselves up and were trying to decide which part to start on first. I imagined my father at his workbench looking at this same magazine, and I felt myself stir and, immediately, my face burned. I closed the magazine. As I got down from his chair, I stubbed my toe on the wood-twirling machine, sending a red stream of pain into my foot and up my leg.

I grabbed his transistor radio from the worktable and carried it off, through the house and past the City, to my tent, holding my thumb on the place on the dial where he had left it. My toe throbbed. I fell asleep to my father's scratchy, incomprehensible station.

After my father left us, my mother changed. All the dance went out of her. She got very quiet and still and listened to my father's old Bob Dylan records constantly. I thought Bob Dylan sounded like a sarcastic tree stump or some kind of enchanted troll lurking under a bridge. He haunted our house day and night with his endless sorrows. We made it through the first winter because my mother's two older sisters kept bringing things over, casseroles and gloves and hats, and they must have brought money, too, though I never saw them giving it to my mother. We had to keep the heat down low, which made my nose run. The raspberry silk seemed to darken and sag with the chill that was always in the air.

I asked my mother, "Where did he go?"

She said, "To California, the creep. The coward."

"What's in California?"

"Nothing."

"Can we go?"

"No."

She put the casserole in the oven and slammed the door shut. She picked up the scissors to continue cutting out Buy One, Get One Free coupons from the newspaper, though she never did use those coupons. They piled up on the kitchen counter, week after week, like drifts of leaves, acquiring coffee stains and soap spatters.

Why is it that people get so much bigger when they disappear? When he lived with us, my father had always been like an extra planet that had somehow strayed into our solar system: rare, awkward, uncanny. He had never fit, exactly, but now his absence was everywhere, it got into everything, like the sound of Bob Dylan. Gone, he loomed. The car made an ominous noise because of him; the stray cats got into the garbage because of him; the house was cold because of him; idiots looked at my mother in the grocery store because of him and then she dropped the bag on the way to the car, spilling groceries into the slush, and then she burned her finger on the stove when she got home and was just trying to make herself a goddamn cup of herbal tea.

He was like a ghost, bent on some kind of revenge against us. A long time ago, my father had been his high school's football star and even with the curly brown beard and the loose jeans he had seemed formidable, strong. He had once run with extraordinary grace down football fields from Newton to Medford; he could hurl a spinning football for miles; he moved, my mother said, like a panther, which was also the name of his school's team: the Panthers. Even later, long after that glory, you could see the panther in him from time to time. After a few beers, he smiled a panther's smile. His eyes were blue. My mother, curled in his lap in the good years, had looked like a slender beauty to my father's beast, resting unafraid in his power. They looked famous together, then. He never knelt down to hug me; he always picked me up, lifting me high, holding me against him effortlessly. Once he was gone, I wanted him to come back, but I was also afraid that if he came back he would do us all some terrible harm, he would spring, tear us apart with his ferocious paws, claw the lining out of the sofa, sink his teeth into the curtains and shred them, shred us, before springing back into the night.

I asked Caroline as we walked home from school, "Do you think he's coming back?"

She shrugged. "Who cares?"

I started to sniffle, blinking back tears.

She stopped dead, putting her knapsack down on the snowy sidewalk. She took me by the shoulders. "Listen to me, Gabriel. You can't be like that. Things are going to get worse. We're screwed."

"How do you know that?"

"Mom told me. We don't have any money. We don't have any credit cards that work. People are suing us about work that Daddy didn't finish."

I had never exactly thought about money before, not in any concrete way, but our not having any suddenly seemed like an enormous pit into which we were about to fall, and I was afraid. My father had dug the pit. I began to cry, and then I peed myself, the hot pee running down my leg and into my sock. I cried harder as it reached my toes. I felt I might pee forever, that I'd engulf the world in pee, a yellow tide washing over everything, flooding all the cities, drowning all the people.

"Gabe, shit. Stop. Stop it."

"I can't." Panic engulfed me, made my ears hot, though it was so cold outside and the pee was already chilling my foot. I tried desperately to stop peeing, which only made me pee more. "Are we going to die?"

"Only if I kill you for being such a retard."

"I hate him."

"Take a number," Caroline said, picking up her knapsack. I stopped peeing, more or less, and we trudged home in silence. My pee and my tears dried on my skin. Why hadn't I heard his truck that night, pulling away? That truck was always so loud. I could have banged on the window, gotten everyone up.

Sometimes I imagined that my father had had another family the whole time, even when we were in Bishop, a secret family. And that they all moved to San Diego together; he finally chose. Maybe that was what my mother had meant by "coward," or maybe she meant something else. I no longer understood what she meant by anything. My father had done that, too: scrambled language. It was all so unfair, so wrong. I lay in my silk tent at night and imagined that he was with his other family, building big houses and throwing footballs to his other sons on the beach, who caught every throw in their big, meaty arms, and I hated what I thought of as *his fucking guts*. He could have his stupid fucking California family, I thought with voluptuous contempt, like shooting arrows high into the air.

But my arrows didn't matter. As the winter dragged on, we were caught in his enormous, spectral grip. It dimmed the lights and thinned the soup, burned the pancakes, turned over the garbage cans, knocked the City flat, put the needle back at the beginning of *Blood on the Tracks.*

One damp March afternoon after my father left, I was sitting on the floor in the kitchen trying to get one of my papier-mâché dinosaur's legs to stay on with more glue. It had fallen off during an epic hundred-year dinosaur war. Bob Dylan was complaining about everything on the record player. My mother, in a kitchen chair, had her back to me. The chair had an uncertain leg, too. My mother wore her hair in a long braid all the time now, like a red rope reaching down for a red anchor. Her face was bony. She had on two sweaters, both very fuzzy and bright white. I thought she looked like the North Star. She was also wearing a pair of my father's huge, old slippers with woolly hiking socks. She wore those slippers every day, big soles slapping on the wood floors.

Aunt Sheila said, "Mary, Kathleen ran into Mark the other day."

I glanced up. My mother was sweeping crumbs into a little design on the table with a forefinger. I wondered what the design was: a whale? In my memory, the light in the kitchen was yellow, but I don't know if that's possible, if it was really yellow.

"Remember Mark?" continued Aunt Sheila. "He went into the Peace Corps?"

"I remember," said my mother. "Mr. Earnest Mustache. Mr. Saltwater Conversion. Isn't he gay now? Maybe that's what happened to Jeff. Maybe he went gay." She laughed roughly.

"Mary," said Aunt Sheila, leaning forward. I could see the tip of her sharp nose. "You really have to focus."

"Well," said Kathleen in her gentle, reasonable way, "I ran into Mark at the Galleria and your name came up. Anyway, his uncle has this property—"

My mother's red braid didn't move, no part of her moved, as she said, "A property?"

"In Florida," Kathleen said. "A motel. He needs a manager."
She paused.

"It's warm there," said Sheila. "The kids can swim."

I took the dinosaur leg off, put it on again, backward. I
thought about what it would be like to be a dinosaur with a
backward leg, if that leg would walk backward on its own.

Sheila said, "I'll sell the house for you. I won't take a com-
mission. We can get you something, at least, for the house. You
might be able to break even, after they clear up Jeff's mess."
Aunt Sheila, twice divorced, was a real estate agent.

My mother didn't say anything. Her red braid remained perfectly still. After a while, she said, "Did you tell Daddy about
this?"

"Daddy thinks it's a good idea," said Kathleen softly. "Considering."

My mother shook her head. She rubbed her face with her
cold, small white hands. "And where is it that we'd live exactly?"

"There. On the property," said Sheila. "That's the way they
do it. There's a school right down the highway. Mark says it's
kind of a nice little town. You could start over."

"Jesus," said my mother, which startled me. She never came
close to swearing. "Jesus Christ. A motel."

There was a silence.

"Oh, man," said my mother.

"Mary," said Aunt Kathleen, gently.

"Mary," said Aunt Sheila, loudly, as if trying to wake her up.
"Your life is shit. Jeff isn't going to send anything, you know
that. He's not coming back. You have to think about your
kids."

Sitting on the floor, my thumbs covered in glue, I somehow had the idea that we'd be taking the house with us, that
the whole house would move to Florida with us inside, rattling slightly from the motion, like the house in *The Wizard of
Oz*. I just deleted the "sell" part. And then, since it was warm

in Florida, I thought I could put up my raspberry silk tent in the yard and stay there all the time, eating oranges. We could make the City outside, in the dunes. I thought there would be dunes.

A few months later, the house in Bishop got smaller and smaller in the rearview mirror, then disappeared. I wasn't sure if we were running away from my father, or if we should have left him a note saying where we were going. We didn't take his unfinished guitars. They went to an excited high school boy, cheap, at the tag sale. As we drove down to Florida in our old car, I noticed how everything outside was getting not only warmer but bleached, all the color draining away as we headed south. I held tight to my father's radio, the dial fixed on his station. The shouting men broke up and faded away; eventually they were replaced by a scratchy Jesus Christ, who, like Bob Dylan, was always upset.

The motel was two stories high, in a town called Brewster. The name of the motel was the Sunburst. It had a tiny pool in front. There weren't any dunes. In front of the motel was a two-lane highway, and on one side of the motel was a store called the Surf Shack. Mannequins in neon-colored bikinis waved from the window of the Surf Shack.

"Shit," said Caroline slowly.

My mother got out of the car and stood in front of the motel, her hands on her hips. I watched from the back seat, waiting to see what she would do, what we were supposed to do next. Caroline got out of the car, marched up and down the length of the motel, then went to where our mother stood and said something to her. She nodded in response. The two of them looked up at the second story, pointing. My sister pulled her black hair into a knot and came back to the car. "Come on," she said to me through the window. She was already sweating, her forehead damp. "We're here."

I wish I had never gotten out of the car. I wish I had stayed in the car until I grew up, that they had passed me my meals through the car window and maybe a comic book or two now and then. The car would have been better. Purgatory would have been better, though it *was* purgatory in a way, dim sandy purgatory by the Surf Shack. The house we had to live in—it wasn't exactly a house, more like a hived-off part at one end of the motel—was the only place in Brewster that wasn't sunny; it was dark, with linoleum floors and bad windows and someone else's television set, left behind on the dining room floor. In the shower were bars of thin motel soap, and in a closet there was a stack of thin, white motel towels. Every towel that I unfolded, then refolded, had a shadowy, indelible stain on it.

"A single man had this place before us," said my mother. "That's what Sheila said. He had some kind of trouble." She walked toward the kitchen, which wasn't really a kitchen; it was just a raised place between the living room and dining room with a stove and a sink. My mother opened the two thin, white cabinet doors, closed them again. For an instant I wondered if that single man was my father. Maybe we had luckily, coincidentally, followed him, like in a movie. Maybe he was at a diner in town, having a cup of coffee.

I went to plug in the television set, but found that the cord was cut, like a bobbed tail. Ragged bits of wire stuck out of the stump that was left. Why, I wondered, would someone do that? Would my father do something like that? But I couldn't convince even myself of my story. I had gotten so much older on the drive down. I knew he hadn't been there. It wasn't him. He wasn't waiting for us at the diner, or anywhere else. Aunt Sheila was right: he wasn't coming back. I set his radio on the kitchen counter.

"Whoa," said Caroline, walking around, making a hollow noise on the linoleum. "Whoa."

Sometimes I ask myself if it would have been different if we'd never had to move. If I would have been different. Maybe

I mean the opposite: if we'd never had to move, I wouldn't have changed in the way I did. And did the change begin in Brewster? Or before? Things have a way of flowing on, one rivulet leading to the next. I can't make it all out. When I go back in my mind, I see a gate connected to nothing, a house with a City inside, five unfinished guitars, and then all the rest, eventually bumping down to Florida like a ball bumping down a staircase. It's only in retrospect that it all seems inevitable, that I seem inevitable. Maybe it happened because we were in Brewster for such a long time, longer than I ever would have thought was possible when we got there, when I was eight. We were there so long that the house in Massachusetts started to seem like a dream, a dream of a City made out of wrapping paper where purple rivers ran over ice and City Hall was an overturned Jupiter Telescope box and lions twined themselves around chair legs. Or maybe it was always supposed to turn out the way it did. I don't really know.

What broke my heart was that my mother and my sister seemed to have forgotten the house in Massachusetts, and the City, and the symphony in the kitchen sink, to have forgotten everything that mattered. Somewhere on the long road from north to south, possibly while I was sleeping, they had let our life melt away, like ice in the sun. Instead, they were always busy. My mother took charge of the Sunburst Motel with a vengeance. She and my sister got up early every day to mop the floors, turn on the cash register, kill any snakes that needed killing. They saved change in a coffee can. They briskly washed the sand off their feet at night; they painted their toenails; they watched *The Love Boat* on television every week. Every day, I dragged myself off to the stable for broken-down nags that was disguised as Brewster's elementary school. When the teachers talked, all I heard was whinnies. At night, I lay in bed and watched the shadows moving restlessly over the ceiling: bears chasing girls in pigtails, clouds that might be ships, puffs of smoke. I tried to will myself up there, where they were, but I always failed.

Maybe it was because I couldn't make it up onto the ceiling with the bears and ships, but at the time it felt like I started breaking into houses because it was easy. Nobody locked their doors in Brewster, not back then, and I didn't even take anything at first. All I wanted, at the beginning, was to slip inside other houses, try them on, haunt them a little. I was about eleven the first time, still runty and skinny with big eyes, and I knew I could say I was lost, or fake a limp as if I were hurt, if anyone came in. I could try to pretend now that I was tired of getting beaten up, but that would be a lie. I was tired of the endless, bloody wars at school—they felt longer than any dinosaur war—of my role, you might say, but to be honest, I think I would have done it anyway. I had a yearning. And a talent for it.

That first house was a cozy house, for Brewster, with bright blue decorative shutters and a clothesline in the backyard hung with clean white T-shirts about my size. I used to cut through that yard on the way home from school, and one day I just strolled in through the open back door. I carried a paper clip in my pocket so I could quickly jab myself in the leg if I needed a little bleeding injury. But inside, not a soul was home. The air was still. Someone liked roosters and chickens: ceramic fowl lined the windowsills and crowded together on the counters. The clock was in the shape of a crowing rooster; the oven mitts were rooster-shaped, too. Inside the refrigerator was a bowl of blackberries with a white paper towel resting lightly on top. I ate a blackberry; it had a dark, slightly malevolent sweetness and it crunched at the center. The blackberry tasted like joy, a secret, stolen joy. It emboldened me. It thrilled me. It led me deeper into the house, through the small, dim, neat living room with the flowered drapes drawn against the heat, through the dining room where a porcelain rooster with cold black eyes perched in the center of the dining room table. I couldn't believe how easy it was, as if I had acquired special powers. I knew — suddenly, wildly — that no one was going to stop me.

I wandered toward the back of the house. An adult bedroom, with a flowered bedspread that matched the drapes. Next to it, there was a room with a set of bunk beds and a *Dukes of Hazzard* poster on the wall. On the dresser was a hairbrush that had a cartoon picture of flying pink ponies taped on the back. I picked up the hairbrush and, looking at myself in the mirror, brushed my curly red hair. It made me feel strange, and mean, and related. These girls — twins? — would find a strand of bright red hair in their hair and brush it away, unthinking. I liked that: being almost a part of them. A presence in the house that had just disappeared, that the people, when they came home, could almost sense, but not quite. One blackberry gone from the bowl. One strangely bright strand. They would miss me, the way the Darlings missed Peter Pan. They would wish I would come back without having met me. Or so it seemed to me as I ran one finger down the hard, unmoving feathers of the porcelain rooster. I don't know how to explain it, but that's what I wanted: to be missed, but like a dream you can't quite remember the next morning. None of them would be able to tell the others that they had dreamed of a wonderful boy, a boy with curly red hair and long eyelashes, and in the dream the boy lived there, right there in the house, but he always disappeared in the morning.

That cozy house with the roosters and flying ponies was on Dragonfly Drive. There were others, on Locust Lane and Cicada Court and Ocean Drive. I slipped into them all, whoosh, swish, then away again. It was romantic to me — dangerous, faintly pointless in the way of many dangerous endeavors, lonely. I was some sort of reverse rebel: I didn't run away from home, I ran away to other people's homes and stood around.

When I looked at myself in other people's mirrors, the world was my diorama: *Early Gabriel I with Pink Pony Hairbrush on Dragonfly Drive. Early Gabriel II on Locust Lane. Early Gabriel III on Cicada Court.* I discovered that spying on Brewster was much better and more interesting than actually living there. When I was spying and sneaking around it, the entire place took on a glow. I took on a glow. I could see that I was getting taller in other people's mirrors, house after house.

Meanwhile, my mother and Caroline were slowly becoming part of the same army, the Braid Brigade: one red, one black. The two of them marched around the motel like sentries. Caroline kept the books. You'd think my mother would have been flattened, like an origami bird on the highway, but instead she got tight and wiry. She began having long conversations on the phone with Aunt Sheila, jotting things down. The woman who had been so dreamy and impractical in our other life, before, never stopped moving now, like the dancer in *The Red Shoes.* She learned to play bridge, and began playing with a bridge club in town. She must have started in the hopes that she'd meet a new man that way, but instead she just got incredibly good at bridge. She sued my father for child support, though she wasn't sure where he lived. She licked the stamps and slapped them down, wrote FIRST CLASS on every envelope and sent them to the address in San Diego.

She drank black coffee all day. I'd see her, with her straight spine and her small feet, standing on the Sunburst balcony, drinking black coffee and closing her eyes in the sun. She refused to protect her fine skin, letting it crumple like a piece of paper in some invisible hand. It was her revenge on my father, I think. Part of her revenge. Her love. We didn't make the City anymore, or anything else. There didn't seem to be time. We were always busy. My mother and Caroline took turns telling me what to do, which was fine with me. I had no intention of claiming that place; being the hired help was great. I never let myself into any of the motel rooms to steal a look or a trinket, because by definition anyone staying at the Sunburst was beneath my contempt. I wouldn't do them the honor of breaking in.

No. I was after something else. As I said, at first I didn't take anything. I wandered around, free: no one could stop me from going anywhere, from looking at anything, from touching anything. I opened drawers and medicine cabinets, I ate things from out of other people's fridges and kitchen cabinets. I would eat one or two Fudgsicles or Pop Tarts so when the people in the house next opened the box, they'd think, *Weren't there more in here before? Trevor, did you get into these before dinner?* I ate sugar from out of sugar bowls with my hands. I stood inside people's showers and looked at all their soap and shampoo. I could hop out a door so quickly and silently that if you walked in the room just after I'd been there, you wouldn't suspect anything more than that a stray breeze had blown in the window. People going into their own houses are mostly pretty loud and insensitive, especially in Brewster. They don't think of who else might have been there. They don't imagine anything. But standing in their houses, I imagined them, in detail. I thought that sometime maybe I'd just stay in one of the houses, be there when they got home as if I belonged there, sitting on the sofa with the family dog, eating a Fudgsicle. All the dogs always liked me; I never got bitten once.

I grew, and grew. The other kids stopped beating me up; it was as if they knew that I had changed, that I got up to something bad outside of school. I think I had acquired an aura. Some of the girls at school said to the girls who could be counted on to whisper it to me that I was foxy. They invited me to make-out parties. Some of these girls' houses, of course, I already knew. I had rummaged through their kitchen cabinets, their record collections, lain down on their beds. It made me feel sweeter toward them; I got a reputation for being a really good kisser. I knew that some of the girls would have liked to go steady with me, but I wouldn't let them, which got me invited to even more make-out parties. Around school, everyone started calling me "G." When I slipped into houses, I felt like him, like G, the sly fox. A day shadow, swift, just slipping out the back door. Around the time I began to go to the make-out parties, I started taking things. Little things. Souvenirs. The kinds of things that would never be missed, that were treasure only to me. Once I slipped them into my pocket, they acquired a magic. It was as if they were all ingredients in some spell that hadn't been revealed to me yet.

The Sunburst never turned into an architectural masterpiece, but through sheer force of will my mother and sister made it cleaner, brighter, crisper, almost profitable. I was becoming profitable, too. Treasure was flying into my hands: lighters, lanyards, Mickey Mouse pins, kids' watches left on kitchen counters, cheap bracelets and earrings (I liked to take just one), and definitely any stray cash. I kept it all in shoeboxes under my bed. I'm sure my mother thought I had porn in there, because she was incredibly careful not to touch my room or anything in it. She was trying to do the right thing by me as a boy; she went into Caroline's room unannounced so often that Caroline finally got mad and put an extra lock on the door. But in that way she left me alone, so at night I closed my door and pulled out a shoebox and looked at what I called my Collection. My stash. It was almost like being in my tent again, with the desert outside.

Late at night, I would pull out some of the shoeboxes and arrange things in a particular way. If you opened each box and looked into it from above, it was like looking into a single house or apartment with the roof missing. I would move around the objects inside according to how I thought they should go together. For instance, the gold pin in the shape of a Christmas tree, with little red stones, like lights, at the tip of each branch, could be propped in a corner of the box, and then ranged in front of it, as if lolling on the floor, several of those bracelets and necklaces that spelled out names in fat cursive: *Laurie, Anne, Traci.* This was the family with the fat, cross-eyed triplets. A big men's watch was propped in another corner, yawning, its thick black leather straps undone. In the next box I might toss some shiny barrettes in a glittering pile on one side, then put in a lighter, a little stuffed ox with glittery silver horns, and one of those tiny plastic tubs of grape jelly you get in diners if you order toast: these were the hippies. I could do this for hours, loving my Collection, my glittering pile of junk, more than anything. My box village grew, and relations became complicated among the inhabitants. I whispered things to everyone, chat and various ideas and possibilities, events. I felt as if they were all my citizens, or my subjects, and I was as tender toward them as a good god.

My master plan was that when the time came I would sell my Collection and fly away. By a backward alchemy, turning gold into common coin, I could get us all back to Massachusetts. The bright gold necklaces that said *Laurie* or *Anne* or *Traci* would become the old house locked in the ice up north. I was going to buy our house back from the imposters who lived there now. My Collection wasn't exactly the City, it was more like a refugee camp outside the City; the City was where my box people—especially *Laurie* and *Anne*—wanted to go. They couldn't wait to get there. We would all go together. I felt like Robin Hood. I was stealing for a good cause, for the sake of beauty. What did it hurt the universe if a few ugly cufflinks in the shape of the American flag were traded in for something so much more important?

I might have gotten a little carried away when I started moving people's belongings around among actual houses. I'm not sure how that started. Probably something, a comb or a silk flower I had cut from a fake bouquet in another house, fell out of my pocket onto somebody's floor during an afternoon's prowl and I thought how nice it looked. It must have been an accident. Turn of fortune's wheel. Like Benjamin Franklin and the kite. Newton and the apple. G is for the gift I'd leave behind. I was always careful to scatter things casually, subliminally. I also hid various items in closets and the backs of drawers where no one would notice them: a mother-of-pearl tie clip tucked behind those big, gauzy bandages that no one ever uses in the medicine cabinet. An earring added to a box already overflowing with costume jewelry. Ties, in fact, were great for this kind of reorganizing, because so many ties look alike and most men don't know if they have three dark brown ones and one black one, or the reverse. Every once in a while I'd have a little fun and tie the relocated tie on a hanger, but if anyone ever thought it was odd, I didn't hear about it. Life in Brewster went on the way it always did: a long, hot, scrubby drive to nowhere. I moved a yellow throw pillow with red fringe. I moved a square green vase with those bubbles in the glass that look like boils, adding it to a house that already had one, so they'd have a pair. I thought that was very funny. It was just a game, an extended game. I don't know how you'd call it stealing, really. What kind of thief puts things into your house? I was making things magic, part of a spell, and then spreading the magic around, for free.

It was because my Collection had become so brilliantly vast, an underground cave full of treasure, that I went to Jenny, and then all the rest of it. She and I were in the same tenth-grade class. I guess Jenny had a gland problem or something, because she was huge and always either sweating a river or shivering in Brewster's sticky heat. She had cornered every black market in school, maybe from sheer size. Jenny was the go-to girl for everything, including all kinds of gossip, so it made sense to me that she would know where I could start fencing my hoard and begin getting us back our house. She came home to the

Sunburst with me one day after school and huffed down onto my bed.

"I'm hot," she said. "You guys own this place?"

"No." I was trying as delicately as I could to reach behind her thick legs and under the bed to begin pulling out the shoe-boxes, which she was threatening with the straining springs. "We're from Massachusetts." I pulled out my best, richest box first, the one with the diamond rings in it.

Jenny took off the lid as if she were pulling the icing off a cake and peered inside. "What is this shit?" she said.

"It's not shit," I said right away. "It's great."

"Gabe," she said wearily. She dragged her hand through the box and picked up one of the diamond rings. With a thumb, she popped the diamond out. It fell like a tiny worthless thing onto the linoleum. When Jenny stepped on it with her big sandal, not even that hard, it broke apart. "It's shit," said Jenny flatly. She yawned. "Do you have any Mountain Dew?"

I looked at the little pieces of glass on the linoleum floor. My heart and my eyes and my stomach hurt. "I stole it," I said. I tried to sound hard and careless. "I stole everything in there."

Jenny picked up a gold wedding band—one of my best finds; somebody had forgotten it on a dresser top—and bit it.

"Hey, stop!" I said. I was afraid she was going to eat it.

She took the ring out of her mouth. I don't think she knew what that biting gesture was; she must have seen it in a movie or read it somewhere. But gamely, like a pro, she tossed the ring back into the box and lay back. "It's all shit," she said calmly. Jenny had incredibly pretty eyes, indigo blue, which was part of how she confused people. Because you weren't sure what you were looking at: a mean, fat girl who had just told you that all your treasure was junk, or a pretty girl who was on the brink of getting out of the cage of her body. It was like she was enchanted, and if you brought her the right treasure, she would be free. Or maybe she was an ogre who would chomp your head off.

"I stole money, too," I said in my new hard voice. I was starting to like the sound of it.

Jenny studied me with her indigo eyes. "How much?"

I reached under the bed again, all the way in the back, and with great difficulty extricated the shoebox with the cash. I wriggled upright, took the lid off the box, and handed it to her. "Look."

Jenny pawed through the bills. "You got all this by yourself?"

I nodded. "Yeah."

Jenny held a twenty up to the light, rubbed it against her cheek. Carefully, respectfully—Jenny was no fool—she put the twenty back in the box. "So what do you want to do with all this dough?"

I shrugged.

"Want to get more of it?" She looked happy, almost relaxed.

"Sure."

"C'mere, I'll tell you."

I clambered up onto the bed beside big Jenny and we began our famous partnership. Famous, anyway, at Brewster High, which wasn't ready for one thin, pale, dreamy kid with capital and one big, fat girl with gorgeous eyes and no scruples at all. I invested in her business, she made me a partner, and we went wild. I mean wild. There was no drug we couldn't, wouldn't, get. Jenny was fearless and, in her way, protective of me. She was always the one who would take the bus to Fort Lauderdale to meet her connection, and she never told me who the connection was. She'd come back with her pink Samsonite suitcase full of goods, and we'd giggle uncontrollably, thinking of all the money we were about to make. I was great for business, because the popular girls liked me. At make-out parties, they'd reach into my pockets for the little plastic bags, sliding bills where the plastic bags had been. Jenny never said she minded that I got invited to parties she didn't. She never even mentioned it, except to make sure I had enough product to sell.

Now, it occurs to me how dangerous it must have been for Jenny, and maybe that was why she stayed fat. Wherever it was she went in Lauderdale, they'd be more likely to leave the fat girl alone, especially in that big, shapeless, cherry-red windbreaker she used to wear. I didn't sample the goods except for a little weak pot once in a while; Jenny helped herself to one magic mushroom every few months, which she savored, including the crying jag she always had the next day. She was a good businesswoman. Smart. I kind of loved her, in a strange way. I was always curious to know what her big breasts looked like, but I never tried to see them.

I don't think she would have liked that, anyway. Once I got to know her, I could see that Jenny was a funny one, underneath. Really, she was shy, like me. She collected stuffed animals, teddy bears and soft lions and Raggedy Anns and pandas. When you went into Jenny's room, a million glass eyes stared at you, unblinking. Her parents were like two thick snakes, circling each other. Jenny said she could hear them having sex at night, for hours. She liked to talk about it. Jenny's father had indigo eyes, too; he sold auto parts. I like to think that maybe Jenny's married somewhere now, with kids; I like to think that she has a business, maybe selling handmade teddy bears, called Jennybears or Bigbears (because her husband is a big, sweet guy)—something like that. Or stuffed pandas. She treasured her pandas. They were exotic to her; they made her feel rich. She made money, obviously—she took a seventy percent cut, because, she said, she was the original owner of the business—but I never saw her spend it on anything except her stuffed animals. The rest: I don't know what ever happened to it. Maybe she buried it somewhere. Of course, if it's in the ground, it's less than what it was, or rotted. Jenny didn't know about investing. I sometimes have to remind myself that she was only a high school kid, too; she seemed so much older to me, decades older.

Together, Jenny and I made money, and more money, and more money. I moved the watches and wedding rings and gold cursive necklaces into one or two shoeboxes to make room for the money, and to sort it: singles in one box, then fives, tens, twenties in others, all neatly rubber-banded. Coins in a box of their own. When I shook the heavy coin box, it made a sound like an army marching over ice. I liked to hear that on hot nights, alone in my room with my money. I liked it when I went to bed knowing that I slept less than a foot above all my neat boxes of cash. In the beginning, I fanned the money out, made designs with it, stacked it on the long side like ancient walls, but that got boring. It was how it added up that mattered. My heart was still broken, of course; sometimes I'd turn on the light in the middle of the night and count my money, full of melancholy. I knew that there was still nowhere near enough yet to buy back our house. It was like trying to build a ladder to the moon. Eventually I was going to have to do something else, something bigger, though I didn't know what.

In the meantime, I found another way to add to what was in the shoeboxes. Jenny and I were taking the local bus to the big bus station in Fort Lauderdale. Probably it was a Monday, after school; Jenny usually made the Lauderdale run on Monday afternoons. The pink Samsonite suitcase sat between us on the floor, empty, bobbing lightly. Jenny rested a hand on it. I had the roll of money in my pants. I liked to be the one to carry the money to the bus station, and Jenny, indulgently, let me.

"Rain's coming," she said, looking out the scratched window.

"Tornado?"

"Don't get your hopes up. Brewster's never going away. We're almost there." She licked her lips, zipped her cherry-red windbreaker to her chin.

I touched the bulge of money on my thigh with my thumb.

"Do you want me to come with you?" That's what I always said.

"No, asshole." That's what she always said, but she smiled, because she liked to have me ask.

The grimy bus stopped at the grimy bus station. The bus door opened and humid air swept in, breaking the seal of the interior. People stirred. I stood up first, hopped down the steps, and waited for Jenny on the hot asphalt. Rain tapped my face. She pushed the big pink suitcase ahead of her; I gave her my arm as she alighted, steadying her. I walked her through the bus station to the line for the Lauderdale bus on the other side. Short, dark ladies speaking Spanish; a skinny white girl carrying Rollerblades; old people in sun visors: Florida's finest. And Jenny, square and solid, her hair freshly washed, as always, for the Monday run, the rest of her draped in cherry-red nylon. You couldn't miss her. As the line started to move, I pressed myself up against her, reached into my pocket, pulled out the roll of cash, and slid it deep into the pocket of her jeans.

"*Mi amor*," she said, winking.

I bit her earlobe. "Hurry back, honey bunny."

"Can't wait, love bug."

"You have no idea, sweet thing."

She patted the cherry-red nylon over her heart, bent her head. "Forever," she whispered, wiping away a nonexistent tear.

I grabbed my crotch. "Yeah, baby."

The skinny white girl with the Rollerblades narrowed her eyes, looking at Jenny, looking at me. The line moved into the darkness and Jenny waved to me from the top of the bus steps, clutching the big pink suitcase. I watched as she rammed it into the overhead rack, then sat down firmly in the first seat. I blew her a kiss; she closed her fist, pressed it to her heart. The bus pulled away.

Still laughing, I wandered into the men's room to pee. I was beguiled by the tiles over the urinal — they were a surprisingly subtle, washy pale blue, with scattered rays of gold, weirdly beautiful, was one loose? — when I noticed that the man at the next urinal, still unzipped, hard, was smiling at me. He was a compact man, salt-and-pepper hair, exophthalmic hazel eyes, uncircumcised, a gold band on the ring finger of his left hand. He glanced down appreciatively, two beats too long. I stroked my dick lightly, but it was already way ahead of me, yearning, pointing. He lowered his gaze, as if to say, *You're too much. You've got me.*

I nodded — how did I know how to do that? it was as if I had dreamed it — and he quickly dropped to his knees and sucked me off. I came so fast it was ridiculous, almost embarrassing. I think I made a sound. His hands on my ass and his thick thumbs pressing against the front of my hips made me hard again and he sucked avidly, pulling, until I thought I might faint. He stroked himself, kneeling there on the filthy bathroom floor, his wedding ring flashing up and down his dick. I came again into the strong pull of his mouth and then I did stumble, falling forward. He caught me with one arm, coming into his other hand; we teetered awkwardly, off balance. "You're a mess," he said softly. "Look at you. You're a mess, kid." I leaned against him, clutching the top of his head, panting.

We stood like that for just a second, my hand in his salt-and-pepper hair, my jeans at my ankles, him holding me around my legs, steadying me as I had steadied Jenny stepping down from the bus with her clattering pink suitcase barely fifteen minutes ago, but in that second I woke up. I remembered all my dreams. "Fuck," I said. "Fuck." I said it as if I were surprised by what I had done, as if none of this had ever occurred to me before.

He glanced at the door, zipped himself up, smoothed his hair. Shaking slightly, I reached down for my jeans, pulled them up, zipped. He handed me a twenty. *"Ciao,"* he said, and he was gone, the bathroom door shutting hard and loudly behind him.

Altogether, perhaps five minutes had gone by. A man on a walker shuffled in. I began to cry helplessly, clutching the creased twenty. I hoped I wouldn't pee myself. The man on the walker shook his head as he passed me. On the bus home I kept taking the twenty out, smoothing it on my leg, putting it in my pocket, then taking it out again and pressing my palm against it. It felt like magic, like a ticket to another galaxy.

After that, whenever I saw Jenny off at the bus station, I'd stop in the men's room, and then I began going to the bus station on my own sometimes. I never told Jenny. I knew she would have felt betrayed, and then she would have wanted a cut. There was a certain balance between us; she was sensitive. Also, when it came to anything involving money, she was pretty mercenary; I didn't trust her to understand what it was like for me. The sweating businessmen, the sun-reddened guys who had just gotten off their shifts doing construction, the old guys in polyester shirts, all on their knees—like *Laurie* and *Anne* and *Traci*, like the stuffed ox with the glittering horns and the men's watch with its straps undone, I collected them, and I loved them, in a way. They were nicer to me, actually, gentler and more ordinary than you might think. They were grateful, a little sad, fervent. When I put my hands in their hair, maybe tugging a bit, I felt like Superboy. I felt as if I was giving them something special that they would take back, secretly, into their everyday lives, in the same way that I had added the vase with the bubbles in the glass, the silk flower, the ties, to the houses of strangers. That night, they would remember me when they saw the red creases on their knees from the dirty tiles; the next day, they would remember my taste; a week later, they would remember me standing by the urinal, and hope that I would be there again. As I came into their mouths, I understood why my mother kept sending out those envelopes marked FIRST CLASS: she was launching a vibe into the universe, a message in a bottle. Maybe the waves would bring a message back.

I dutifully put most of the bus station twenties into the shoeboxes, but every now and then I'd spend all of what I'd made in an afternoon on the stupidest stuff you can imagine: candy, ice cream, a super-size panda for Jenny, Pac-Man. Never anything useful, never anything I could keep. I certainly couldn't show up at home with big, glaring new sneakers; my mother and Caroline counted every penny in the coffee can and their ethical system was very rigorous. When I think of those afternoons, I mostly remember being half sick on sugar and trying to force down dinner anyway, so my mother wouldn't suspect anything. Then I'd go to my room and count my day's earnings and listen to my father's transistor radio, turned down low. In Brewster, his station was big band music. I would think: *I can do this. I know how to do this.* It was comforting.

I didn't break into houses anymore. I didn't have the time. I needed to stay focused. And after about a year, I had amassed $7,000, which is a lot of money for someone in high school. Or it was then. I began to devise some schemes. I felt the distance to the moon getting shorter. I looked at my mother and Caroline marching around the Sunburst with their checklists and thought about how much happier we would all be once we were back on Tinker's Way, how foolish and unreal Florida would seem.

Caroline, who had definitely become a weird girl, with much too much long black hair for Florida and only three friends—a strangely tall guy with a big head, a ferocious short girl with a faint mustache, and a pen pal in Sweden—was a senior, but she refused to apply to any colleges, which made our mother furious. "I plan to travel" is all she would ever say. It didn't help. She missed dinner more than once, came home with scratches on her arms, tangles in her hair, bruises on her knees. Our mother spited her by refusing to ask where she had gotten them. Caroline bought her own Ace bandage, wrapped one ankle in it; a week later, her wrist.

At school, Caroline more or less acted as if she didn't know me, but she left a note in my locker one day that said, "Gabriel — are you so sure about your new friends? Love, Caroline, your sister." For a minute I thought she meant the guys at the bus station, and I was terrified, but then I realized she meant Jenny and all of that. I tore the note up and slid the pieces into her locker. If she didn't understand, I wasn't going to explain it to her. She didn't mention it again. The point is: we all had secrets. Secret places, secret agreements, secret things we did. My mother's entire heart had become a secret, for example. What did she care about bridge? That was just her cover, like an alias. All she really cared about were her envelopes that said FIRST CLASS. She sent them out vehemently, furiously. And maybe she knew I wasn't an angel anymore, that I was a bit of a devil. Only an angel to the guys in the bus station bathroom. Taller than her by now, with red hair like hers, but the hair was everywhere, and sweat that stank. Or maybe she didn't know anything. Maybe she made Cities by herself at night, then kicked them all down before we woke up in the morning.

I didn't know. I put it out of my mind. When Caroline was in a good mood, which was rare, we'd say we were going to the beach in the next town, the bigger town with the bigger beach. But then we'd drive past it, Caroline hanging one hot arm out the driver's side window. We'd go three towns, four towns, passing one strip mall after the next. She would never tell me where we were headed, because that was part of it. We had to be like explorers in uncharted territory, although I guess I was the only one who really was; she knew where we were going. We'd pull over to some edge, or down a dirt road, and when we got out of the car Caroline would spray me all over with bug spray until I was shellacked. She was very serious and thorough, spraying me down to the fingertips, the earlobes.

Florida has swamps. More of them than you might think, some not far from the highway, some a stone's throw from a shopping mall. I thought they were a secret, too, the swamps, Florida's secret. Caroline loved them. After a while, truthfully, I knew that our expedition was always going to be into a swamp, but I pretended to be awed and surprised because I didn't want her to stop taking me. It was the one place she'd let me go with her, out of all the times she took the car and drove away. I wondered if this was where she'd gotten her scratches and bumps, but she was so careful when we were there together, so delicate, almost reverent. She walked lightly.

"This way, Gabriel. In here." And in we'd go, walking right into solid green. If someone had been looking, they'd have seen us disappear, as if we had walked into a time machine. But it was really that Caroline knew how to part the dank branches in such a way that the swamp would let us in, then close behind us. The sound of the insects was phenomenal, like they could eat the entire earth. If you walked as delicately as she did, it was almost as if you were walking on water, because the land was so tenuous and boggy. Caroline walked ahead of me, slender little flying bugs with bright blue wings studding her black braid. She stepped lightly. I stepped lightly, too, imagining that I was walking inside her footprints. We'd both be sweating in the long-sleeved shirts she made us wear, stepping in our cheap sneakers like flamingoes.

"Look." In her hand, maybe, a small damp frog with yellow spots on its back.

She put it on my palm. I cupped my other hand over it. The tiny webbed feet of the frog seemed to adhere to my skin, and its belly moved against my palm like a beating heart.

"Shhh." She leaned down and peered at the frog in my hands. "Little swamp guy. Okay, let him go, Gabe."

I bent down so he wouldn't have too far to hop.

As you go farther into the swamp, things change. You might think it's getting more and more impassable, but then all of a sudden you're in this incredible light and the water is moving. There are alligators. Caroline taught me how to spot their snouts. She told me they carry their young in their mouths. When you get in farther, some of the earth-eating insect noise dies away, leaving a thin curtain of insect sound between the outer world and this world, a world on swamp time. Swamp light is sweet. Many people don't know that, but Caroline knew it. She knew the swamp's secret: that inside the thick, dry shell of Brewster was somewhere beautiful and strange and very slow. You could imagine that inside an alligator it might be beautiful, too, gorgeous strong tendons and a translucent, cool, jade-green alligator heart. In case you ever got swallowed by one, you could look around in the jade-green light and see what was in there. Pieces of garden hose. Baby rattles. The bottom curve of the cool jade-green heart, like a sun hanging on the horizon of another planet. But when I was with Caroline in the shimmering swamp, I knew the alligators would leave us alone.

As we wandered, Caroline would tell me the names of things and all about them. "You can eat this one, Gabe." Holding up a long leaf. "But *not* this one." Holding up a leaf just a little less long, but with more of a sheen on it. "At night, you have to learn to sleep in a tree. We should be practicing."

"I'm hungry."

Sometimes she let me have one of the sandwiches she'd brought, but sometimes she'd say, "Look around. What can you eat that grows here?"

There was bark with a rich, dank taste, somewhere between old coffee grounds and sardines. There were leaves not unlike kale: tough, but nothing special. Crayfish, if you can manage to build a small fire on top of a tree that has fallen into the water, take a long time to boil right, and I always got that metallic taste from Caroline's tin cup, blackened from many fires. The boiling doesn't make the spindliness go away, but back then I thought the spindliness was interesting and I was proud of myself, eating crayfish out of the swamp. Water has to be carried in with you; you'd be a fool to drink swamp water. I never did learn to sleep in a tree, though I think Caroline could. She was good at teaching herself things like that: ice-skating backward, finding north without a compass, holding her breath for minutes at a time underwater, waking up at a certain hour without an alarm clock. I guess she was practicing for when she was far away, in places where they ice-skated backward and didn't have alarm clocks.

My hoard grew. At one point, I had close to $9,000. Think about it: if I'd invested that $9,000 in 1987, let's say in a CD with a reasonable rate—and remember, interest rates back then were high—I'd have had five times that much ten years later. I was a minor. I could have said I'd saved it mowing lawns and doing odd jobs—who would have asked anything further? Especially in Florida. They like cash in Florida. All my subjects in school—geometry, history, the tragicomedy of my French class, gym, English—were puny compared to what was in the shoeboxes under my bed. Classes were just talk. I had proof of that, mostly in small bills. For the first time since we'd moved, I felt hopeful. There was even one girl, Felicia, who I thought could maybe be my girlfriend. She was lush and happy, and she drew these great pictures of jungles. They looked like album covers. She kissed in a really deep, not shy, way. She put her hand on the crotch of my jeans—lightly, firmly—and kept it there. I thought Felicia and I looked good together, like a picture in a magazine.

When I looked in the mirror, I liked what I saw there, too. I liked my curly hair that was just a little too long, I liked that I was getting ropy in the arms and legs, I liked the way my jeans hung. I thought that if I sneaked in Felicia's window one night, like a sly fox gliding over the sill in the dark, she wouldn't mind. I thought about how that would be, so easy. One good thing about Florida is that it's generally warm at night. Every day, it was as if I was hard all the time, even when I wasn't. It was as if I had an axis, a trueness. I knew what I was doing. $9,250. $9,565. I skimmed a lot less off the top than I could have, considering how much Jenny had come to trust me. I think she might have had a crush. She even showed me which panda she hid all her money inside of (it was the one with the red hat). I hit $10,000 like a Triumph taking a curve.

Meanwhile, every day my mother paced the concrete corridors of the Sunburst like a queen pacing her battlements, wreathed by cigarette smoke. She gazed outward, like a queen looking at the sea, but you couldn't see the ocean from where we were, just scrub on the side of the highway. She looked at the scrub accusatorily, but, honestly, I still thought she was so pretty. Once, when I saw her standing there, frowning in her cloud of smoke, I almost told her. I almost brought out the boxes and opened them for her and said, *Look*.

But I didn't do that. Maybe I should have.

Instead, Jenny and I made plans. The pink Samsonite suitcase bulged with product; we expanded to the high school in the next town. We talked about Miami, how we could live there. Jenny said she was going to go on a diet. In the afternoons now, I'd go over to Felicia's huge, freezing, empty house. We drew album covers for bands that didn't exist. I unhooked her bra incredibly slowly; I left perfect hickeys on the insides of her upper thighs. I felt like I was going places, finally.

When I got home from Felicia's one afternoon, my lips sore from kissing, my mother was waiting for me at the kitchen table. Her braid was tighter than usual, as if she'd just rebraided it before I came in. Caroline was standing behind her, silent.

"Gabriel," my mother said, "I've had a call from the police."

Caroline shook her head, put her finger to her lips.

"The police?" I gazed at the ceiling. I began to sweat. Not one of those guys had ever asked me how old I was; I could say that; I got ready to say that.

My mother looked at her hands, which she had laid flat on the table. "They picked up Jenny at the bus station." I exhaled with relief. She hesitated, then drove herself forward. "Gabe, you need to show me what you've been keeping under your bed."

The universe folded in on me. "No," I said. "No, no."

She didn't care. She marched down to my room, threw the door open, and hauled out all the shoeboxes, the covers falling off as she shook their contents out onto the bed. She was a giant, tearing up the refugee camp. *Laurie* and *Anne* went flying, crying; they'd never make it to the City now. When my mother saw all that money, it was as if she had been hit. I thought she was going to be physically ill. I had left my body and become a fly. I was hovering somewhere around the ceiling fan, my spirit getting dizzy as the dusty blades circled. My small, once delicate mother stood surrounded by tumbling stacks of grubby money, her sun-baked face in her hands. Then she lifted her face from her hands and hauled off and smacked me in the face as hard as she could. It hurt: I was no longer a fly, just a cruddy fifteen-year-old boy. "You little shit," she said. "You rotten little shit." She pushed handfuls of money at my eyes, at my mouth. "For this? Are you kidding me? What is wrong with you? I didn't teach you this. You fucking creep. You horrible, horrible kid. You little bastard. You're an asshole, just like your fucking father. You're a thief."

I didn't say anything. The ceiling fan whispered, *It's not my fault, it's not my fault, it's not my fault.*

"At least I fucking did something!" I yelled. "At least I cared! Screw you! How were we ever going to get back—we can't live here. This is a terrible place. I almost had enough, too. You ruined everything. We never should have come here."

39

My mother looked at me as if one of us were at the bottom of a well, with no rope. Then, regally, she stepped through a spill of money on the floor. "You shit," she said quietly, and walked out. She slammed my door behind her, but it bounced back open, because it was a cheap door.

I stood there sweating. The necklaces, the little plastic tubs of grape jelly, the lanyards and Mickey Mouse pins, and everything else, my whole glittering plan for the future, was scattered across the floor. There was money everywhere, but it wasn't mine anymore. It wasn't anyone's.

I picked up a ten and began folding it into a small green and white bird. I hadn't forgotten how. I pointed a green and white beak.

Caroline, frowning, came to my door. "Come on," she said.

I set the money bird carefully on my dresser to guard my wrecked room and followed my sister down the hall, out of the Sunburst Motel, and into the parking lot. Our mother watched silently, expressionlessly, from the balcony as we headed to the car. She threw the keys at us over the rail, hard, metal striking gravel. Caroline picked them up, we got in, and she drove, not looking at me, one arm out the window on her side of the car. Her black hair flew up all over from the hot wind, like she was jumping down a chute. I felt as if the pressure inside my head was changing, as if my ears were popping, though the road was as flat as ever.

We went down a road I didn't know and pulled off at a place I'd never been. The ground seemed firmer than in the other swamps. The water, when I put my hand in it, wasn't cold, but it had another note in it, a darker note. The sun kept moving in and out of clouds, as if it was restless. Caroline walked ahead with slow, intent steps.

"Let's go back," I said.

She didn't reply. Usually, the swamp opened up at a certain point, and it was like being inside some sort of primordial green plum. But this swamp was narrower, the trees overhead thicker and more entwined; when I looked behind us, I wasn't certain I could find the way out. Dismally, stupidly, I wanted to go home, though I knew we couldn't go back until our mother cooled down. I wondered if she was making a bonfire of the money, throwing bills into the flames one by one. My sneakers felt heavy on my feet. My balls itched; I discreetly scratched them. Caroline began whistling "Row, Row, Row Your Boat," and it made a pretty, thin sound there in the swamp. There wasn't much to eat that wasn't poisonous in this one: a few stringy purplish leaves. I knew we couldn't live here; I didn't need Caroline to tell me that. Maybe, I thought, we could live in the car and buy food in plastic packages from rest stops. I could earn our keep along the way. Maybe we could start driving and never go back. Maybe we could head north until we turned into ice versions of ourselves, with snow for hair.

Caroline was peering at the trees. She seemed to be counting. "This way," she said tersely, plunging to the left. I followed her like a leaky balloon on a string. I felt like I was bleeding to death, invisibly.

"Okay." She stopped at the foot of one of the taller swamp trees. A brown fungus covered one side. The tree listed slightly. Grasping the trunk, Caroline began climbing it, reaching high above her head for the lowest branch. She pulled herself up, looked down at me. "Come on, let's go, Gabe. Get up here." She rested easily in the tree, as if they were the best of friends, leaning back to back. She scrambled up, reached above her for the next branch. One of her sneakered feet disappeared into the leaves.

I was afraid she might leave me here forever, keep going straight into the sky without me. I grabbed onto the trunk and pushed and pulled, scraping my arms, scraping my knees through my jeans on the wet, tough swamp bark. I followed her into the tree. She twisted ahead of me, going up gracefully, fast. When she got about halfway up, perhaps ten feet from the ground, she stopped. I made it onto the branch next to her, huffing.

"All right, Gabe," she said. She looked straight into my eyes with a raw solemnity that she rarely let me see these days. This, I knew, was her deepest secret. I squirmed, not sure I really wanted to know her deepest secret. She reached into her back pocket, took out a plastic bag, dipped her hand inside, and briskly rubbed something all over her arms, as if she was putting on suntan lotion, though it was nearly dusk in the swamp, the day's light rust-colored, shadows lengthening around us. She grabbed my hand and put something in it, a dab of some mushy, grainy stuff. "We don't have that much time before it gets dark." She closed her eyes, balanced perfectly on her branch, and extended her arms, turning her palms up. Her hands and arms were shining. "Shhhh."

Straddling my branch, I limply held up my palm with the mushy grainy stuff in it. I kept my eyes open. My sister was so weird, I thought. I wondered if my mother was crushing all my treasure, tossing it out the motel windows, putting it on the road and letting cars run over it. I imagined it shining on the asphalt, and then the crunch of the cheap metal under tires. The tires blowing out, cars skidding sideways, killing everyone inside. Bloody, whimpering dogs. The swamp smelled of life and rot, and my sister, on the branch next to me, gave off the calm alertness of a swamp creature blending into its home turf. Her crazy black hair seemed to have been pulled from the shaggy tree we sat in, and to be reaching to retwine itself among the branches. It was hot in this swamp; it seemed hotter than it had been outside of it, as if the heat of the day had collected and condensed in here, caught and held by the abundant undergrowth, waiting for the tide of night to cool it. Where we sat felt like the exact edge of day and night, heat and coolness, earth and air. The tree against my back was sticky and sharp, holding and biting me at the same time.

We were both sweating, but Caroline was smiling, a look of concentration, of will, wrinkling her brow. I tried not to think about how high up we were. I wondered if she knew how strange she was. No wonder she didn't have any boyfriends. Mosquitoes began biting me as the dusk thickened. Outlines blurred. I slapped at my arm, and Caroline again, sternly, hushed me. "Fuck you," I said, but then I was quiet anyway. The sooner she was done, the sooner we could go home and I could see if any of my treasure was left. I particularly wanted to see if any of the Christmas trees with the rubies at the top—even though I knew they weren't really rubies—had survived. I focused on how bored I was and how stupid the swamp was. Gingerly, I licked at the dab of stuff Caroline had put in my palm. It was greasy and sweet; I sort of liked it.

They weren't there, and then they were. They seemed to arrive so suddenly that I might have said they emerged from her hair, that the ends of her black hair had turned into small black birds with yellow wings, but of course that isn't true. They flew to her and landed softly on her outstretched hands, her arms. They settled on her shoulders and the top of her head. They seemed to bring a light with them, but maybe it was a sound, or a motion. Or it might have been a feeling, or something that they knew all together. Caroline smiled, winced as they pulled at her hair, keeping her eyes closed. They jostled one another, dipping at her shining hands and arms. They were the most gorgeous things I had ever seen, and my sister seemed to be dissolving into them beginning with her outer edges, undoing herself into a flock of small birds streaked with gold. Her arms were their branches; her hair was their nest; the black-and-gold birds were her thoughts whirling in the air around her. Her eyes were closed. She had become something else. She was so beautiful. She was elsewhere. The gods had chosen her, they had changed her, they were changing her before my eyes. More than anything in the world, I wanted that to happen to me.

I held out my hand with the stuff in it. I did it like Caroline, wincing, palm up, but with my eyes open so I could see what to do next. She didn't move, so I didn't move. I wanted them to cover me the way they covered Caroline, to fill my arms and shoulders with their wildness, to pull on my earlobes and tug at my hair and tell me their secrets and take me with them. I held out my hand, waiting, trying very hard not to cry or fall out of the tree like an idiot. A few of them hovered near me but didn't land, wings whirring. "Caroline," I whispered. "Hey."

She frowned, making a short sharp sound, like a bark, that meant I was supposed to shut up.

I was damp with sweat and longing and the first swelling of rage. If they didn't come to me, I might be stuck in the swamp, petrified, for eternity. My arm was beginning to quiver, but I didn't give in. I could stay here as long as she could, longer, as long as it took. I squinted, held my breath. They were so close. Caroline's branch was inches from mine. Their cheeps were like small tears in the night, shreds of bright noise from another world very close by where it bent briefly, recklessly near to ours. I wanted to see it so badly. I needed to sneeze, but held it back for fear it would scare them away. I was pierced with jealousy, because I knew now that this was where Caroline had been going. She'd been practicing with her relentless fervor, and she was way ahead of me. I knew both that she was doing me a favor, giving me her best gift, and that I might never, ever catch up.

I concentrated as hard as I could on keeping my arm steady. At last there was the tiny pressure of a bird's foot, a few quick pecks. Then gone. The memory of the unbearable brightness. My empty hand. Caroline opened her eyes and smiled at me, and in a rush, as if a bell had rung, all the birds rose and flew off, a few with strands of Caroline's wavy black hair trailing from their beaks. Caroline exhaled loudly, wiped her hands on her jeans, and pulled her hair off her forehead into a rough knot on top of her head.

44

It was over. She was her usual weird self again. I realized that we were both covered in swamp dirt and tree junk and whatever that sticky homemade crap was, that we were sweaty and filthy and bitten to shit by mosquitoes that had feasted on us along with the birds. When I scratched my arm, I scratched up skin and mud together, indistinguishable. There was bird shit on one of Caroline's thick eyebrows.

"See?" she said. She was so happy.

I nodded. I did see. And it was already gone. Leaving just a bright spot, like a mirror, in me, waiting for the reflection to return, like the sun sliding into view across the mirror's face. I knew it might be a very long time, with all the trouble I was in. Fucking fat Jenny. My fucking bad luck. But the bright spot: I could live there until they came back for me.

"Okay. Look out climbing down. That's when I always slip."

I clambered down ahead of her as fast as I could, swinging from branch to branch, monkeyish, letting go of the second-to-last one too soon and slamming heavily into the swamp dirt.

"Goddamnit, Gabe," said Caroline, making her way down carefully, back to being the peculiar nerd she was. "I told you."

I just laughed, lying on my back in the swamp. My knees and my spine were banging with pain by the time we made it back out in the dark, but I was calm.

The motel was quiet when we got home. My mother had locked me out of my room, but I didn't care. I let myself into an empty motel room and slept on top of the scratchy covers. I dreamed that my light was sliding in and out of a large darkness. The next morning, Caroline and I didn't talk about where we'd been. Our mother didn't ask. When she let me back into my room, it had been swept clean. Nothing under the bed at all.

And then the way it worked was this: since Jenny was the one going to the dealer, and since she was older (which I didn't know until then, that they'd held her back more than once, she was actually almost eighteen, her real name was Genevieve, who was she?), if I testified against her she'd be under more pressure to turn in the Fort Lauderdale guys. Which I did. And which she did. The court sent her to juvenile detention. It sent me to a different high school, where I had to talk to an ugly counselor every day for a month.

I was a man in exile.

I didn't go to the bus station anymore. I wondered if they missed me, my kneeling men. Who did they kneel for now? Who had they knelt for before?

The cops took everything that was in the shoeboxes. I'd still like to know what they did with it all, how they spent my money. I could feel the cold hollow, the invisible ruins, where the shoeboxes had once been, under me as I slept. It gave me bad dreams. To ward them off, I slipped into my mother's room one day when she had gone to one of her endless bridge afternoons. Her room was extraordinarily neat, like she had joined the army. The white sheets, the two modest pillows, were crisp as salutes on the high, single bed. The venetian blinds shone like clean blades. She had an antique mahogany dresser with curly feet that she'd refinished with great determination; on the dresser was a small, square mirror in an oak frame. The floor was no-color linoleum, just like everywhere else in the Sunburst, though hers was scrubbed until it was almost a not unpleasant beige, with maroon stars. When had she become so selective? No more paisley. Velvet banished. Though we lived in Florida, she had never saved a single shell.

I looked at my face in her small square of mirror: *Gabriel, Brewster, midafternoon.* The funny thing was that I couldn't see G anymore. G had vanished entirely. I wasn't sure if I even missed him. I was Gabe now. Gabe the fuck-up, the skinny red-headed kid who lived at the Sunburst Motel and got expelled from Brewster High for dealing drugs.

At first I couldn't find what I was looking for. I looked on the bedside table, in its one drawer—an old *New Yorker*, a stick of lip balm, and a calculator. I looked under the bed: nothing but scrubbed linoleum. I was sure it was here somewhere, and I knew it wasn't downstairs in our little tilted motel living room, where we almost never opened the curtains, since we were on the ground floor. The dresser scowled at me, warning me off. With a certain amount of trepidation, I opened her closet door. Inside, set precisely heel to heel, toe to toe, were her work shoes: black, laced, no heel, thick sole. White insoles that bore the faint impression of her feet. A slight bump on the left shoe that marked her bunion. In the back, a cheap pair of heels with silver buckles, a few pairs of sneakers splattered with paint and stain, the soft gray slippers Caroline and I had given her for Christmas that she never wore. They still looked new. A belted coat, a blue dress, a poncho the color of an Appaloosa pony that I remembered from the Bishop days, all on hangers.

I was tall enough now to reach the high closet shelf. I felt around. I was sure that, secretly, she had kept it. She couldn't have thrown that overboard. No matter the sharp-cornered white sheets, the square of mirror barely big enough to see your face: she was inside somewhere, like a spirit in a rock. I felt carefully past boxes, a phone book, a flashlight, then there it was, its crumbling spine in my hands. I was almost crying as I took it down, so gingerly, from the high shelf. I stood by the window and let it fall open, as if magically: there was the fleeing girl, Daphne, her arms twining and leafing, her untied sandal; Phaethon tumbling headfirst from his chariot with the sun and moon and stars all whirling chaotically above him; a bull (Zeus, in disguise) with a vast span of lethally sharp horns swimming in the swirling, thick lines that were the sea. Last, most thrilling, the savage Tereus becoming a bird—crest of his head, beak of his nose, sword in one hand, feathers sprouting almost obscenely from the other. The feathers were etched, cartoonish, aggressive. I turned the pages with my dirty, nicotine-stained hands, entranced.

I picked up a few stray navy-blue scraps of spine that had fallen to the floor. I wouldn't leave any traces. Although my mother wasn't home — no one was home except the spacy, pregnant girl who worked the desk on weekdays — I tucked the big, old book against my chest, under my shirt, and spirited it away to my room, where I covered it in plastic wrap and slid it between the mattress and the box spring. I didn't have any cheap porn under there; my life, as far as I could tell, *was* cheap porn. Instead, I had the book from before, the most important one, the one that told all about how the gods took pity on those who were inconsolable in their grief, turning them into animals and trees and stars. I wished the gods would take pity on me and turn me into something, into anything.

But I never did go back to that swamp, that certain tree, the one the gods clearly knew about. I told myself I didn't know where the tree was, I didn't know how to make that stuff that summoned them, which was true, but it was more like I was saving it for some other time, in a better future somewhere else. Keeping it a secret, even from myself. Instead, now, between me and the cold ruins where the shoeboxes used to be, I had this middle earth of incredible stories, this metamorphosing populace. I felt them all furling and unfurling underneath me at night, bumping into me with their horns and fins and branches, murmuring and clucking and lowing. They comforted me almost as much as masturbating did, and when I had my cock in my hand I felt them draw close, closer, closer still, drawn by the scent. In this way, for a little while every night, the gods did take pity on me. Stiffening, I was a beast in that magic bestiary, an animal, all the animals, and all the trees, and all the rivers. But in the morning I was back to being the same guy.

On my second day at the new school, I got a girlfriend with

ratty blond hair and screwed her all the time. I failed as much as you could fail and still graduate, just for the hell of it. I used the diploma for rolling papers. Jenny wrote me some terrible, mean letters from juvenile detention. I couldn't have been all the things she said I was, but I suspected that maybe I was a few of them. I wore dirty jeans and felt as if I were an old plastic bathtub toy in a condemned building, a dolphin flecked with rotting spots. Felicia called, but I didn't have much to say. My new ratty girlfriend loved to hear about the shoeboxes and the whole affair. I left out the bus station bathroom part. "I can't believe you did that, G," she'd say admiringly, and pinch one of my nipples. She thought I was some kind of sexy, foreign criminal, a hard case who left girls crying in doorways in their underwear.

I went from ropy to skinny, no longer a sly fox but a mangy dog. The ratty girl couldn't wait for me to get up enough energy to break her heart. I blew smoke rings into her brittle yellow hair like I was sending a message to someone, somewhere. Find me. Inside, I stood on the bright spot, waiting to be beamed up. *Gabriel in exile: Florida, Earth.*

But I knew we'd never get back to Bishop.

I knew the City was gone forever.

I never had enough money anyway, and now it was gone. My father had put us into a debt that could never be repaid.

Caroline was gone, too. She graduated from high school and went to Morocco for what she said was a year. I knew she would never come home again. She'd gone AWOL from the Braid Brigade; she'd flown off with the strangely tall guy and ferocious short girl; they were a flock of weirdos. My mother cut all her hair off, and permed what was left. Many of her curls were gray; the rest were a dull near-brown. With a cigarette in one hand and a cup of coffee in the other, her skin seamed by the sun, she looked like she was made of bark, like a leafless, lightning-struck tree.

We didn't talk much. In the evenings, she determinedly did her laps in the small, warm pool and then, with her short, permed, gray hair—it looked like poodle fur—still wet, she did the motel's accounts, making neat marks in the oblong book with the thick yellow grids inside. One of her FIRST CLASS missives finally came back with a message scrawled on it in pencil: *not here—moved to mexico sorry.* She tucked the envelope into the back of the oblong book and closed it, her face empty of expression. I couldn't wait to leave her. I didn't care where I went as long as it was far away from the Sunburst Motel. She had become its gargoyle, and I didn't love her anymore.

The pregnant girl had her baby, so after school most afternoons, I worked the desk. I fixed the wheels on the maid's cart. On the weekends, I went on beer runs in vans with guys at school. They thought beer was a big, questing adventure. I told them things about the ratty girl that weren't true, and when I was in a really bad mood I told them things about her that were true. I looked exactly like a guy from Brewster: sunburned, skinny, horny, and dull. Flip-flops and stretched-out T-shirts with stupid slogans on them. No one knew anything about me. I was a cur, slouched in the back of the van with my nose in a comic book. I was the best belcher, the master of the fastest, most disdainful wank that never missed its aim. God knows I had practice.

I made up a boy in my mind, a tall, smart boy a little older than me with shaggy black hair, and I thought about him while the ratty girl was blowing me. As the ratty girl worked away, I had extended conversations in my head with the made-up boy in which I explained what happened, how it wasn't my fault, none of it was my fault, and he was very understanding, he understood it all, he'd nod, and together we'd begin cutting things out of construction paper: trees, lions, swans. Then, usually on the floor of the ratty girl's family's rec room, near the pinball machine that didn't work, I came.

"Yum," the ratty girl would say. The smart boy with black hair vanished.

In that brief, pulsing instant, I always felt more alone than ever. The indoor-outdoor carpet in the rec room grated on my scalp.

At night, I lay in my bed, stroking, and became other things, making my way around my own personal zodiac. First I was a small brown swan, gliding down a deep blue stream behind a larger snow-white swan, my feet cold in the water. Then I was a twin astride a flying pink pony. Then I was a fox leaping out a window and slinking into the shadows of an afternoon. Then I was a nymph, bathed in rays of gold, worshiped by a ring of hunters. Then I was a mouse, like Stuart Little, carried by a blackbird. Then I was a great eagle with huge, strong wings. Then I was a dolphin. Then I was a dog, rutting and snapping. The black-haired boy breathed into my mouth. I was the sun. Then I wasn't.

I'd start over again at the swan, trying to figure it out, make it all come out differently this time. Twin. Fox. Nymph. The ice machine in the hall clattered. A woman laughed. Mouse. Eagle. Dolphin. Dog. Swan.

Swish went the traffic on the road outside. *Swish* went the wind where the City used to be.

2

The Boxes

IT CAN BE SO DIFFICULT, looking from tree to tree, to understand where the sound is coming from or what it means. You think you know, but the shape, the light, are different from what you've seen before. You drop an arrow, then another.

I got into exactly one college, a tiny place in Arizona called Arroyo D'Orado College. My roommate was brain-damaged — that's not a joke. Brian was actually brain-damaged, I think from a car accident. There had been a large settlement, so he had the best of everything: the latest chunky Mac, a clock that talked, special orthotics in all his special shoes. Everything was difficult for him — language, what time it was, where his body was in space — so he labored with monkish concentration just to get through the day. He was a broad-shouldered, handsome guy, and he was universally adored at Arroyo D'Orado. Students were constantly in our room, helping him study and secretly wondering if the damage had affected him below the waist as well, and what the ethics were of boning a brain-damaged guy. He probably got more pussy than anyone in the state of Arizona.

I was Brian's creepy, skinny, snide roommate. I was also the campus drug dealer. In some odd way, I felt like I was repaying Jenny for all the time she did in juvie by running the risks alone that she had run for us—driving to Phoenix to meet my sad-ass connection, a red-headed guy with a birthmark on his forehead who lived in a leaky condo and looked like I would in twenty years, post-melanoma; driving back with excessive caution; delivering the goods to various dorm rooms. There was just one other student on campus who was gay, or admitted to it. We had sex now and then. His name was Tim, he was small-boned and inquisitive, and he liked to talk about the universe: how big it was, when it started, when it would end. I didn't mind lying next to him while he talked about time and space, but I didn't love him, and he didn't love me, either. He was in love with Brian, actually, and I sometimes suspected Tim was having so-so sex with me to get closer to the earnest, damaged penumbra of my roommate. I dyed my hair flat punk black. I wore combat boots with chains around them and, on a fairly regular basis, eyeliner. I looked the part of whatever it was I was pretending to be.

One of the people on my route was Arroyo D'Orado College's sole art history teacher, a slightly burned-out guy named Bill Bauman. He was a regular, so I took his class—Introduction to Modern Art—and he showed us slides of Joseph Cornell boxes.

They struck a chord in me I had barely known was there. I sat in the darkened room, surprised. Clanking over to the art room, I began constructing my own boxes. They were like Cornell boxes, but weirder. More intense. Moving parts in some of them, and peculiar hybrid plastic animals I melted together out of kids' barnyard sets, scraps of type from books, fossils, elaborate pop-up apocalyptic landscapes, Mary Jane

candy wrappers, snot in a tiny brown vial that I'd found between the sofa cushions when my connection went to take a
leak. There were remnants of a white powder inside. I snorted
the powder. The snot was mine.

The art room was the best thing about Arroyo D'Orado; it
was a small, well-sited geodesic dome, donated by some hippie
alum who'd gotten rich making mesquite-flavored corn chips,
and at the top of the dome was an oval skylight. The gradu-
ates of the college tended to go into accounting, marketing, or
medical schools in the Caribbean, so, needless to say, the art
room was mostly empty. The easels had never been touched.
The tables were eerily immaculate. An enormous triangular
window at the back of the dome framed a picturesque triangle
of mesa, creek bank, and a cottonwood tree on the other side
of the creek.

One afternoon during the rainy season of my sophomore
year, I was in the art room alone, as usual. I was tinkering with
one of the gears from a broken pocket watch, using a tiny
screwdriver to bend the tiny brass teeth in an alternating pattern. The art room smelled of chalk and new plastic; the air
was cool, dampish; the overhead lighting was very bright. I put
down the tiny gear and the tiny screwdriver and rubbed my
eyes, focused on the cottonwood tree across the creek. I walked
over to the great triangular window and flattened my left palm
against the glass. Between my fingers, the tree twisted upward
toward the sky.

I needed a smoke. Pulling on my hooded sweatshirt, I left
the art room and went around the back of the dome. I had
tossed a few cinderblocks into the creek for occasions just like
this one; I crossed the creek block to block, teetering, pleased
to see that I was getting my chains wet but nothing else. I took
a giant step up the bank and leaned against the tree, carefully
striking a match in my cupped palm. Across the creek, through
the triangular window, the still life of my momentarily abandoned project was scattered over the art table: the tiny screw-

driver, the broken watch, the brass gears, a soda can. I contemplated it, smoking. It looked like a sentence to me, like a rebus —*screw time circle bubble.* I couldn't quite make it out. Was it a line from a Morrissey song? I squinted. No. But I felt the space between the random items on my art table as a bar of music, and I felt this odd opening in my chest, as if the smoke from my cigarette had turned white, cold, and propulsive. My left hand began to feel as if it was burning.

Down the creek, something was whirling. The air darkened, bent; it made a low, booming sound. The whirl was wrapped in rain, like the invisible man. It was the wind in the arroyo, became two whirls. Three. I could see them all rushing, keening, moving rapidly up the creek. My left hand burned hotter; my ears popped. I was afraid, but I couldn't move. The hair on my arms stood up as if yearning. The whirls, and everything around the whirls, rolled toward me, thundering my heart, my ribs, my knees. They weren't my sister's cloud of golden birds; they were bulls, they had hooves; and yet they weren't animal at all. They were something else. They were enormous, nearly pushing me over. But when they arrived, I couldn't see them. Instead, a heavy, warm rain strafed my face. I desperately grasped the trunk of the cottonwood tree with both hands; I clutched it to me like a lover. I didn't care what I looked like or who saw me. As their massiveness descended, they filled me and moved me, they pressed at my eardrums and hardened my cock. Instinctively, like a smaller animal caught in a stampede, I pushed myself up into the tree, the rain falling hard on my face, falling on my hair and inside my collar, slithering down my spine. I made it onto a low branch, climbing roughly, scattering bark with my boots as I went, digging awkwardly into the tree. My left hand was still burning. More or less perched in the tree, holding on to the trunk as hard as I could so as not to be blown into the air and lost forever, I closed my eyes. I let the whirls talk to me.

I surrendered. I took their breath into my breath, shivering, my cheek pressed so hard to the bark that I nearly became the bark, stiffening and cracking. They filled me, and then as quickly as they had arrived, they swept up out of the tree and away, leaving me drenched, shaking, and cold. I made my way down from the tree. I crossed the creek, wading right into the water, my chains tangled with mud and silt. In my wet jeans, my wet sweatshirt, I trudged back across the creek and into the dome. I took my wet boots off and the muddy chains smacked the floor. I took my soaked socks off. In my bare wet feet, I stood with my head bent in the center of the art room. My left hand was cool. I began to cry. I thought it had happened—that I had been changed.

From that day on, I nearly lived in the geodesic dome. I felt like I was in my own space station orbiting another planet when I was in there. I was full of inspiration. I brought in my father's old transistor radio. In Arizona, it got a mixed schedule of born-again rantings, call-in advice shows, and oldies. I listened for hours and hours at night as I carefully taped and glued in tiny watch gears or pubic hairs or teeth or little heads I cut out of tin, or I wrote a sonnet in an interior corner of the box in minuscule handwriting that couldn't be read unless you were a mouse hanging upside down. I made a Tereus box out of feathers and bones that I'd found along the trails outside, plus some arrows I pulled out of a souvenir Indian maiden's tiny suede quiver. I made a Phaëthon box with a half-melted Ken doll and a Hot Wheels car in it. I built the boxes myself out of manzanita that I cut into thin strips, planed, sanded, and nailed together with delicate, expensive nails I ordered from a supplier in Belgium. You can't get nails like that anymore; they had been used to make wooden microscopes. I spent all the money I earned from drugs on those nails. It seemed like a fair trade.

Praise the Lord.

You're on the air. Can you turn your radio down?

Oh, my love, my darling, I've hungered for your touch.

I assiduously collected interesting junk, filling my pockets with pebbles and wire and old nails: the stuff of transformation. I didn't care if I ended up living in a tin shed, or if no one discovered what I'd done until after I was dead; I didn't care if I became a hermit who never shaved. I toyed with the idea of dropping out of school to go live way out in the desert and do my art all day, and I almost did it. Professor Bauman said it was a great idea; he knew some great people who lived in the desert. But ultimately I decided that I liked the dome too much. No one was ever in there, and anyway, my mother was happy enough to pay my tuition. I thought of her as my first patron.

I bent to my boxes. Calluses grew and toughened on my hands in the tender junctures where I gripped my tools. Looking at myself in the mirror one day, I realized that I now bore more than a passing resemblance to the smart boy with shaggy black hair whom I had once imagined as I lay on the floor of the ratty girl's rec room next to the pinball machine. I was elated. That boy, I realized, must have been my vision of my own future.

One afternoon in the rainy season of junior year, the door of the geodesic dome opened and a girl in green wellies blew in on a gust of rain. She was carrying a small paint-stained leather suitcase with silver buckles, which she set on the floor. Her face was a long, pale oval; she had a high forehead. Her wavy hair, damp from the rain, reached to her waist; it made her look like a pioneer. Her skirt was long and shapeless. Her sweater was strange. I wondered if she had it on backward.

"Yo," she said. "Who are you?"

"Gabe."

"Are you in here a lot?"

"Yes," I said proprietarily. "All the time." I put the dried cicada I'd been moving from spot to spot in a new box all morning in my pocket. "It's not locked."

"Good," she said. "I'm a transfer. Sarah." She looked around. "Jesus Christ. Look at this place. It's like a church. Can we open that?"

I turned the crank on the triangular window. I turned it patiently, as if I were humoring her. Sarah sniffed, held out her pale, thin hands in the wet air. "Cattle. Love it."

"What?"

"Can't you smell it? There must have been a ranch here."

"Here?" I took a deep breath. Sage. Gasoline. Glue. "Cattle?"

"Yes. A lot of them, I think." She tilted her head. "Maybe there was a fire."

I sniffed again. "I don't know."

"You've felt it," she said. She heaved the suitcase onto one of the immaculate tables and unbuckled the silver buckles. "They know you're here." Inside the suitcase were myriad crumpled tubes of paint, brushes, rags, pencils. "I like cows." She began taking everything out and busily spreading it across the table as if it were some sort of puzzle, or maybe the parts of a car that could be put back together. "Let's bring them some sugar tomorrow."

"Cows like sugar?"

For the next two years, we piled sugar cubes for the phantom cattle on every surface in the room, listened to the radio, and watched the sun and the moon pass back and forth over the oval-shaped skylight. The accreting walls of sugar made me think of the bus station and how happy I'd been there on those long, humid afternoons. Though the guys I had been with generally didn't say much; there was often a wink, a shared smile, a sense of affinity. Being inside the geodesic dome with Sarah was a little like that, an echo of that kind of being together and not being together at the same time, working away in silence. I dreamed about the cattle. They jostled me, they lowed, and in my dreams they not only had a thick cattle scent, they had names, too, like minor deities.

Soldier Boy.
Louie Louie.
Michelle, ma belle.
Jesus.

By senior year, Sarah had moved on to sculpture. She built
—or tried to build, it was an ongoing epic with many verses
of lament—columns that reached from the floor to the top of
the dome, while looking as if they had grown from the dome
downward, like stalactites. I remained devoted to my labor-
intensive Cornellesque inventions, but I began to sense something else, something larger, though perhaps not literally, that
I wanted to do. I hung around the cottonwood tree a bit, waiting to see if the bulls would come again and lean down and
touch me, tell me what the next thing was, but they didn't.

Still, I could feel it humming at the edge of my consciousness, and of my ability. I didn't think it was painting, though
it had the thick sinuousness of oil paint; I didn't think it was
sculpture, though it displaced air, made gravity visible, the way
sculpture did; I didn't think it was drawing, though I dreamed
sometimes that my hand was opening and I was looking at
the lines in my palm. In the dream, my hand was burning, as
it had burned that day of the cottonwood tree. I knew that I
was meant to see something in my hand, and I tried very hard,
without success, to make out what it was. Sometimes in the
dream my hand burned away entirely as I stared at it; at other
times it became transparent, outlined in black, like a cartoon
hand. I had no idea what those images could mean, and when I
woke up I clenched and flexed my ordinary hands, relieved.

A month before graduation, Sarah and I sat in our favorite
bar, the Flying Horse, drinking Coronas with lime. It was the
beginning of April and already 95 degrees by lunchtime. My
jeans were heavy on my sweating legs; my elbow dripped sweat
on the laminated fake-wood table. The Santa whose light was
always on stood merrily on top of the bar, next to a few of his
variously wounded and tilting reindeer. A few flies buzzed

slowly around the leis and Mardi Gras beads hung around Santa's neck. The television over the bar was turned to QVC: diamonds! sparkled on red velvet.

I moved a red checker. "San Francisco," I said.

Sarah moved a black checker. "My family lives there. No way."

"But maybe I could fall in love there."

"That's a cliché." She peered at the board. "Did you steal one of my checkers?"

I took the black checker—half a black checker, actually, maybe one of Santa's reindeer ate the other half—out of my pocket and held it up. "Santa Fe."

"That's worse than San Francisco. God, you're pale. Don't you ever go outside?" She leaned over and wiped a smudge of eyeliner under my left eye. Her thumb was heavy.

I pulled away. "Cut it out. And don't change the subject. We have to go somewhere. And Sarah, this whole thing with Bauman—it's not healthy. You two have to get away from each other."

"Oh," she said, suddenly downcast, as if I were saying something that had never occurred to her. She sighed. "I know. He is such a *liar*." She twisted the lime from her beer and stabbed it with a toothpick. "He's a narcissist and an asshole."

I put the half a checker on her side of the board. "My sister's in New York. Let's go there."

Sarah brightened. She began stacking the checkers into a tower, the black and red circles making what looked like an odd vertical code. "Yes. Okay. That's it." She frowned. "Bill loves New York. Do you think I should let my eyebrows grow back?"

"Maybe."

Her hands hovered around the wavering but upright stack of checkers, not quite touching them. "Look how it balances," she said with the unguarded joy that always made me love her.

She'd gotten so thin. Her wrists were like the wrists of a child. "See that? Don't move, Gabriel. Shhh."

Think of the next decade or so as a series of boxes. Think of me as the man who was trying to get the right people and things into the right boxes. In the first one, put the three of us—Caroline, Sarah, and me—in the apartment on East Seventh Street. For me, use a Mr. Potato Head: remove my eyeliner, the chains around my combat boots, the boots themselves. Take off my flat black hair and put my wavy red hair back on. Give me a new pair of boots, Doc Martens, sans chains. For Sarah, a Little Mermaid. Give Sarah back her eyebrows (lightly, though—eyebrows take longer to grow back than you might think) and put her on the pull-out sofa in the living room, which never got really dark at night, or so she said, as she lay there awake, her mermaid's tail thumping restlessly under the sheet night after night. Mark her tears with a thin bit of charcoal; make them trail all the way down to the floor, and then out the door, like the footsteps in a dance studio. For Caroline, a paper doll. Paste a thought bubble above the frowning Caroline paper doll's head that says, "What a drama queen."

In this box, put a bike lock key (bike messenger), a paper coaster (bartender), a hundred-dollar bill (waiter, my best night, and my first one with Leo), a snippet of sweaty T-shirt (construction), a coat check (I absolutely *did not* steal from the checked coats, no matter what rumor was spread), a pink While You Were Out slip (office temp), another coaster—a stack of coasters.

In this box, write LEO and nothing else.

Pile this box with snow, the next with rain, the next with all the heat waves that seemed as if they would never break. Put the Cyclone in the heat-wave box, and at the very top of the highest curve, I'm not kidding, put Leo, saying, "I think I need some time alone," his words half carried away by the wind as the roller coaster cars crest and tip down.

Make a box of nights, and on the sides write all the names of all the bars in order of genealogical succession—the Anvil, the Mineshaft, the Tunnel, the Lure, Jackie 60, the Cock, and manhunt.com. Add pop-up line drawings on cardboard of penises everywhere, of every shape imaginable, and in every degree of popping up. Outline certain ones in gold. In the corner, very faint, one sketchy girl with small breasts and blue-tipped hair. Randy? Brandy?

In this box, put the yellowed plastic clock that is embedded—still embedded, I'm sure—in the top of the stove on East Seventh Street. Make sure to fix its hands somewhere between 4:37 and 4:38, because that is where they have probably stood for the past forty years and where they'll stand for the next four hundred. Put unidentifiable crud in the edges of the clock. In a circle around the clock, in white chalk, write *Caroline moved to Berlin today.*

Make a box of haircuts, with swatches of differently dyed colors of hair pinned up in rows like butterflies. Put a mustache or two here, too. A set of long sideburns.

In this box, put the curve of Leo's arm as he throws a stick for his big, happy black dog in Tompkins Square Park while his boyfriend (you could tell), a thin-faced guy with glasses, laughs. Add a stack of coasters in the lower right-hand corner. On the underside of one of the coasters, deep within the stack, write in a circle, in black ballpoint pen, *What am I doing with my fucking life?* Glue all the coasters together.

Make a box of Sarah and Gabriel Discuss Whether or Not Love Is Possible.

gabriel says I really think so of course it is think of
sarah says You're dreaming bud

Nail doll-sized wooden chairs to either side of the box, on lower inside corners, but paint the box's interior in a color that gradually changes from, say, black at the bottom to a washy mauve at the top. On a tiny chip that will play if you press it, include layers and layers of street noise.

Make this box a mirror.

Fill this box with things left on the floor of the East Seventh Street apartment after parties: bits of balloon, a Percocet, a bright red bangle of Sarah's, half a birthday candle, condoms used and (once, maybe twice) unused, a silver belt buckle with a mustang embossed on it, Johanna curled up in the fetal position and snoring, a field of sprung corks, part of the chocolate skull of a chocolate snowman, a page from a datebook with an unknown phone number scrawled on it, a dark plum lipstick, a cracked R.E.M. CD, one playing card (six of diamonds), a few date pits.

Why do the remnants of people's parties all look the same? That's the ironic question this box asks, though it's not a question I ever asked myself at the time. I wasn't ironic at all, except in the things I said. I loved to throw parties. There were always several cakes, no matter the occasion. I thought I was Gatsby, Pollock, Peggy Guggenheim, somebody. I threw a thirtieth birthday party that went on for a week, traveled upstate, and finally ended, at daybreak, at the Saint. I kept thinking I should go visit Caroline in Berlin and throw a party for her there so she could see how good at it I'd become, how life-changing a great party could really be. I tried to explain this to her in a letter, but it sounded wrong somehow, so I never finished it. Actually, I never wrote it, except in my mind. Put that letter in this box, too.

Fill this box with shredded pages of *The Hudson Times*, the almost-disappearing, half-assed tourist newspaper on Wall Street where I got a job as the assistant to the obituary editor, a crumbly old guy named Skip. See the pictures of the dead I found for Skip; see me spending a great deal of time cropping the pictures just so with lengths of cut-up manila folders. The pictures of the dead were like playing cards: the baseball player, the bookie, the entrepreneur, the woman who swam the Hudson in 1938. I shuffled them, filed them, scanned them into the computer and made a digital archive of them called Dead New York, or deadny.org. Toss a few of the cards—the shrewd bookie, the happy-go-lucky baseball player, the intrepid lady swimmer—in this box.

In this box, put my father's radio, still tuned to the station he listened to in Brewster. In New York, that was all classic rock. *Layla. Gloria. Angie.*

In this box, paste a cartoon of the towers falling. Sketch them with a pencil; turn the pencil on its side to make the plumes of smoke endlessly rising into the air. In another panel, sketch Sarah and me sitting by the East River on the Williamsburg side, watching those same plumes, the next day. We are quiet, two in a long line of quiet people watching at the edge of the river, which slaps softly at the ratty, junk-filled vacant lot of a shoreline. Sarah is sketching the plumes; she is turning the pencil on its side. She has kicked off one of her sandals, and the river laps at her dirty toe as she draws. I watch her draw and wonder why it is that I don't want to be drawing, why it is that that would never occur to me: to put my pencil on this moment, to feel the fulcrum of fate in the soft gray line that extends from my hand. I am uneasy about this. I look at my hand, at my palm, and it is not my hand from the dream—not burning, not transparent, not outlined in black—not at all. It is so ordinary. I look back across the river and I think: All of those people are dead. With a terrible sinking sensation, I realize that when I go back to work, which is a five-minute slanted walk away from the towers, I will be passing through a city of the dead. They will be everywhere now, too many to be cropped into place on the back page of *The Hudson Times*. Dead New York, indeed. I think that I should really quit, that it would be holy or something to quit. Sarah bites her lip, leans closer to the paper, going over the plumes she has made. I turn my palm over on my knee. If I quit, what would I do for money? I realize I don't want to go back to bartending.

In this box, paste a pay stub dated September 21, 2001, because I don't quit. Everything feels weird. New York is suspended in time: vertiginous, a necropolis, a bubble. The gods have struck us, burnt us. Some story is happening in the heavens that we can't see. Next to the pay stub, paste a scrap of *The Hudson Times*, and on that scrap sketch me slouching reluctantly down an ash-filled Wall Street with a paper cup of takeout coffee a few weeks later, as the dead, crowded on the sidewalk, still in their business clothes, look on silently, jealously. I am completely freaked out. A few days later—in a coincidence worthy of the stupidity of *The Hudson Times*—the real obituary editor, Skip, dies. I spend hours trying to crop his picture; we give him a full-page obit. They offer me his job, which I take, because the world is ending, and I didn't draw the plumes of smoke—why didn't I?—and maybe Sarah and I will move out of New York anyway. Go back to Arizona. Go live out in the desert. On another scrap of newspaper in the lower right-hand corner, sketch me at thirty-three, sitting at the old obituary editor's desk, looking out the window where he used to lean on his elbows to smoke a surreptitious cigarette, thinking that I should put it on a T-shirt: *The towers fell and all I got was this lousy job.*

In the next box, put the cake the two postmenopausal copy girls made for me to celebrate my taking the job as obituary editor. The cake is in the shape of a tombstone, with my name, date of birth, and an unfulfilled dash engraved in black frosting on the top.

In this box, write *Leo* in invisible ink, but on top of it write *Janos* in florid, purple cursive. Add a snippet of black silk from Janos's cummerbund, one of his dark hairs, my key to his townhouse in Gramercy Park, Monopoly money for his real money.

Leave the last box entirely empty. This is the box of the

enormous things I kept expecting to happen to me that didn't quite happen. I didn't have a word for what that thing, or series of things, might be. It was the same feeling I had had as a little boy, staring out through the gate connected to nothing at the end of our curving brick walkway at the house on Tinker's Way; the same feeling I had had in the swamp with Caroline when her hair turned into black-and-gold birds; the same feeling I had had alone in my bed at night in the Sunburst when I was in exile; the same feeling I had had in the geodesic dome at Arroyo D'Orado College when I felt the winds charging at me, and away. This is, in other words, the box dedicated to the gods. They had changed me once, but since then, capricious, they hadn't thundered back. They might have struck the city, but they hadn't touched me on the forehead. The years went by, box by box, my resolve to make them waning, and I was still waiting for the gods to notice me, waiting to cross their path on my way to the subway or in a kiss or in the face of a stranger. I was waiting and waiting for them to change me again, to find me. And then they arrived.

3

The City

You don't know which one is the goddess. She hides her face among the others, and it's dusk.

So there I was, in the city of the dead, on a Tuesday afternoon in the last few months of my thirty-seventh year. I looked out my dirty window at *The Hudson Times*. I could see the place where the East River bent into the Hudson River. The river was just beginning its daily transformation. The small, gray waves were tipped with light. The clock at the top of my computer screen said *4:58.*

I typed out, "May Goddard, Rockette and Contortionist, 97."

Our crammed, dilapidated offices were on the eighth floor of a small, still elegant stone building at the corner of Wall Street and Water Street. South Street Seaport was a few blocks east; the massive, cream-colored stone façade of the New York Stock Exchange was about three slanted blocks west. Catty-corner from the exchange, a statue of a benevolent-looking George Washington being sworn in as President of the

United States stood outside Federal Hall, a relic from the days when New York was the fledgling country's capital. Two centuries ago, when necessary ships had docked at the wharves along South Street, *The Hudson Times* had rivaled the many other New York dailies, packed as it was with the freshest news of tides and captains and voyages and the arrivals of mighty schooners and brigantines and, later, steamships.

Back then, our *Times* came out twice a day and was printed on massive presses on the ground floor, which these days is occupied by a chain fitness center and a Starbucks. In the middle of the twentieth century, it was still a real, thick, daily broadsheet, and everybody drank heavily over lunch at the Killarney Rose, on nearby Beaver Street. By the end of the century, the paper was much thinner and the type larger. At the beginning of the twenty-first century, we were bought out by a Los Angeles–based media conglomerate, and *The Hudson Times* became a free shell of a paper, thirty-six pages on a good day, about the size of a folded dishtowel. The content was premasticated wire stories, Hollywood gossip, LASIK surgery ads, and a dash of local color—i.e., my section, the obit page, which was devoted to dead New Yorkers and the occasional dead world leader. The newspaper existed solely for the tourists who swarmed fatly around the stores, like Banana Republic and Old Navy, at South Street Seaport, had their pictures taken in front of the New York Stock Exchange, and lined up to watch the blasted World Trade Center site slowly morph into a mall. Everyone on the staff knew that our days of being printed on actual paper were numbered; the conglomerate was eager to move us entirely online. We were a joke, a fake newspaper that nobody really read and that could often be found littering the cobblestones on Fulton Street. Soon we wouldn't be paper and ink at all; we would just be light. But by then I'd be across the river, across the place where the East River swirled into the Hudson, and inside my house with its crooked gate.

I wrote, "Goddard retired from the Rockettes in 1943. Her final show was the Christmas Spectacular. She took her last bow dressed as a tin soldier." Leaning against my cubicle wall was the scratched and fading picture of May, holding her soldier's hat with one hand and swanning with the other, bowing straight-backed from the hips. That May—she'd almost made it to a century. Barely five feet tall, with a strike-up-the-band smile, she had begun her career as "The Little Butterfly," tossed into the air in pink and purple wings off the upturned feet of her older brother and caught by the upturned feet of her middle brother in the Goddard Family Flyers, a vaudeville act that couldn't get work by the time May was nineteen. So she hoofed it. Became a Rockette, dated a few minor gangsters, married Roy, the owner of a furniture business in Queens, and died in her sleep. Roy went in 1979. I wondered what May did all those years, surrounded by Roy's furniture that slowly, then quickly, aged, just the way Roy had. Tap, tap, tap up the stairs, down the stairs, in her small, echoing house. It wasn't my house; it was May's dream house. I knew how she felt; she died there, in her sleep.

5:11. Past the close, as usual, I thought, and then the managing editor, Sydnee, IMed me: "gabe come on we need to get goddard to copy hurry up." Fuck this fucking local rag, I didn't write back to Sydnee, she of the suede miniskirts and sharp little white teeth and talking points. Fuck this fucking bullshit city of the dead for tourists that it was my job to maintain endlessly, like bailing out a leaky boat. Like painting a bridge. Even if I had known what I was doing, I couldn't have kept up. Nobody could. The city of the dead was always expanding, while the circulation of *The Hudson Times* was always shrinking.

The obit section was called, cutely, "Local Heroes," as if dropping dead were an exceptional act, and I was encouraged, via e-mail from Los Angeles, to cover the passing of "real New York types, Gabe, the kinds of colorful guys and gals that make your city unique!" I was supposed to churn out two-para-graph sentimental tributes, written at an eighth-grade level, to ghostly Noo Yawkers who had lived in buildings that had long since been torn down, eaten in Automats that had dissolved, held jobs that no longer existed: telephone operator, dance hall girl, coal and ice man. May fit the bill so well that I wondered if I had made her up. Yet there she was, faded but real, bowing in her sequined tin soldier's hat.

I typed, "Goddard ran May Goddard's School of Dance on Elmhurst Avenue until 1971, when it was bought by the Ar-thur Murray chain." Even I could write a basic sentence like that, plus the subjects were always dead. It wasn't like they could complain. The light at the tips of the waves lengthened, deepened. Across the dirty river was the open arc of the Prom-enade in Brooklyn Heights, the buildings like enormous stair steps, the dense green trees. It looked like the land of the liv-ing, where happy people pushed happy babies in strollers and walked happy dogs on good leather leashes, while where I was felt like the land of the dead. But this land of the dead had brought me to Fleur, and Fleur would get me across that river, sooner or later, and really change my life.

5:13.

I worked in ruins. I don't mean only the literal ruins of the World Trade Center, though they were not so far away and you could still come across that suspiciously thick dust in odd, overlooked places. I mean that as soon as you got off the train down there and began making your way along the wind-ing, close-set streets—as narrow and intimate as streets in old European cities—you found yourself in a kind of ruin, or in a confused, half-remembered dream, of not one but several ancient civilizations. The temperature dropped ten degrees. These blocks were always in shadow, whether it was noon or seven o'clock at night; the sun couldn't find its way in. Once upon a time, the big money guys who made the city believed they were gods, and they built their enormous banks here, a stone's throw from where their ships came in, in the style of Greek temples, or what they thought Greek temples were. Massive columns and domes modeled on the Pantheon ornamented even more massive stone buildings trying to outdo one another on the serpentine streets: Wall Street, New Street, Beaver Street, Pearl Street, William Street, Ann Street, John Street, Stone Street. The flora and fauna, kings and queens, of another time. Gryphons, myriad Neptune's tridents, the heads of gods, and winged horses were carved on pediments and grand doorway arches. On top of one bank was a seven-story pyramid that could be seen only from the sky. Reigning high above the entrance of the stock exchange was a statue of Integrity, wings sprouting from her head, guarding the kneeling figures of Agriculture and Mining on her left, and Science, Industry, and Invention on her right. All the kneeling guys were cute.

But who the hell ever heard of Integrity? Why were there wings on her head? The Roman Forum had nothing on Wall Street when it came to being history's junk heap; antiquity was an odd-lot jumble in the penumbral gloom down here, mixed and matched with impunity, half of it now covered in scaffolding as the bankers' temples were being converted into luxury hotels and condos, much of it barricaded against terrorists by wrought-iron fences. Armed guards and soldiers in blue uniforms with *Special Ops* embroidered on their collars stood, bored, in the spaces between the Ionic/Corinthian/Beaux Arts/ Art Deco columns. And all along the face of one nineteenth-century structure, in gigantic, television-ready lettering, gold as a stripper's tassels: THE TRUMP BUILDING.

The perpetual chill, the stone, the cheap gold, the chipped winged horses and old tridents and temples scattered helter-skelter everywhere: it was a tumbled mausoleum before the towers went down, and it was a tumbled mausoleum where the dead burned for weeks afterward. The smell was terrible. A few years later, in the time that I'm writing about, the sound of jackhammers was constant and construction workers vied for sidewalk space with tourists speaking German or Chinese or Dutch and the floor traders in their blue smocks, numbered badges hanging askew, loosely pinned near their hearts.

I didn't know why I was here, and I hated it, but sometimes I wondered if there had been unforeseen luck to it. Because, after all, this shadowy, jumbled place where two rivers met was the home of the money. Short, crooked, and cobblestoned, Wall Street was filled with secret entrances to the money. It's a small street, no more than a five-minute walk from end to end, and day and night it had a peculiarly hushed, suspended, inward-looking atmosphere. It was populated by men at work on two kinds of things: the buildings, which you could see, and the money, which you couldn't. Money was the aquifer. Since the destruction of the World Trade Center, the New York Stock Exchange was closed to the public, but none of the temples down there had ever really been open to the uninitiated.

For years, I saw the men (and they were, still, almost all men) from these temples smoking, hurrying, eating salad out of plastic bowls on the Federal Hall steps, wearing Bluetooth earpieces, getting into helicopters at the heliport or disappearing into the subway, but they didn't really see me. When I went down to Wall Street at lunchtime, guys my age in shirtsleeves and ties stood in line at the hot dog carts or fruit carts or pizza carts, punching at their BlackBerrys, talking on their cell phones or to one another, saying things like, "It was a motherfucker to put something in place to make the transaction," or, contemptuously, "Twenty-five million, forty-five, sixty—whatever." I stood next to them, listening, trying to figure out what was going on. I almost could be one of them, but I wasn't quite, and sometimes when they noticed me listening they dropped their voices and turned away. It was like they knew I was still a bartender underneath.

Sydnee IMed again: *what the hell are you doing move it.*
5:20. The river brightened. My heart beat faster.

I had tried to blend in. When I got Skip's job, I went to Brooks Brothers the very same day and bought a tie: brown, with a discreet black stripe. The next morning, I put the tie on for the first time. I wasn't sure that I'd tied it right, it had been so long, but immediately I liked the feel of it. In the tie, I was a different man. It made me want to smoke and drink at lunch and call women "skirts." The tie snapped things into focus: it translated reality into the most linear, boring terms. I began wearing the tie to work every day as sort of an homage to Skip, sort of a joke, sort of my cover. It became my signature, because none of the other guys at the paper wore one. To the outside world, the striped tie was a sign of respect, even deference, but to me it was so excessively normal that it meant (secretly) *I'm just kidding. Psych.*

None of the shiny pods on the new corporate management team got the joke. The suspiciously, egregiously normal tie; my slightly too long hair with the retro-ironic *Teen Beat*–esque red waves that I firmed up every morning with the help of a peculiarly effective product called Bedhead Manipulator; the slouchy way I wore my belt, my low-slung jeans reminded me whenever I looked in the mirror in the men's washroom that this wasn't really me, this wasn't my real life. My life, as such, hadn't started yet. I thought it had, but I'd been wrong. I still looked like an artist; like a bartender (and there were days when I missed that job, the thick roll of cash in my pocket at 3 A.M.); like a guy in a band, though I'd never been in a band; like a guy you'd meet in a graduate seminar in philosophy, or on the plane to Goa, though I'd never been to either of those places.

I let the tie take care of things. The tie could float to work in my place and probably no one would notice. Probably the tie would do a better job. The tie would care. The slouchy belt, the retro-ironic hair full of Bedhead Manipulator: they laughed at

73

the tie. I always wore my heavy black Doc Martens—the same ones I'd worn ten years before to clubs where I head-banged all night—with my work clothes. Still, I admit that after I got Skip's job, when I walked down Wall Street, passing the men on cell phones, the men in construction helmets, the men with *Special Ops* embroidered on their collars, the men with guns, the men getting into limos, and the men with numbers pinned sideways, as if carelessly, on their smocks, I led with the tie. I conspicuously loosened it as I walked along, as if to say, *Hard day. It was a motherfucker to put something in place to make the transaction. Twenty-five million, forty-five, sixty—whatever.* But the guys in shirtsleeves and ties standing in line at the carts still kept their voices down, murmuring numbers to one another.

Wall Street ended at the East River. At the top of the block, the street was capped by the busy, democratic push of Broadway. There, Trinity Church, straight-backed, offered its blessing, raising its delicate spires to the sky, but the spires were dwarfed by the enormous office buildings shoving in, around, and over the top of them to get close to the money. The real soul and presiding deity of this entire zone was the huge bronze bull that tossed its horns and pawed the ground on Bowling Green. Last summer, a prankster had covered the bull's head with a papier-mâché bear's head; the cops tore it off. I felt like that bull: frozen in motion. Here and not here. Perpetually ready to charge, and unable to move.

5:27. Finally. From the small, dirty window where Skip used to hold his cigarette aloft eight stories up, I watched the river turn to gold. It was that sliver of time between day and evening when the river lit up and looked like something scalloped but solid, like you could walk right across to Brooklyn on it. I couldn't see anything on the Promenade, but it seemed that there could be a big white dog there, and a man leaning against the railing holding the dog's leash. My dog would be a small spotted dog named Chester; he would have an expressive face

74

and be quick and light on his feet. When we walked along the Promenade, he would jump up to put his paws on the rail and bark madly at the air.

As if that bark had woken me up, unfrozen me, I grabbed my jacket and knapsack and ran out of the building. It was Tuesday, how had I forgotten? Visiting day. "Coffee!" I yelled into Sydnee's office on the way out. I hurled myself into the elevator and up the darkening curve of Wall Street, past the benevolent figure of George Washington, past the exchange, past the earnest, lacy church. The carts were folding themselves up for the day, getting ready to drive off. Though everything was cleaned up these days, though the ash from the attack was gone, the windows replaced, the smell long since dissipated, I felt as if I was being watched by the dead, that they clung to the corners of the buildings, sought in vain for their own reflections in store windows. They liked sweat; their presence was thicker in the summer. It made me glad winter was coming. The wind ruffled my hair; I chased it down the subway, where wind from an oncoming train rushed up. The wind that came to meet me was surprisingly warm, intimate, like a baby giant's breath. Almost a whirl, but not really.

I pushed onto the train, one of the new silver ones with the narrow blue seats. A woman in a pink pashmina shawl jumped out of her seat as I was getting on, so I nabbed it. A few stops later, the train lurched and puffed to a stop under the river. In the silence, a fat man resolutely read his *New York Post*, legs spread, taking up two or three of the concave blue spaces. A baby slept in a stroller; a young Hispanic woman standing by a pole in the middle of the car held the stroller's handles, glaring at the fat man, who pretended not to notice. Above their heads were oblong cardboard advertisements for bunion surgery and English lessons, a flyer offering the services of a psychic named Teresa, a poem by Ezra Pound, a photo of a glamorous Scotch bottle, and an ad trumpeting the most recent book

in the wildly best-selling *Stolen* series by Fleur Girard; this one
was *Stolen Blossoms*. Miranda, Leah, Natasha, Anna: each young
woman's face was embedded in a holographic flower. Together
they formed a shimmering constellation, a sisterhood of abuse
and victory, hovering near the ceiling of the N train. I smiled
to myself, knowing my smile was inscrutable to anyone else on
the train. They couldn't see my money spring, although it was
right there in plain sight.

The only people talking were two pale, limpid guys in their
twenties with pierced tongues and torn, low-slung, skinny
jeans, slouching by the dark door at the end of the car. One of
them was saying, ". . . from the gym . . . an ostrich." I caught
a glimpse of myself in one of the car's darkened windows, su-
perimposed over a bit of shaggy tunnel wall. In the window, I
looked to myself like a watercolor, like you could put your hand
right through me. *Gabriel, thirty-seven, somewhere underneath
the East River.* A fairly good-looking guy with sparky, longish
hair in a suit jacket and backpack, no briefcase, but wearing a
brown tie with black stripes that his father might have worn, if
he had had a father. Though I'd never seen my father in a tie.
He must have been about the age I was now when he walked
out on us. Where did he go? Was the river above me still gold,
or had it turned to black?

As the train sat suspended underground, I wondered, just
for a heartbeat, what was going to become of me. It occurred
to me that I couldn't exactly say how all my time in New York
had gone by so far. All I knew was that every day I was trying.
Looking up at the plucky, unsinkable *Stolen* girls in their stars,
though, I wondered if maybe I had drifted. Rallying, I thought
that my girl May had probably caught glimpses of herself, too,
in windows like this one. May had ridden these trains. She
had been a young woman, then an old one, then quite an old
one, getting smaller and smaller in these dark tunnels. She had
lugged her life around these subway cars like all of us, like the

woman with the pink pashmina shawl, like the baby with his florid baby dreams, like the guys with their ostrich. She had held her sequined soldier's hat in a box on her lap on the way to Radio City. May would have drawn herself up to her full five feet. Shoulders back. Chin up. March. I squared my shoulders and reminded myself that there was still time, plenty of time, everything would turn out fine, I had a lot going for me. It wasn't like I lived in the city of the dead. I just worked there, for now. The train shuddered and lurched on.

I got off at Clark Street and came up through the St. George Hotel. It was actually condos, but the sign remained, as if the hotel were a shell, a portal. I went up through the St. George Hotel that wasn't a hotel anymore, and there I was on the other side, in the land of the living. The sun, I saw with relief, hadn't set yet. From Clark Street I could just about see the river, but more important, I could feel it. I could see the big sky over the East River at the end of the leafy block, and the way the street seemed to bend imperceptibly toward that expanse. The people on the street looked brighter because of the light from the big sky. The fall afternoon was warm. I took off my jacket and loosened my tie.

On Clark Street, birds were singing, but otherwise the block had the muffled, languorous feeling you get in Manhattan only at four in the morning. It was all brownstones or Victorians on this stretch. The light was a strong amber that gave all the colors extra depth, as if they were made of thick oil paint. A heavyset woman with curly gray and blond hair, changing a light bulb in the black iron lamp in her yard, smiled at me as I walked by. I ambled along, down Henry Street. I passed a yellow house, a blue house, a gray house, all with stoops. The people on the stoops of the yellow house and the blue house next door to it were laughing together, their front doors open to catch the last of the season's warmth. A man held a plump dachshund, standing on its hind legs, in his lap, one hand on the dachshund's round belly. The toenails of one of the women were painted a strong, shiny red. A hot-pink tricycle with pink and purple streamers dangling from the handlebars sat by itself in the middle of the sidewalk.

I passed a small, nondescript alley incongruously called Love Lane, then turned down Pineapple Street. It was so fanciful, like something out of a children's book. *And they all lived happily ever after on Pineapple Street.* It was even quieter on Pineapple Street than on Clark Street; it was still as a mews. Halfway down Pineapple Street, I stopped to have a smoke. I noticed that there was a scaly red patch, about the size of a quarter, in the crook of my right arm. It itched. I scratched it. Tapping out a cigarette, I glanced, as if casually, at the house across the street. My house. For one irrational moment, I was gripped by anxiety, but then there it was, as always. My house.

The house wasn't markedly different from the others of its kind on Hicks Street or Joralemon Street or Cranberry Street, or any of the others in Brooklyn Heights, or Park Slope, or Cobble Hill. It wasn't a brownstone. It was wood-frame, three stories tall, faintly—very faintly—Victorian. It was painted green. There were houses that were grander, more embellished, stranger. The house, in fact, was far from perfect. It was too skinny. It slanted a bit to one side; its porch looked tenuous, scruffy. On top of the roof was a lacy widow's walk, painted gray. The peak of a skylight was just visible on the roof as well. There was a section missing on the widow's walk (did a widow plunge over the edge?) that had been badly filled in with an unpainted two-by-four—it looked like a wooden leg. Under the widow's walk, on the third story, there was a row of windows that were shorter than the windows on the first and second floors; just below the roofline, between two of the short windows, was a round, black metal plate with the raised shape of an anchor, and below the anchor, also raised, was the date 1853. In front of the house on Pineapple Street was a wrought-iron gate, and around the gate twined a vine of blue flowers, just like on Tinker's Way in Bishop. That gate—if the blue flowers twined around it had actually spoken when I first spotted them a few years back, on my way to a yard sale for box treasure, they couldn't have called my name more loudly. *Old friend*, they said. *Old friend.*

A nice African-American family lived in that house. A mother with long dreadlocks, a square-faced father, and a tawny girl of seven or eight with loosely kinky brownish-blackish hair and blue eyes. The little girl was generally dressed in many colors, many layers; her expression tended toward the grave. It had always been that way, even when she was a toddler. She was growing up so fast. The name of the family was Fisher, and, as if in homage to this name, on the heavy green door was a brass knocker in the shape of a fish, tail up. The garden in front of the house was modest: a few pansies, a bit of purplish ground cover. As I say, the house was far from perfect, and apart from its imperfections it was fairly ordinary. Its charm—which was almost certainly apparent only to me—lay in the indefinably insouciant way it sat on its little plot of ground, the subtly pleasing space between the windows, the particular broadness of the front steps. It had a soul. I loved that house. I just did. Seeing it was like seeing my own face in the mirror: familiar, inevitable, flawed, reassuring, sublime. The old glass in the parlor floor windows looked like still lakes. I couldn't believe they hadn't replaced that two-by-four. Maybe the square-faced father had been busy at the office.

No matter. I breathed in the umber air on Pineapple Street, breathed it in deeply. Clearly, the Fishers weren't home right now, but they would be home soon. They would be making dinner, telling one another about their day, watching a little television. The father would be thinking, for the hundredth time, *I really need to fix that spot on the widow's walk. Saturday.* The mother would be asking the daughter if she'd done her homework. The daughter would be skipping in the living room. (She would skip with a serious expression.) I was quite respectful toward the Fishers; I had never crossed the street, but always stayed, invisible hat in hand, leaning against the lamppost, smoking just one cigarette, getting one good, long hit of the house. On this Tuesday, feeling infinitely better at the sight of it, I finished my cigarette, stubbed it out on the curb, and turned away.

7:03. Back at the half-empty office, I wrote that May was crowned Miss Rockette of 1939 and a few other highlights and sent the obit off to copy. *Click.* The Miss Rockette part and several of the other highlights weren't true, but the fact checker—we had only one, cost cuts, and we weren't so heavy on facts anyway—was usually so tweaked on triple espressos from the Starbucks downstairs that he confirmed everything in a manic rush to get through as many stories as he could in the shortest possible time. He never questioned any of my extra sentences, overwhelmed as he always was with anxiety about closing on time, though why he thought that it mattered if we closed on time, or even existed, was beyond me. We all had ways of convincing ourselves that the paper wasn't a fraud, that what we did was necessary, that we weren't about to be erased altogether; adding a few extra medals here and there was mine.

Sometimes I wished those medals, like the Cowardly Lion's badge of courage, could convince me that I still cared. Sometimes when I walked past the frozen bull, I remembered the three whirlwinds that had rushed up the creek toward me and filled my ears, I remembered my father, I remembered the City rising from the living room floor in Bishop. Sometimes there was a whisper, a rustling of leaves, when I was in my apartment looking at what I called my art wall. I'd never been able to afford separate studio space, so when Caroline moved out eleven years ago, I ripped out the shitty cabinets on what I could see was a pretty good, pretty big wall in the ratty kitchen. I went to the lumber yard on Avenue D and got eight six-foot-long pieces of plywood, brackets, runners, thick screws, and plastic anchors. I hung the eight shelves, floor to ceiling. On the shelves I put my precious Belgian nails, my tiny jars of paint, my hammer and cracked screwdriver and needle-nose pliers, my stash of manzanita, wire and glue, and all sorts of treasure.

The city, I had discovered right away, abounded in treasure. The streets were paved with it. On the upper shelves, the ones I couldn't reach without a ladder, I put the boxes I had finished. They made the kitchen look like a curiosity shop or an apothecary. On the floor, underneath the first shelf, went issues of *Artforum* and *Art in America*, catalogs from shows I'd liked, my art history textbooks, and a few issues of *Butt* magazine and *Bound and Gagged*. I bought four huge green plastic storage bins and stacked my random collection of dishes and silverware, cereal and spices, in them. I labeled the lids.

My wall was fantastic, and I never failed to feel a glow when I regarded it. It was a really cool wall, my art wall, and it had only improved over time. Sarah thought so, too. It looked like a vertical archaeological dig. On the very top shelf were my Pineapple Street boxes: Pineapple Street in summer, Pineapple Street in winter, Janos and I at the door of the house on Pineapple Street, carrying enormous fish in our arms: these boxes were sentimental, secret, true. I made them rarely.

Sometimes there was more than a whisper in the shadow of the art wall. A week before the time of which I'm writing, for instance, I called in sick to work one day—I felt really tired. I went to the bathroom and rubbed in a good handful of Bedhead Manipulator until I got my hair the way I wanted it, which made me feel more awake. I went to the kitchen, took down my tools and the peculiar figurine I'd been attempting to whittle for months. My whittling energy felt incredibly strong. Today I might finally be able to get the figurine's strange face right. I had already tossed a dozen bad versions of her into the scrap box. I turned on my father's radio, sat down at the kitchen table, and set to work, shaping her large jaw line with my best, smallest knife. My plan was to make her blue with big, curving, bluer horns, like rams' horns, on her head. Sort of like Integrity, or maybe it was Mining. I might whittle her a deer for a companion. The deer would be blue, too. I had just invented this great thing, pagan realism. No one had ever done that before. It would be my signature. I dug into the wood with the knife edge, turning it just so, delicately. At last the wood responded. It gave me a yielding, exact curve, another. I unearthed the left side of her jaw line, the beginning of the point of her chin. I felt her small, solid weight in my hand.

I was happy, whittling and listening to Nirvana. I had a vague urge to have a wank, but I wanted to finish the line that was flowing so well, like reeling in a big fish. Her chin pointed. Luck ran from my shoulders to my fingertips, guiding the knife effortlessly. It was the right thing to do, calling in sick. And I did feel sick, in a way. I was about to have a fever. In my feverishness, though, I had grace. This one, the blue goddess, might even get me into a juried show in Queens that Sarah and I were entering. I knew what the blue figurine's box was going to be, and her vibe alone was already amazing. I sashayed to the right side of her jaw line. Then the knife slipped, cutting deep and clean into my forefinger. Blood everywhere, and the pain came, a sickening throb. Motherfucker. I ran to the kitchen sink and turned on the cold water, which turned red, then pink, then red again. I wrapped my finger in a dishrag and sat down heavily in the kitchen chair, feeling slightly nauseated. The rag soaked through. Fuck. Fuck.

Three hours, one shot of Novocain, one tetanus shot, six stitches, and two extra-strength Tylenols later, I sat in a plastic bucket seat in the emergency room of St. Vincent's while Janos asked questions about the discharge instructions. I looked at my hand with its one grotesquely large forefinger wrapped in gauze. I couldn't feel my fingers or my palm. Sensation, uneasily, began at my wrist. Maybe my hand was paralyzed and I could quit my stupid job. I opened and closed my other hand, pinched it below my pinky. It felt. Good, I thought; I have one, anyway. My wanking hand, luckily. I wiggled my toes in my shoes, stretched my neck. I swallowed a few times. All systems go. I stayed at Janos's that night, went obediently in my tie to work the next day (I was sick, I was injured, after all).

Everyone in the office said I looked wan, which was satisfying, and told me to go home early. I still felt like I might have a fever coming on. When I got home to the afternoon quiet of my apartment, the half-formed figurine, like a totem, was lying next to the bloody knife on the kitchen table. She was spattered with blood. And I hadn't even started on her horns yet. I washed the knife, but I didn't wash her. If she wanted blood, she could have it. With this blood offering, she would get me into the show for sure.

It was a strangely exciting day, cuspy and painful. The stitches felt like they might let something in or out, but then it passed. Days like that had become rare. I sensed that my whirlwinds were dying down, slowly unwinding, like a clock whose spring had stretched over the years.

Ciao, I IMed to Sydnee. I checked out the Advances queue, where the very important living were laid out in their finest achievements, ready to meet their Maker and the next day's close. As far as I knew, they were all still dully alive. A familiar melancholy brushed me. I clicked around online for a minute, like May clicking around the kitchen linoleum to the radio after Roy died. I was hungry; my eyes hurt. The gauze on my finger had been replaced by a modest beige Band-Aid. The cut was taking a while to heal. May, on her way to print, was already fading away, like the Cheshire Cat, leaving just her showgirl smile behind. Her spirit pressed close; I almost thought I could hear her voice, her accent; then it dwindled and disappeared. All her unlived lives, tap-tap-tapping away.

I sometimes thought that I needed a new job. A new life. I had been unusually tired recently, like the air was slowly leaking out of me. My fake job at the fake newspaper was draining my real, vital forces. I looked out the window again. It was dark. The river had disappeared. I quickly logged out and left the office, trotting up Wall Street again. All the cart guys were gone. Like the traders with their badges, the cart guys were a determined bunch. What did I care about? I wished I could walk over and ask the bull. I certainly didn't care about *The Hudson Times*, though I liked hearing the dead people's stories and cropping their pictures. I was finding it increasingly hard to care about my boxes. And, in my most secret heart, I didn't know if I cared that much for Janos, though he cared so much for me.

Janos was huffing impatiently at the entrance to the New York State Theater at Lincoln Center, standing underneath a banner with an enormous image of a ballerina in a feathered tutu, her long neck arcing back, her arms extended midflutter. Next to him was his mother, a tiny, ancient Hungarian woman, straight as an arrow in a silver beaded suit with matching heels, standing up proudly gripping her walker, glittering. Janos was on his cell phone, frowning, but he gestured at me to come on quickly, pulling the tickets out of the breast pocket of his fawn-colored cashmere overcoat.

"Hello, darling," Janos's mother said to me in her thick accent. "Janos is closing a deal." She beamed. Despite two hearing aids that were practically bigger than her ears, she was stone-deaf.

"Hello, Margit," I yelled, kissing her on the cheek.

"You're late!" Janos said, flapping the tickets at me, his accent a faint imprint of his mother's. He snapped the phone shut. "Are those the only shoes you have?"

"The swan dies," I said. "Let's go get dinner."

"Very funny." He led the way through the crowd, my lover, Janos: a short, strong, dark man in his mid-fifties with a rough, irregular face, wearing, under the cashmere overcoat, a white Egyptian cotton shirt open at the neck, suit pants and jacket, no tie. Excellent black shoes. He pushed efficiently through the sparrow-like elderly ladies in sparkling embroidered jackets, the skinny high school girls in too much makeup, the doctors and lawyers who were already bored and looking at their watches as they waited in line at the elegant bar for champagne, the handsome young men with good haircuts. He was like a tugboat steaming through a harbor filled with yachts and bright sailboats, albeit a tugboat draped in cashmere, clearing a path for his mother.

I followed with Margit on her walker. She took a step, glanced to her right, her left, like the Queen Mum, took another step. I pulled off the brown tie, rolled it up in my jacket pocket, unbuttoned my collar. From my other pocket I pulled out the signet ring Janos had given me and put it on. Bulky, heavy, with excessively swirled initials (mine), it fit me perfectly. Did I love him? I wondered, slowly escorting Margit, encased in steel, across the thick carpet. When we had taken our seats (orchestra, fifth row, his mother on the aisle), and he was impatiently flipping through the program with that same feathered, arcing, dying ballerina on the cover as if he were looking for a phone number in the yellow pages, and the murmur of the audience was mixing with the bleats of the oboes, the long notes of the violins tuning up—when we were settled in I turned the heavy ring around on my pinky and wondered, Do I love him? Is he just one more of my kneeling men?

Right before the intermission, I leaned over and whispered in Janos's ear, "I have to go."

He frowned, shook his head.

"I'll call you later. I'm not feeling well."

"Gabe," he whispered heatedly. "*Gabriel.*"

I squeezed his hand, quickly kissed it, and turned away.

Margit, transported, smiled radiantly at me as I carefully stepped over her light, gleaming frame and headed up the aisle and into the open air. Outside, the evening was chilly. A line of limos waited on the service road; the drivers stood together in twos and threes, chatting and drinking coffee out of paper cups. With a sigh of relief, I went down to the train station with its colorful mosaics of dancers and musicians, whole and untouched by graffiti, inlaid on the walls.

I turned the heavy ring around on my pinky and again I wondered, Do I love him? Or is it just a daddy thing? I did like to be adored, time expanded deliciously in those moments — though now, waiting for the train, this fantasy felt pale, threadbare. But it wasn't like Janos was a simple man. No grateful construction worker, no guilty married accountant. Not easily dismissed. He was known for his kindness and generosity, but his arms seemed to be slightly longer than his torso and his eyes were quick, black, beneath a firm brow. Those eyes put you on notice that he was someone to reckon with.

That had turned me on at first. He *was* someone to reckon with. As he often remarked at dinner parties, as he'd remarked at the benefit dinner where we'd met, he came from pure Hungarian trash: gypsies, gangsters, drunks, thieves. "One scoundrel more handsome than the next," he liked to say. "Except me. Not only am I the ugly runt, but I'm honest. An embarrassment to my entire family." Everyone always laughed, because they knew he was rich and successful, and they hoped, just a little, that he'd stolen or cheated his way into at least part of it. For many years, until I came along, he had been the single man at dinner, the walker, the confidant, the fixer. Silly boys came and went. He rarely bothered to introduce those boys to his friends. But *We're so glad to meet you*, his old friends had said to me, earnestly pressing my hand. *We're so glad Janos has met someone finally.* They murmured in his ear that I was adorable, charming, and never, ever remarked on the age difference. They always asked me about my art projects. Several of them had bought boxes from me and hung them in their foyers and hallways. I signed the back of each box with a flourish. My work, I said when asked, was mostly in private collections.

Janos had cheated to get rich, of course. But not that much. I knew that I should love him for that. Did I? The train came and I got on it.

Forty minutes later, I was in Williamsburg, pushing open the chain-link gate in Mrs. Wieznowski's yard, which led to Sarah's little crooked rental house behind Mrs. Wieznowski's house. All Sarah's floors tilted away from Mrs. Wieznowski. As I opened the front door, I could hear the strains of "Goodnight, Irene," Sarah's signature piece, coming from the living room. I paused a minute in the low, musty, water-stained hall to listen. It was beautiful. I never got tired of hearing that one, which worked out well, because Sarah played it often, with variations. Goodnight, Irene, goodnight, Irene: that was our waltz. No swans in tutus in it.

I went in. Sarah was sitting in her straight-backed practice chair, embracing the gleaming accordion. It looked like she was playing an air conditioner, albeit a handsome navy-blue air conditioner with shiny silver fittings. The accordion was the newest, shiniest thing in the tilted house; it made the house look even smaller. With her high, pale forehead and thin, flat fingers and delicate collarbone, Sarah looked as if she could barely lift one of the accordion's heavy buckles, much less play the thing, but by bending all the way into it, she was able to produce quite a sound.

She smiled at me, bathed in the light of the secondhand

green leprechaun lamp. Across the room from the straight-backed wooden chair where she sat was her makeshift sofa: random cushions piled onto plywood on cinderblocks and covered in a vast length of brown fake fur that trailed onto the cold floor. On the bumpy living room wall above the furry sofa was the frilly pink vintage dress she had pinned there for decoration when she moved in eight years ago; the dress was dusty and the lace around the hem was torn. She used to wear that dress, with flip-flops, in Arizona when she went out to bars. Sarah pushed, grimacing, at the keyboard as she leaned into the last, sad notes. The accordion was the right instrument for her, though I was never sure that she was serious about getting famous by playing it. I still liked her eerie ceramics pieces of a few years back. I still liked her stalactites. I still liked her paintings from junior year at Arroyo D'Orado College, for that matter. She played the last note of "Goodnight, Irene." I clapped. Underneath us, an L train went by, rumbling for our attention, as if it were our pet.

We ignored it. I kissed her forehead, helped her out of the heavy accordion.

"Damn," she said playfully, "maybe I should have gotten one of the littler ones. The fucker is heavy."

"It sounds great." I sprawled on the fake fur sofa, kicking off my shoes. "You're a star."

"Doesn't it? So much richer than that other hunk of junk. It's like playing a whole different instrument." She bent her head to rub one shoulder. Along the part in her hair, where gray strands had appeared, there was now a streak of magenta. She had recently engineered a way of twisting and braiding her long, dark hair so it looked like topiary, or hair from outer space. She put her armful of wooden bracelets back on. "I just need my own Sherpa to carry it, I guess. How was work?"

"Absurd. I need a new life. Or vitamins or something. I have this cruddy feeling all the time. My joints ache. Maybe I need a new boyfriend. And"—I shook my head—"I think my ears are ringing." They were, faintly, as if a large bell, like the Liberty Bell, was ringing far away. "I went to see my house today. It was great."

Sarah leaned over to push my hair out of my eyes, bracelets clacking. "You're such a freak." The lines around her eyes were kind. "What you need is a haircut." She sighed. "I'm sort of cold," she said. "Aren't you?" It was always drafty in Sarah's house. The cold seasons arrived there first. "Let's have a bath."

Up the tilting stairs, there were two rooms: the bathroom on the right and Sarah's tiny bedroom on the left. In Sarah's room, a desk filled half of the space and a loft bed took up most of the other half. Under the loft were a few dressers painted different Day-Glo colors. The bathroom, hilariously, was bigger than the bedroom, with an old clawfoot tub and dark wainscoting. It was as if someone had fixed up the bathroom back in 1936 but didn't even try with the rest of the crooked house. And since Mrs. Wieznowski couldn't be bothered to wreck the bathroom with a bad plastic built-in shower and flimsy drywall, that one room had remained great. Sarah indulged in thick, soft towels for it; she kept a shelf of books in there, a low-slung rattan chair with a flowered cushion. You could stay there for hours, decades.

Sarah closed the door, leaned over to turn on the tap, hot, the way we liked it. I leafed through a warped paperback of *The Portrait of a Lady*. I felt panicky. The ringing persisted. Maybe I hadn't been lying when I told Janos I wasn't feeling well and left the ballet. Maybe the age difference between us was shrinking—that happened with men, the younger one seeming to age more quickly than the older one, trying to catch up. While Sarah ran the bath, I thought firmly: It's all right. There's still time. There's plenty of time. I took off my jacket, my shirt. "Oh, hey," I said. "I brought you a present." I handed her the picture of May taking her last sequined bow.

Sarah studied the picture. "Look at her! She's beautiful.

Thank you, honey." She stuck the photo in the corner of the mirror on the medicine cabinet. "Where did you get it?"

I shrugged, winked. She laughed. We got undressed. I unlaced my boots, pulled off my button-down shirt. Sarah took off all her bracelets and rings and put them in the aqua ceramic dish that rested on the windowsill next to the rabbit skull, the rialto with its happy little skeletons playing guitars and an accordion, and a tiny painting she had done of a man she'd loved years ago. The blob of white paint that was the cigarette hanging out of his mouth. I added the signet ring to the ceramic dish. The curve of Sarah's long pale back as she stepped into the tub was like the opening note of some song I'd known forever. I knew that mole, too, and the other, lighter one just near it. The stretch mark on her hip.

"Have you lost weight?" Sarah eyed me as she held out her hand. "Come on."

I climbed in behind her and she lay back against me, splashing the water's heat over us both. Our two sets of legs looked so easy together, so domestic, my rougher ones around her smoother ones, like parentheses. Her back against my chest was warm, firm, and damp. Her topiary hair was like thin, soft ropes.

She clasped my hand in the water. "I'm glad you're here. What's up with Janos?"

"He's at the ballet with his mom. I've seen it before."

"Yeah." The curve of Sarah's ear, near my lips, was delicate. Her face was damp from the steam. I could hear the wind outside the house, pushing and knocking at the old walls. In the quiet bathroom, in the clawfoot tub, it was as if we were in a berth on a ship at sea. I felt snoozy, attenuated. "How's your old lady?" murmured Sarah.

"Still paying me. I'm her man."

"That's cool. That's good." Sarah reminded me that it was time to send in our slides for the juried show in Queens. "We can't be late, Gabe." She sighed. "And, God, did I tell you?"

"What?"

"They promoted me. I'm an art director." She made air quotes around "art director." Sarah worked as a graphic designer for a fashion magalog aimed at preteen girls. She made beguiling things for the catalog on her computer; she knew all about fonts, and tiny invisible measurements that apparently changed everything, and how to make preteen girls feel special.

"Cool." I made the money sign with my wet thumb and forefinger. A pang troubled my wrist. I lowered it into the hot water.

Sarah splashed an aimless splash. "I guess." I soaped her back. Janos was probably helping his mother into the limo about now. The driver was folding the walker. Margit would be very happy; she adored the ballet. I was thinking that maybe I should turn around and join them at dinner when Sarah began to cry. She felt so terrible, she said. She'd been mean to some other man, an avant-garde puppetmaker, in this very tub, just the night before.

"Jesus, Gabe," she said. "Am I a monster? Am I?"

Of course not, I told her, and to prove it I held her tenderly for a long time in the bath, my penis as silky and limp as a calla lily. Unlike, I had no doubt, the wooden penis of the puppetmaker. Sarah's men were generally assholes. Sarah cried for a while, adding salt to the bathwater. I turned on the hot tap so she wouldn't get cold, kissed her high forehead, her thin, wet fingers. I rocked her in the way she liked. "Shhhh," I said. "Shhhh." The ringing in my ears stopped, as if I had soothed it, too.

"Gabe," she said tearfully, "am I going to end up like Mrs. Wieznowski?"

"How is that even possible?" I said, but I knew what she meant. I tried to sound sure of what I was saying. "Of course not." I held her close while she cried about the puppetmaker. Janos and Margit, at La Giraffe, would be ordering from the bald waiter. How old, I wondered, did I look to the waiter? I should ask him, in a joking way, the next time we went. Janos would be having the duck, longing to turn on his cell phone. I ran the hot water until it ran out.

"You know," she said, sounding foggy from crying, "sometimes I want to go back to Arizona."

"Yeah, me too."

"Really?"

"Really. It's so much cheaper there. We could both have huge studios out in the desert. Live in pod houses we built ourselves from a kit."

"That would be so great." A tear straggled down her cheek. "Why don't we do that?"

"Okay. We'll go back to Arizona."

"After we get into the show," Sarah added.

"Yes. Okay. I didn't finish my piece yet, did you?"

She nodded, still crying. "Yesterday."

I clambered out of the tub and held up one of Sarah's thick towels. "Don't cry." I dried her off, helped her into her grandmother's tattered red silk robe that always hung on the back of the bathroom door. One of my old T-shirts hung on the same hook. I put it on.

Looking into the steamy bathroom mirror where May was now bowing in her sequins, Sarah quickly retwisted her hair into its outer-space twirls. Had May played an instrument? Did she have any talent? Rosy from our bath, we went downstairs, and by the light of the leprechaun lamp Sarah played me her latest variation of "Goodnight, Irene," her tattered red silk sleeves gently fluttering as she pushed the keys, her topiary hair with the magenta streak at the part falling over her shoulders. She looked pretty and strange and something else — angry, maybe. Combustible. She had a sharp chin, tended to have dark circles under her eyes even if she was in a period when she was sleeping well.

My Sarah. She was one of those constantly dissolving women, like sugar in vinegar in a jelly jar. I hated it that from certain angles I could see the woman whom men were drawn to, slept with, and ran from: the smart, edgy, artsy girl with the accordion, in the wacky little tumbledown house behind the house. She had been so excited to find it; she loved living in the footnote house. She had found it the same week I had found mine, on Pineapple Street, though she actually lived in hers, of course. She had footnote men, too—their main text was usually about someone or something else. The worst of her suitors, in my opinion, was Rodney, the married civil rights lawyer who called her from airports to talk dirty on his cell phone and liked to fuck standing up. He was much worse than any drug-addicted drummer or arrogant artist. Not that I had the right to comment, but still. He was.

I hated it even more that from certain angles I could see what we looked like, how we were fading away, disappearing from the land of the living. Once upon a time, we went to parties or gave parties where we were the two people, our shirt cuffs dangling unbuttoned over our wrists, who whispered in each other's ear, two not quite good-looking people exchanging superior glances. Castor and Pollux. From certain angles, angles that were more spiritual than strictly physical, we looked as if we might be brother and sister, or at least cousins. We were the sort of people who looked as if we were saying mean things about other people at the party, and usually we were. But not always. Now we didn't go to many parties, and we both worked at fake magazines, ironically doing fake jobs that seemed to be becoming ominously real. My bull was bolted down to the middle of a traffic island.

Why was I so moody tonight? I smoothed down the curling edges of the Band-Aid. That little blue goddess had really fucked me. Or maybe May was haunting me, playing a trick on me. The dead had to find something to do with their time. Maybe I shouldn't have stolen her picture.

Sarah proudly held a note, her long fingers tensed. The song was sadder now, something she'd changed in the phrasing. The sound of the new accordion was as silvery as its fittings, fine, resonant. It sounded like it was distilling the fresh sorrow of the world as she played, humming along softly. I clapped again.

We made a huge amount of spaghetti with olives, the good kind that Sarah savored as if they were truffles. After dinner, we ate marshmallows out of the bag and watched three *Law & Order* reruns we'd both already seen. I rolled my panging wrist around. There seemed to be pins in it.

During a commercial, she said, "I feel like hell. Will you stay? Is that all right?" She bit her lip. "Maybe you want to go to Janos's."

"No." I felt very tired all of a sudden. "I'll stay. Is my toothbrush still here?"

"Yup."

"Well then."

After watching the local news, we went up to bed, tumbling into the creaky loft that was like the crow's nest of a ship at sea. The white sheets were cool and soft as leaves; like the towels, the sheets were where Sarah spent her money. The rest she saved; like me, she was a hoarder. She was saving for her future. She tucked up her long legs and slid quickly under the covers beside me in her tattered red silk robe. Drafts, like ice fairies, skittered across our faces. Sarah turned out the rickety light that was clamped to one side of the bed.

She curled up, fast as a wingbeat, against me in the dark. I held her slender body in my arms. She hooked her leg over mine. I pulled her close, stroking the long curve of her back. I twined one of her soft ropes of hair around my hand. She sighed, resting her head on my chest. We were who we'd always been. Her shoulders were small, silken, narrow. She was much more naked under her robe, somehow, than a man could ever be. I felt like her brother; like an animal in a den with another animal; like I was keeping watch. I needed Sarah without wanting her, and maybe to some people that would be a kind of sin. Worse than me and Janos. But she felt so real, the fact of her, her hard heels, her surprisingly strong arms. We had been friends, star twins, for such a long time. She pulled my arm around her, firmly interlacing her fingers with mine. It wasn't as if I wanted to go home that night, anyway. My wrist began to ache again.

Sarah breathed against me. We warmed up. The thing in me unlatched; the thing in her unlatched. Drowsiness began somewhere at the nape of my neck, seeped through me from the inside out, submerging my sore wrist. Her fingers, spread against my ribs, released, opened. I could smell the damp warmth of her hair. The short strings of time, of schedules and trains and deadlines, unraveled. Janos, in his townhouse near Gramercy Park, turned out the lights, turned on the security system. Sarah grasped one of my fingers, murmured something about Arizona; she, who usually slept so badly and whose dreams were bad, too, was already asleep. In the millisecond before I fell asleep, I heard that sound again, the ringing of a bell. I thought that a bell had rung, in fact, somewhere in the house. But Sarah didn't have a doorbell. The bell—though it was more like the echo of a bell—rang again, more faintly. I pushed at my ear, shook my head. Silence. I returned to basking in sleepiness, in the warmth and endless roll of it, the clean scent of Sarah's neck. With her so near me, I knew that there was plenty of time. Oceans of it. We were already rich. We'd both get into the new artists' show. We were going there, to the warm island, together.

Much later, sometime toward dawn, I opened my eyes in

the gray light to see Sarah, in a sweatshirt and socks, at her desk. Her long runner's legs were bare. She was busily writing, with the aid of a pocket flashlight, on a yellow legal pad. I hung over the edge of the loft for a few minutes, watching her. "What are you doing?" I finally said. The bell was ringing in my ear again, making my temples ache. Maybe it was telling me I needed more money.

"Writing a letter." She didn't look up.

"Who to?"

"Shhh. I'm concentrating."

"Is it to me?"

"Yes."

"What?"

"Yes, it's to you. Be quiet."

"Can I read it?"

"No. I'm not done."

"Can I read it when it's done?"

"Maybe. Hush, I need to finish. I have to work tomorrow afternoon."

"Come back to bed."

She didn't answer, intent on her task.

"Sarah," I said, "Sarah, do you love me?"

She turned her head and regarded me seriously. "Yes, Gabriel," she said. Her ropes of hair had come undone, and her hair hung down her back in long crimped strands, like a girl's hair, or a grandmother's. In this light, the magenta streak looked like unnecessary emphasis, like an arrow pointing out where she was. But she was right there, as always. "I do love you," she said. The bell went still. Then Sarah returned to her letter.

The next morning, Sarah and I drank too much coffee until she was late for work at the magalog, then we pushed our way onto the jammed L train. Back across the river, dutifully, in the ordinary way, like ordinary mortals. But the sensation persisted that I was fading, that I was losing density, that my bones were going hollow, open to the winds.

Maybe this is why, or how, I started to change. Maybe it was my way of trying to remain in the world, to turn from fake to real.

Of course, I could blame it all on Fleur and her stolen girls.

On a chilly afternoon a few days later, I sat in my usual place on the hard, spindly chair with gold legs. Fleur was in her usual place as well—on the divan, a grand piece of furniture that was like the inside curve of a conch shell, tremendously magnified. The divan was upholstered in a gold brocade so dense that it looked as if a thousand suns had conspired to weave it. Scattered over the divan were various little oddly shaped pillows in gold silk with gold and silver tassels, and cashmere and mohair throws that over the years appeared to have grown together, like kudzu. Somewhere underneath all the throws was the cat. A white cat's paw or tail would appear from a curve of mohair from time to time, then disappear. I had never seen the entire cat—for all I knew there were two cats, or six—and I had never sat on the divan myself; I think that if anyone besides Fleur had reclined there, spontaneous combustion would have been the instant result. The room was otherwise empty except for an ancient, no-color metal file cabinet in the corner and a dirty glass ashtray on the floor. Venetian blinds hung lopsidedly in the two small windows. My cut finger, still healing, hurt. My ears were ringing again. I shook my head like a wet dog, but then I felt dizzy.

"Let's go," she said. Her *s*'s were very soft these days, almost completely melted. Fleur—I never called her Becky—was slight, a pencil sketch. Her hair, cut just below her ears, was sharply gray, definitive. I think she was seventy-five, though she admitted to being only sixty-six. Sometime in the past, she must have had work done, but the work had slid, unevenly. It was like her not to have it redone, or repointed, or whatever it is that they do. She cultivated a certain ferocity, even now. The immobile curl of her left hand lay on one of the mohair throws. Her right hand was poised on the keyboard of a laptop computer that rested on what I assumed was her tiny, scrickety lap, like a bird's nest, far underneath all the expensive bedding.

I took out the pages and the flash drive from the breast pocket of my suit jacket, which I always wore when I went to Fleur's. I read the pages aloud to her in a clear, strong voice. Fleur pecked at the keys vaguely, as if she were typing, smiling with the half of her face that could smile.

"And listen," I said, "I've been thinking about how Miranda could get out of the nuclear reactor."

Fleur listened hard, a charged filament. She held out her hand for the flash drive.

I had met Fleur by accident, when she was full-strength. Her sister the congressman's widow had died, and Fleur—though I didn't know she was Fleur then, I thought she was Rebecca —was the last of the four gorgeous, poor, fast-talking Sharp girls. They got around, those Sharp girls. When I first phoned from the paper, we hit it off. We met for coffee, then dinner, then another dinner; she would send a car for me; since she never mentioned having had any sort of job, I thought she must have marriage money, maybe divorce money, like her sisters, who had all married or divorced well. She was clever and tough in ballet slippers, with a lingering trace of a Brooklyn accent.

"I was born Becky Sharp," she said over chanterelles at Chanterelle, "can you beat it? My grandfather's name was Abe Sharpstein, but who's counting?"

"Not me." I gave her my best crooked, wolfish smile. I figured she probably liked a touch of the rogue. I winked.

Maybe because of the wolfish smile, or the wink, or maybe

because she felt like it, she revealed to me that night who else she was. I was astonished. Fleur Girard! The *Stolen* series! You couldn't get on a subway or bus without seeing someone, usually a tired woman in pantyhose and sneakers, reading one of the *Stolen* books. There were eight of them out then, eight installments of the adventures of the Stolen girls: Miranda, Leah, Natasha, Anna. (*Stolen, Stolen Again, Stolen Victories, Stolen Moments, Stolen Blossoms*, etc.) People couldn't get enough of them. I told Fleur that—not that she was surprised that I said it, but she seemed as blushingly pleased as if she'd never heard it before.

"They're my muses," she said unironically. "We've been through a lot together." She shook her head, as if remembering things she couldn't say.

I was impressed. "I've read them all," I blurted out, and then regretted it. It was almost too much, on top of everything else, to let her know I was a fan. It embarrassed me. And the *Stolen* series, of all things; it was so uncool. Of course, that was exactly why the tired women in sneakers and pantyhose, reading their way from Queens to midtown and back again every day, liked it. And why I liked it. Those four dewy coeds—now, eight books later, young women with demanding, super-high-powered jobs that involved much clicking of high heels over expertly polished marble floors and cream-colored La Perla lingerie cupping pert breasts under tight-fitting business suits —had been abducted by white slavers from their college suite, driven to revenge, reabducted, tortured, driven to revenge, cyberstalked by international cartels linked to white slavers and worse, and driven to revenge yet again, more than you might think was possible in fifteen or so years. But the women on the subway didn't care. I didn't care. Entire forests vanished so that Miranda, Leah, Natasha, and Anna could click-click, or crawl in silk lingerie, through the hidden seraglios, dark alleys, and boardrooms of the world.

The *Stolen* girls might have been gossamer and cardboard, but they were hard to resist. I could say that I myself had read all eight books for a laugh, but that wouldn't be honest. I read them because I couldn't put them down. There was something about those girls. You wanted to be close to them. You wanted them to win. You wanted to be them, click-clicking through Singapore in a ripped teddy, with the secret code written in invisible ink high on your bruised inner left thigh.

"The little bitches," said Fleur warmly. "But they bought me some great houses."

After that moment, that unmasking, over the chanterelles, I began to hang out with Fleur. We had some fun. I learned that she had a husband of many years, Morty, who didn't like to go out much, so sometimes I escorted her to an opening or a show —always in my best white shirt (I had only one that good), smoothest pants, a suit jacket, and a blue tie with a darker blue stripe. I never so much as kissed Fleur on the cheek, but in the evenings when I was carefully ironing my shirt, straightening my blue tie, I felt as if she was dressing me. Smoothing the shoulders of my jacket. Looking me over proprietarily. I liked the feeling. I was her walker, sure, but I knew that I also looked a bit like her gigolo to other people, and I liked it that I looked that way to them. It made me laugh, and it also made me feel that anything, any life, was possible.

The morning that Morty called, I knew something was wrong. Morty had never phoned me before. "Can you come over?" he said. "Becky wants to talk to you." My heart tightened. I had never been to Fleur's house before, either. Usually I waited on the street for her with the chauffeur. I found my shirt and tie, my jacket. I took a cab to Central Park West. A maid led me through room after room of a bellowingly huge apartment. We passed French Provincial tufts and swags and porcelain and big paintings of springtime meadows and ornamental bronze things with curlicues, knickknacks everywhere, twin vases with flower arrangements the size of headdresses on Vegas showgirls. Anything that didn't gleam, puffed; every ornate knickknack was an event, possibly a catastrophe. There were more end tables than there were ends. It was very quiet. The maid didn't say anything.

Morty materialized in a long hallway. He was a very lean, grizzled, unshaven man of sixty-five or seventy in an ancient pair of baggy-assed jeans and a Clash T-shirt. He looked like an old rocker. Fleur had told me he imported rare clocks; he supposedly had a shop in the East Fifties. "This way," he said in deep Bronx tones. "She's awake now."

He led me to a room in the back and left me there, closing the door behind him. Fleur was reclining on the gold divan that day, too. She looked very slight, just a ripple in the layers of cashmere and silk. Her face was like an ax blade, resting against a silver pillow with gold tassels. Her eyes were half closed. I couldn't tell if she was asleep or awake. There was nothing in the room but the divan and a laptop, open on the floor, its screen dark.

With an eerie feeling I realized where I was. I had entered the sanctum sanctorum, the place where Becky became Fleur and vice versa. The source of all of it, the stories and the cash. The air in that room felt flatter, dustier; it didn't have the faint scent of lavender and furniture polish that permeated the rest of the apartment. There was a dirty glass ashtray on the floor. I hadn't known she smoked. I tried to put together the cruddiness and randomness of the room with the elaborate, single piece of furniture in it, but I couldn't. It felt more intimate here than if I was in her bedroom, with the old venetian blinds on the window and thousands of dollars in shiny fabric on — well, who knows what it was under all that? Maybe it was a few desk chairs and a lot of pillows, all lashed together with a clothesline. A silver and ebony cane with the price tag still on it leaned against one wall. Nervously, I shot my cuffs. "Gabriel," Fleur said, speaking slowly with a new, slight slur. "It's nice to see you. Sit down."

It was only then that I noticed that her face appeared to have broken in half and been carelessly glued back together. That one of her hands was curled stiffly in her lap, like a small hoof. That her usual light was dim, flickering. She'd had two strokes, she explained slowly, two cock-s-s-sucking strokes in a single day. *Two.* She held up two fingers with a certain amount of pride. One measly stroke could never take her out. He needed an accomplice. I took her uncurled hand and she grasped mine tightly. I could feel the sharp, surprisingly strong points of her bones on my fingers. She gave a raspy sigh.

"I need some help," she whispered. "I have a strict deadline. They won't wait! The m-motherfuckers."

"All right," I said, still unclear as to what she meant. Fumbling with one hand, I found a pen and a scrap of paper in my jacket pocket. "Shoot."

She nodded. She gave me an outline. Because I knew the books so well. Because she trusted me. Because—she didn't say this, but I knew it was true—she just wasn't ready not to be Fleur Girard anymore. She wasn't ready to go back to being Rebecca Sharp; she knew what the next stop on that train was.

So. I took it all down in the tiny handwriting I used to write poetry in the corners of my boxes. She nodded again. One side of her mouth slanted now, pulled down by an invisible force. Her face looked like the joined masks of comedy and tragedy. Suddenly, irrationally, I wanted to pick her up and hold her tightly against me; I wanted to say, *Don't go. Please don't go. Don't turn back into Becky yet.* If she turned back into Becky, I would turn back into—well, I didn't know who, exactly, but I resisted it with all my might. I didn't take my hand from hers, though she was hurting me. She was stronger than she looked, as if she'd been boiled down to pure will. She intertwined her fingers more closely with mine, pressed harder. "Don't fuck it up," she whispered. "I'm trusting you, Gabe."

"Okay," I said. I looked at the outline, which I'd written shakily, as if I were the one who'd had a stroke. The scrap of paper, I noticed, was an ATM receipt for forty dollars, plus the two-dollar fee. "Why me, Fleur?"

She closed her eyes, pursed her lips, considering. "I need a young man," she said. "A discreet young man. Can you be discreet?" All her *s*'s were soft at the edges.

I looked at her, fallen there, crumpled, on the gold divan: the littlest Sharpstein girl, the last one, the one with a temper. If I say I kind of fell in love with her at that moment, that wouldn't be accurate; but it wouldn't be accurate, either, to say that what we entered into was purely a business arrangement. As with Sarah, and those kneeling men long ago in the bus station bathroom in Florida, I don't know what Fleur and I became that afternoon, in the cruddiest room in one of her several well-appointed houses. I know that we became something. I know that she changed me. No whirlwind of bulls, no sonic booms. I just found that I couldn't let go of her small, cool, powerful hand, which was nearly transparent with age and ambition and bad habits, and she couldn't let go of mine: our bones had fused. At the same moment, something fluttered inside me, like a little red bird on the tip of a slender branch: opportunity, illuminated. An opportunity I'd figure out how to use later.

"Absolutely," I said. "Very discreet." I folded the ATM receipt and put it in the breast pocket of my jacket.

The side of her face that could move relaxed. "Good," she said. She released my hand. With an effort, she reached under a gold pillow with silver tassels and pulled out an envelope. She held it out to me. "There. Come back in a week."

Two minutes later I found myself standing on Central Park West, feeling somewhat bewildered and shaken. What had just happened? Fleur's building, behind me, was massive and white, awninged and heavily ornamented, fully stocked with doormen and footmen and jesters and what have you, but it felt as insubstantial as an image projected on a screen and as if it could dissolve as quickly. I turned around to make sure it was still there. It was. The doorman frowned at me. I reached into my jacket pocket and pulled out the envelope Fleur had handed me. It was full of cash. Three hundred dollars in clean, flat twenties. Wrapped around the twenties was a note in shaky handwriting. *You help me*, it read, *and I'll help you*. I slid out a twenty and stroked its smooth surface. It wasn't creased or dirty, like the twenties in the bus station bathroom, but it felt as charged, as magical, as illicit. I carefully slid it back into place with the others, put the envelope in my pocket, patted it, and briskly walked away from the building.

It turned out that it wasn't all that hard to imitate Fleur's particular mix of speed, violence, cunning, and rough sex. Style wasn't her strong suit anyway. Her writing was slapdash, but it was propelled by unstoppable drive. You knew from page one that the book in your hand was going to get where it was going like a shot. She always outlined the action for me. Once I got the hang of it, the actual writing was pretty easy, like painting by numbers. And by now I could slap a sentence together as well as the next person. We finished *Stolen Kisses* (bonus! an extra silver brick!) and began on *Stolen at Twilight*. It was a goof. And month after month, my freezer slowly filled with nice, cold, foil-wrapped bricks of money. They delighted me. I could buy anything with them, go anywhere I wanted. I tried not to think too much about the fact that, since Morty had ushered me into Fleur's writing room over two years before, I hadn't seen her off the gold divan. I sometimes wondered if there had been yet another stroke, a further neurological step down that she'd kept even from me. I purposely stopped short of imagining that in any detail.

• • •

On this chilly day, Fleur considered my suggestion about the nuclear reactor and the ramp. "Yeah," she said. "That could work. Write that down."

I wrote it down.

She smiled her half-smile. "Ah, the little bitches," she said. "Gabe. What do you think? Should Natasha get raped over there in the corral?"

"Again?" I asked delicately.

Fleur looked confused, then annoyed. "Miranda then. Write that down."

I wrote it down.

She nodded and resettled herself on the divan. "Good boy." Her eyelids began to lower. A minute later, she was asleep, faded away to a streak of silver in all that gold. The white tip of the cat's tail thumped once against a patch of brocade, then disappeared into a fold of white cashmere. The immobile curl of Fleur's left hand, with the flash drive in it, rested on that same white fold.

She was so small now on her throne, so frail. I doubted she weighed as much as a hundred pounds. I wondered if Morty came in after I left, to pick her up and put her on one of the mammoth, tufted white sofas like clouds in one of the countless other rooms. That ebony cane with the price tag on it was leaning exactly where it had been leaning a year ago, collecting dust. I knew that it might be leaning in the same place a year from now. And then one day, just like May, Fleur's light would go out. Her voice would diminish to a rough-edged point, then disappear. There wouldn't be any more *Stolen* books. Our time together would be over. *Gabriel, broke.*

"Fleur? Fleur?"

She snorted, woke. "Rape Natasha. What do you think? Would that work?"

"I'm not sure," I said. "What about Miranda instead?"

She nodded slightly, like a general acknowledging a foot soldier. "Possibly." Her *s*'s slipped, leaned drunkenly against one another. "Not a bad idea. Gabe, when's your birthday?" She pushed herself up the slope of shining pillows, wide awake now.

"November."

"Tell Morty we should throw you a party. Listen. Did I ever tell you what Morty was doing when we met?"

I sat back. "No, what?" I said. I liked this one.

"Fixing my sister's car. Yeah. He was a car mechanic, dating my sister Myra. He doesn't know shit about clocks, except the big hand is on the hour and the little hand is on the minute. Even that, I'm not so sure." She laughed.

"Was he a good mechanic?"

"That he could do. He got Myra's motor running, that's for sure. She almost killed me for stealing him." She laughed again, ruefully. "God, I miss her."

"I know."

"Longest legs you've ever seen. Like a dancer." Fleur sighed. "Ovarian."

"I'm so sorry," I said. "I hope she didn't suffer."

"She did suffer," said Fleur. "She suffered terribly. You can't imagine how much she suffered. Now Barbara, she was the smart one. She invested *very wisely*. Guess what in."

"What?" Recycling.

"Recycling. Is that amazing or what? Very forward-thinking." She tapped her forehead with her good hand. "Pancreatic."

"Oh, Jesus," I said. "Horrible."

"It was. Like being hit by a train. Her kids are nightmares. If they ever call you, don't call them back." A melancholy expression crossed her face.

"What about Linda?" Linda had been the oldest, Fleur's favorite.

Fleur brightened up right away. "Oh, she was kind. Biggest heart you ever saw. She did everything for us. Brushed our hair, got us ready for school, told us what was what. She figured out a way to send us all to summer camp upstate, sewed our names on our shirts: Linda, Barbara, Myra, Rebecca. Us four girls, we were a team. Couldn't get a piece of paper between us. You know what happened to Linda."

"She died in her sleep," I said. "The day after Christmas."

"That's right. When's your birthday?" With her good hand, she fussed at a bit of cashmere. "Too hot."

I covered her good hand with mine. "Fleur."

She frowned. "I'm sleepy."

"My birthday is in November. Fleur. You know I'm an artist. Or trying to be." I winked in the roguish way she liked.

She yawned. "Yeah." Her eyelids were lowering again.

"And you know how tough that is, how I work all the time. Fleur?" I jostled her lightly. "Fleur. It's tough. And art supplies are so expensive." I waited, but nothing happened. She watched me, half asleep, half awake, like the white cat I never saw. "I'm wondering if we could double my fee? Since I've helped you out so much?"

"No," she said, quite clearly.

I tightened my grip on her good hand, to keep her from slipping away into sleep. Her gaze widened. "But the thing is, well, you know, I really have helped you a lot. And that's a private thing between us, how much I help you. How much I want to keep helping you. I love the *Stolen* girls—I can't wait to read the next one, even though I know what happens. I worship you, Fleur. I admire you tremendously. But if it were ever to become *less* private, this thing of ours"—I gestured to the invisible bridge between us, to our unseen fused bones—"then I wouldn't be able to help you anymore. And that would break my heart. You can't imagine how much I look forward to our time together. It's my secret life. But, wow, it really has to stay a secret, doesn't it?" I clucked my tongue. "You're the star. I want to make sure we keep it that way."

"Linda," she said, taking her time to enunciate the syllables. "Barbara, Myra, Rebecca. I'm the last one." She shook her head against a gold silk pillow. "Jesus Christ. Gabe. Jesus Christ."

I didn't say anything, maintaining my grip on her hand. With an effort, she withdrew her fingers from mine, reached behind one of the gold silk pillows, and pulled out an envelope. Then, slowly but deliberately, she reached back in and pulled out another. "Here you go, my boy. When are you coming back?"

I took the envelopes. I gently plucked the flash drive from the curl of her left hand. "How about in a week?"

"Make it two." Her eyelids began to lower again.

"Fleur. Thank you."

"Forget it, kid. Did we say Natasha or Miranda?"

"Miranda."

"All right. All right. Come back in a week."

"Okay."

"No — make it two." She reached for my hand, grabbed it, and squeezed. Her small bones pressed hard against my fingers. "We'll throw you a birthday party in November. Big party."

"Great." I saw myself through room after silent room. In the room with the grand piano, I spotted an intricate cut-glass pineapple. I slipped it into my pocket. I continued on, past the enormous white sofas like clouds, down the ornate elevator, through the echoing lobby, and out into the street. Central Park West regarded me with its wide, blank, guarded stare. I patted the reassuringly heavy envelopes in my breast pocket. I loved the money, I loved the money, I loved the money. Fleur and I had that in common. She loved the money too. Underneath, she understood why I had to do what I had to do. Why should Morty get it all? To buy more clocks? All I was doing was borrowing against the time we might not get to have together, because of an accident of age and the body. Time wasn't my fault.

I made my way home, pleased. Third Avenue, Second Avenue, down Seventh Street, up my battered stoop and the cracked marble stairs in the grimy hallway with the fluorescent ring lights (two were always out) and into my precious rent-controlled apartment. Caroline's name was still on the mailbox in her blocky handwriting. Fifteen years ago, the three largeish rooms had needed a paint job; now they needed that and plastering, too, but I had no intention of alerting the landlord to my existence. I still signed Caroline's checks, a small hoard from an ancient bank account, for the rent.

In through my heavy front door. Early evening. The gate over the back window, rusted shut, threw shadows on the floor. The plastic clock hovered, as ever, between 4:37 and 4:38. All the furniture had been salvaged from the street—great finds, amazing finds—except for one expensive throw pillow ornamented with a plain blue triangle and a wall clock that looked as if it had been made out of bicycle spokes. I think it actually was made out of bicycle spokes, and it had been quite expensive, a gift from Janos. I looked around without turning on any lights. My house. It looked as if it was all made out of shadows.

I took the cut-glass pineapple out of my pocket and put it on the windowsill, as if to ripen, next to the other *objets* I'd collected from Fleur's house—trinkets, really. She would never miss them; some overpaid interior designer had selected most of them. But as I eased the pineapple into place, a porcelain milkmaid with spreading, deep blue skirts fell and broke. Her head rolled under the radiator. Damn. On hands and knees, I retrieved her head, covered in under-the-radiator crud, but her neck was hopelessly shattered. I set her head, rolling awkwardly, next to her smooth porcelain body. Then I took the two envelopes of money Fleur had given me out of my breast pocket, wrapped them first in tin foil, then in a plastic Gristede's bag, then in another layer of foil. I opened the freezer door and added the thick, oblong aluminum bundle to the others and tapped it into place. The silvery bundles were stacked, mute and heavy, in neat rows, shrouded in ice. The freezer was nearly full. I needed to push a bit to close the freezer door, but at last it clicked shut. It was going to go twice as fast now. I might have to get another freezer, maybe a little portable one, just for the money.

In a way, it was the money wrapped in aluminum foil that drew me into the wrong grove. Money has its own animus, its own gravitational pull, its own will to live. I worked on Wall Street, after all; the evidence surrounded me every day of how willful money is, how it gathers force as it accumulates, like a creature assembling itself out of the dust, bit by bit.

Money has its own ideas, its own plans. Hadn't it frozen the bull in place on Bowling Green? And I liked the money so much. At the beginning, I had half thought, or told myself, that I could use it to buy some time to work on my boxes — I knew I should want to use it for that — but after the first few months of stacking silver bricks on old freezer ice, I had had to admit that I didn't want to spend it yet. I liked thinking of things I could do with the money. I liked the secret weight of it, liked the fact that no one knew I had it, in the same way that I liked the trinkets of Fleur's that I'd curated and set out on my windowsill. It had been just over a year that I'd been stacking up silver bricks, and I didn't want to stop. Ever.

It was part of another world, that money — a world that no one else could see and that wasn't entirely visible even to me. But I could feel that world, its curves and spires, pressing against the inside of this one. I glimpsed it from time to time. And it wasn't like the money had been *given* to me; I didn't steal it, either. I'd earned it, and I was overdue for a raise. Fleur's books, including the one I'd helped her write, sold boatloads of copies. It was all on the up-and-up. The money, shiny and cold, was simply an *if*. The *if* was a door. As the money stacked up, it had persuaded me to enjoy the idea that I could, one day, swing the *if* open. The money wasn't wrong. I mean, wouldn't you want a door like that? Wouldn't everyone? Money knows that. It knows all about you and what you really want. It knows, for instance, that you'd rather not be caught off guard, helplessly peeing in your pants on a cold day. It is never, ever still but always moving, always changing: now an open door, now a mirror, now a loyal dog, now a busy city, now you, now me.

And then the door did swing open. A crooked door, that small, grave girl: that's all it took to pull me across the river for good.

I stared out my dirty office window in the city of the dead on a Tuesday afternoon. Wall Street burbled and bustled below, businessmen shoving right through the ghosts on the sidewalk, elbowing them out of the way as they wolfed down sandwiches from the carts and gossiped about what money was getting up to today. My gaze had to leap the South Street Viaduct, the ferry slips, the gray river, the Brooklyn-Queens Expressway, but then there it was: the land of the living, bounded on the south by the Brooklyn Bridge and the enormous tan building with the letters that read THE WATCHTOWER, that badly printed weekly booklet handed out on streets and at doorsteps by Jehovah's Witnesses; and on the north by industrial buildings.

One day not long after I'd gotten my raise from Fleur, still feeling restless and ill at ease, haunted by I didn't know what, I stared across at the city of the living and willed my spirit onto those wide, leafy streets, willed my body to follow my spirit somewhere, anywhere. It didn't. My spirit snapped back into my body and landed with a dull thud. I was in my same old cubicle, with the same fuzzy, beige half-walls. I still had the Band-Aid on my finger. The kneeling figures of Agriculture and Mining were nearby. I straightened my brown tie. It was 4:56.

I played some online poker (I lost), cropped a picture or two of famous people who weren't dead yet, and then, as if blown by a gust of wind, grabbed my things and left the building ("Dentist appointment!" I yelled into Sydnee's office), sending my body in search of my spirit. People on those long rides under the river from Manhattan to Brooklyn often doze, lulled by the motion and the length of the trip home. I liked it. I let other people lean drowsily against me as I watched the stops tick by. I got off at Clark Street. As soon as I came up through the St. George Hotel and saw the great brownstones, like ancient towering redwoods, I felt that satisfying click, that release. Yes. Here.

I made my way down Clark Street, Henry Street, Love Lane (Love Lane! Who would dare it?), and then, whistling, onto Pineapple Street. I took out my one cigarette, getting ready, and hurried to the lamppost. I turned up my collar; chillier today. But as I cupped my hands and bent to the match, I noticed something. Two things, actually. First I noticed that the widow's walk had been fixed. That two-by-four had been replaced by a nicely turned white post that nearly matched its fellows except for a slight brightness, like a new tooth. Good, I thought, but then my gaze fell on the other thing, the hand-lettered sign in the front yard: FOR SALE BY OWNER, and a phone number written underneath.

I shook the match out, the unlit cigarette between my lips. The uneasy thrum I'd been feeling for weeks deepened, intensified. The red patch on my arm (which had been getting bigger, it needed some cream or something) itched ferociously in protest. I scratched it. My ears began to ring. What would a house like this go for? For sale by owner. Something about that phrase bothered me, suggesting as it did a certain greed. Or was it an opportunity? My pulse quickened. The hair on the back of my neck stood up. I felt a sudden urge to piss.

The dark green front door opened. The little girl walked

out of the house. She was wearing purple and white leggings, a pink skirt, a second, turquoise skirt on top of the first, a stretchy yellow shirt with orange sleeves and a big blue dog appliquéd on the front, five plastic bracelets in tropical hues, and a red macramé beret on her head. Lavender high-top sneakers. In her hand was a lighted square of computer that seemed to be singing; an intricate design coiled and uncoiled on the screen. She walked down the steps and stood at the gate. On her face was an expression of anticipation mixed with melancholy. She looked up the street, down the street. She ran her hand along the top of the gate, closed her eyes in the manner of a child making a wish, opened them.

She sighed. Just that: a sigh, the smallest sigh of a child waiting at a gate, a sigh I knew so, so well.

I began to shake. My left hand burned. FOR SALE BY OWNER. That bell rang in my ear again, but now, with an almost euphoric blend of sadness and joy, I welcomed it. There should be more bells, a row of bells, all ringing together, to herald the moment when I had glimpsed, at last and unexpectedly, my proper future. *Gabriel, on Pineapple Street, in autumn.* It was here, it had been here all along, waiting for me to recognize it, just across the river. It had pulled me here today, beckoned me to the land of the living. I was going to cross the Hudson to it on a walkway of icy, oblong silver bricks. (When was the last time I had counted them?)

As my hand burned, my life passed before my eyes. I saw it all so clearly: I had sold a box here and there over the years; I had gotten a grant or two; I was in a show called "Boxes." I had gotten by, hanging on to my day job. But it was as if I had lived not in the apartment on East Seventh Street but in my own boxes all this time, tapping my dwindling stash of Belgian nails into manzanita wood from the inside, arranging found objects artfully around me, looking at the city's washed-out night sky with my head pressing against the top edge of the box and my feet curled against the bottom edge. And now, all at once, I found that I was reaching up and out toward that dark horizon, that there was no end to my reaching, and it seemed that without knowing it I had been reaching like this always. Manzanita wood splintered around me.

I didn't know how it would happen, but this life that I saw on Pineapple Street was the life I had always wanted, and somehow I was going to get it. The light in the lamppost went on, a joke, but it was all I could do not to weep. How had I ever forgotten? FOR SALE BY OWNER: this was my sign, my chance, my past, and my future.

The little girl at the gate was regarding me in her grave way.

I smiled what I hoped was a non-threatening, non-child-kidnapping, invisible, distracted, grown-up sort of smile.

"Hey, are you Mr. Bender?" she called out.

I made a show of stubbing out my cigarette, though it wasn't lit. "Who? I'm just—"

"We're waiting for Mr. Bender," she said somewhat accusatorily, as if I'd eaten him. "He's my new Latin teacher." Did they speak Latin in Brooklyn now, on top of everything else? What was this place? On the lighted square of the girl's computer, the intricate design appeared to turn inside out and chuckle.

"No," I said. "I'm not Mr. Bender. Hey, listen. Who do I talk to about your house?"

She narrowed her eyes. "Who are you?"

"My name is Gabe." I moved to cross the street to the house, then thought better of it. The little girl folded her arms, eyeing me up and down.

"We don't sell to crackers," she said. "Our house is *nice.*"

I shrugged. "Maybe. Maybe not. I'd have to take a look." I tried to slow my breathing, seem casual.

The little girl didn't care, or notice. She remained at the

gate, kicking one lavender sneaker in the dirt. "Fat chance," she said. "Dream on." She kicked the gate. "We're getting a rottweiler when we move."

"Sounds good. They're good dogs."

We eyed each other from opposite sides of the street, like gunslingers. The back of my neck began to ache. My vision blurred, resharpened, blurred. I was dizzy, thirsty, beside myself—literally, it felt like I had split into two versions of myself and neither of them was me. I wanted to sing. I wanted to vomit. I desperately hoped I wouldn't pee in my pants.

The front door opened again. The mother, in a business suit, leaned out. "Alice, come in here."

I had never known what her name was.

Alice gave the gate an aggressive push. It clanged, clashing with the ringing in my ears. "Bye," she said.

"Bye."

She walked up the stairs backward, still looking at me. "Don't come back, cracker."

I shook my head slowly, as if I was appalled by her bad, childish behavior. Then I turned away and plunged down the block, repeating the number on the sign over and over to myself until I had it memorized. I didn't look up or pay attention to where I was going until I realized I had arrived, as if by instinct, at the river.

Dusk was coming in. The peaks of the small gray waves were hooded with light, marching toward me. I held fast to the railing on the Promenade. I needed to focus. I closed my eyes, trying not to cry. I opened my eyes and watched the seagulls squawk at one another over trash: a bit of hot dog bun, a grimy French fry container. A big, dingy gray seagull sat on the rail with the lordly expression of one who had already eaten well. Others wheeled hungrily in the air. The light deepened; the river seemed to flatten out into a long glow. Pulling out my cell phone, I dialed the number. "This is Carl," said a recorded voice. "If you're calling about the house, leave a number and I'll call you back." So the square-faced father's name was Carl. I left my number and folded my phone into my palm with a click.

Across the illuminated river, I could just make out the modest, shadowy rectangle, like a headstone, of the building that housed *The Hudson Times* amid the mammoth glass-and-steel buildings that towered over it. I tried to imagine that it was my past and to summon up a rueful tenderness, but instead, just like earlier in the day but in reverse, my spirit seemed to be stuck over there while my body was here on the Promenade. On the shabby eighth floor, the lights were on. The river turned entirely gold, solidified. I could barely see the building now, it had dissolved into the last blaze of light, but I could feel the taut stretching, the hollow in my chest that pulled me toward it. I was suddenly tired. With a sinking feeling, I knew I couldn't stay here, that I was going to have to go back. For now. Before the tug of sleep overtook me altogether and the river went black, I picked up a little stone and put it in my pocket for the journey across the river. Souvenir, theft, ballast, return ticket.

Carl, I discovered two days later, had a few threads of gray in his modest beard. He wore a plaid shirt and khakis. Inside the house, the rooms were small, with drop ceilings and wallpaper ornamented with blue and white figures in Colonial dress, walking along country lanes and dancing merrily. The floors were wide-planked, uncarpeted, and buffed to a high sheen. The air smelled of freshly baked cake. Every window was elaborately curtained in several layers of filmy white fabric. We sat in the living room as Carl explained the history of the house, the work he had done on it himself, the copper pipes, the new roof, the double-paned windows, the central heat. On the tour, I had seen the Jacuzzi in the master bathroom, the neat rooms upstairs, the immaculate attic. The kitchen was old, and the basement was wide, dry, clean-swept. New hot water heater. Sitting in a wingchair, I listened, nodding, imagining in detail how spectacular the house was going to look after I gutted it, ripped down the upstairs ceilings, and punched holes in the roof for three or four cunningly slender skylights.

Carl leaned back. "Do you have any questions, Gabe?" I had told him to call me Gabe, since we were all on a first-name basis now.

"Well. Why are you selling, Carl?"

Carl chuckled. "This house," he said, "was left to me by my grandmother. I have no mortgage, so my wife and I have decided to move up to Chappaqua with Alice. The schools are wonderful up there. That's why the Clintons moved there. I've been in Brooklyn my entire life—I want to have grass. I want to have trees. I want to see stars at night. And Alice is getting to be quite the rider." He chuckled again. "Sorry. Long speech. It's just . . . we've had a lot of great interest in the house, and I'm eager to get going. Can't wait."

"What, um, price did you have in mind?"

Carl put his hands on his knees, making himself into a small, solid, plaid square. "Two point five," he said forthrightly.

"Two point five?"

"Two point five," and he added, as if I didn't know what he meant, "million."

What a greedy bastard. He had to be kidding. "Listen, Carl," I said. "I'm an artist. I could never afford that much. But this is my house. I've been watching—" I stopped myself. "I love this house. It's very special to me. *Very.*"

"Well now, Gabe, it is a special house, you're right. And that's nice, that art thing. But." He shrugged. "This is business. And, to be quite frank with you, I don't expect it will stay on the market for long."

"You're bleeding me," I blurted out.

He tilted his head. "I don't even know you." He stood up, held out his hand. "Good luck to you and your art, Gabe. I'll keep an eye out for your name."

"No, no," I said. "No."

"Yes," said Carl. He gestured toward the door. "I have another appointment coming."

Shattered, I managed to get to my feet, shake Carl's hand, and stumble down the front steps. Two bearish guys in baseball caps, one with a baby in a Snugli on his chest, were coming up the walk.

"Wow," said the one who wasn't carrying the baby. The other one waved at me in a friendly way. The baby cooed.

"The rooms are small inside," I said. "Very small."

They ignored me, climbing the front stairs with heavy, bearish, big-assed footsteps.

Back home, I took all the money out of the freezer and heaped it up on the floor in a glittering, melting silver pile. I unwrapped one of the bundles and counted the chilled cash inside: $300, just like the first one Fleur had given me. The plastic Gristede's bag was clammy; the aluminum foil, like a carapace, lay stiff, wet, and empty on the floor. I tapped the rest of the bundles, but none were light, and then I counted how many bundles there were. More than I had thought: $25,520. I stepped over the pile and opened the small filing cabinet in my bedroom. I found a relatively recent 401(k) statement from *The Hudson Times:* I had another $7,863.29 in there. So, altogether, that was about $33,000. I glanced at the trinkets on my windowsill—the cut-glass pineapple, the antique copper Buddha, the Steuben starfish, the gold-handled grape shears, etc.: $3,500, perhaps. $5,000? $8,000?

It didn't matter. It was nowhere near enough.

I sat down on the floor next to the melting heap of money, fighting despair. What would the *Stolen* girls do? They would be clever. They would be resourceful. In miniskirts, tied up with clothesline. Like the scrappy working gals they were, they would find a way where there seemed to be no way. I wondered what that way could be. Because it just wasn't fair. The market was so horrible! How were middle-class folks like me, working artists, strivers, people with families, ever supposed to get a toehold? The city had been ruined by September 11, sure, but hadn't it been just as thoroughly, if more slowly, destroyed by its hyperinflated real estate market? Eaten away from the inside, co-op by co-op, condo by condo, thousands of dollars a square foot, even a square foot of air. I didn't exactly blame Carl, but what he was profiting from was evil, and he was turning a blind eye to that fact. What if I had been a *black* artist? Would Carl have lowered his price? My instincts said no. So that was on Carl, too: all he cared about was getting his, the rest of the race be damned. Had that been his grandmother's intention when she left him the house she'd probably worked her whole life to pay off? That he would sell it to move to some white suburb?

I doubted it. I doubted it very much. My face burned; my fever seemed to be coming back, or maybe it was the fire of indignation. My joints ached. On the kitchen table above me, the figurine, which had one good horn now and the thick beginnings of another, sat serene, eyeless, blood-stained. Methodically, I rewrapped the money I had unwrapped, and stacked all the silver bricks back in the freezer, fitting them neatly on top of one another, making room for more. I knew I was defeated, for now. But the *Stolen* girls knew how to bide their time and plan. I would figure it out. I sat down at my rickety kitchen table, turned on my father's transistor radio, and began whittling the figurine some eyes. Three, I thought. Three eyes for her, all in a row, all open.

The odd thing was that it began to look, evening lamppost after evening lamppost, as if Carl had been wrong. The market wasn't flowing in his favor after all. Three weeks after I had first seen it, the FOR SALE BY OWNER sign was still taped to the window. I tried the number, and the same outgoing message answered.

As if in response to my unrequited longing for the house, the patch in the crook of my right arm grew, turned scaly, circled around my elbow to meet itself, like a rough red bracelet. I put cortisone cream on it, but it stubbornly remained, as if someone had tied a piece of twine very tightly there. The tether of my love.

But one day, as I took my usual place against the lamppost, I saw that the house was completely covered in grayish-white fabric, or perhaps it was thick plastic, wrapped up like a Christo installation, even over the widow's walk, which threatened to poke through the wrapping. Since Carl and his family couldn't possibly be inside unless they were mummified (I didn't go so far as to wish for that, not yet, anyway), I left the lamppost and walked up to the house, pausing at the gate in the manner of a curious passerby. The vine was a twisted stick now, the blue flowers gone underground for the winter. The house was mute, blind, cold, wrapped in its grayish-white shroud. I thought I could smell it from where I stood—the scent of baking cake, the floor polish, the heat rising through the vents. But I knew that wasn't true. There was no scent at all coming from the house, though there was a low hum, like the sound of a fan. Around the perimeter of the house was a series of signs, spaced about six feet apart, and on each sign it said the same thing in large red letters: WARNING PELIGROSO DO NOT ENTER NO ENTRAR FUMIGATION IN PROGRESS FUMIGACIÓN EN DESARROLLO STAY BACK ALEJATE KING EXTERMINATION.

I tilted my head, reading the words over and over. When I got home, before I began my Fleur work for the evening, I spent a bit of time online. Research can be so helpful.

For the next two weeks, while the house cured, I went to work every day and did my job, chin up, shoulders straight.

I bought a new tie, a black one with a brown stripe. I sent my mother a pretty card with a note in it—*Thinking of you, maybe Janos and I will come down in January*. I sent Caroline and her boyfriend, Carsten, in Berlin, a box of Harry & David special pears—*Thinking of you, maybe Janos and I will come over in February*. I arrived at work on time, and if I was still there at 6:00—the days were getting noticeably shorter—I closed the blinds until 6:24. I barely glanced at the river for the rest of the day. I did not go to Brooklyn.

On the way from the train to the office, and the office to the train, I passed the motley row of newspaper boxes, some free, some that asked for coins, yellow or red plastic, black or forest-green metal, all dinged up and huddled together on the corner like day laborers waiting for work. *The Hudson Times* box was never empty, though the box didn't ask for any coins. There had been no snow yet this year, just a cold that seemed to deepen every day like dye setting into fabric. I carried my Metrocard inside one of my big black flipper gloves so I could get at it as fast as possible while exposing a minimum amount of flesh.

I wore two pairs of socks and my indestructible old Doc Martens. My injured finger had healed, but the red patch on my arm hadn't gone away. It was joined by another, behind my knee. I was starting to look like a leopard. My toes ached sometimes, and my elbows, and the back of my neck, as if I'd been marked by a bad tide. Suddenly my hair seemed ridiculously *Teen Beat* and foofy, so I took Sarah's advice and got a haircut at the barbershop down the street from work. The barber's name was Ted or Fred or Sal. He cut hair like he was shearing a dog, and when he was done I could have been any guy, in any office, in any town. Cut that short, my hair barely looked red, or any color for that matter. It was like a distant reflection of hair. My face, without the foofy waves, looked bony. With my head shorn, I could see that my hairline was receding. "You're a fine young man," said Sal or Ted or Fred. "Give her a kiss for me." He winked. I wasn't sure if he was being sarcastic or not—*young man? her?*

When I got home that night, like any night, I did my yoga stretching routine, microwaved a frozen hijiki burger, watched a few minutes of the news, and put my plate and fork in the sink. I did my Fleur homework. I knew the drill: there had to be vengeance and life-threatening situations and disguises and triumph in tattered dresses, blah blah. The tired women on the subway wouldn't have it any other way: the bloody *Stolen* girls, clothed in torn lingerie and framed in stars, were their heroes, and there were certain obligations that adhered to telling those heroic stories. It was like tending the temple of a powerful goddess and her muses.

Since I didn't need it anymore, I threw away my tube of Bedhead Manipulator and did the jobs I was supposed to do. I turned out pages for Fleur after dinner, went to bed early, drank black coffee in the morning, tidied the lives of the dead all day, let the gathering fall wind bite my ears and scrape my shorn neck on my way to the train in the dark. I acted like a man who knew his place, a penitent, a messenger, scurrying from temple to temple, tie flapping. And at last the house was unwrapped again, sitting immaculately imperfect, scruffy, mine in November's darkness. FOR SALE BY OWNER. With a bit more time, just a bit, I knew I could figure it out.

I sat in the spindly gold chair next to the magnificent divan. Fleur held the flash drive in the immobile curl of her left hand. I read the new pages aloud to her. Sex, death, sex, death, sex, death, priceless pearls scattered on terrazzo, a shot rings out, Miranda races through the corridors by night, the vial tucked between her milky white breasts, sex, death, sex. Death.

Fleur nodded. "Good," she rasped. "Good boy." The ax blade of her face rested amid the gold and silk; under the web of expensive throws, she was tiny but alert. Today her eyes were bright. She turned her head to look at me. "So."

"What?" I kept my voice and expression neutral, like an amanuensis, a lowly scribe. As if I was afraid of her. Which I was.

She flicked her sharp gaze over my face, my newly shorn hair, my hungry soul. I reddened, keeping quite still.

"Something," she said. "The extra money—it's not for your art."

I looked at the floor, at my feet in the heavy Doc Martens, the purplish scuff on the toe of the left one—what was that?

"And it's not enough," she said. "Right?"

I nodded, not lifting my head.

She laughed. "It never is, my boy." She pushed herself upright among the layers of shining fabric. The points of her sculptural gray hair fell smartly, expertly to her jaw line. Her *s*'s weren't sliding so badly today; they almost held their outlines. "Is it love?"

I nodded again. "I think it might be," I mumbled. But it wasn't love. It was payback.

"Hmmm," she said. "Love." She said the word as if she'd never heard it before and was testing out the sound of it. "That's a mistake. Never throw money at love. Look at Elizabeth Taylor—not a happy woman."

I wasn't sure what Elizabeth Taylor had to do with it, but I nodded anyway.

"I liked your hair better the other way," said Fleur. "You look sad now."

"I am sad," I said softly.

"Why?"

I shook my head. "I can't talk about it," I said, even more softly. "But Fleur—" I glanced up. She was regarding me coolly. "Fleur—"

With the side of her face that could smile, she smiled. "It won't be enough. You understand that, don't you?"

"I know." I ran my hands over my scruffy, reddish scalp, loosened my tie. I sighed. I was careful not to look at her as

she reached beneath the pillows and extracted three envelopes
—maybe the entire divan was made of money, maybe she kept
all her money in there, somehow I wouldn't have put that
past her—though I caught her eye and ducked my head shyly
when I took them. She was right that it wasn't enough, but
then again, it might be. I had learned a thing or two from the
Stolen girls. I tucked the money into the breast pocket of my
suit jacket, patted it. I grinned and then leaned over and gently kissed Fleur on the forehead. "Thank you," I whispered.
She had a delicate, flowery scent, surprisingly feminine. Like a
rose. Was that why she had named herself Fleur?

She closed her eyes. "*De nada*," she said. "Leave. I'm tired
now."

I plucked the flash drive from her hand and saw myself out.
Because it was my birthday in a few days, I picked up a beautiful pair of swans, one silver and one gold, each about three
inches high, with onyx eyes and swooping loops of neck, from
one of the inner living rooms. The swans were heavier than
they looked. They pulled at my coat pocket as I rode the elevator down to the ornate lobby, but when I put them on my windowsill at home they were perfect, silver loop of neck lovingly
overlapping gold loop of neck, as if they had just glided over to
greet each other.

By contrast, the glass jar with the holes punched in the lid
wasn't very heavy at all. It rested easily in my coat pocket,
visible to the few other riders on the dreary subway only as
a slight lump. It could have been a jar of homemade jam. Of
course, three in the morning is sort of late to be bringing
jam to a friend, but this was New York. Some people surely
ate jam in the wee hours, spreading it thickly on homemade
bread, laughing, listening to cello music and entwining pin-
kies. That would have been much nicer than what I had to do,
which was slink down Love Lane and then Pineapple Street in

the cold, dark night, hop the old iron gate without making any noise, crawl like a thief across the dirt to the house's foundation, ease the jar out of my pocket, unscrew the lid, and shake it firmly—though my own hands were shaking, gloveless and raw—and then, nearly gagging, reach inside and push the termites out. For some reason, the critters didn't want to leave the jar. They had Stockholm syndrome or something. I knew there were about eighty of them in there (not cheap, either, let me tell you, not easy to come by), so I shook and shook, holding my breath, trying not to make a sound.

The house was quite dark, unwrapped, and silent in a way that felt as though no one was home. But that bastard Carl—he could be in there with a flashlight and a shotgun, awake. Prepared to shoot on sight. The things we do for love and our destiny! Fleur had been right. When the jar was empty, I stood up to go. But as I rose, a searing pain struck me at the knees and elbows, as if I'd been hit with an iron bar. I gasped. Was it Carl, invisible? The house was still and silent, Carl-less. I took a deep breath. The pain passed, mercifully, and I hurried out of the small yard, back over the gate without a sound—G, *the night shadow*, and once again, I was a strange kind of thief, actually *adding* something to the house, not taking anything out of it—and up the street. The terrible pain haunted me all the way home, and I felt it whispering through my joints as I fell asleep, chilled and exhausted but hopeful, in my own bed. I felt sure that I had bought myself some time. Two, three weeks, maybe a month.

That's when I began blackmailing Fleur in earnest. I was an impatient, jealous lover, still young in so many ways. Foolish. And I was nervous. I thought the termites had betrayed me, because the house, when I checked on it, remained peculiarly ordinary and unchanged, as if it had been enchanted. The old glass in its windows was placidly wavy as usual, like still lakes. No fumigation tent. Once, when I had crept closer than I should have under cover of night, I saw Alice dancing with her mother in the living room. The curtains were open. Brightly lit inside the house, the two of them were pogoing away to some song I couldn't hear. They looked so happy. Alice's mother's dreads swirled in the air and bounced around her shoulders; she grabbed Alice's hands and they jumped up and down together, laughing. If things had been different, fairer, I could have told them that I knew just what that was like, that I had thrown my head back and danced with my mother once too, but of course I couldn't do that. There was a canyon between where I stood on my side of the sidewalk and the living room where they danced. I wiped away a tear.

The next day, I explained the situation to Fleur—how hard it had become for me to keep our arrangement private; how embarrassing and potentially legally complex it would be if it came out; how easy it would be to pick up the phone and call her editor; how obvious it would be to anyone who came to see her, considering the current state of her health, that she wasn't really writing these books, not to mention the evidence on my computer at home and on the flash drive in my pocket at that very moment. I patted my pocket. (I had another flash drive, which was sitting on the windowsill in my apartment, between the copper Buddha and the Steuben starfish. I wasn't an idiot.)

All of that was true, but I was banking on something more subtle, more psychological, the reason she had asked me in the first place: Fleur, née Rebecca Sharp, would do anything to go on being Fleur. Honestly, I think she would have paid more, even. She had no intention of allowing anyone anywhere to see her like this; I had no doubt that her plan was to drop dead one day and have the last laugh on all the suckers who thought they could get the better of her. The worst thing I could have said, the ace I had up my sleeve, was that I'd quit if she didn't give me what I needed. Fleur didn't trust many people, and she'd spent months grooming me, allowing me in, inch by inch. She didn't have the time, the strength, or the coherence to start training another young man to be her prosthetic writing arm.

While I waited for her reply, I reminded myself that I was fully prepared to produce my ace, and that I was prepared to make good on it, to walk away from the table. I hadn't slept well the night before; I still felt teary. I didn't, under any circumstances, want to cry in Fleur's sanctum sanctorum. Who knew what would happen to me if I did that? The smiling side of her face frowned. "How much?"

"Forty-five thousand." I didn't say, For this book. And forty-five for the next one. And so on. We would cross that bridge when we came to it. I felt giddy, surreal. I couldn't believe I was doing this, yet I felt that I was finally demanding some of the respect I deserved, that I was acting like a man for once. Why should they all get to bleed me just because they'd caught a break with fate? Carl's grandmother was the one who did the work for that house. I was the one churning out the pages for Fleur. I had started writing the books as a lark, but life was more serious now, I was getting older, and I hadn't thought when we started that nearly two books later I'd still be crouched on that spindly chair next to her magnificent divan, building her already considerable fortune. Ghostwriters make a lot more money than what was filling up my freezer. Invisibility is expensive. Fleur knew that.

Or, it seemed, she must have, because she nodded grimly. "Gabe," she said, "could you put that throw, the one with the fringes, around my shoulders? It's freezing in here."

It was boiling in the room. I disentangled the fringed white cashmere throw and settled it around her, up to her frail chin. She smelled so sweet, like a grandmother. Though she was the wolf, of course. I sat back down in the spindly chair, my hands on my knees. This is the moment, I thought. Breathe. Breathe. The world is going to turn one way or the other.

"Hand me that computer."

I picked up the platinum laptop from the floor and handed it to her.

"Give me my glasses."

I got them from the little gilded table behind the divan. Sighing, she put them on. They were almost bigger than her entire face. "Number."

I told her the number of my leaky dinghy of a checking account. She pecked at the keys for a minute or two with her good hand. Then she leaned back against the nest of silver and gold pillows, clearly exhausted. "All right, you little motherfucker," she said. "Don't ask me again. I'll have your legs broken for you." Eyes closed, she continued, "Take my glasses off and put them back on the table. Put the computer on the floor. Leave. Come back in ten days with pages or I'll hunt you down and kill you."

My hands shook, but I did as she said, gently closing the door behind me. I hurled myself out of her apartment, through the living rooms and sitting rooms; past the maid, holding a small white towel, regarding what looked like the Queen of England's silver service piled on a dining room table; past the springtime meadows. I was moving so fast I didn't even stop to grab a keepsake, though it would have been nice, I thought later that evening, to have had a memento of this day, the day I took charge of my life. I burst from the building, past the doormen and liverymen and footmen, dashed across the street, and paused by the old stone wall around Central Park, trying to catch my breath.

I still had a long way to go, but I was surprisingly content. It was one of those rare evenings when the moon had risen before the sun set: the moon hung high in the blue, a faint, crisp curve of white; the sun sat low on the horizon, amber and taciturn. For that moment, with my hand near my heart, I felt lighter than air, perfectly balanced on the world's fulcrum with the moon and the stars wheeling at one end and the sun and clouds glowing at the other, like the silver and gold swans poised on my windowsill on East Seventh Street. As if from a great height, I saw everyone I loved most: Fleur asleep on her divan, Sarah measuring very small things at work, Janos murmuring very large numbers into his cell phone. Far away I saw my mother, mall-walking in Brewster; even farther, Caroline and Carsten, asleep in Berlin. I saw myself, typing in the lighted names of the dead onto dissolving reams of paper in the place where two rivers turned into the sea. On Central Park West, cars proceeded along, obedient as cattle. Bending down, I unlaced the grimy Doc Martens, took them off, and hurled them over the wall into the park. They went *thud, thunk* in the dirt. Today, I thought, I became a man. It was time to buy some real shoes. I could afford them.

No one on the train remarked on my stockinged feet. I needed new socks, too, I noticed. The other riders probably thought I was just another homeless guy who wouldn't stay in a shelter. I looked at my sober, bony-faced reflection in the subway window and smiled. *Gabriel, thirty-eight, at Fifty-ninth and Lex. On his way home.* When had that thin but perceptible line appeared between my eyes? My hair was about an inch past penumbral. After work the next day, wearing my new black lace-up shoes, I got a haircut from Sal. That was his name: Sal. *Gabe*, I said, holding out my hand for Sal's firm grip, as if he was pulling me to the shore of manhood.

In a muffin shop in Brooklyn Heights, I ordered two of their huge muffins and a double latte — I could never quite wake up these days, and I was hungry all the time — and found a seat by the window. My house on Pineapple Street was unchanged, which was both a relief and not a relief at all. What was up with my fucking lazy termites? Were they fake? Had I been gypped? I wondered what a spell cast by a *curandera* would cost, and how to find the best one. I could Google it later. It was humid and warm in the muffin place, like being inside a muffin. The butter was soft in the little plastic tub. Rock-and-roll from twenty years ago was playing—Duran Duran. I thought about Arizona. The curve of Tim's small, indifferent white ass. Was the cottonwood tree still there? I buttered one of the muffins, licked the remainder of the butter off the knife. Three women with babies in strollers sat at the next table, talking excitedly about a blog they wanted to start. The shop window, glazed with condensation against the cold outside, glowed. It was all about half a size too small, which was what I liked about it. I could *be* here, effortlessly.

The shop bell tinkled. Carl and Alice walked in, walked right past me. Carl was on his phone. Alice was hop-hop-hopping into the store like a rabbit. "Three!" said Carl into the phone. "That's love, that's definitely love. Oh, my."

Alice, at the counter, peered up and down, side to side, at all the types of mega-muffins. She was wearing a red coat with a hood, like Little Red Riding Hood, and white patent-leather boots. She pulled at her father's sleeve. "Marble. Daddy. Marble."

He put a hand on her head, still talking, but so softly I couldn't hear what he said. He turned around, squinted, nodded. His gaze met mine. He frowned, then he pointed. My heart sank. My God, I thought, he knows—oh Jesus, oh fuck. I felt as if termite trails were etched on my hands; I shoved them into my coat pockets.

"You," he said.

"Me?"

He waved the phone. "You still interested in the house?"

"Yes," I said fervently, "yes, I am, I really am, I was just going to call you, actually."

"Well, you better start dialing. It's a bidding war." He smiled broadly. "I can't believe it. After—never mind. What's your name again?"

"Gabriel."

"Gabriel, if you want in, you'd better make an offer. This thing is *moving*."

Alice, leaning against the glass front of the counter, said, "I don't like him."

"This is business," said her father. "It doesn't matter about liking or not liking."

"Yes it does," countered Alice. "That's our house. He can't have it."

Her father looked at her tenderly.

"Please, Carl," I said. "I'm begging you. Two days. Forty-eight hours. Let me try to get a bid together. I love that house so much." I assembled my most solemn expression to conceal how desperate I felt.

Carl gave me a long look, one hand on Alice's head. He checked his watch. "This time Friday," he said. "And then it's over."

"Thank you," I said. "Oh, thank you, thank you. You'll be hearing from me."

But the problem wasn't just the money, or Carl, or Fleur, floating on her golden bed of cash. The problem was that I had waited too long. The metamorphosis had progressed too far, though I didn't know that yet. What I thought I knew was that my rash seemed to be spreading—the top of my foot, the back of my neck—and I was exhausted, dizzy, weak. The winds were in me.

I had so much scheming to do and so little time to do it, but that afternoon found me lying on Janos's sofa, with a fever, whittling away at the blood-stained figurine. I began on her left horn, working gingerly with the knife. Janos sat in a chair nearby, reading a book about the history of Prussia. A fire was burning down in the fireplace; the room smelled faintly, comfortably, of smoke. Near the fireplace, the worn Oriental carpet had an even more worn-down spot, like a shadow, where

Sofia, the little dog, used to sleep on her plaid cushion all day. The huge stone square of coffee table was scattered with books, newspapers, magazines, a pad on which Janos had scrawled a few notes, a glass with melting ice in it, a plate containing my half-eaten sandwich, and a bowl of soup. I twirled one wrist in the air, then the other: they ached as though someone was sticking pins in a puppet with my name on it. I had a set of fever blisters, like the Pleiades, burning inside my mouth. I whittled my figurine, slowly piling wood shavings into a hollow in the blanket on my lap.

"What is that going to be?" said Janos.

"A being." I was hot, I was cold, I was floating around in an irritable way, feeling itchy at the ankles. I was bursting with my news about the bidding war. "I bet I'm dying," I said. "I feel weird."

Janos turned a page. "You have the flu." He closed the history of Prussia. "Live with me, Gabe." He gestured. "There's plenty of room here for you and all your . . . beings." He smiled.

This was my opening. "Listen, Janos, I have to tell you." I set the figurine and the whittling knife on top of the shavings in the soft blanket hollow. "Something so amazing has been happening." I spilled it all out, everything about buying the house on Pineapple Street, my chance meeting with Carl and Alice in the muffin place, my destiny, my vision of the future, our matching Vespas full of *cava* and oysters going back and forth over the Brooklyn Bridge, what it would mean for my art. How it could be for us. I left out the blue goddess, the termites, and the blackmailing part, but I did say I was so close, so close, unbelievably close. I had almost $80,000. I needed maybe another $200,000. I felt my face grow hot as I talked, from the beauty of it all. I might have cried, just a little. I insisted. I begged. I left things out. I put things in. I asked for $280,000.

Janos set the history of Prussia on the coffee table. He regarded me for a long moment and then said, "No, Gabriel. I am not helping you buy that house. Not in this market. You can live with me or you can fend for yourself. I have asked you so many times, and we are getting older here, have you noticed? Both of us. You're almost forty. I'll be sixty before we know it. We're going to end up being two old men going to see each other in taxicabs on Saturday nights. It's ridiculous."

I stared at him, furious. I didn't know what to say. I didn't know how I felt. What a fucking bastard! Just like Carl. Out for himself.

As angry with him as I was, though, I had to admit that I still admired him. He was a self-made man; he had earned, more or less, everything he had. Like my mother, who now owned the Sunburst Motel, he was scrappy. His scent was espresso and the special expensive dirt in the townhouse's atrium and laundry starch. He always wore white or light blue button-down shirts: the white-collar businessman's uniform. For Janos, lightly starched dress shirts were a sign that you recognized the worthiness of your opponent, that you didn't think you were any better than the average lowly trader on Wall Street hustling futures for a Christmas bonus. He would never have allowed himself to put the knife in while wearing anything else. His cuffs were immaculate. His taste bordered on the old-fashioned, the Continental, though he'd grown up in Newark.

If I hated him so much, did that mean I loved him as well? Why didn't I know? Maybe it was just a daddy thing. But if he was my daddy, how could he have said no? Was it because we were looking closer to the same age? Somehow forty didn't seem as far from sixty as thirty-five had from fifty-five. My spine hurt. My eyes ached. "Maybe I should go home," I said.

"Maybe you should. Maybe that old bat will die tomorrow

and leave you all her money. Maybe you should have saved some of what she's already given you."

"Maybe she will," I snapped. "Someone has to help me. My art!"

He picked up his book again. "What is it, exactly, that you're holding out for, my love?"

I knew what he meant, but I had no answer. I hated him, but I did love him, of course. I loved his irregular face, his formidable will, the long years of his life before me. I loved his wrists, his shrewd way of eyeing the world. I had never hesitated to use the word "love" with Janos. I was searching for some other word, a word I didn't know yet. Until I knew that word, I couldn't live with him, whether I loved him or not. That word was somewhere in the house on Pineapple Street, written high up in a corner, but just for another forty-eight hours. Then I would be lost.

"Goddamnit, Janos." I took my blanket and shuffled huffily in my stockinged feet into the atrium at the center of the house. The glass atrium door made its soft *thush* as it closed behind me. Inside, there was real dirt and grass and several tall, thin trees. A carefully calibrated humidity permeated the three stories of air. At the top of the atrium was a round skylight, a disk of smoky, white-gray sky. There was a small stone bench inside the atrium, and hanging just above the bench was a hand-carved birch feeder for the two little, exquisite, carnival-yellow birds who had a nest among the ferns and flowers and the tall, thin trees. The birds were some sort of rare finch; Janos called them both Tweetie. If you sat on the bench, sooner or later one or both of the Tweeties would skiffle down and sit near you, or perch by your ear on the length of perfect birch, and you'd feel visited, graced, until they skiffled away again.

I sat on the bench with a handful of birdseed, my skin feeling quilted with fever. I could hear the Tweeties high above me, gossiping, but neither of them came down. I opened my hand wider. From inside the atrium, the rest of the apartment looked like a scene from a movie, colorful but weightless. I could see Janos's foot in its black silk sock, the light from the long window. Was it love I was holding out for? Was I waiting for a higher love to walk through the door with his shining, irresistible face? Was my true love's name the word written high up in the house on Pineapple Street? Did he live in Brooklyn? Or was the word something else? Would I ever know what it was? Burning, despairing, I held my hand open, waiting. The gods were clearly nearby, hovering over Pineapple Street. Maybe they would whisper the word or the name to me. I waited and waited, but they didn't come.

But the gods, as we know, are fickle. Sometimes they take the shape of wild boars or swans or waves. Other times they inhabit lowlier creatures — termites, for instance. Which wasn't the word Carl used when he called to tell me the bidding war was undergoing a temporary cease-fire. "We have a little problem to take care of," Carl said. "I'll be in touch in a few weeks, Gabe." I smiled through my tears. Already, I knew, that house was shrouded, white, mute. Carl and Alice and Alice's mother were out of it. With the help of the termite gods, I had done it: I had stopped the clock.

The cake was gorgeous. Red velvet with white icing, festooned with multicolored icing flowers, an extravagant set of red, molten sugar loops — *Happy 38th birthday, dear, dear Gabriel* — that began at the base of the cake, ran up the side, across the top, down the other side, and off the cardboard disk. It shone brightly in the crowded Chinese restaurant, excessive as a spaceship. Sarah's and Janos's faces beamed at me. From Sarah, a soapstone box filled with clock parts and foreign coins — art material. From Janos, a complete set of small, exquisite woodcarving knives that cleverly rolled up in a length of canvas, with canvas handles stitched into the center. I kissed Sarah and Janos with loud smacks and cut them big fat pieces of rich red cake. Sarah laughed. "We're going to get high on this shit."

Janos turned to her. "It's so nice to see you, my dear." He patted her hand. "It's been too long. You look wonderful." Which was a lie. She looked tired; her chin was pointier than ever. Subtly, he pulled his BlackBerry out of his pocket and glanced at it.

Sarah made a face. "*Mezzo mezz'*. I think I'm going to break up with my boyfriend."

"What boyfriend?" I asked. "You don't have a boyfriend."

She dropped her gaze to her slice of cake. "Sure I do. The puppetmaker."

"The puppetmaker? He's your boyfriend? Janos, this cake is *amazing*. What are you talking about?"

Sarah ate a delicate bite. "It doesn't matter, because he's not my boyfriend anymore. I'm going to tell him tonight."

Janos put the BlackBerry away and turned to give Sarah a keen look. "And why is that, may I ask? That you're breaking up with this man, this toymaker."

"Well." She considered, eating icing. "Okay, first, he's not a toymaker—he's an artist. His puppets were in the last Biennial. He's a serious guy, pretty much. He went to Brown. That's not the problem." She sighed.

"So what is the problem?" asked Janos.

"He wants to marry me." Her face crumpled, and I thought for a minute that she might cry, but then she regained her composure. "Like, married. This cake really is great. Where did you get it?"

I looked closely at her. Even after all this time, and all the baths, and the curling up to sleep in her drafty house behind the house, she could duck behind an inner door—the girl door, I called it privately—and out of my sight. Always, she seemed quite young to me when she did this, perhaps five, in a white party dress, crying for a reason no one else would ever understand. Just now, for instance, all I could make out was the lacy edge of a white skirt. "Honey," I said, "do you want to marry this guy?"

She shrugged miserably. "I would have to move to Vermont. He got a teaching job there."

"What?" I nearly choked. "You can't do that."

"Well." She set her hand flat on the table. Her tone was flat, too. "That's what a lot of real artists do, Gabriel. They teach. He's lucky to get it."

Janos, sitting back, said nothing. He ate his cake slowly.

"What do you mean, 'real artists'?" I said.

"He's a real guy, Gabe," said Sarah in a tone I didn't like, "with a real job. He was in the *Biennial*."

"Screw the Biennial," I said angrily. "Since when do you care about things like that? Everyone knows the Biennial is a fraud. Jesus, Sarah." I was furious with her, but at the same time I was thinking with pride of my beneficent termites, who had intervened with time on my behalf. I cut myself another thick piece of birthday cake. "Okay, you know what? Fine. Throw away your own art. Marry the puppetmaker, move to Vermont, have ten kids, milk a cow or two, get fat and resentful, ruin the kids' lives with your bitterness. Good plan."

Sarah, still eating icing, began to cry. "I'm the one who's bitter?" she said tearily.

"Gabriel," said Janos. "Gabriel! Apologize."

"No," I said through a mouthful of red velvet cake. "We know each other too well for that. I mean, come on. She won't even say his name. How serious could this be?"

"Peter," said Sarah. "Peter Priest."

"Peter *Priest?* That's not a name. That's absurd. Peter Priest the puppetmaker? That's a joke."

Sarah looked at me coldly, tear-stained. "It is, in fact, his name, Gabe. He didn't choose it."

"Gabriel," warned Janos again. He gestured for the check. "What in God's name is wrong with you? Are you having a stroke?"

Sarah tapped her fork against her plate. "No, really, this is helpful." She raised an eyebrow at me. "You being such a total fucking asshole makes me see it: I don't want to break up with him at all. I like Peter Priest. I like him a lot. He's incredibly gentle."

Burrowing into my bad behavior like a hungry termite, I snapped, "So you're going to be Mrs. Priest? Is that where this is going?"

Sarah stood up. She looked tall and pale and thin; her topiary hair, scattered over her shoulders, was regal. Her high forehead was flushed. Almost against my will, I knew why Peter wanted to marry her. There was something in her that burned clean.

"I really don't know," Sarah said. "And screw you." She kissed Janos, squeezed his hand, nodded at me. "I'll call you tomorrow," she said to me, "and you can apologize. At length." She left the restaurant.

I stared straight ahead, thinking of my termites. I counted them, began naming them.

Janos set a small pile of bills on the check, weighted them down with a little glass pitcher of soy sauce. He boxed up the remainder of the glorious cake. He rolled up the canvas with the exquisite woodcarving knives tucked inside. He gathered the watch parts and foreign coins from the pink tablecloth and put them into the soapstone box. He stacked it all in front of himself like a man waiting with his suitcases for a train, but he didn't move to go. He checked his BlackBerry again, glanced at me, glanced away.

I was embarrassed, of course. But something was tearing inside me, as if my ribs were pulling away from my lungs, as if my shoulder blades were broadening, stretching, cracking. I didn't feel right. I couldn't explain what was happening to me. I didn't know why I hadn't told Sarah about the house: my first big secret from her. This Peter was her first big secret from me, apparently. Unless there were others. I felt slightly queasy, and stupid, and stubborn, and obscurely wronged, though I was, by any measure, the asshole at the table.

Janos said, "When I was your age, I had already been poor and rich and poor again and I was scratching my way back up. I wonder sometimes if this is an American thing, this drift. This *attachment* to drifting. I don't understand it."

"I'm not drifting." I wondered if I was going to throw up. My breath shortened, strained. My teeth hurt. "I have a plan."

"Gabriel." In profile, Janos's craggy face was leonine. His cufflinks were thick, plain gold bars. "Gabriel, my dear. Buying a house you can't afford is not a plan."

"I think something's wrong with me," I said. How much cake had I eaten?

"No," said Janos. "It's just life. It pulls quite hard."

But he was wrong. It wasn't life, or not usual life, anyway. It was the change. It was on its way, moving toward me, already lifting me. I thought it was the glowing windows of the house pulling me toward them across the river, and I rowed as hard as I could toward that light.

On a gray, freezing Thursday during which nothing was happening at *The Hudson Times* and my section was tidy as a freshly mowed lawn, the dead docile in their boxes of type, I got a tense call from Sarah. Could I come right now. Please.

I arrived at the crooked house behind the house to find Sarah sitting in her living room on her makeshift sofa. The fur had slipped down to reveal the black cotton futon beneath it. Sarah was biting a nail, looking as beautiful and undecided as I had ever seen her. There was a smudge over her right eyebrow. The floor was covered in boxes, some closed, taped, and labeled, others with clothes or shoes or pans sticking out of the tops. The curtains had been taken down and were lying in a crimson heap on the floor. The unfiltered light was brighter than usual. There was a pronounced draft. The room felt shaken molecularly, as if a rhino or a hippopotamus had just galloped through it and away, out the back door. Sarah wore a gold band on her left ring finger. Her brown eyes were wide. She was wearing jeans and a plain blue thermal shirt and a long indigo scarf around her hair, as if she was an ordinary woman in an ordinary old house with water-stained walls where the air was already going flat.

I sat down next to her and she nestled against me. Her familiar scent. "Where are you going, honey?" I said. I thought she must have found another, cheaper apartment. Or, I tried to think that I thought that.

"Vermont. I married the puppetmaker."

I nodded slowly. "Okay."

"The moving van's coming soon." She put her head on my shoulder.

"You should finish packing."

"Yeah."

The makeshift sofa was soft. The heat banged in the pipes against the cold. For an instant, I thought that maybe if I fucked her, I could get her to stay. But no part of the rest of me was interested in that. I was her brother, at best, chaste and melancholy, with pale, midwinter hands. I pulled her against me and I could feel her, her quivering. I didn't forgive her. I went upstairs to pee. The windowsills in the bathroom were empty, with grimy patches. The tub was scrubbed clean and white.

Then we sat side by side on the sofa. I tapped her new, hard gold ring with my finger. It was the plainest of bands, blank and simple against my fingertip. "Wow. Very real."

"Yes," she said. "You'll like him. He's just a person. He has a beard, sort of."

"I didn't get into the show," I said.

"Me neither." Sarah rubbed her eyes. Then she got up as close as she could to my ear and whispered, "Gabe. I'm sorry we had a fight. I love our story, but it's time." I wondered grumpily which kind of time she meant—mythic or historical. Though I knew, of course, she was right. And women, poor things, had that ticking clock, cruel taskmaster, inside them. "And Gabe," she said, "if you get in trouble, ask Saint Margaret. You know where she is."

"Saint Margaret," I said. "God, we haven't been there in a while."

Sarah shrugged. "I'm just saying. She helped me." She turned the wedding ring around on her finger. It was slightly too big.

The van came, but she left most of her stuff behind. She left the makeshift fake fur sofa and the dusty pink dress with the torn lace on the living room wall. She left a coffee-stained cup on the kitchen table. She left one emerald-green high-heeled shoe. She left a half-empty box of sugar cubes in the refrigerator. She didn't, however, leave a thick, Sarah-sized, epic, devastating letter anywhere, addressed to me or anyone else. When she got into the van, next to the man who would drive her to Vermont to begin her life as Mrs. Priest, the puppet-maker's wife, she first set the accordion, wrapped in three blankets and tied with lots of twine, up front on the floor on her side. Maybe, I thought sourly, she'd play "Goodnight, Irene" for her children. Maybe they'd dance around the living room, build a castle out of sugar cubes in the dining room, pour food coloring over ice in the kitchen sink. Send me Christmas cards they'd made themselves, gluing eggshell Santas with cotton-ball beards to colored construction paper. I'd send something clever and tasteful, and too expensive, in return. I knew my part. She clambered in around the accordion and closed the door. She waved a little wave through the window.

After the van pulled away, I went back into her tilted house, walked through the echoing, water-stained rooms one last time. I put the emerald-green high-heeled shoe on the top front step, arranging it carefully, jauntily, as if any minute she'd come running back, laughing, to slip the missing shoe on her bare foot. But the emerald-green shoe just sat there empty. I felt like the Prince with a runaway Cinderella. I closed Mrs. Wieznowski's rusty gate behind me. In my pocket I had a long piece of torn pink lace. I took it out and wound it around my fingers as I rode the subway back to Manhattan.

I looked at the faces of the people sitting opposite me. They seemed tired, worried. That Pound poem was on a placard above their heads, but the subway car didn't seem anything like a wet, black bough. It just seemed like a subway car. It rattled the way it always did. On the subway floor, something had spilled, turned grayish black, and gotten a newspaper page stuck to it. The half-page sports section of *The Hudson Times*. When I got home, I sat down in a kitchen chair. I still had my coat on. I pulled the length of dusty-rose lace across my palm, straightening its thready rows of tiny flowers.

I put the length of lace down on the kitchen table and went to Janos's. I waited in the downstairs living room until he came home from work. The fireplace was cold. The coffee table was swept clean. On it was a note from the maid: *Need more Bon Ami please and soft sponges thank you mr janos.* Feeling strange and hollow, I took Janos's enormous, regal fur hat, his ally against the impending winter, from its wrought-iron hook in the entryway and put it on. It clasped my head in its heavy embrace, still so warm it might have been breathing. The rich black fur tickled my ears and neck. Janos's head was bigger than mine, so the hat tilted, unable to get a solid footing. In the mirror, I was a surprisingly attenuated, pale figure, with sharp cheekbones, large eyes, my penumbral hair like a prisoner's, and the majestic black fur hat tumbling into my eyes. *Gabriel, at Janos's, on Sarah's wedding day.* Something bothered me. Something seemed to be missing. I moved closer to the mirror to try to see what it was, or where the missing thing should have been, but I couldn't make it out. Just my own blurry face. The big, ungainly hat tilting, uneasy as an ill-fitting crown, above it. Poor hat, I thought.

The front door opened. Janos came in. "Gabe," he said. "What are you doing?"

The hat slipped over my eye. "It's Sarah," I said. My voice cracked.

"Is she all right?"

"She got married. She's gone." I stood there awkwardly. "Neither of us got into the show, either."

Janos gently took the hat off my head. "Ah," he said. "It will be all right, you know? You will visit. There will be another show. Next time, you will win."

But I knew that none of that would happen. I just knew. The blue figurine was not a kind spirit, as it turned out, but a vengeful one. A dark knowledge, like an anchor, dropped from my center straight down into the earth. I rested my forehead against Janos's and felt his force, his warmth, the lines in his forehead. I kissed him, both because I wanted to and because I didn't know how to explain that I was panicking. I didn't know how to say *I think I'm losing. I think maybe I've already lost,* so I kissed him again, more forcefully this time, and I tasted the espresso in his mouth and pushed his coat off and unbuttoned his shirt and moved my hand inside it. His chest was warm. He pulled me against him with the lonely, hungry sigh that never seemed to get less lonely or hungry no matter how long we were together, and that always made me think of those rows of Hungarian boys in their beds in that tattered Catholic boarding school, Janos staring, awake in the dark, his thin scabby legs.

We went upstairs and moved together. My belt, his belt, clattering to the floor. The flesh of his belly was undergirded by muscles that even now seemed strong as drawbridges, thick bands that could move whatever needed to be moved. I tasted the crepey skin of his balls, the smooth hardness of his dick. He lay back on the bed with his hands behind his head and his brow furrowed. I wanted him to stay hard forever, and I also wanted him to come forever, until my jaw ached and the streets turned from glass to rushing water. They almost did. Then I lay in his arms and curled around him, my ear to his heart. It beat, and beat, and beat, quickly, and then more slowly, just like hearts do.

"So are you ready to come home to me, my love?" he said into the dark. I pretended I was already asleep, my knee on his thigh. I didn't answer. In the morning, I thought, I'll ask him again about the bid. I was so close.

But in the morning a feather brushed my cheek.

I was drinking the coffee Janos had made me. When he made coffee it always tasted as if it had been made half out of rust—that's the way he liked it, rusty and sweeter than sweet, like the Manhattan Bridge immersed by a tsunami of sugar. He was on the phone: some market was already open, or just closing, somewhere. He was speaking in German, though not necessarily to Germany. I decided to go into the atrium with my coffee and see what the Tweeties were up to. I sat down on the stone bench, sipping the rust and sugar.

The Tweeties were in one of the thin, three-story trees. I could see the delicate upper branches swaying from their tiny weight. I was running over what I knew about the habits of goats for Anna, who was in hiding in a convent, tending the nuns' goats. I really wanted to finish *Stolen at Twilight* and get more money. Maybe Fleur could advance me for *Stolen in Flames*. Outside the glass, Janos paced back and forth in boxer shorts, scratching his ass and pouring himself more coffee. Inside, the sounds were so subtle you wouldn't hear them unless you were alone and still: a branch shaking as a Tweetie hopped onto it, the almost subliminal whir of the fan that was hidden somewhere. And another sound—I don't know if it was sound, technically—of three stories of air distilled in a lush green column.

You couldn't eat any of these trees, so Caroline wouldn't have liked the atrium; she would have thought it was artificial. That's why she said she left New York, because the city had become too artificial and manicured; it had lost its wild, secluded areas, its productive wreckage. She said Berlin still had great wreckage. Berlin, she said, was New York in the sixties. It had mystery. It was obvious to me that the real reason Berlin was better was that Carsten was there, though Caroline wouldn't admit it. The only thing better than Berlin, she said, was Cracow. Anyway, I was content in the atrium. I could have lived there, almost. Slept there, definitely. I wondered why I never had.

The Tweeties, who tended to travel together, glided down to the birch feeder, careless streaks of yellow chattering away, and at first I was thrilled when the wing of one brushed my face, a feather on my cheekbone. But then a voice that I barely recognized as mine was screaming with pain. It was as if that feather had sliced me open to the bone.

Janos hurled open the glass door, his phone clattering to the floor. When he reached me, I was doubled over, the birds peering down at me from high in their Three-Story Tree, cheeping inquisitively. He couldn't know that I was on fire, that a feather had incinerated me. I felt his hand on my chin. He peered into my eyes.

"I—" I said. I was in so much fucking pain. I was in so much fucking pain.

"Lean on me," he said. "Come out of here." Janos was not a large man, but he felt vastly sturdy to me at that moment. My knees were exploding. My skin was salted with lye. My hands were cinders. Yellow birds were trapped in my lungs, piercing them with the scrabble of their sharp, dry feet.

"Ah," I said.

"Shhh," said Janos, grabbing up the phone. "I'm calling an ambulance."

But already, before the ambulance came, a flower of blood was blooming under the skin on my right forearm. I have to say, it was beautiful. It was purplish blue. I thought about how much Sarah would have liked it, how she might have painted it, just before they covered the flower with gauze. We jolted through the city to the hospital, Janos holding my incinerated hand gingerly between his two cool, strong hands and looking questioningly into my eyes. Another flower bloomed on my left arm, near my wrist. One on each side of the gate. *Old friend.* My head ached dully, then ferociously, then dully again.

They admitted me for observation and began testing me for everything. I knew it couldn't be HIV—I'd recently had that test—but it felt bad, and large, and dark, as if a ship had sailed in between my ribs. Janos wangled me a private room. They gave me a pill for the pain, and a dinner that had grainy mashed potatoes with it. A nurse tried to turn on the television set for me, but Janos stopped her, and he was right. The pill had lulled my skin and bones to placid quiescence, but not my ears—they got confused if there was too much noise, like wild animals in traffic. Janos made low-voiced phone calls to other doctors, better doctors, who said they'd be there the next day. In the quiet hospital room, I felt sweetly sad and oddly composed, like a clean, folded white shirt. Outside the windows, the city was dark.

"Janos," I said, "will you read to me?"

He frantically patted his pants pockets, as if a book might be concealed inside, then sprinted down to the gift shop. Laughing, he came back with Fleur's first book, *Stolen*. The four girls on the cover, like whorish paper dolls. Eighties hair. "It was this crap, the Bible, or the *Enquirer*," he said, waving it, with its garish cover, in the air. "I'm not sure there's a difference." He shook his head.

"It's okay. That one's my favorite." I felt nauseated; my bones felt fragile, as if they ached down to the marrow.

He turned off the glaring overhead fluorescent light, turned on the bedside lamp, and sat down in the orange naugahyde visitors' chair. Putting on his glasses, he opened the cheap paperback and pressed the thin pages down. "We were all stolen," he began in his smoky mongrel accent, "stolen right out of our shoes." I closed my eyes and turned on my side to listen, though I already knew it by heart.

When the other, better doctors arrived the next day, they crowded into the room and went over every inch of me with various instruments. They sent x-rays of me overseas by computer and then huddled around the computer, pointing. They agreed. They disagreed. It took all day.

"Well," they said as evening fell. "Well."

"Am I?" I said.

The oldest better doctor, who was technically retired but had flown in from Seattle, stood at the end of my bed with his liver-spotted hands spread on the metal footboard. "Gabriel," he said, sounding like Walter Cronkite, "we believe that you may have what we call a lazy cancer." He gestured shyly in the air. "It's—"

"Take it out," I said.

The other better doctors looked at me sympathetically. The one who wore stylish glasses bit her lip. "We can't," said the oldest better doctor. "It's in your blood."

"My blood has cancer?"

The oldest doctor shook his head. "No. It's actually somewhere between leukemia and a cancer. It's very difficult to diagnose—there is a margin of error here. We do feel reasonably confident that we've gotten it right. But, Gabriel, the good news is that while it's not quite curable, it's only fatal now and then."

The doctor with the stylish glasses gazed at the floor, folded her arms. Janos looked relieved. "So, the treatment," Janos began, but I interrupted him.

"What does that mean, 'now and then'?" A ferocious itch, like a little flame, broke out at the base of my spine.

The oldest better doctor looked me in the eye in a practiced, gentle way. "There can be opportunistic infections. Heart problems. Liver failure. Things can develop, but usually they develop quite slowly, which is why we call it lazy, or indolent." He nodded confidently in Janos's direction, including him in the medical team. "We'll have to keep a close eye on you, and you may find that your pace of life slows down somewhat. You're going to have to rest, and there may be flare-ups, as with rheumatoid arthritis, that are restricting and even painful. You may have an odd growth or two, perhaps a lipoma. We'll have to watch that those aren't too close to a lymph node. Usually this strikes people much later in life — you must be an old soul, Gabriel."

"I'm barely thirty-eight," I said. The flame burned higher, angrily. "Look, am I living or am I dying? You know, I work right near the World Trade Center, maybe that bad dust—" That fucking blue devil, I didn't say. I should have known when she cut me the first time. And what about my bid?

The oldest better doctor didn't flinch. "I can't say about the dust. Today you're living. But I won't lie to you, Gabriel. Cancer, even the laziest cancer, is like a lion. Lions spend enormous amounts of time sleeping, did you know that? If you go on safari, all the lions are usually asleep in the shade. But then sometimes they wake up. That's what we'll be watching you for. To see if the lion has woken up."

All the other better doctors smiled, as if this was a brilliant metaphor, except for the one with the stylish glasses, who turned her head to look out the window at the night. I wondered what the river was doing, if it was gold or already black. In the glare of the overhead fluorescent light, the room was stark and dull. The windowsill was piled with papers and laptop computers. Oh, I thought. So this is what it's like. This is how it starts. "So it's neither, then," I said. "I'm not living or dying." Maybe I was blooming. I wanted to peek under the gauze and see if the blue flowers were still there.

"Don't be silly," said Janos. "We're all dying, everyone in this room is dying, we begin to die the minute we're born—we're like butterflies."

"No," said the oldest better doctor. "You're being metaphorical." Clearly, he would be the chief maker of metaphors in this room, and it would be lions, not butterflies or flowers. "Gabriel has a real medical issue."

"Sort of real," I said.

"Not 'sort of.'" The oldest better doctor frowned, beginning to grow visibly impatient. "It's very real, I assure you." He patted my blanketed foot in a kind way that made my heart sink. "They'll do a bone marrow test to confirm in the morning, but I don't plan on being surprised."

My visitors began gathering their things, sliding their laptops into their clever cases, zipping the cases shut. Janos kissed me on the forehead, which was cool now. Nothing hurt anywhere on me. All the better doctors in their white coats fluttered out behind him to be put in taxis. I was alone in the room with my lion inside me, which might or might not wake up at any minute and eat me. I tried to believe what the oldest better doctor had said about my lion being sleepy, but I kept seeing the downcast eyes and the carefully folded arms of the doctor with the stylish glasses. Staring at the light green floor as if it were her job to keep an eye on it.

Late that night, lying awake in my hospital bed, I saw things. The fever must have come back. I saw colors, as when you press your fingers over your closed eyelids: red, blue, lines of super-bright white. My mother dancing in a circle, her long, wavy red hair sticking straight out behind her, as if pulled by a fierce wind. That swamp tree flying up toward the sky. The crested head of Tereus, looking spiky and electrified. I got tangled, snared in the sheets. Sarah used to shout in her sleep now and then, and I heard her cursing out ghosts, the way she used to. I saw her sleeping on her back in the summer, her belly large. I saw a ruined house somewhere, maybe on an island. The ruined house was made of stone; huge windows cut from the stone, now glassless uneven rectangles, looked out onto an emerald-green sea. Fleur stood in one of the windows, smiling, young. My mother stood in another, Caroline in another, Sarah in another. They looked like four face cards, four serious queens hanging in the air, bordered by stone. There was another window on the side. A sad bear appeared in that window and then loped away. Goats ran over what was left of the stone walls and windows and dug around in graves behind the house. They stood on top of the tombs. They were kind of joyous.

I saw a long bolt of pale yellow fabric burning. I saw a black man who walked a white dog. A tiny, cloaked figure crossing a stretch of desert. The elbow of a river where it opened into the emerald sea. A sand-colored lion with a flame-colored mane asleep under a tree. And birds, flocks and flocks of birds, mostly large and black, but some bright blue, a silver one, a gold one, two that could have been the Tweeties, though they were larger and more muscular than the Tweeties, a flock of dancing swans, five or six seagulls, and one bird that looked like an egret, white and long-necked and intent. The birds were everywhere, they filled the hospital room, they flapped at the windows, they skimmed the ceiling and roosted on the veneered wardrobe in the corner, they crowded together along Caroline's outstretched arms, making a dreadful noise. But I knew, with a mix of terror and happiness, why they were here.

They were the vast thing I had been waiting for. Finally, all these years later, they were coming for me, to change me once again. I didn't need to wait for all the better doctors to get all their better heads out of all their better asses. I knew what was happening to me. I could feel the feathers moving under my skin, pushing their way up.

4

The Sun and the Moon

SHE STRIKES SO DEEPLY, when she strikes, that you can't remember having been struck. It is as if you have always been like this, that this was how you really were all along, gasping, wounded, endlessly bleeding.

And even now I wonder, did I stumble into the wrong grove or did I rush into it? Or was it a different sort of motion altogether? Sometimes if you get on the subway going the wrong way, you can go quite a few stops before you notice. The rhythm is so familiar, the opening and closing of the doors, the other passengers with their bundles and children, the tourists with their bottles of water and their guidebooks in other languages; you know this place, these orange plastic seats, this forward motion. When you finally hear the announcement of a stop with the wrong name, at first you think the conductor has made a mistake, and then you realize with a shock that no, it's you, and you jump up and run for the closing doors as if your life depends on it.

· · ·

Caroline and Carsten came tumbling into my apartment on a Saturday morning like a merry-go-round crashing through the ceiling.

"Why are you here?" I said, standing at the old door in my bare feet.

"Janos called us," said Caroline. "Gabe. Oh, Gabe." She hugged me tightly. "Have you told Mom?"

"I'm busy," I said. I was still holding the calculator.

"We're coming in," said Caroline, releasing me. "You look awful."

She and Carsten carried in their many pieces of black luggage, all of which were zippered, with complicated closures and peculiar bulges. Carsten began stacking the bags in one corner of the living room. He pulled a cable out of a side pocket. "We need a converter," he said to me, though this was the first time we had met.

From Caroline's e-mails, I had imagined a tall, thin, serious man. But Carsten turned out to be short, in his late forties at least, with a wandering right eye, Ben Franklin hair, and a dense sexual charge that hovered around him like a cloud of buzzing bees.

"Gabriel," I said, holding out my hand.

"Yes," he said, shaking my hand brusquely, as if we were businessmen sent by our superiors to sign a deal. His palm was quite warm. His right eye, gazing off, seemed like it was looking into the fourth dimension. I liked him. "You are having an eclipse," he said, wagging the cable.

"No, it's just a health scare—"

"No. This city. It is having an eclipse. We are going to shoot it and then fractal it. But we need a converter."

"What?" I said.

Caroline waved her hands, said something to Carsten in German, then, to me, "We're here for you. There *is* going to be an eclipse next week, but that's not why we came."

"How long are you staying?" I tried not to sound alarmed.

"As long as we need to be here," said Caroline, taking off her thin red gloves. "Shut up." She took off her coat, glancing around. "We're ridiculously jet-lagged. Can I smoke in here?"

I shrugged. What did it matter? And when were they leaving?

Caroline lit up. She'd long since bobbed her mane of black hair to chin length; it scribbled interestingly, in sprung black and gray curls, around her face. There were lines at her eyes, her mouth; her face had gotten thinner with age. Over the years, she'd acquired an odd gravitas—where had she gotten that? Had the birds brought it to her in the swamp? She wore a long, straight skirt, like a twenties bluestocking; a leather belt with a large silver buckle; big clunky shoes you could tell were stylish and citational in Berlin, though one of the shoes had a patch on the side. She wore glasses now: delicate, rimless. The left earpiece slanted a few degrees, giving her thin face a tilted, vulnerable cast. I brought her the antique brass ashtray from the windowsill, the one with the gryphon's head with diamond eyes. I was pretty sure the diamonds were real; Fleur preferred real jewels in everything.

"I can't believe you still have this chair," said Caroline, sitting down in it and stroking the frayed arm. "I bought it from the guy who used to live upstairs," she explained to Carsten, who had stretched out on the sofa and closed his eyes. "He was an actor."

"Oh, he's still there," I said. "I think he was just in a play in Rhode Island."

"I used to be an actor. Guerrilla political theater," said Carsten. He was appealingly ugly, like a smiling gargoyle. He took his shoes off, sighed. "I am fried." The word "fried" sounded breaded in his German accent.

"Carsten used to be a lot of things," Caroline said to me. "He's full of stories."

"Listen," I said, "I'm not, like, *dying*. Janos shouldn't have called you."

Caroline gave Carsten a drag off her cigarette, then took it back, inhaling deeply, blowing smoke toward the ceiling. "Are you taking your pill?" she asked.

"None of your business! Janos should know better. Go back to Berlin."

"No," she said.

I did my best not to give myself away by looking over to where the black bottle, like a black-clad nurse, clasping its hideous yellow pills inside, stood on the windowsill between the ancient copper Buddha ($15,250) and the Steuben starfish ($4,800)—I'd looked online.

"And," she pressed on, "what about the transfusion? I read up on it. They say—"

"I don't care what they say. I can't afford it, Caroline. It's not like I have health insurance."

Which was true. But I didn't say the other part: that it's a lot of work turning into a bird. I needed all my strength for it— not to be so nauseated I couldn't stand up straight, not shitting uncontrollably, not half sleeping the day away as the light in the apartment grew dim. The ovoid yellow pill, with its dashing black thunderbolt design, exacted its price. I would pay it, but later. Meaning: after I got the house, which was, at the end of the day, the real reason I was sick. I had been sick, I had been carrying the sickness within me like a seed, ever since we left Tinker's Way. I knew that now. I concentrated on my left femur, thinking *lightness lightness lightness.* I pinched the bridge of my already peaky nose, trying to increase its peakiness.

"You need a haircut," said Caroline.

"I like it this way," I said. I couldn't go back to Sal anymore; I couldn't face him. I felt that I had failed our pact somehow. And anyway, I liked my hair. I liked to feel it grow.

I sat down on the sofa opposite my sister in the frayed armchair she had gotten from the excitable guy upstairs, whom, as she might have forgotten, she had slept with. And she didn't buy it. The chair had been his love poem to her, rejected in favor of Berlin, a city that took down walls only to build others, higher and grander. I didn't say that, either. Instead, settling in, tossing the old calculator on the older coffee table, which wobbled, I said, "So, what's a fractal?"

A fractal is a pattern that repeats, identically, all the way down to its tiniest incarnations. A snowflake is a fractal. So is lightning. Circles within circles, squares within squares, mirrors within mirrors—all fractals. They are infinite, which is either a blessing or a curse, depending on your mood and the windmills of your mind. Fractals can be made on the computer, using a mix of technology, math, and vision. That's what my sister and Carsten were doing; they were part of an intense Berlin fractal/new-media art scene. They used fractals and other images made out of computer programming that moved like schools of fish; the images also reproduced and made a funny kind of atonal music on their own; Carsten and Caroline lived in a mathematical jungle with endless, secret pathways. Fractals were the most common flora there; they grew everywhere. I think that the gods are fractals—Zeus is always Zeus, whether in the form of the smallest hoofed creature or a moth or a hurricane. Cancer is a fractal. Memory is a fractal. The house on Pineapple Street was a fractal, infinitely receding in my dreams to smaller and smaller versions of itself until it was the size of a matchbox, with teensy-weensy people inside, and then it got smaller than that, until I couldn't see it anymore no matter how hard I peered.

As I watched the thickets of technology grow in my living room, I thought how ridiculous—sweet, but ridiculous—my sister and her German boyfriend were. They commandeered my television set as a monitor and hooked up cables and widgets and keyboards and speakers no bigger than apples or quarters or canaries from which peculiar noises emerged constantly. When I left to go to work in the morning, the two of them were sitting close together in front of the monitor, aka my old TV set, fervently typing, speaking half in German and half in English, watching a dotted line swing like a rope across the screen. When I got home at night they were still there, or sometimes one of them was standing by the open window, smoking and looking frustrated, dropping ashes on the gold or silver swan while the other, in headphones, stared bleakly at the monitor. The smell of whatever they had cooked for lunch—meat, usually—filled the apartment. The dotted line might be stalled in the middle of the screen, or bunched up to one side, as if treed. Sometimes they gave up on the dotted line and watched their electronic fish have electronic fish sex. The fish made beeping whale sounds as they combined and drew apart.

How the eclipse was going to figure into all this wasn't obvious to me, but then again, I thought their whole fractal/new-media trip was basically dumb, like psychedelic black-light art. A billion dotted lines. A billion busy schools of mathematical fish. A billion eclipses. Who cared? Would it help get me that house, the house that had been growing in me since the moment we'd lost our house in Bishop? I didn't want to watch the Pineapple Street house travel toward infinity. I wanted to have it. And I was so close.

Alone in the kitchen later that night as Caroline and Carsten snored on the air mattress in the living room, I pulled the stopper out of the small, dark blue bottle labeled *Rose of Acacia: Ebnaflorum* and released three or four drops into a glass of water. I watched the color disperse, like a black veil falling through the sky. The inky swirl reminded me of the food coloring ribboning over the ice in the sink in Bishop, the melting tendrils of purple, of green. I couldn't tell my mother, not yet. There was a tender spot on the inside of my left thigh. I touched it, oddly pleased by the pain. It felt like a pebble in a creek. I was clearly still here. The feathers on the back of my neck were new, stiff. I drank the swirl down in one gulp. Sitting at my rickety kitchen table, I imagined it swirling inside me, painting my ribs, my heart, my lungs, suffusing my blood, cleansing it. So much better than the yellow pill, so much cheaper, and it gave me a peaceful feeling, which was nice.

I had a lot to do. While Caroline and Carsten gazed deep into the computer's black abyss, I had everything with the house on my mind—the clock was about to start ticking again any minute—and then there was the matter of becoming a bird, which, counter to the house's yang energy, was a yin state, incredibly dreamy.

No transfusion could have changed me more. For instance, I couldn't stop looking at the sky. People who say you can't see the sky in New York are wrong. Of course you can see the sky; it's right there. What you can't see are the changes beginning at the horizon: rain, snow, lightning, a bevy of new clouds coming in. If you're looking up as you walk—well, that's just it. You can't only look up. You have to glance down every few steps so as not to run into people, and between the glancing in front of you, so you don't inadvertently kick off a riot, and the buildings framing and interrupting the sky, it can seem as if dark gray is suddenly spreading all at once, like a blot. Or that brightness is everywhere. Your view of the sky is so partial that weather, light, darkness seem to have no starting point. They simply are, now. In New York the sky doesn't give up its secrets easily. Instead, the ordinary arc above continually surprised me, enticed me, seduced me, flickering between the buildings like a film with missing frames. It was always shifting, playfully building cloud palaces, only to dismantle them the next minute. Whenever I looked up, something up there was moving, some vast motion of which I could see only a small part.

Mercurial though it was, the sky had come to seem so true

to me, more real than a lot of what went on here below. It mattered; how had I not noticed before how much? The range of blues, grays, blacks—paler toward the horizon, richer straight overhead—was extraordinary. And there was a taste to it, an ice-cold, acrid sweetness that I craved. Something waited for me there; something leaned down to me. A sunny sky was good luck; a cloudy sky meant a day of shooting pains in my bones, hard breathing, and creeping exhaustion. Partly cloudy meant Reply Hazy, Ask Again Later. But unlike many other things, maybe even most things these days, the sky wasn't only a barometer of my luck. It was also sanctuary. I had the feeling that I could find my way across it, like the four *Stolen* girls marching single file through the desert; that if I needed it, the sky would rescue me, hide me from marauders and enemies behind its seamless blue doors. It was part of my becoming a bird, of course. It was my element. After a few minutes of gazing up at it, I felt as if I was floating there, at home. It was hard to leave a place where time was different, and sound, too.

While I was up there, I looked down and saw—why had I never noticed before?—letters painted on the bricks, now faded, at the top of many apartment buildings. For instance, on a former tenement not far from my apartment: *Emil Talamini Real Estate PA6-3367.* The letters were so faint that you could barely see them. Two buildings away, another, a whisper of white paint: *Haddad Carting We Take It Away!* In cursive, no less. *Holiday Handbags.* And another, barely perceptible, facing the handbags: *Rubin's Fine Suits for Men and Boys, 850 Second Avenue.* In fact, I began to notice many more of these faint impressions, like grave rubbings, advertisements for the past. *Egyptian Gardens. Franklin Furs.* It was like an aerial archaeological dig, these ghostly invitations to businesses, and probably buildings, that didn't exist anymore, phone numbers to heavenly phones—heavy, black, with thick plastic dials. I loved Talamini, Haddad, and Rubin as if they were my ancestors.

159

I nodded to them on Avenue A, lifting my face to the sky. Talamini, Haddad, and Rubin looked down at me from it, smiling. Around them was a strong, clear blue like open water, waveless. On a good sky day like that, I wanted to make a box. Put Talamini, Haddad, and Rubin in it, up to their necks in tympanic blue. Put the phantom Egyptian Gardens in it. Put a primitive telephone as big as an anvil in it.

But even on a bad day, I knew the sky was there. I could hear it, feel it on my skin, taste it. Alone in my cubicle at work, watching the helicopters take off and land, the yellow water taxis cross the river, I moved my empty shoulder blades back and forth, back and forth, as the nubs grew. I perched on my bad chair, my legs folded under me. My chest bowed out. Secretly, I stroked the tufts growing there. I pushed at the tender spot on my left thigh until it bruised. Hungry as I always was these days, I ordered in BLTs with double fries and chocolate milkshakes for lunch. The food tasted salty, sweet, promising. I licked my pale fingers when I was done. I had stopped shaving my balls; the hair was growing in, red, feathery. It itched. I liked the itch. Now I was glad I worked at *The Hudson Times*, because it was so close to the river that the sky was big, open. All day, the enormous sky hummed and crackled that much closer to me, just outside the window.

But down on the street, there was a lot going on that needed my attention. Root issues: body, home, ground. Carsten affectionately called me a *luftmensch*, a sky man, a man who lives on air. He liked to get me to eat more by saying, "A second helping for the *luftmensch*." But I didn't live on air. (And Carsten's cooking, I discovered, was excellent. Meat is good. I gained a pound the first week he and Caroline moved in, and kept gaining.) On the contrary, I felt more strongly than ever that I had to get my body into that house across the river, that the broken temples and chipped winged horses and shadowy streets of Wall Street, the weightless electronic rows of dead people from a vanished city, my old apartment that was now overflowing with cables and monitors and a reluctant dotted line—all these, I knew, were dragging me down and killing me. At night, as Caroline and Carsten slept peacefully, entwined in each other's arms on the air mattress in the living room, I cracked open the freezer door and counted the icy silver packages inside, though I knew perfectly well how many of them were in there. I counted them anyway, over and over. I was almost there.

I left a message for Carl. This was my bid, I said, for when the clock started ticking again. I named a number. A sky number, maybe. But I was different now. If I could get cancer, why couldn't other extraordinary things happen to me? My ideas about limits, about what was possible, had changed.

Over a big meal at my little Formica table, Caroline tried to explain to Janos what their art was about. Janos looked bemused, but willing. He had even turned his phone off for dinner. He often came over these days; the center of gravity in our relationship had tilted toward my apartment. Also, I think he warmed up to Caroline and Carsten because they were Europeans, like him. I sat at one end of the table, hungry as ever, restless, but also happy that everyone was together. The lamb was superb that night.

Caroline was patient, slicing into her meat. "We're really just surfing the edges, these places"—she steepled her hands—"where bio-mimesis, data, and chaos meet. Math is an organism; art reproduces itself; music and image can grow of their own volition. In real time, no less. New life forms are everywhere. Robotics—"

"It's the future!" said Carsten. "These will be like cave paintings in a hundred years! I hope they still have the technology to view them!" He looked both despairing and titillated by the prospect. "There's a collective in Norway doing things with bacteria and artificial life that you would not believe. They nearly took down the government last year."

"But how do you make any money?" asked Janos.

"Oh, you know," said Caroline. She laughed, adjusting her rimless glasses.

Carsten lit a cigarette.

I tried not to slide my gaze over to the freezer, though it was a peculiar thing to know that, not three feet from where we sat, there were probably enough ice-cold bricks to get that dotted line out of its corner and swinging into the future. I poked at the potato gratin with my fork.

"Are you getting tired?" asked Janos tenderly. The three of them appraised me. I caught Caroline and Janos exchanging a glance. So they'd been talking about me when I wasn't there. E-mailing? Text-messaging in German? On the phone when I was at work? Carsten began to clear the table, stacking the dishes in a big messy pile, his cigarette stubbed out in the mint sauce.

I shrugged, putting down my fork. I was tired. My bones ached. "No, no, I feel great," I said with as much brightness as I could muster. "Is there dessert?"

"Listen, Gabriel, the transfusion—" Janos began, seeing his advantage.

"Stop it. Stop it about the fucking transfusion. Not now."

Caroline touched Janos's hand, raised an eyebrow. As much as I loved them, I hated their guts at that moment.

In the ensuing silence, Carsten produced a *tarte Tatin*, like magic, from the refrigerator.

"He cooks when he's nervous," said Caroline. "We can't get our thing right. There's a deadline."

"I'm not nervous," said Carsten, putting down the dish with a clatter. "I have a point to make. Now listen, all of you." Carsten, impassioned, mapped out what had been on his mind, by way of Leibniz and phenomenology, using the salt and pep-

per shakers and a few pieces of dirty silverware. "This is existence," he said, slamming the ketchup bottle down in front of
him. "This"—tented fingers on the surface of the table—"is
consciousness." His wandering eye, excited, wandered farther.
The evening brightness fell across the open bottle of wine, the
empty dessert plates, the uncut *tarte Tatin*, the paper whites
sprouting in the brown dish in the center of the table (Caroline had bought them), their bulbs like knuckles in the shallow
dirt, and our four faces: it was a gilded still life of precious ordinariness. I knew it, too. Even without the paper whites, with
only the ketchup bottle, I would have known it. "We are *puck-
ers* in the energy field." He kissed his fingers together, unkissed
them. "Like that. Poof. All life is artificial life in some sense."

Janos nodded, laughed. "Yes, all right, but even a pucker has
to eat, right? Even a pucker gets old."

Carsten elaborately fell out of his chair onto the floor and
kicked his feet. We all laughed. Later that night, I heard him
and Caroline out on the blow-up mattress. A soft guttural
noise from Carsten. A delicate sound from my sister. I stayed
awake, listening, comforted, pushing at that spot on the inside
of my left thigh; the spot was slightly swollen. I had to admit
that I'd been feeling better since they had arrived. Maybe Janos had been right to call. Their noises and cigarette smoke
and ridiculous concerns, like someone banging on pots and
pans at a campsite, must have been keeping the lion at bay. I
was sorry when the guttural noise, the delicate sound, stopped
for the night. There was a shout in the street, then nothing. I
rested my fingers on my clammy chest, above my heart. The
tufts were definitely thickening. And I liked my old blood. I
didn't want new blood, a stranger's blood.

I got off the train in midtown. The regular doctor in the regular office, with issues of *People* from two months ago in the
waiting room, talked about my numbers. They weren't rising,

he said. They weren't falling, either. That place on my thigh, near a lymph node: they had to keep an eye on that. He apologized for the side effects of the yellow pill; it was, he said, the best they could do. I said I understood completely. I said I was trying to reduce my stress. I said that I was reading up on my illness. I said that my partner had made an appointment for me to see a special doctor soon, the top man in the field. The regular doctor nodded approvingly, palpating the lump on my thigh. "He's brilliant," he said as he measured the lump. "Good for you." Then he smiled at me the way a stranger smiles at another stranger on a subway platform. And, in fact, half an hour later he passed right by me on the subway platform. He was walking quickly, head down—a lunch date? an assignation? an appointment with his tailor? Since getting sick, I had begun to be a little psychic, but my newly burgeoning psychic powers failed me now. I couldn't read anything off the regular doctor, and he didn't notice me as he hurried to the other end of the platform.

James, a tall Asian man with four dark blue bands tattooed on his right arm and with perfectly clean, bare feet, lifted the big white lid. On the wall behind him was a hologram of a rainbow, and underneath it was written, in big iridescent block letters, SPIRIT LIFE COLOR. He helped me step into the tank. The salty water lapped at me: warm, geological, indifferent. Even at these prices, many other people had lain where I was lying now, leaving no impression on the shallow oval of sea.

James closed the lid. He rapped on it once, making my salty world ring. "Okay? You ready to ride?"

I rapped back as hard as I could. "Yeah!" I shouted. The salt began nibbling my skin; my spine extended. I floated up. Inside, it was darker than dark ever is: no stars, no stray light from distant cities. Closing your eyes was redundant. There was a faint, pervasive, clashing scent of eucalyptus and damp wood and chlorine. I missed being in Sarah's tub in the drafty house behind the house. I moved my toe, which already felt far away, in the warm water. I would tell her soon. Goodnight, Irene, goodnight, Irene. I added up my frozen money as my feet waltzed away and my ears became enormous echo chambers, like caves where waves swirled. I was upside down, inside out. A collection of random points. One toe. A rib. They might connect, make a really long, curving backbone. A long, curving prow of nose. Long arcs of arm bones, lightening. In the oval of salty water, DNA came undone for a while, refashioned itself. Like taking apart a chandelier to be cleaned and reassembled. Like the schools of mathematical fish, coalescing and disintegrating. *Shhhhh*, went the caves that were my ears. It was trippy in that humid pod. My fingers clenched, reached in the dark water for some other shore. The salt brocaded me.

In the tank, I felt optimistic. My yeses and nos fell away, leaving a blurry radiance. Everything seemed salty, possible. And, oh joy, my elbows were crooking up, the bones of my fingers fusing. It was only a matter of time. I'd be well, better than well. But as I floated in a soup of undone DNA, divine in my metamorphosis, Alice tapped me on the shoulder. Her kinky brownish-blackish hair streamed behind her where she stood before the house on Pineapple Street, at the gate with the blue flowers twined around it, regarding me gravely. Because of the perspective, Alice looked larger than the house. Behind her, the crooked house shimmered, wavering in its outlines. Was she in wind or in water? I was pierced, shot; my insides jackknifed. Homesickness. The house, shrouded in its white tent, bride-like, was waiting for me at the altar. But Alice's enormous shadow fell across it. And that expression on her face: she knew something I didn't know. The breath left my body.

I banged on the inside of the lid as hard as I could. I slammed the panic button with my elbow. "James! James!"

James's strong, tattooed arms appeared immediately, the

square of light very bright. He lifted me out, dripping salt water, wheezing. He wrapped me in a towel.

"Whoa," said James, gripping me tightly, sopping though I was, a wet terry-cloth bag of bones. "Whoa, Gabriel. Breathe. Breathe, man. Come on."

I gasped. "I had . . . I think I had a vision."

James laughed a rich baritone laugh. "Second vision in that tank today. Must be the eclipse coming."

I shivered. James pulled the towel tight. He placed my fingers on my wrist. My pulse thrummed fast, light, avian. "Feel that? You're okay."

The acupuncturist put the needles in slowly, gently, precisely. Several in my spine. One each on the backs of my knees. One on the bottom of my left foot. A few, like a crest, running up the back of my head. At intervals he turned the needles. I felt like I was being tuned. The swollen lump on my thigh ached. I could hear them outside the window, calling for me. *Caw*, they said. *Brrr. Cheep.* Whoosh of feathers. Along the slender wires of the needles, I could feel a humming: the cerulean paths were opening. I didn't need to waste my money on borrowed blood when I could feel this so deeply in every nerve ending, this opening and blossoming that ran from the soles of my feet to the top of the sky. It was painful, but there was an ecstasy to it.

I arranged the objects on the windowsill to balance the energy, sort of like the acupuncturist's needles. The headless porcelain milkmaid (I had never been able to get her head back on, no matter how much glue I used), the silver and gold swans, the Steuben starfish, the intertwined platinum letters *FG*, an imposing pair of grape shears ornamented with silver clusters of testicular grapes, the ancient copper Buddha, a small bronze bell, three cloisonné brooches, an imitation Fabergé egg encrusted with semiprecious stones (real? I couldn't tell), a gold-handled letter opener shaped like a miniature samurai sword, and a transparent clock, very modern, very strange to look at, to see its mechanical heart beating. The windowsill had gotten a bit crowded. I might have to start another one.

The milkmaid's jagged head rested in one of the cozier piles of more ordinary though still significant things that had developed around my apartment, on a bookshelf, on top of the refrigerator, on the back of the sofa: collections of shiny objects, feathers, small animal bones, cheap unraveling knit hats, and so on. This treasure had come not from Fleur's house but from the street. I thought these things might become part of a box one day, but I hadn't been able to interest myself in a box since I'd gotten out of the hospital; really, they were all emblems of my luck. I told my fortune from them. My vision for finding small things on the ground had sharpened considerably. Right on the sidewalks and streets, I'd discovered, were so many glittering stray things, and each item had my fate in it, yes or no. Well or ill. Living or dying. Thumbs up or thumbs down. One second to spot it, two seconds to see if it was a good sign or a bad one, two more to snatch it up before the juju drained out.

You'd be amazed how many talismans of fate are lying around city streets: single lost earrings, half-flattened pen tops, inscrutable and intriguing bits of metal, cowrie beads on a string, coins, lone keys, crosses, a curvy initial in gold plate (T), an intricate silver flower no bigger than your littlest fingernail, a star made out of rhinestones on a string covered in rhinestones. I grabbed all the yeses I saw shining on the concrete. I got incredibly good at it, incredibly fast, pecking at the pavement with lightning speed. I figured that between the flattened pen tops and the Steuben starfish, I had the range covered. Fate, manifested in seemingly innocuous objects, had no haven: I would find it and drag it from the immaterial to the material world.

My system covered events of all sizes as well. Three sunny days in a row meant I might be getting better, ditto finding a nickel heads-up on the street, or seeing a license plate with my initials on it. I wished on stars, eyelashes, wishbones. I threw coins into fountains. I decided, though I knew this was dicey, that if the smiley, dark-eyed Hispanic girl at the Starbucks near work waited on me, then I'd have a good day, but if it was her generally unsmiling, heavyset twin, who worked at the same Starbucks, then it would be a bad day. Sometimes I'd dump the latte made by the unsmiling twin into the gutter and go back in, hoping to get the smiling twin. (It didn't count if I asked for her.) Oh, I'd say in an abashed way, can you believe I dropped it the second I walked out of here? I must have been distracted. Winking, brushing at my pants, roguish smile.

I moved the black plastic pill bottle to the back, behind the headless milkmaid. I picked my way through the jungle of cables and made myself a maitake-extract protein shake and drank it down while glancing at the *New York Times* online. A picture of a sad polar bear on a tilting ice floe, a picture of an Iraqi soldier running from a burning building—nothing good. Slight chance of snow. It had been a snowless winter so far, another bad sign. In the lower right-hand corner of the screen, the coming eclipse moved through its phases, back again, then re-eclipsed. In the corner of my living room, the dotted line, mute and motionless, hung in the middle of the television screen. Caroline and Carsten had gone to meet with some people in Greenpoint who were doing amazing work with noise, they said. I walked over to the windowsill and picked up the little bronze bell, rang it. Hello, universe. Hello.

No answer.

I put the bell back in its place. The protein shake tasted like damp, crumbling cardboard. I sat down on the sofa and watched the moon cover the sun, pulse of darkness, uncover it, pulse of light, cover it, uncover it. The gears in the transparent clock went *tick tick tick*. The moon covered the sun, pulse of darkness. Then it uncovered it, pulse of light.

"Gabriel, take the money."

"No," I said firmly. I tightened my lucky red scarf around my neck.

Caroline and I were walking down Henry Street. It was a weekday, but I had called in sick. (Well, now I really was sick, wasn't I? And the dead would still be dead tomorrow.) People passed us on their way to work, hair wet, some holding a child in one hand and a briefcase in the other, some already doing business on their cell phones. A stout black woman pushed a small, fragile curl of a very elderly white woman, covered in sweaters and blankets, in a wheelchair. The white woman looked like a seashell. The sound of hammering came from an upper floor in a grand white wood-frame house.

"And you haven't called Mom, either, right?" Caroline said.

"I've been busy." Wishing on wishbones and counting clouds, scheming to get my latte from the right twin at Starbucks. Going in and out of the tank, diving down through layers of being. James had said my aura was much improved. "Plus, you say 'take the money' like Janos is handing me cash in a paper bag. That's not what he means. He means move in with him."

"What's the difference? He wants to support you. He wants to help you get better. Dependency is not a dirty word, Gabe. If you moved in with him, you could save the rent money and use it for the transfusion. They have this new kind now, they mix it—"

"Oh, my God, shut up about the *stupid* transfusion. How many times do I have to say it? Do you know who I really want to tell? Who I really want the money from?"

Caroline looked mystified. "Who? Did you tell Sarah?"

"No. Dad."

"Dad?"

I smiled. It was hard to startle my unsinkable sister; I got pleasure from getting a rise out of her. "Yes. Dad. Remember him? We have half his DNA?"

Caroline snorted. "That train wreck. What a waste. Anyway, I think the man must be dead."

Now it was my turn to be startled, and angry. "That is a horrible thing to say. God, Caroline. He's not *dead.* Can we sit down a minute?" We sat down on a stoop just before my knees gave out. The lion was like that, clawing unpredictably.

"When did you become such a fan? He walked out on us two days after Christmas, for God's sake, in that falling-down dollhouse with the mice and no heat—"

"The Bishop house? The Bishop house was great. It was so beautiful."

"What planet are you on? That house was a shambles. The plumbing was a disaster, the basement was always flooding. Some contractor he was. After we went to Florida, Mom practically had to give it away, it went for so little. At least it was warm in Florida. You could be outside all the time."

"What planet are *you* on? Brewster was a hellhole. Mom became a zombie. She never read us Ovid anymore—"

"Ovid? She never read *me* any Ovid. She was always in a rage. That's what I remember. After he left that winter, she kept me awake for hours telling me awful stuff about their marriage I didn't want to know. Sex stuff, even. Talk about myths. I hated it. Ovid?"

I nodded, embarrassed for both of us. But I couldn't stop myself from saying, "And the City. Remember the City?"

Caroline smiled ruefully. "Oh, right. She was always clever with the scissors and construction paper. She had an eye. Man, the two of them: how many dreamers can one marriage stand? But Gabe, that's why you have to tell her. She's impossible, but she's had such a tough time in the world, poor nervous thing.

To lose the husband and then—I'm sorry to say it, but I have to—maybe the son."

"Why do you keep talking like that? He walked out. It's not the same thing at all."

"Gabe." Caroline shook my shoulder. "Gabe. Wake up. Doesn't it ever strike you as odd that after the first year or two we never heard from him? We heard he'd moved to Mexico and then . . ." She made a dial-tone sound. "People don't just morph. Things happen to them. What, did you think that all this time he was leading some other life as a circus clown in Arizona or something? That Zeus turned him into an antelope? He went to Mexico or some shit, who knows, and we never heard from him again. What does that sound like to you?"

The morning collapsed in bright pieces around me. "I don't know. I don't know what it sounds like."

Caroline's expression softened. "Honey, do you think you can find him and tell him about . . . what's going on with you? Is that what you're saying? What would it matter?"

"He's my father," I said. "Don't you think he'd want to know, that he'd want to help me out?" I let her think that I meant the transfusion.

"Some fathers, maybe. Not him." She stretched her legs down the stoop, pointed her toes. "I don't know who you've made him into in your mind, but to me he was one of those guys who's hiding out all the time. Behind the beard, in the garage, out who knows where at night. He was a scuttler." She shuddered. "And then he left all those beautiful guitars behind." She shook her head. Case closed. "What did he think he was going to be? A rock star? The next Bob Dylan?"

I felt sliced to the quick. "You're wrong."

"He did leave them behind, Gabe," Caroline said softly. "You know that. Listen to me. Let Janos help you. You can't live like this. That apartment with all the creepy junk in it—"

I tossed the end of my lucky red scarf over my shoulder and

stood up. "Stop lecturing me, Caroline. I told you, I've been feeling better. And even if it isn't true, it doesn't help anything to make me feel worse. I'm trying to maintain a positive attitude. The mind-body connection — heard of it?"

"You're an asshole," she said, but she followed me down the stoop to Pineapple Street anyway, like a reluctant shadow. I showed her how to stand by the lamppost up the block. I positioned her so she could get a full view. "I'm so in love with this house. Now look like we're talking."

"What? Did you break into it or something? Is that where all the knickknacks came from? Is this like before?"

"No. Shhh. That was a long time ago. Come on, look like we're talking." Though I was angry at her, I couldn't help but be excited. I kept my bid to myself, my sweet, pulsing secret.

"We *are* talking. All right, all right. Which one is it?"

I pointed, delicately, with a lift of my chin. I peeked at it over my shoulder and from under my eyelashes.

But instead of my house, with FOR SALE BY OWNER written on the sign outside, I saw a skeleton. Someone had carefully, methodically taken apart the house since I'd been here last. Someone — a giant, with a giant's hands, a giant's strength — had skinned it. For a second I thought my father must have come back and done it while I was sidelined in the hospital.

The front of the house was stripped to the sheathing. The porch had been removed, and in its place was a rough wooden staircase, braced in the dirt by long, raw pieces of wood, leading to the hole where the front door had been. The yard was bare, muddy, with big truck-tire tracks in it. The iron fence and gate were stacked in pieces, like firewood, along the right side of the yard. Most of the windows were gone, and in their place was thick, clear plastic. The plastic made the house look as if it was hibernating. The siding had been removed from the left side of the house, too, and in one part there were a few — well, what were they exactly? I couldn't tell. They looked like large square tiles with a pinkish hue to them. If I had to guess, I'd say they were porcelain, but was that possible? Whatever they were, they made an odd mix with the old wooden widow's walk, still perched, like a battered hat, on the top of the house. The anchor was still there, and under the anchor it was still 1853. The large window on the lower left, one of the windows that had previously been the dim surface of a lake, was now a single, bright sheet of glass that stood open on the diagonal, like a sail. The house was sailing away.

Oh, God. I put my hands over my eyes. How had this happened? When could it have been done? This was what Alice had been trying to tell me in my vision. Termites wouldn't help me now. Nothing would help me. I plummeted.

Caroline, next to me, shifted her weight from foot to foot. "Gabe. This is *someone else's* house, right? Isn't someone else doing all this work?"

"Yes," I said. "This is someone else's house."

"Oh, man, you're just like Mom." Caroline shook her head and walked away, back up the block and out of sight. I stared at the skeleton house until my vision blurred.

I called Carl and explained a few things to him, things I thought he should know, certain impressions, certain emotions. I tried to be quite clear.

Carl said, "You are crazy. If you ever bother me or my family again, I will have you arrested for harassment. Business is business. It's over, buster. Lose this number."

I threw my phone over the railing of the Promenade into the river. If Pluto found it, I thought bitterly, he could fucking call me.

That night, at Janos's, I had a nightmare. In my nightmare, my old blood was emptying out through a tube, but there wasn't enough new blood coming in through the tube on the other side. The plastic line was pinched in one spot. And I was hungry, so unbearably hungry. In my dream, I couldn't get enough to eat.

I woke up with a start, rolled over in bed, still terrified by the pinch in the plastic line, and put my arms around Janos, pressed his strong shoulder blades against my chest. The hair on his thighs was reassuringly thick, alive. The back of his neck smelled like starch and a hint of sweat. No pinch, I reminded myself. Look. No pinch anywhere here. Indeed, Janos was warm, solid, his blood flowing unimpeded through his veins. I wondered if I was actually hungry, if that was what had woken me up, but I wasn't. On the contrary, I felt slightly nauseated. My sour blood, I thought dismally, was making me sick. My fright, like my hunger in the dream, expanded, inflating just beneath my ribs until it seemed one might crack. Oh fuck, I thought, oh fuck, oh fuck, oh fuck.

I got out of bed, naked. Janos's house was dark, the furniture hooded by the night. A few glowing red dots near the living room ceiling indicated that the security alarm was on. I wanted to run out of there as fast as I could, just run until I reached the top or the bottom of the island, plunge my arms into the water, splash the filthy, beautiful river water on my face, but instead I rushed into the atrium. The glass door went *thush* behind me. I leaned against one of the glass walls, my face in my hands. Oh fuck, oh fuck, oh fuck. My ribs hurt. The swollen nodule on the inside of my left thigh seemed bigger, and it hurt. I crouched down, ass in the dirt. The Tweeties were asleep, heads tucked into their feathered breasts. *Brothers*, I whispered in bird language, but they didn't stir. The fan was off. Nothing moved. The air was just barely humid.

Through the skylight above, I could see the luminous quarter moon, gathering its strength to spring and bite the sun. My ass, my balls, settled into the ground. My right big toe itched. I looked down. In the gloom, I could make out a small, scuttling shape—a pill bug? a centipede? a roach?—moving purposefully over my toe. It traversed my toenail, moved over the downward curve of my big toe, crossed a patch of dirt, and began the journey up the side of my long second toe. I didn't brush it away. Instead, taking quick, shallow breaths, I watched the determined bug, half wanting to eat it. I put my hands in the dirt, which was nearly as warm as a body. *Don't fall asleep, don't fall asleep, don't fall asleep.* The bug made it to my third toe, victorious.

At the Metropolitan Museum, the statue of Saint Margaret emerging from the body of a dragon was easy to overlook, especially if you were hurrying past, hungry, as people usually were. Saint Margaret was too close to the café to be noticed. She was a small figure, perhaps two feet high, carved from brownish alabaster. Her typewritten cardboard label said she had been made in 1475. Her arms were gone, as was the head of the dragon from which she was rising with a benevolent, loving, untroubled expression. The rubies on her headdress, however, were intact. They glittered in the dim gray light of the medieval gallery. She wore a long, simple dress with a full skirt and a robe that fell in folds around her small shoulders and over the back of the dragon, who was rather stout. Her head was inclined to one side and her eyes were closed. Her long wavy hair was loose, her forehead was high, her chin was pointed. She looked so young—too young to be afraid of the dragon or surprised that she had emerged, whole, from within it. Anyone could see that she loved the stout dragon and the dragon loved her, too. They were still one, inseparable at the base; the dragon's sturdy, scaly paws were braced against the ground, ready to move, to take the little saint where she wanted to go.

In the past, I had come with concrete requests, like a child waiting to sit on Santa's knee. Sarah had asked Saint Margaret many things over the years and received many astute replies. But today I felt within me a vague, windy rushing, a striped wheezing, like the accordion before it found a note. *Saint Margaret*, I thought, *tell me who I am*. The little saint, still half dragon herself, continued her silent contemplation of everything.

From here, it all seems so clear. I see myself, an anguished, energetic figure rushing and hopping busily over the curve of the world, full of self-importance and worry, thinking I could read the sky. I studied it every day, took its temperature, ran it over my tongue. I collected endless treasure from the ground and assembled it into what seemed to me patterns and designs that would attract the maximum amount of luck. I burned incense. I made sacrifices—my cell phone, for instance. I made a rule that I could wank only every three days. I hurried down Wall Street, head bent, past the temples. I tended the dead dutifully, if without any particular emotion. I kept my trove of silver bricks intact, hidden in the freezer. That house was gone, but maybe there was another one, a better one, waiting to reveal itself at dusk. I played all the angles, in other words. What else could I have done? What else does anyone ever do?

I sat in the spindly chair next to Fleur's magnificent curve of divan. She was sleeping. A silver streak, she looked as if she was about to dissolve into the gold pillow beneath her head. I turned the flash drive over in my hand. This was the end of *Stolen at Twilight*, though I had some good ideas for *Stolen in Flames*. I should probably raise my fee again, I thought. Morty, his hair standing on end, his ancient jeans sagging, peeked in.
"She didn't wake up yet?" he said.
"No."
"Oh, she will," he said, and shuffled away.
I touched the damask throw, fingered the silk. They were

truly divine. Being rich made a difference. I held a bit of cashmere to my cheek.

Fleur's eyes snapped open. "Put that down," she said.

I dropped the divine fabric, my face red.

"Give me the thing." She held out her curled hand. Stung, I dropped the flash drive in it. She was in a terrible mood.

She pulled herself up until she was almost sitting. She frowned. "I know about you," she said. "I know what you did."

"What are you talking about?"

"You." She pointed an accusatory finger with the uncurled hand. "You stole my swans."

"Your what? No, I didn't steal anything."

She narrowed her eyes. "You little bastard. I know you did. I know all about you. Those. Swans. Were. Mine. You take my money. You lead me on. You help yourself to my knickknacks, some Steuben shit. That's bad enough. But those swans were a gift from my own sister. Linda gave them to me when I finished my first book. They've brought me all my good luck, all my silver and gold. All this"—she waved her skinny good arm—"is because of those fucking swans. And you are going to pay, you rotten shit."

"I don't know what you mean," I said, as forcefully as I could manage. "I don't have your swans! I've never even seen them!"

"And now you're lying, on top of it. Let me tell you something. You are done here. We are done. You will never, ever come back here. You will never get another dime from me. And I'll tell you something else. I know about you, your disease. I put my man on you."

"Morty?" I almost laughed at the thought of Morty ducking behind cars and lurking in doorways, but then, seeing Fleur's broken face, I didn't.

"Not Morty, you idiot. The man I pay. The one who checked you out for me in the beginning." With the side of her face that smiled, Fleur smiled bitterly. The other side maintained its frown. "I know what you have. You deserve it, and you"—she pointed again, her narrow finger an inch away from my nose—"you're going to die from it." She spat on the floor. "I curse you."

I felt the blood leave my face. "Jesus Christ, please don't curse me, Fleur." I held out my hand. "Please." I was afraid. Darkness opened beneath my feet. I whispered, "Okay, I'll give them back."

"Too late," she said. "The damage is done." She stared at me, unforgiving.

Without a backward glance, I ran. Past Morty listening at the door, past the springtime meadows, past the white sofas like so many clouds, down the marble hallways, slamming out the front door, careening down the hall with its flocked wallpaper, the clanging fire stairs, running running running past the liverymen and footmen and jesters. Nearly in flight, my feet on the verge of leaving the ground, I ran into the oncoming dusk of Central Park West, where, two blocks down, I finally stopped, bent over, breathing hard. *Mama, take this badge off of me.* I looked at my open left hand, empty of the flash drive. Only its same tilted, wavy lines in it, which I couldn't read. I pressed it to my face, breathing in, breathing out. *Knock, knock, knockin' on heaven's door.* My feet unmistakably on the ground. If only, I thought, that door would open up and let me in.

When I got home, I found Caroline sitting at the kitchen table with a cigarette and a cup of black coffee, her hair pulled tightly off her face. In front of her on the rickety kitchen table was a silver brick, but the brick was split open by a jagged tear. The green bills were bursting through the torn plastic wrap and tinfoil.

"I was looking," said Caroline in a low, terrible voice, "for some sugar." She flicked her fingernail against the split-open brick. "Fuck you, Gabriel. Fuck you, big-time."

I hadn't taken my coat off. "Let me explain."

Who knew the Furies could be so cold when they raged? "No. No. No. I counted. There's enough here for the transfusion. There's enough here to move. And I know you. If there's this much in the freezer, there's another stash somewhere else, isn't there? Enough for so many things. While we worry about you, and cry, and talk it over endlessly, and sneak off to do research online and *wait*, Gabriel, we fucking *wait* for you, you're so *fragile*, we have to be so *careful*. We *choose our battles*. We *manage*. We tiptoe. And what do you do?" She picked up the brick, shook the cold money onto the dirty floor. "You do this. You have got to be kidding me. You are heartless. You haven't changed at all. You never will."

"It was for my house," I muttered, about to cry. "I was saving."

"There *is* no house, Gabriel," said Caroline, tapping her ash. "I bet you got up to some shit there, too. But let me explain something to you: there never was a house in the first place. You were trying to steal back what never existed."

"Maybe not for you," I said, and then I found myself flattened against the door from the force of Caroline's glare.

"You stupid, stupid little boy. You selfish fuck." She shook her head. She looked old. She was getting jowls, though her black and gray curls seemed springier than ever, electrified by anger. "I'm a fool. But not anymore." She lifted her chin. "I'm taking my name off the lease. You're on your own. Maybe that will pull you back into reality."

The back of my neck itched. A feather emerging. Inwardly, I smiled. Outwardly, I returned Caroline's stare. "Do whatever you feel to be in your best interest, Caroline," I said. "Just like you always have. And, by the way, when are you leaving? And until then, please stop smoking in here, will you? It's not good for my health."

Caroline dropped her cigarette into the dregs of her coffee. "We leave in two days. We want to get that footage of the eclipse." She adjusted her glasses. I swept past her into my room. I shut the door and curled up in bed, thinking *lightness lightness lightness*. I rubbed at the back of my neck where the feathers were thickening. They were thick and reddish now on my balls, too. I had a wank; my come was thready, like egg white. Then I fell into a deep sleep.

The rocks along the shoreline were mammoth and jagged, and we made our way along them slowly, weighed down by the bundles we each had to carry. I grasped a rough declivity, pulled hard, and slipped, scraping my ankle. The wet burlap sack on my back slid perilously to one side. Sweating, I hit it awkwardly with one arm, batting it back into place. A rusty can of tuna fish fell out, clattered down between the rocks. I ignored it. There wasn't time: the sun was setting. I was drenched, salty, shivering. Up ahead, I could see that Caroline was tiring, too. Her wet calves trembled as she hauled herself up a rock so tall and steep it must have had a local name of its own. She clung to its side, gripping, making progress an inch at a time. My ankle was bleeding and already starting to swell. There were two in front of me, three behind me. No one spoke. I lowered myself down a rock in preparation for the next climb up. The tide was coming in. My ankle, I knew, was broken. Caroline, wiggling on her stomach, rolled over on top of the huge, steep rock and sat up, breathing hard.

"Gabe!" she called out from atop the tall rock, the wind tugging her black hair against her mouth. "Gabe! Gabe!"

I woke up covered in sweat. Switched on the light: 2:30 A.M. I reached for the glass of water, the aspirin. I held my hand up to the light: my hand was pale, my fingers thin. White spots flecked my fingernails. My heart raced. I put my hand on my clammy chest, entreating my heart to be still. I flexed my feet, ankles intact. I pinched my beaky nose. The nodule on my thigh was bigger, harder. I made myself concentrate on what I could see from my bed: the curve of the mirror, clutter of keys and change and the black plastic pill bottle on the dresser, the woodcut print of the city skyline on the wall. In the street, someone shouted a name—Derek or Eric. Then silence. Dead of night.

Next to the aspirin was the small, dark blue, stoppered bottle of Rose of Acacia. I pulled out the stopper, squeezed up a dropperful, and released the inky drops into the glass of water. I drank it in one swallow. I turned my pillow over to get the cool side, lay down, and switched out the light. I didn't dream again that night.

As fate would have it—and who said fate has no sense of humor?—the next morning, Janos took me to my appointment with the most special doctor, the top doctor, who was seeing a very select group of patients at the hospital, in a colleague's office. A nurse drew blood; we waited. Another nurse drew a bit more blood; they gave me bright orange peanut butter crackers. We waited some more. Janos made calls. I was hungry, even after the crackers. I wondered if that was a good sign or a bad one. Finally, the top doctor, a tall, bony, snow-white man, called us into his office. On the desk was a photo of a black family, smiling next to a pyramid. The family of the doctor whose office it was, obviously.

The bony white doctor had a few numbers scrawled on a prescription pad. "These numbers," he said, "are very sobering." He corrected himself. "Mr. Collins, Mr. Laszlo, these numbers are bad." He held up the pad, but I couldn't understand what the numbers meant, and anyway, they didn't look bad or good—they just looked like numbers. Threes and fours, mostly.

Janos put his head in his hands. His pant legs rode up, exposing his black silk socks.

"So, do we need to do the transfusion?" I asked as my glittering pile melted. I surrendered. *Mama, put my guns in the ground. I can't shoot them anymore.*

The light in the room dimmed. I thought it was my eyes, my anxiety, but the bony white doctor looked out the window and said, "You know what that is? That's the eclipse." He checked his watch. "It's a beauty. A big one." He turned on the desk lamp. "I'm sorry to say that we can't do the transfusion. We have to go straight to chemo."

"What?" said Janos. "Oh, no."

The top doctor explained that I should be admitted within twenty-four hours, thirty-six at the most, to begin a rigorous round of inpatient chemotherapy. Of course there must be things I'd want to put on hold, bills to pay, but I needed to come in for a while. He said "come in" as if I was a spy and the hospital was the home country where I could relax, speak my native tongue, not be shot at.

"I've seen this movie," I said. "You're always the guy not to trust."

The top doctor smiled. "I'm sorry." He asked me if I'd been taking the hideous yellow pill. Absolutely, I said. Every week. They gave me a calendar. The top doctor shook his head. He repeated how sorry he was. He said they'd be very aggressive with the chemo. I was a young man; that was apparently in my favor. I could handle a bigger dose of drugs, but of course the side effects would be worse. The light in the room brightened and the doctor turned off the lamp. "The next full eclipse is in Peru two years from now. Rare things."

Janos was not to be distracted. He set his jaw. "We're getting another opinion."

The top doctor said, "Mr. Laszlo, this isn't a matter of opinion."

Out on the street, the vast blue sky shed its light without distinction on all the passersby. From the street, the hospital looked bland, professional. We went to the corner to hail a taxi, where three newspaper boxes leaned against one another. All these things would be here, I thought, whether I was or not.

A taxi stopped for us. "Barneys," said Janos. He called Caroline from the taxi and didn't try to conceal what he was saying. He used no code words.

As we neared Central Park, I noticed loose groups of people straggling out of it. A few of them had circles affixed to their foreheads, half white, half black, like yin-yang symbols. A line of schoolchildren, all in luminescent vests with thick goggles dangling around their necks. A man with an intricate design of flames and stars painted on his face and naked chest, wearing a skirt made of camouflage material and carrying a flute. A gaggle of white kids with shells and beads woven into their dreadlocks carrying pots and pans, drums, noisemakers, and cymbals. Something resembling a zither, carried by a fat boy with a limp, an ecstatic expression on his face. A woman in business clothes, her jacket over her arm, talking excitedly to the man in the skirt. A man pushing a cart full of camera equipment. The sky was clear, ordinary, healed, as if nothing had happened. I tasted it: licorice, ice.

"Wow, look at them," I said. "I guess it was a big deal, like the doctor said."

Janos shrugged, resting his forehead against the window.

"It will be okay," I said, though I didn't really think that.

The taxi stopped and we got out. Janos could be very indulgent. It was an interesting thing about him and money: he didn't particularly like to keep it where he could see it, the way I did, stacked up in the freezer. Instead, he liked to watch it move and change. He liked to make it go around, turn it into other things: buildings, factories, thousands of acres of oranges, airports that would be built in 2051. Cashmere slippers, an expensive leather jacket, a jet-black Prada suit. "For the ballet," he said, adjusting my cuffs. "It fits you perfectly." In the three angled mirrors, I looked like a tubercular young man on the way to his wedding, or maybe his own funeral. Strange how being unwell made you look both much younger and much older. A changeling. *Gabriel, thirty-eight, Barneys dressing room, 3:32 P.M.* The jet-black suit fit me perfectly. I looked like a blackbird. Or maybe I was a fractal of a blackbird. Maybe this was just three of the Gabriels; if you cut me open there'd be more and more, receding endlessly. I stood up straight in the jet-black suit, shoulders back, thinking of May the Rockette, of the blue goddess, of Fleur. Which one had done this to me? And for what crime?

When we left Barneys, I said to Janos, "I'll meet you at my apartment. I want to walk a minute by myself." He nodded, taking all the shiny black-and-silver shopping bags.

I went straight to the Met. Early, raw spring was in the air. I stood before Saint Margaret in my lucky red scarf. Poised halfway outside her dragon, she inclined her head. I closed my eyes, kept them closed. Footsteps echoed around me.

When I got back to my apartment, Caroline, Carsten, and Janos were sitting in the kitchen, wreathed in cigarette smoke. A bottle of Hungarian wine stood open on the table. They'd taken down my three good wine glasses and used the little chunky cut-glass vase for a fourth. Caroline stood up immediately and took me in her arms. I didn't resist. I didn't pretend not to know why. I held her tightly, feeling her elbows, the back of her neck, her sprung curls against my cheek. "I'm so sorry," she said in my ear. "About everything. We'll stay. As long as you need us."

I shook my head in her embrace. "I want you to go home," I said. "Please."

We clung together. I wasn't angry anymore, or sad, or hopeful. I wasn't anything I could name. I was simply with her, my dear sister, until finally I let her go.

Carsten poured us all glasses of the wine, which was surprisingly good, and Janos took cheese and grapes out of the refrigerator. When the wine was finished, Carsten made a large, dense omelet and a salad. We opened another bottle of wine and ate the food. Caroline and Carsten said they had gotten good footage of the eclipse and the eclipse watchers. "Makes you remember film," said Carsten mournfully. The black-and-silver bags rested, forgotten, by the door.

While Janos cleared the dishes, Caroline and Carsten lit their customary after-dinner cigarettes. Caroline patted my knee, then she and Carsten got up from the table and moved my three pieces of living room furniture out of the way, clearing a large square. "We'll build it here," she said. "But wait, don't start yet. I have a plan."

I nodded, contemplating the bare, scratched-up portion of floor. While Caroline studied the empty square, I pulled the cardboard tubes out of the rolls of paper towels that I had. I pulled the smaller cardboard tubes out of a four-pack of toilet paper, too, leaving the four squishy white carcasses in the dry tub. I dug up a few shoeboxes, a bunch of fancy shopping bags, two pairs of scissors, half a roll of tape, and, from the front closet, what turned out to be yards and yards of wrapping paper in holiday colors, festive prints, with stripes, with stars, with squiggles. Eleven years' worth, it seemed. Along with the cardboard and scissors and shopping bags, it was a start, anyway.

Janos finished the dishes, Carsten opened the third bottle of wine, and we began. Around ten, Caroline murmured, "We need Legos." She'd gathered her hair in a big knot on top of her head and secured it with a rubber band and was drawing with great concentration on sheets of typing paper.

Carsten, puffing exuberantly, cross-legged on the floor, was laboring to make an elaborate, shiny, swooping thing — a roof? a patio? — out of one of the Barneys bags. The roof said *eys* on an angle. Next to him was a substantial purple lake imprinted with white stars; on the lake sailed the silver and gold swans; in the center of the lake, like a gazebo, sat the imitation Fabergé egg on its ebony stand.

I was cutting small headstones out of shoebox cardboard, which is harder to do than it sounds when your scissors are dull and one third of a blade is missing. I knew exactly where the graves would go, and had cleverly given each one a tab on the bottom so it would stand up, leaning back a little, the way headstones do. I also had a secret plan for the string of multicolored paper lanterns I'd found under my bed. Everyone would be amazed. "Maybe there's an all-night toy store somewhere," I offered.

Janos stood up from his wind farm, scattering rejected paper-windmill prototypes. "I'll go," he said. He put on his shoes and left. The apartment walls rattled as the front door closed.

Carsten heaved himself up and poked through one of my little nests of special things on top of the refrigerator. He returned to the floor, clinking together an assortment of earrings and special bits of curvy metal in one hand. "No," he said firmly. "What we need is a good glue. Like a glue that is super." He set out his sparkly finds on the dusty floor and studied them intently. Then he got up and added the bronze bell and the platinum letter opener to his pile. I didn't mind. The City was already rising around us. A tubular house with long windows by the radiator. The purple lake filled with stars. A green plastic soldier guarding a silo covered in fluffy, red-cheeked Santas.

My thumb hurt, but I was very into it, too. "Maybe there should be catacombs," I said.

"Mmmm," grunted Carsten.

"Under the castle," said Caroline.

"What castle?" I asked.

"Shhh. I'm doing that next. Over there. Fuck." She grabbed the cigarette from Carsten and took a long drag. "I should really quit smoking."

"Where did you get all this crap, *luftmensch*?" asked Carsten. "Some of it is very nice."

"I stole it," I said, high on City and on how well my cemetery was turning out. I was modeling it on Père-Lachaise. "From an old lady I used to work for."

"Gabriel should have been a spy," said Caroline from her corner.

"Caroline," I said, "remember the year we made the elevator? With the pulleys?"

"Dad did that one," she replied, not looking up. "Dad always did the cool machine stuff."

"My lake," said Carsten with satisfaction, "is exceptionally deep. Dinosaurs swim on the bottom. It is called the Midnight Lake."

"Gabe," said Caroline, "you have to call Mom. Promise me. Before they admit you."

I cut a window in the shape of a cross into one of the mausoleum walls, curved the wall, and taped it down to the foundation. "I swear. Before they admit me. Look how great this is. The mayor will be buried here."

Janos came back forty-five minutes later with a big bag of Legos, as well as a fleet of miniature buses and trains, which he set down on the burgeoning, twisting City streets. Caroline grabbed the Lego bag and dumped all the pieces next to her in a heap. Janos knelt down. "Where is the courthouse?" Under his light blue shirt I could see a slight paunch, though it wasn't much more than a crescent of flesh. He would be fifty-eight in a month. His back was as wide and square as ever. His arms and legs were as strong as they had always been. He was aging, it was clear, from the middle outward, like a tree cleaving a rock. Whereas I—I might be crumpling, like a blue flower at a gate. A bird with an arrow in its breast. "I will make us a courthouse," Janos said, and set to work.

We didn't stop until nearly three in the morning, and by

then we all believed we had actual bricks and mortar; it had become that real to us. Plus, it looked fantastic. Like Sydney crossed with Tokyo crossed with a dream city. I made a river winding through the middle of it, like the Arno, and a flock of ferries, cut out of toilet paper tubes, crossing the river. That's how the people in this City got around, tacking from shore to shore. Janos adjusted the spacing of the ferries on the river to accommodate the evening rush. We built a castle out of chopsticks and Scotch tape and pieces of beautiful Japanese paper Carsten had produced from the pocket of a suitcase: creamy white, imprinted with dark blue cranes, flying in place. "Cranes are for long life," said Carsten. Carefully, we set a votive candle in a glass and put the glowing glass inside the paper castle, turned out all the lights, and, by the light of the shining paper walls with the cranes forever in flight up the sides, talked about the past, the present, and the future, until the sky outside began to lighten and the candle went out.

An hour or so later, while everyone was still asleep, I slid out of bed. The lump on my thigh twinged as I pulled on my jeans. I dressed, went to the freezer, and, as quietly as I could, removed all the foil-wrapped bundles, stacking them neatly in my old black knapsack, zippering it. I took my passport from behind the box with the vengeful blue trickster goddess and her blue deer. I looked the goddess in her three eyes for a long minute. I latched the suitcase Janos had packed for me for the hospital and picked it up. It wasn't very heavy. He must not have expected that I would stay there long. On the kitchen table sat the three good wine glasses and the little cut-glass vase, stained with the dregs of last night's wine. The jet-black Prada suit was neatly draped over a kitchen chair, because we'd cut up and used the suit bag. Scattered across the kitchen table next to the stained glasses were three plastic toy soldiers, a cracked pink button, a seashell, an open pair of scissors, a gold hoop earring, and a cigarette butt. A still life, a box with no walls. It looked like I'd had one of my parties from the old days. A going-away party, perhaps.

I took a deep breath, standing in the kitchen with my knapsack and suitcase. The paper-towel-tube entrance to the City also marked the entrance from the kitchen to my old, crumbly living room. Caroline's too, I supposed, since her name was still on the mailbox. On one side of the living room, Caroline and Carsten were curled up on blankets outside the City, big as sleeping gods, dwarfing the Lego walls. Carsten's arm rested across my sister's waist, his hand open on the dusty floor. My sister's face, in sleep, was lovely. The City lay next to them, motionless. The gold and silver swans were suspended in place, necks curved and fixed, on the navy-blue surface of Midnight Lake. The cardboard headstones no bigger than dominoes tilted in the cemetery, caught and held on the brink of falling over. The citizens penciled on typing paper were frozen in midstep on their way to work and school. The castle walls were solid again, because the votive candle inside the castle was extinguished; the dark cranes on the castle walls were stopped in midflight. The ferries waited between shores in the middle of the river. The big bronze bell inside the church — it filled the church, actually — wasn't ringing. When I got up, Janos had been sleeping on his stomach, his left knee bent, left arm crooked. I hadn't dared kiss him goodbye for fear of waking him.

The yellowed clock on the stove said 4:38. Time to go. My hand on the suitcase was pale and thin; my pulse was light and fast; my eyes were tired. The back of my neck, where the feathers were well along now, prickled. I can't say that I expected to find him. I didn't know where to begin looking. I had no idea what I was doing. But I took my father's transistor radio off the shelf anyway, as if it was a homing device that would tune him in once I got to Mexico. I put a piece of masking tape on my father's station and tucked the radio deep inside my suitcase.

I just had to go. That was all I knew, really. Before I *came in*, I had to go where he went, even if the lion got me on the way. I burned for it. I leaned down, gently straightened one of the paper towel tubes at the City's entrance. I left the jet-black Prada suit draped, empty, over the kitchen chair.

I pulled the front door shut for the last time, the door of the yellow taxi closed a few minutes later, the long looping curves of the BQE, hours of nothing in the waiting room, then finally feet up, the force of acceleration as your wings extend and your feet leave the ground, the propulsive rushing, lifting, and the air. JFK, which used to be Idlewild, below. Evening clouds coming in orange and pink. The entire sky, like being able to see, able to breathe deeply, at last. Heaven's door opened. It pulled me in and welcomed me. I was a warrior, like Tereus, a sword in one hand and feathers sprouting from the other. I flew away. The metropolis getting smaller, every tender building and tender ghost-building, the two silver rivers like necklaces abandoned on the sidewalk, the lions frozen in front of the library, the golden seahorses eternally plunging into the air at Fifty-ninth Street, the endlessly somersaulting polar bears in the zoo, the enchanted bull on Bowling Green, the long rectangle of trees and water in the center of the island. Wings long, white, and wide. The sudden, innate knowledge, strong as the strongest imaginable smell: this way. This is where we go. Ping.

Night falls over the city.

5

The Sky Below

YOU DESCEND.

I turned upside down. That was how it felt. Maybe it was the altitude. Maybe it was the wind in Ixtlan, which never stopped blowing. Maybe it was the fact that I spoke so little Spanish; being in a continual state of semi-comprehension was strange, vertiginous. I didn't understand Mexico. Not just the language. I didn't understand the place itself, how it worked and what things meant. Such as: Why was NEUROTICA written in multi-colored, ballooning letters on a stone wall that the bus passed on the way out of Oaxaca? Why were there so many VW bugs on the road? Was it 1969? As the bus made its way up, and up, and up into the mountains, how did those little open buildings with long tables covered in red-and-white oilcloth manage to cling to the very narrow space between the road and the sheer drop down to the valley? How did the bus stay on the mountain at all?

Every time we rounded a sharp corner, the sky below us appeared through the windshield. I thought I was going to be sick. And it wasn't as if the other people on the bus—the short, indigenous men in cowboy hats and women in knee-length skirts and long black braids—didn't mind. They braced their feet against their bundles on the floor, looking worried. One stout middle-aged woman crossed herself every time we made it around a curve. CONSERVA EL BOSQUE said a sign nailed crookedly to a tree. Beginning with that one, maybe. PARCO ECOTURISTICO LUVI. COMEDOR "ELI." Convoys of soldiers rattling past. A woman cooking by the side of the road. Light shooting off a CD tossed in a ditch. A smiling woman with a Chicago Bulls hat on and good balance walked up and down the bus aisle selling walnuts, tortillas, and cans of Pepsi.

I didn't understand how the hyperreal, glowing colors on everything from billboards to the sides of gas stations to the bedspreads I'd seen hanging in the big *mercado* in Oaxaca could coexist with the dirt. They seemed to be made of such different stuff, woven of dissimilar atoms. How could one place hold them both? I felt as if I was in a dream. But the weight of my own body rocking back and forth on the curves as the bus climbed reassured me that this was real, I was real. This was Mexico, a real country. The other people on the bus were probably going to work or coming from work. The road was the road. We seemed to be making it up the mountain without dying. The bus pulled over at one of the open buildings, Comedor "Luisa." The middle-aged woman who had crossed herself gathered her thick plastic bag that said *Refresquería Rosita*; colorful plastic bracelets clacked on her arm as she lowered herself down the bus steps. Maybe she was Luisa.

I didn't know where I was going, but as we continued up the mountain, the feeling grew in me that I was revolving, that my head was turning toward the earth and my feet toward the sky. Have you ever woken up in bed and been unsure, for a minute, where your body was in space? That was what it felt like. As if gravity was ambivalent: it might hold me or it might let me go. For the time being, it was turning me upside down, as if to empty my pockets. The blood rushed to my head, though I was still rocking gently against the soft, dark blue bus seat, trying not to look out the window at the drop.

Begin with Julia. To remember. I know that now. There are times, now, when I'll be doing something or going somewhere, seeing the Taj Mahal for the first time, crossing the street on an ordinary day, breathing the air, noticing a slant of light, and, pierced by it, I think, *Remember this. Remember this moment. Now.* As if all of this was for that, in the end.

I remember Julia.

When I got off the bus in Ixtlan, I heard that roaring, echoing wind for the first time, the wind I would come to know so well. It sounded like the wind at a beach, though we were far from any coast. Was it the wind from the arroyo in Arizona, had I followed it to its source? The roaring wind in Ixtlan snapped the flags in front of the municipal building, blew the skirts of the elderly Mexican women against their legs as they lined up to get on a school bus painted dark blue, wrapped around the enormous church on the hill above the bend in the road where the bus stopped, tumbled along the concrete basketball court in the center of town. Michael Jordan gazed soberly over the empty court from a glowing red and orange mural painted on the concrete wall at one end. A rooster crowed. There was the smell of something burning. The town wasn't very big. I could see where it trailed off into stone steps going up the side of the mountain to the north; the highway was its southern edge. The tallest object on the eastern limit was a satellite dish on a low rooftop; on the western edge the town tilted slightly downward, revealing a patchwork of red roofs. Ixtlan seemed to be deserted; I didn't understand that, either. A tan dog trotted by, looking purposeful. The dark blue school bus full of elderly women pulled away. The emptiness of the town made me feel as if I was inside a balloon. Ixtlan had a tympanic quality. That wind roared through it.

Had he come here? Why would I even think that? But I felt quite strongly that he had gone somewhere like here—maybe a little farther up the mountain, or up a different one, or maybe a town along the coast. He wouldn't have stayed in a big city; he'd never have lasted in Mexico City. He would have ended up, I thought, in a place like this. Wherever this was. He would have put his bag down, sighed, rubbed the back of his neck the way I was rubbing mine now, although I was feeling my feathers. He would have looked around for a place to eat, maybe a bar.

Most of the little stores around the *zócalo* were closed except for a storefront with air conditioning and wall-to-wall carpeting that offered Internet access. I sent an e-mail to Janos and cc'd it to Caroline, Carsten, and Sydnee. The e-mail said, "Dear loved ones, Due to my health crisis, I have decided to take a short trip to try to get my head together. I have arrived safely and will be in touch soon. Please do not worry. This is just something I have to do. Sydnee: the section has tons of stuff, just run it. Caroline: I hope you're back in Germany. Don't hang around waiting for me. Janos: I love you. I'll be home soon. (All of) yours, Gabe." I hit the send button.

Then I headed up the hill toward the massive church. It dwarfed every other structure in sight, organizing the landscape around itself. The vast churchyard was dusty. A man was leaning idly on the open church door. Five men in cowboy hats ambled past, talking and laughing. An *Å 1734* was carved on the stone arch above the door. I went in.

Even inside the church I could hear that wind. Otherwise, it was hushed. A cricket chirped. The altar was a gilded extravaganza, a hundred times the wattage of Fleur's divan; it seemed to be not 3-D but 5-D, with elaborately worked figures and faces everywhere, huge carved wooden doors, and saints in glass cases, like Barbies. A Jesus standing nearby wore a long brown wig and what looked like gold lamé hot pants. Some of the cherubs carved into the wall behind him had on the same hot pants. These hilarious elements didn't make the church any less imposing. Oddly, they made it more imposing. The church had its own idea of the order of things, what went with what. I had to admire that—the saints in glass boxes were fantastic. I approached the altar to get a better look.

In a pew toward the front, a little girl of perhaps eight was kneeling, head bowed, in a torn Communion veil. The rip began in the middle of the veil and ran straight down. The girl's bare feet stuck out of the veil's hem, her soles and smudged heels edged in white lace. Sort of white lace. The veil, in addition to being torn, was smudged and stained. It might have been a tablecloth, saved from the rag bin. The little girl was murmuring fervently, her folded hands pressed tightly against her forehead. Her dirty toes wiggled. Her ankles and forearms were pocked with insect bites. Besides the veil, she was wearing several variously patterned and wildly colored skirts and shirts, piled on haphazardly. She looked like a piñata.

She raised her head. "*Qué quieres, señor?*"

"Alice?" I said, in shock, because this girl looked so uncannily like the Alice of Pineapple Street: the same tawny skin, the same loosely kinky brownish-blackish hair, the same guarded, slightly regal expression in her eyes, the same small point to her chin.

"No. No Alice. Americano?"

"Yes," I said.

She adjusted her veil, peered at me, first skeptically, then confidently. She nodded. "I know who you are," she said in English that was barely touched by an unlocatable accent. "I dreamed you were coming. I dreamed all about you."

I peered skeptically back at her. "Oh, really? Then what's my name?"

She stood up. "You don't have a name yet. My name is Julia. Come on."

As I say, I had been turned upside down. So I simply followed her, torn veil fluttering, up the aisle and out of the church.

The truck shuddered out of town and up the mountain. My suitcase banged from side to side in the truck bed. Julia, still in her veil, sat next to me. Next to her, driving, was an old man wearing shorts held up with a length of clothesline and filthy huaraches. His bare chest was narrow, ropy, and mahogany from the sun; his mahogany arm, shifting gears, was strong. He had a full head of shaggy white hair into which were wound feathers, tinsel, troll dolls, small bones, a headless baby doll, fern leaves, and several brightly colored model cars.

"How did it go?" Julia asked.

"Not too bad," said the old man. He had no Spanish accent, but he did have a Chicago timbre to his voice. "I think they're beginning to understand the vision." He turned to me. "Jabalí."

"What?"

He pointed to his ropy chest. "That's my name. Jabalí."

"Oh, okay. Nice to meet you."

Julia giggled, pulling her veil over her nose. "A *jabalí* is an animal. It has *tusks*."

"What?"

"Wild boar," said Jabalí. "A jabalí is a wild boar."

"It's his *name*," said Julia.

Jabalí smiled, shifted gears as the road got steeper. "We'll explain later."

"I dreamed him already, *Papi*," offered Julia, putting her dirty bare feet on the dashboard. "I told him he can't have a name yet."

Papi? Father? That word I knew.

"Cool," said Jabalí.

On our right as we slowly chugged up the mountain there rose a spectacular estate at the end of a long, tree-lined drive. It was a mansion, low and rambling, with an expanse of undulating red roof. The walls were composed of stones so large I could make out their irregular shapes from the road. The entrance to the estate was an enormous curved door; a fountain burbled on a grassy oval in front of the entrance. To one side of the main building stood a small stone chapel with a cross on the steeple. Tennis courts were visible, as were the aqua squares of three swimming pools set into terraces on the mountainside, one above the other. Water flowed from the edge of the pool at the top into the one below, which spilled in its turn into the pool below it. A white horse, sunlight winking off the silver on its saddle, stood riderless near the fountain. A discreet wooden sign at the beginning of the tree-lined drive said LA HACIENDA.

The truck rolled to a halt as Jabalí fussed with the gearshift.

"Jesus," I said. "Is that where we're going?"

"Hah! Those motherfuckers," said Jabalí. He wiggled the stick and we jolted forward. "Assholes."

We left La Hacienda behind us and continued for perhaps a mile, where we turned off the road and drove down a much smaller, pitted one, past a few cinderblock buildings. Raucous music pounded loudly, permeating the air, but there were no people in the street.

"Benito Juárez Day," said Jabalí.

I didn't understand anything, but the sensation was curiously pleasant. In fact, it made me feel hopeful. Upside down, so much was possible that might be impossible right side up. I might see my father's face in a pool of water, come upon him sitting in a meadow. Did Mexico have meadows? Could Jabalí really be Julia's father? Who was her mother?

We left the cinderblock buildings behind as well and bumped

down a long, quiet road with fields on either side. We stopped at the tall iron gates of a church. Jabalí got out of the truck and Julia scampered after him in a blur of colors and lace. Slowly, I climbed down from my side, got my dusty suitcase out of the truck bed. "Here?" I hesitated by the truck's rear bumper. Dusk was coming in; the air grew chilly. From far away, I heard traces of the pounding music. I looked back down the long road. No cars in sight. A white dog loped along the empty field. The wind wound itself around us.

Julia jumped on one of the tall gates and rode it as it swung open. "*Aquí! Sí!*"

Jabalí, the headless baby doll and feathers and model cars bouncing in his shaggy white hair, was standing at the open gate. The church rose behind him. He held out his hand to me. "Come on," he said. "It's all right."

Now, here, any reasonable person might well ask, Why did you go in? What were you thinking? The answer is, I don't know. I wasn't thinking. You might say that the echoing wind made the decision for me, carried me through the tall gate into the stone courtyard. That's not quite right. It's more like the wind had entered me long ago in Arizona; it was part of me. It had already happened. I had already gone in with Jabalí and Julia, gone through the little sanctuary where a clutch of local women were praying aloud in unison in the pews, gone back behind the gilded altar, gone down the hallways with broken plaster walls, past the stone rooms stacked with boxes, past the radio playing softly on a card table (a rhyme with mine, good sign), already gone into the interior courtyard, sky-roofed, ringed with the small, wood-beamed stone rooms that felt, even after I'd been there a while and understood more, penitential.

Jabalí led me to a room in the corner. I put my suitcase down. It smelled dank. There was one little window at the back, a bare bulb hanging from one of the beams, a single bed, a few open wooden crates stacked on top of one another. I looked around as if I were deciding, but the wind had already nodded my head, the wind had already said, *Thank you. Gracias.*

Here's the odd thing. No one ever called it anything but "the ex-convento." Which means what it sounds like—the small, crumbly rooms that ringed the church's interior courtyard had once been a convent, and it wasn't one anymore. Behind the church was a ruined library that was also a chicken coop; a compost heap; and a small stone building that had been an ice house, then a fallout shelter, and was now a toolshed, and most of the tools were rusted and broken. The church was built in the sixteenth century, so many generations of nuns had slept where we slept, ate where we ate, passed through the halls we passed through. The last nun to live in the convent had died there in 1943.

Mexico is actually full of ex-conventos; they're not rare. If you said to someone, *It happened at the ex-convento,* that person would reply, *Which one?* And yet, for all his vision, his many, often contradictory visions, Jabalí never gave the ex-convento or the ragtag group that inhabited it a name. Maybe he thought it shouldn't be limited to one name. Or maybe if he named it, that might give the group a starting point and, potentially, an end point, a moment when he would have to know whether or not he'd failed. Or maybe he just didn't get around to it. So it was always "the ex-convento." If you knew about it, you knew which one it was.

I set my father's radio on top of the stack of wooden crates and turned it on. A man speaking Spanish in the deliberate cadences of a speech, arguing some point. I turned it off. I sat down on the bed and looked up at the rough, uneven plaster on the ceiling. It was dull red in some places, yellow in others, and it was falling down. It looked like scabs. In the corner of the ceiling, the building's lath was exposed. The walls seemed to be made out of papier-mâché, layer upon crumbling layer, and they were cold. My bed was made up with clean white sheets, a modest pillow, a blanket folded at the foot. I was tired. I'd been traveling so long. I leaned against the wall and closed my eyes. The gravity in my body was still shifting; I felt as if I was spinning.

"Hey." I opened my eyes. Julia stood in my doorway in her many skirts and shirts, folding one dusty bare foot against the floor. "Hi."

"Hi, Julia. You can come in."

She did a sliding step into the room, picked up the radio. "Did you bring this?"

"Uh-huh."

"From where?"

"New York."

"New York," she repeated. "I knew that. That was in my dream." She jumped and her colorful skirts flounced, then she sat cross-legged in the middle of the room. "Do you want to pray?"

"I'm not religious. Do you have to be religious to be here?"

She shook her head decisively and smiled broadly at me. For the first time, I saw her buckteeth. I hadn't noticed them in the church, and in the truck she had kept her veil across her nose. Her teeth were terribly uneven and practically perpendicular to her head. "You can be here," she allowed. "I dreamed you."

"Oh." Along with everything else, I couldn't understand why no one had asked me who I was or what I was doing here. They had just taken me in, as if I was expected. "So, do you like to pray in that big church in town?"

"I have things I have to do there," she said.

I tried another tack. "Julia," I said, "what did you mean that I can't have a name yet? Do you give people their names, too?"

She regarded me as though I were an idiot. "Of course not. You pick your name. When you're ready."

"Ready for what?"

"To stay with us."

"Oh," I said, "honey, I'm not planning to stay here. I'm . . . looking for someone. But then I have to go back to New York."

"Maybe," she said in the imperturbably superior tone that only an eight-year-old can take. "You don't know."

I began to feel annoyed. "No, Julia," I said, "I do know. I live there. I'm going back."

"Who are you looking for?"

I didn't want to go into it. Who were these people? It seemed best to change the subject again. "Is Julia the name you picked for yourself?"

"I haven't picked my name yet. It's almost time. I have a list." She paused. "You can't see it, Stranger."

I was so tired. There was a fog in my head. "Stranger? No, my name is—"

Julia cut me off with a laugh, jumped to her feet, hopped up and down a few times in her skirts, and did a little heel-toe dance. "Here," she said. From her dirty fist she produced a red jujube. She set it on the blanket. "This is for you." Then she scampered out of the room. Her footsteps pounded away down the hall.

I ate the red jujube, which was delicious. A bell that wasn't inside my head rang; I later learned that it was the dinner bell, but that night I fell asleep sitting up in my clothes. Wherever it was I had ended up, I didn't care. They were a bunch of weirdos, but so long as I didn't get beaned by any falling six-teenth-century plaster, I'd probably be all right.

I woke up a few hours later, chilled, hungry, my belt buckle cutting into my waist. I undressed and got into bed. The cool night air seemed to get cooler as it drifted across the stone floor. A coyote howled outside. In the courtyard, a few people were speaking Spanish in low tones. What did the nun think about, lying here so long ago? Did she really think only about

Jesus? At least she knew what her life was about, that Mexican bride of Christ. I imagined she was short, serious, studious, with an unfortunate nose. I pulled the surprisingly soft, dense wool blanket around my cold shoulders. It was scented with lavender. I wondered if everyone had gotten my e-mail and if they'd written me back yet. Even if they were mad at me, I hoped they missed me, too, a little. Surely they understood the pressure I was under, and that I had to do what I had to do.

I remember the sacred tree. It was a tall, spreading tree in the middle of a field that could be seen for miles around. Caroline would have liked it.

And I remember — still, with such happiness, such delight, were they not the biggest sign of all that I was doing the right thing? — I remember my wings. My wings! How they arched above my head. Their weight on my shoulder blades. Their conductivity: heat, cold, wind. Like getting a seventh sense.

But days spent in the sacred tree were long, and trying to find a spot on the branch that didn't stab me in the balls, the ass, or the thighs was a continual head-on collision with futility. The wings didn't help; my shoulders ached from the leather straps, and I was sure something was living in the tip of the left wing. Something with a lot of legs and antennae that also could bite. The wings were filthy and they smelled of old glue and the sweat of the person who'd used them last. They were also heavier than shit, made of real white feathers from what must have been an entire flock of birds, and highly sensitive to wind currents. Every time a breeze came up, I almost fell out of the damn sacred tree altogether. Julia, who was generally perched on the branch above me in her pretty, ultralight, modern moth wings that were made out of polyester and silk thread, never tilted as the breeze merely ruffled her hair, shimmered her moth wings.

When Jabalí had put the big wings on me in the courtyard of the ex-convento and explained the project that first morning, I was thrilled, flattered that he'd let me participate, but I also suspected that this was a test, which amused me. Here was Jabalí's explanation: "We're pantomiming the animal origin in the sacred tree of Ixtlan. Another time, we would do this as part of a *velada*, but CNN wants to shoot segments around the world on eco-protests, so . . ." He shrugged. "We'll be an eco-protest. That they can understand." He rummaged through a bin on the east side of the courtyard.

I rolled my shoulders around in the wings. They were heavy and reached down to my knees. They stank. They were real. The straps already, satisfyingly, hurt. "It's not an eco-protest? What's a *velada?*"

"Yeah, sure." He pulled a moth-eaten monkey mask with eerily lifelike fur out of the bin and held it to his face. "Phew. We're protesting, our whole *life* here is a counterargument. If they can see it if we call it a protest, it's a protest. Do you know the work of Maria Sabina?"

Was that Julia's mother? "No."

"Very, very important shaman. I came here to study with her, to experience *velada*. Extraordinary woman."

"But what is *velada?*"

He shook his head. "It's hard to put words to it. Come on, let's go. Don't trip."

By day four in the tree, sweating, shoulders aching, I was exasperated enough to venture, "I don't think they're coming. Did anyone call to confirm?"

Jabalí, eyes closed, leaning against the trunk on a lower branch with his monkey mask on, murmured, "You have to be patient."

Malcolm X, who was short and plump with very large breasts and wore a squirrel tail, said, from near the top of the tree, "Julia, go get us some sodas? *Por favor?*"

The others, in their bits of fur and fin, were quiet. Meditating maybe. Or simply bored speechless. The wind rocked us in the branches. Julia, in her ultralight moth wings, clambered down onto my branch. She leaned against me, smelling of sugar and sweat and jalapeños. A mosquito bite by her knee was puffy and red. "How are you doing, Stranger?" she said. "Do you want a name yet?"

I adjusted the strap that was making me sore. "I like my old name."

"Ha!" said Julia, swinging down to the next branch, and the next. "Idiot." She jumped, flying lightly to the ground, her skirts billowing. She began hopping and dancing. The tree folk applauded.

"Geronimo!" cried Julia, stretching out her arms and running down the field toward the ex-convento. The spots on her wings, the colors of her skirts, flew above the scored dry dirt.

One of the others, a skinny kid in a frog head with a high voice, said, "Maybe he's right. CNN couldn't care less about us, or the planet for that matter. How do you even know that guy was for real?"

"Do you think Julia will bring us back the sodas?" said Malcolm X.

Jabalí laughed. "Listen," he said. "They're coming. Julia dreamed it."

"Did she dream she'd bring us sodas?" asked Malcolm X.

"Did her dream say when, exactly?" asked the skinny kid in the frog head.

"Forget the sodas," said Jabalí. "Listen to the wind."

My wings were killing me. Maybe *velada* meant "to stagger around like a sweaty fool." I pulled a bug out of the left wing and squashed it against the branch. That was one, anyway. The day got hotter. Julia didn't come back with soda.

An hour went by. Another. The road remained undisturbed by any CNN trucks. A few motorcyclists went by, engines roaring. As they passed out of sight, the wind gusted, but all at once I was able to ride it. I felt the lift. I moved my shoulder. The wing flapped. I moved the other shoulder. That wing flapped lightly, with perfect control. I moved both wings at the same time, rolling my shoulders, arching my neck, the wings flapping, flapping, flapping on my back, the heavy tips tracing parabolas in the air. I laughed out loud. I didn't think CNN was coming, I didn't think the tree was sacred, the branch didn't stop stabbing me where I lived, another bug bit me on the neck, but I flapped my wings and was so fucking happy. Let the bugs bite. Let the wind blow. I had been truly transformed at last. I was a bird, a glorious filthy white bird. I stood up on my branch, clutching the branch above me, and crowed.

"Ah-oooo," I cried. "Ah-oooo." Everyone else in the tree laughed. I laughed, too, victoriously. I felt not only well but better than well. Nothing hurt. I had tons of energy. Let the lazy lion pad around below the tree. Let him gaze up, frustrated, at the bird he'd never catch now.

There were eleven of us at dinner that night—seven from the tree plus a short English professor who was walking from Ixtlan to Oaxaca and his very tall ceramicist wife, two teenage boys from the town in soccer jerseys, and their mother, who cleaned the church. We ate in one of the larger stone rooms, in which paintings of saints hung on the walls and a string of multicolored lacy paper squares ornamented the ceiling's center beam. From across the table Malcolm X asked me, "So what brings you to us?"

"I needed a change," I said. "All I ever did was think about money—I worked on Wall Street."

"Really?"

"Yes. Uh-huh." My tamales were limpid, meaty, with intricate spicing. Indeed, the food at the ex-convento was always astonishingly, even hypnotically, good. I've never, before or since, tasted food quite like it.

"So did you see September 11?" In addition to her very large breasts, Malcolm X, who was around forty-five, had a sharp, restless way of looking.

"I was late for work that day," I said, "so I was halfway to the office before I realized what had happened. And then, it was the oddest thing, I didn't turn around. I walked toward the noise and the smoke and the chaos. I was somewhere on lower Broadway and I looked up and saw the Trade Center buildings and then I saw these shapes. They looked like starfish falling through the air. And I thought, Oh, the world really is ending, the starfish are in the sky. It took me a minute before I understood what they were. Then the first tower collapsed, and I ran like everybody else. I think I ran all the way home that day, gagging."

"Starfish," she said with her sharp look.

It must have been that, her way of looking, that made me confess through a mouthful of exquisite tamale, "Yes. Starfish. And you know what? I hated it—the constant smell and the dust and the pall everywhere, for months. And you know what else? Secretly, I think the world did end that day. The sky did fall."

"Could be," she said. "So this is the afterlife, is that it? We're all shades?"

"Yes."

"Well." She laughed a throaty laugh. "You've come to the right place if that's what you think. Did you try the *chicharrones?*"

"Do you think I'm right?"

"That we're all shades? I don't know. But then again, it's in the nature of shades not to believe they're shades, isn't it? They're all still hoping for another chance back up top."

I nodded, considering her point. Who had Malcolm X been "up top"? What had she wanted? She wasn't shy about her breasts, but in her black T-shirt she didn't display them much either, in the way of a woman who might have given up on sex.

Strong shoulders. Expressive hands. A teacher? A shrink? An actress? "Are you hoping for that?"

She smiled, but her smile was sly. "Of course," she said. "Aren't you?"

At the other end of the table, Jabalí tapped his knife against his water glass. "I have an important announcement," he said. We all hushed. He put a hand on Julia's head. "Julia had a nap this afternoon, and she dreamed that CNN isn't coming this week. They'll come later." Everyone clapped. Julia beamed.

"Oh, damn," said Malcolm X.

"What?"

"That means we have to build the latrine. We start on the new moon—day after tomorrow. You'll be my helper."

By now, I had surrendered to not understanding anything, so I said that would be great. On the way to my room that night, I saw my wings through the open doorway of one of the stone rooms. They were hanging from a hook on the wall. Beneath them were the frog head, the squirrel tail, the fox mask, a large shark fin, and a few other hypertrophic animal parts. I stared at my wings with longing, then, darting in, I plucked a feather from the right one and carried it off to my room. I clutched the stolen feather as I fell into a deep sleep.

The next day, after breakfast, I sat on a cracked stone wall in the airy courtyard and spread out my map. There was the big beige hulk of the United States, and beneath it, like a rudder, the curve of Mexico and the countries beyond it: wider, narrower, narrower still, like the tail of the dolorous mouse in *Alice in Wonderland*. So many doors. He could have gone in through Texas, Arizona, New Mexico, California. He could have wandered to Baja and drowned. Most of the map fell over the wall like a thin tablecloth. A stone under the paper made a bump, like the bump on my thigh, in New Mexico. A leaf twirled down and covered most of Guatemala.

Julia, the veil tied around her head, Hell's Angels style,

walked toward me along the wall. She stopped, tapping at Texas with a bare, dirty toe. "*Qué es?*"

"I'm trying to figure out something important."

She tapped her toe on Mexico. "We're here."

I put my finger on New York, which was tiny. "I come from here," I said.

Julia shrugged.

"No, it's great. Don't you want to see other places?"

"Not really. This is *paraíso*." She crouched down on the map, wrapping the veil and her arms around her knees. Perched on North America, she covered it. The Pacific Ocean spread out from under the tatters of her veil. "What's your important thing?"

"It's a secret."

Julia's face brightened. "I love secrets. Tell!"

"Not now," I said. "Not yet." I touched the map, trying to feel for him, where he might have gone. The stone wall was cold under the paper.

The rest of the day before the new moon was dull, drifty. Malcolm X sketched ferns in the courtyard. Jabalí, looking like a cobbler out of a fairy tale, tapped at the heels of a pair of large, cracked leather boots. I pretended to read Pablo Neruda, wandered partway down the road toward the tiny town, got hot, wandered back. Stray dogs lay sleeping in the fields. There was nothing in that town anyway. As I approached the ex-convento, I saw Julia by the tall church gate in her Hell's Angels bridal/Communion/tablecloth veil. She was sitting on an upturned green plastic bucket, back straight, hands folded primly in her lap. The gate was propped open with a brick, but Julia was posted just behind it, her toes on the rusty bottom rail. On her face was an expression of melancholy and fervent expectation.

"What are you doing, Julia?" I said.

"Waiting."

"For what? CNN?"

"It's a secret," she teased, but she didn't move from the gate for hours, staring down the road, until the dinner bell rang.

I remember the latrine pit. I pushed and dug and heaved next to Malcolm X, trying to convince myself that we were falling into a rhythm and were getting somewhere. The dirt was like sand in some places, like iron in others, and at times it shifted unpredictably. How would we ever get to twenty feet? The chickens clucked, watching us from the chicken coop/library nearby. The little library had an odd grandeur, ruined as it was, roof falling in; it must have been beautiful once. My arms ached and my hands blistered within the first hour; my knees began to shake before it was time for lunch.

"Why do they need this? There are bathrooms inside," I said, leaning on my shovel.

Malcolm X sat down in the dirt, lifting the back of her shirt and leaning against the coolness of the earth. "Oh, that feels good. It was one of Julia's dreams. And it's not such a bad idea, because the plumbing inside is ancient, and sometimes we have gatherings of folks here. Extra facilities will be a help."

I dropped my shovel, hard. "What do you mean, Julia *dreamed* it? We're busting our asses in the heat all day because some kid had a dream?"

Malcolm X took off her mud-caked sneakers. "She's not 'some kid.' Don't you know? She's an indigo child."

I stared blankly at her.

"An indigo child is a kid who's been given special abilities and sent to Earth to change the world and lead us into the future. They have prophetic dreams and some of them can read minds, things like that. It's very bad to force them or try to make them conform. When Julia was born, Jabalí saw her indigo aura right away, and he's been careful with her ever since. She's very important."

"Do you believe this bullshit?"

"Well—"

"And is there some sort of rule that indigo children can't get braces? It's amazing the girl can chew her food."

"Jabalí can't afford anything like braces. Can't you see that? That's why he's always going down to Ixtlan to talk to the *communal* about buying the land around the church. He's trying to set up an ecotourist-spiritual center—for Julia. He knows he won't be around forever."

I leaned forward. "Who is her mother?" I said in a low voice. "Doesn't she have anything to say about this?"

"Oh." Malcolm X's usually sharp look softened. "That's a sad story. Let's dig, okay? I'll tell you later."

Unsatisfied, I dug. We got our rhythm, we dug until our hands were in shreds, we talked. Malcolm X had been a political science professor at Berkeley. Up north, she'd left behind years with a gloomy husband, and a baby they never actually had but endlessly fought about. The circumcision question for the phantom baby, she said, had proven to be the final straw. They divorced. And anyway, she had wanted a baby girl, named Laurel. I agreed that Laurel was a pretty name, a name that would be right her whole life, child to woman. No Laurel, though, said Malcolm X. No anyone—she'd had her tubes tied. The gloomy husband, who drank, killed himself a year ago. She'd been an occasional visitor to the ex-convento before, but since his death she'd decided to stay on; she'd taken a name. What kind of father could he ever have been? said Malcolm X, digging and tossing dirt out of the pit. A child would have been swept under by him, his impossible needs. He was inconsolable, she said. An inconsolable man. Bottomless. We talked about names through the afternoon, digging ourselves down past Nathaniel and Margarita to John and Mary until, by the time the dinner bell rang, we had made a pit as deep as Malcolm X was tall.

"Not bad for one day," said Malcolm X, leaning on her shovel. Dirt dusted her all over. "And now we're friends." She smiled. My hands had left blood smears on my shovel handle.

At dinner that night, gauze wrapped around my thumbs and crisscrossing my palms, I watched Julia trot around the room, beaming at everyone with her buckteeth. She was wearing the Communion veil again. Javier, a dark-eyed boy about her age, chased her, running at the veil with his fingers at his forehead like bull's horns, and she shrieked with laughter, wiggling the veil and yelling "*Toro!*" After dinner, as we drank strong coffee and ate *dulce de leche* smooth as spun silk, Julia stood on a chair behind Jabalí and braided more things into his hair: a yellow ribbon, a bit of green paper. "*Papi*, be still," she said. When she was done, she threw her arms around his neck, resting her cheek in his already much-ornamented hair.

Malcolm X and I dug for three days, until the handle of that shovel felt like an extension of my hand, which finally stopped bleeding on the afternoon of the third day. Calluses had formed. We had a ladder now, leaning against the dirt walls of the latrine pit. We had considered the fate of the world, written it off, and offered it a thread of hope, several times over. The pit had begun to seem almost cozy, familiar, ours. Above us, the southern sky was high and clear; throughout the day, from where we stood digging, back to back, we could hear muffled footsteps, the murmur of voices, passing cars.

Malcolm X's rump was close to mine all day, every day, and her rump, like the rest of her, was surprisingly muscular. Feeling companionably sweaty, rump to rump in the pit, I almost told her who I really was and why I was here, but I didn't, for fear of jinxing things. Because every time my shovel hit the earth and I was able to loft more dirt out of the pit, I felt death move back an inch. Another, another, another. I beat my lazy-ass cancer with that shovel. Until death was at least twenty feet away. Twenty feet and a half, for good measure. We scrambled up the ladder, threw our shovels out ahead of us, and collapsed at the edge of the pit, giggling, giddy with fatigue. We drank huge gulps of water out of a plastic jug. It was the shank of the afternoon; everyone was working. I tossed a rock into the pit and listened for the small thud.

"Fuckin' A," I commented. "All this for people to shit? What kind of prophecy is that?"

Malcolm X rolled over and crawled on her belly to the edge of the hole. Resting her chin on her fists, her large breasts scooped between her arms, she said, "Look."

I crawled next to Malcolm X and peered into the pit. A rough column of dirt ending in dirt. I saw what she meant. It looked like art, like an earthworks piece by Michael Heizer (Sarah had loved those), or like a meteor had plunged into the ground and disappeared, or like a door. It looked impossible, ominous, beautiful. It was exhilarating. With a surge of energy, I swung myself around and hopped back down the ladder. Malcolm X, laughing, followed me.

At the bottom of the pit, she turned to me and pressed her body against mine. I bent my head to hers, but we didn't quite kiss. Instead, we stood like animals, nose to nose, quivering. I was shocked to feel myself hardening. I hadn't had sex with a woman in so long that it barely seemed like a possibility anymore. And yet. She unzipped my pants and slowly ran the back, then the palm, of her hand along my dick, closing her eyes, taking it in her hand as if it were a precious object she was weighing. "Shhhh," she whispered, though I wasn't saying anything. "Shhhh." Her shirt, when I pressed my face down into it, tasted like dirt. I unbuttoned it. Her large nipple was as warm as the rest of her and it stiffened in my mouth. Then the other. Her skin tasted of salt. Her breasts were so large I couldn't hold them in my hands, which made me harder, the way a regular guy would get. It was strange to be a regular guy.

Leaning against the wall of the pit, she pulled her pants off and dirt tumbled over us as I hoisted her up with a grunt. She was heavy, braced against the dirt. She tightened her legs around me; dirt fell into my eyes, my mouth, but once I got into her I was all blood and reckless forward motion. Her skin was hot. "Go," she said. Hunched over, I buried my face in her neck and pushed like I was trying to push through the dirt wall. We dug together. Was it still art if you fucked in it? Our dirt house was crumbling over our shoulders, into our hair. I thought maybe it would bury us, but I kept pushing anyway. She wouldn't let me pull out, wrapping me with her short, strong legs, as I got close to coming. The weight of her was almost too much, but it also made me want to fuck her more, deeper, harder, faster. Even in my lust, I noticed that the nodule inside my left thigh didn't hurt at all. The vein on Malcolm X's neck pulsated against my closed eyes; her tears mixed with the sweat and dirt and I tasted mud and salt.

I came. I set her down. We leaned against the walls of the latrine pit as the wind above roared past us. We were both streaked with dirt, panting, sweating. Leaning forward, she took my face in her hands and kissed me deeply, pulling my tongue into her mouth. She held on to my forearm for balance as she stepped back into her pants. A ray of sun shone into the pit, illuminating the side of her face, and I studied the lines there, her skin, as if it were a map that might show me where I was. You Are Here. Where? I felt like I had vertigo. I was a stranger to myself; Julia was right. For a second I wondered if I had dreamed it, but there she was, Malcolm X or whatever her name was, buttoning her shirt over her big breasts, pulling the damp hair off her forehead, starting up the ladder. She had a big ass, too. I held my palm to the soft dirt wall in the place where she had lain against it. The spot was still warm.

Later that afternoon, we began mixing the concrete. She

showed me how much water to add to the cement, how to stir the mixture, how to pour it. The dusty bags of cement were even heavier than she had been. I felt like Atlas, and rather pleased with myself, as I struggled to hoist each one onto my shoulder, stagger a few feet with it, and drop it at the base of the big rusty tin drum where we mixed it. We had been coated in dark dirt before; now we were coated in the gray-white dust of the powdered cement. We looked like survivors of Vesuvius, pouring the concrete slabs that would anchor the latrine. I was unaccountably content and, to my great surprise, got half hard for her off and on all afternoon.

At the end of the day, we went back to the edge of the latrine pit to admire our handiwork. "You're a good digger," Malcolm X said, pinching my ass. "We could use a digger like you around here." At dinner she fetched me my dessert—a flan like a cloud of cream—with a wink.

That night—and for this I have no more explanation than for what happened in the latrine pit—Janos came to me in my nun's cell. I woke to find him sitting upright on the bed, his feet on the floor, gazing down at me. The Tweeties perched on his right knee, sleeping, their yellow heads tucked into their yellow chests. He was in the middle of telling me something, a very long story in Hungarian, and somehow I knew Hungarian, and I was torn between a ferocious desire to know what happened next and an equally ferocious desire for the story, which had every kind of thing in it, not to be over. He talked on and on into the dark, and I held my breath for fear that he would stop. I didn't want to be a stranger forever.

Where are you? I miss you. — G

I walked outside the Internet place. The sun was bright on the zócalo. A group of kids, big boys and little boys, were scrambling on the basketball court, all of them in the baggy shorts and enormous shirts of American ghetto style. Michael

Jordan looked on, inscrutable as Mona Lisa. The burnt-orange ball pounded on the concrete. The boys shouted to one another. In marked contrast to my dream, the virtual Janos in real life had nothing to say to me. I'd checked the Sent queue—no problems there. Caroline had sent me back a long, articulate, pleading, worried missive that I didn't finish reading. Sydnee had written curtly that I was fired. Where Janos should have been, however, there was a blank space. I watched the boys run up and down the court, chasing the basketball. Who did they love? Did any of them love another boy? Could a boy do that in Ixtlan? The tallest one, soaked in sweat, tumbled theatrically down onto the concrete as he was fouled. The other boys gathered around to help him up and jostle one another in their baggy ghetto clothes.

Across the zócalo, I saw Jabalí leave the municipal building. He waved me over. I crossed the square and got into the truck with him. "How did it go?" I said.

He lifted his shoulders, started the rumbling truck. "These things take time. They understand the *ecoturismo*, but this is a very Catholic place." He pointed to the church on the hill. "They're suspicious of gringos with ideas about the spirit." He waved his fingers in a mock-spooky gesture.

"Well," I said, "can you blame them? Consider the history."

He laughed. "Not to mention looking like this," he said, tugging at the tinsel and feathers and other items in his hair. He had, however, put on a clean white button-down shirt, long pants, and decent sandals for his meeting. He looked smaller, dressed conventionally. "To them I'm a madman. Harmless, but a madman."

We left the town and began climbing back into the mountain. I kicked off my shoes. "Did you get the duct tape?" We always needed duct tape at the ex-convento.

Jabalí nodded.

"Can I ask you something?"

He nodded again, shifting. The topmost shimmering pool at La Hacienda came into sight.

"This place, the ex-convento—what is it all about? I don't understand."

Jabalí squinted. "Yeah. I don't always understand it myself, to tell you the truth. It just got a hold of me. It started because I used to have another name. And then for a while I had a number." He gave me a knowing glance, but I must have looked blank, because he continued, "Twenty-five years ago, when I finally walked outside those prison gates, I swore that I would make something better. Not just another fucking prison with prettier walls and a big television set." He slapped at a bug on his wrinkled mahogany neck. "When I go, I want Julia to feel like her crazy old father left her something that matters. Someplace a special person like her can be. Where she can build what needs to be built."

Not wanting to know, at least not yet, or maybe ever, what he'd been in for, I asked, "So it's like a utopia? Like a commune?"

We shuddered around an upward curve. The shining expanse of La Hacienda's grounds came into full view, glorious and pristine. Malcolm X had told me that they had fresh salmon flown in every day. Half of Ixtlan worked at La Hacienda in some capacity or other, mostly as maids, waiters, and groundskeepers. "It's what's next," Jabalí said. "I can't explain it to you better than that."

I stared out the truck window at La Hacienda. It was quite beautiful: someone had dreamed it up, terraced the mountainside, dug the pools to spill water from terrace to terrace. "Twenty-five years? You've been here twenty-five years?"

"Yeah. Never expected to be. I thought I was on my way to Costa Rica. Ixtlan was much less built up then."

"So you've seen a lot of folks come through here."

"Who are you looking for?"

I didn't hesitate. "My father. He came this way, maybe, around twenty years ago. It's just a feeling. I don't have any evidence."

"Hmmm. You should ask Julia. She might be able to pick up a vibration, see something. Do you have anything that belonged to him with you?"

"I do, actually."

That night, after dinner, I brought Julia to my nun's cell. We sat cross-legged on the cold floor. I handed her my father's radio. She closed her eyes, felt the radio all over with her slender brown fingers, turned it on, turned it off, held it against her cheek. She set it in front of her on the stone floor and held her hands over it. My skin prickled; my heart speeded up.

"Who is this?" she said, eyes still closed. "He's a running man."

"My father."

She nodded. "Okay." She tilted her head. "He's a running man. But." She frowned, pursed her lips. "He is sad."

"He's sad?"

She touched the knobs on the radio. "Homesick."

"Was he here?"

She sighed. "If he was here, he wanted to leave again. Homesick."

"So did he? Did he come here and go back home?"

She shook her head. "I can't say. I don't know. I'm getting tired. Javier ate all the extra cookies."

"Julia, please. Tell me."

She opened her eyes, lifted her head. The small radio, silent, sat between us. "They're going. I can't. They say it was a long time ago."

I did my best to conceal my overwhelming disappointment from her. She was only a little girl, after all. "Yes. It was a long time ago. When I was about your age." She looked fractious, exhausted, and as if she might cry. "It's okay, honey. You did great."

I remember the cave. On the day that the concrete was drying in the latrine pit, Julia led the way to what she had said was a special place with treasure inside. She was purposeful in shorts, an Outkast T-shirt that was three sizes too big for her and belted with a white rebozo, and good sandals with a buckle and a thick tread. I walked behind her carrying a knapsack with water and lunch. I was already hungry.

Julia turned around. "Are you tired yet?"

"No."

"Good. We have a ways to go."

The path was wide and well worn. Not far away, the river burbled, creatures scrabbled in the undergrowth, birds called. There was a single sock in the dirt, a bottle cap. We reached the edge of the winding river and Julia grasped my hand as if I was blind and she was going to spell something on my palm.

"That's them," she said. "The Burros."

Five rocks, rising in a dark curve above the water; when I squinted, they looked like a shoulder, a back, a donkey head.

Julia was stern. "They got stuck swimming across. Spit."

"What?"

"Spit right now!" She kicked me.

"Ouch." I spat in the general direction of the river. The current was strong here, rushing over the Burros. It wasn't hard to imagine that they had gotten caught, confused, enchanted. The sound alone would have been bewildering to an animal balancing on hooves.

She sighed. "Okay, good. Come on."

We turned and walked along a path by the edge of the river that lifted us above it, grew thinner, more tangled. The air changed, turning sweeter and damper. The greenery lightened in color and became more delicate. There were fewer tall trees, though it didn't feel as if we were emerging into a clearing or a sparser part of the forest. The path behind us disappeared. The stray clangs and shouts from the ex-convento grew faint, washed away. We entered a long field of ferns. Julia let her hands drift over the big, mitten-like leaves that were nearly as tall as she was. They eddied around my waist, brushed my arms. The green of the ferns was supersonic. When Julia turned her head, I saw that her eyes were closed.

"Julia," I said in my best adult voice, "do you know where we are?"

"Quiet, Stranger. Just come on."

Since I didn't know the way back any better than I knew the way forward, I complied. If we didn't turn up for dinner, I thought, someone would come looking for us eventually. I wanted to sit down and eat lunch, but Julia was forging ahead, bending back ferns, her white rebozo flickering through the green. The air continued to thicken and dampen around us, the supersonic greens grew even greener, and what I really wanted right then was an iced double espresso from the smiling twin at Starbucks, loaded with sugar. Would the Tweeties be happy by this river? I wasn't sure where they were from — it might have been India, or was it Cape Verde? Someone had flown them in from somewhere. They'd landed in the middle of the night at JFK in a special climate-controlled cage. I didn't think they would like this humid, wild zone, though they were the ones who had sent me here, hadn't they? Maybe if I had spit in the atrium, none of this would have happened. I wouldn't be a stranger.

Julia hummed, did her hopping dance, turned us this way and that. The river remained on our right, though sometimes our increasingly impassable route tilted down closer to it, at other times rose up and away from it. Julia cut over abruptly. She seemed to be listening hard, eyes still closed. In profile, she looked older than she was, her future self. Her top teeth stuck out above her lower lip. I could take care of her, I thought. I could get her teeth fixed, tutor her, make sure she left here for school in the States (had she ever been to school?). She could live with Janos and me in the winters, return to Ixtlan in the summers, grow up and be complicated. Jabalí loved her enormously, but he was a total crackpot, and an ex-con to boot. She would outgrow him. She would outgrow this place, and then what would she become? A guide, taking gringos on burro rides into the mountains, telling tourists three times a day to spit in the river? A maid at La Hacienda? Or, worse, she'd stay here doing not much of anything, as fascinating and wayward as the rest of them, growing taller, more odd. Decide on a name gleaned from one of the moldy books holding up the walls in the chicken coop: Heloise, Don Quixote, Bathsheba. I stopped, bent over, breathing hard. It was unbearable to me. Was this why I was here? To get her out?

When I straightened up, I didn't see her. "Julia?" Green everywhere, a thick curtain of ferns. The river was almost inaudible, so we were high up now, far above it. "Julia?"

"Stranger!" Her small, clear voice, like the ringing of a hand-held bell, somewhere to my left. I walked left, forward, wading through the green. "Over here! Close your eyes!"

I closed my eyes. Roots grabbed at my ankles, clutched my toes. The ferns were up to my chest. It was hard going but I persevered, hands held out awkwardly, and then something snapped and I stumbled, because I was suddenly free.

"Here! We're here!"

I opened my eyes. Julia was standing in a clearing, twirling excitedly in the Outkast T-shirt that reached to her knees. The clearing was a downward-tilting spot where the ferns didn't grow so thickly. In the center of the clearing was a shallow declivity ringed by rocks that had once been, or perhaps still was, a fire pit. Behind Julia was the entrance to a cave. I set the knapsack down and walked closer. At first the cave seemed to be a cleft in the rocks, little more than a shadow in the side of the mountain. The air emerging from it was quite cool. A rusted bicycle wheel rested near the mouth of the cave, ferns growing through and around its spokes. The rough sides of the entrance were charred. A striped lizard with a long yellow tail and a stark streak of red by its eye watched me from an outcropping of rock, his shiny underbelly falling and rising. I wanted to touch the lizard but knew that I shouldn't. I leaned forward, curious, tentative. Inside the cave were scorched objects I couldn't identify. A ladder toward the back? A round mirror, half blackened. Something larger. Something smaller with a handle.

"Where are we, Julia?"

She gestured like a tour guide. "This is my mother's house. It used to be really beautiful. There are special things inside."

I stared.

"When someone dies here," she said, "we make a little house and burn them in it. So it goes with them, and all their favorite things, too. She had her cave, so we did it here. I gave her a special thing of mine to take with her." Julia sat down by the fire pit. "I'm not going to tell you what it was. This was her place, Stranger."

I nodded, careful to keep my face still. "Honey, you should drink some water. It's hotter out here than you think, and we've been walking for a long time."

"Okay." A gentleness had come over Julia; now she looked younger than she was, a past self, blurrier, not fully formed. I pitied her. She drained half a bottle of water, stray wisps of hair escaping her braids. Malcolm X had tied them, lovingly but not very deftly, with twine. Her mother should have braided and bowed her hair.

"What was your mom's name?"

Julia shook her head. "You can't say it anymore. No one can ever say your name once you die."

I glanced inside the cave again. Blackened objects, heart-break. The scorched mirror's strange gleam. "And was your mom the first person who died here?"

"Uh-uh. There was an old guy before her. I can't say his name. And a dog."

"Do you burn the dogs, too?"

"Well, yeah, but we don't make them a house. And they don't really have stuff to take with them." Julia finished the bottle of water and smiled up at me. "That old guy had a *lot* of favorite things. He used to be a shoe salesman."

I smiled back at her, but I was distracted. So Jabalí had come up with it. Maybe the prison cell was where he first began inventing all this. It was like him—simultaneously thoughtful, semiplausible, and half-cocked. Burn the dead one's place, burn it off this earth, burn her favorite objects, burn her name, burn the mirror that held her reflection. It occurred to me that he might have been a violent man, before.

"You must miss her."

"Special things in there," said Julia. "They're all mine. Let's eat and then we can go in."

I sat down next to her at the fire pit and unwrapped our lunch. Cold enchiladas, dense and meaty, almost nutty. "Are you sure it's okay for me to be here?"

"Don't you want to see?"

"Sure. If it's okay." Actually, I was afraid. I didn't want to see it at all. I had seen enough, but I didn't want to disappoint Julia, who was being so generous with the most precious thing she had.

When we finished lunch, she got up and walked ahead of me into the cave. Reluctantly, I followed. Inside, it was dim and cool, and the indeterminate blackened shapes were now recognizable as a saucepan, the charred remains of a single wooden pallet tucked beneath one of the cave's irregular walls, a kerosene lantern on its side. It smelled of soot. A burned ladder did, indeed, lean at the rear of this part of the cave, in a curve where the walls tilted sharply upward and continued back into a deeper, danker darkness. The mirror was cheap and thin, about two feet across, unevenly ringed in melted veneer, foxed in some places, blistered in others, while in still others it looked as if small suns had exploded on its silver surface.

Julia squatted down, her nose almost touching the mirror. Then she stood up again, shaking her head. "Sometimes she's in there. Not today, though." She took measured steps around the cave, not hopping or dancing, toes first. In this part, the cave was low-ceilinged but fairly wide, perhaps as big as my apartment on East Seventh Street. Big enough to collect shadows by its walls. Julia picked up the lantern and set it upright, a few inches from where it had tumbled. She bent over again, sniffed, displeased. "Raccoons." She briskly kicked dirt over the area and continued. In the gloom, her white rebozo was a light, accompanying her on her journey around the interior of the cave.

I stood not far from the saucepan, my hands at my sides, sweating even in the coolness, thirsty. My overwhelming feeling was that I shouldn't be here. And it wasn't clear to me that Julia's mother wasn't here, because the cave had an almost unbearable atmosphere, a kind of surface tension, like the air before a storm breaks. I wasn't sure I liked this woman, whoever she had been. What kind of woman needs a mirror in a cave? Julia was standing quite still now, eyes closed, hands over her heart, singing something I couldn't make out, a mix of Spanish and English. Then she opened her eyes and kneeled in the dirt, moving some small objects here and there.

"Look, Stranger. Treasure."

I crossed the cave. On the ground in front of her she had four or five ceramic animal figures of the kind you saw all around that area, from roadside souvenir stands to upscale arty stores in Oaxaca. A pig, a horse, a chicken, a fantailed bird, a llama, a man. She also had a cardboard box, a bit bigger than a shoe-box, turned on a long edge, open in front. Inside, there was a painted landscape and a tiny trough, a plastic miniature ear of corn. Julia picked up each ceramic creature, kissed it, and set it back down against the painted landscape, very precisely, as she had done with the lantern. Whatever design had once been painted on them had burned away, so they were only simple clay figures now, unevenly scarred by black streaks and clouds. Julia, frowning, arranged them with enormous concentration until she was satisfied they were in the right spots. The animals obediently stood, as if grazing, by the painted clouds and trees and mountains—skinned, singed, placid, unaware of their true condition. The burned man, equally oblivious, watched over them.

Julia gestured. I kneeled next to her. "Now we have to say her story," Julia said.

"I don't know her story."

Julia gave me a look. "I know that, Stranger. I'm going to teach you."

"Please stop calling me that."

"When you pick a name, I will." She tapped me on the wrist. "Okay. Repeat after me. She was born." Silence. "Stranger. Say it."

"Oh, sorry. She was born."

"She was born and she was beautiful."

"She was born and she was beautiful." I really wanted to get the hell out of that cave.

"She was born and she was beautiful and she sailed over the ocean."

"She was born and she was beautiful and she sailed over the ocean. Julia—"

"*Shhhh*. Ocean ocean ocean."

"Ocean ocean ocean," I mumbled.

"A bee came out of the waves."

"A bee came out of the waves."

"Jesus Mary and Joseph."

"Jesus Mary and Joseph."

"The bee stung her."

"The bee stung her." Was the smell of soot growing stronger?

"The bee stung her and she died."

"The bee stung her and she died."

"Oh! The bee. The little bee."

"Oh! The bee. The little bee."

"Jesus Mary and Joseph."

"Jesus Mary and Joseph."

"Amen." Julia bowed her head, holding her palms out by her sides.

"Amen." I waited a beat. "Can we go now? I think it's getting late."

"No. Oh, no—we forgot the flowers!" She looked over at me beseechingly.

Glad of the excuse, I dashed out of the cave and cast around in the greenery for anything that might resemble a flower. It was all ferns and peculiar succulent plants up here, probably poison ivy or who knows what poison thing, and useless scrubby bushes. The striped lizard, still on the outcropping, watched me skeptically, motionless, king of this entrance to the underworld. Although I was outside, I was as frightened as if I were still in the cave, and I plunged around frantically, scattering fern leaves. I was desperate not to fail. I had the irrational fear that if I didn't bring back at least a handful of flowers, Julia would be trapped in the cave forever, perpetually eight years old. Going around past the cleft and onto the hillside, I stumbled down the slope and managed to capture a grubby clutch of weeds with a few pink and red blooms on them. They were sub-daisy at best, but they would do.

Panting and huffing, I carried them back into the cave. Julia put her finger to her lips. "We have to be quiet for this part."

We stood in silence together for several minutes, until my eyes adjusted again to the dimness and my breathing slowed to match Julia's. Whatever this was, I wanted to do it right. It was like a game, except it wasn't a game, of course. When Julia was sure I had assumed the proper attitude, she took the flowers from me. "Come over here," she said. My heart sank, but I walked with her over to the remains of the pallet by the irregular cave wall, trying mightily to conceal my reaction to what I suspected was there. "You take one." She handed me a stalk of weed with two red flowers on it.

The charred pallet was a busted box. The figure was half buried in ash and dirt and shriveled, dried-out flowers. Time and fire had made the mortal shapes that were still visible abstract, sculptural. You couldn't know her from what she was now. Next to the phalanges of the fingers was a white dinner plate, cracked down the middle. Julia went first, murmuring her near-song and solemnly strewing pretty weeds on the ribs, the hipbones, the slender white architecture of the fingers. She brushed a brown stalk aside to lay down her last green one, finished her song, and nodded to me. I set my stalk next to hers on an anonymous clump of earth. I didn't like this cave that was also a funeral pyre, and I didn't like the woman who had once been woven around these bones. I saw a muddy, roiling red around her, shot through with lines of a bad, empty, flat white, a deathly white. I was angry at Jabalí for letting Julia come up here alone, as she was obviously accustomed to doing. Even for a child as strong and smart as she was, the forces in this place were too great for her. Even I could sense how dangerous it was.

Julia, though, was intent, standing next to me, rapt, rigid, hands over her face. This, too, it seemed to me, was dangerous; what would stop a little girl like her, with thin wrists and watchful eyes, from slipping into another realm and not being able to get back? That silent one in the pallet had had a jealous spirit, you could tell. But I was a visitor here, a newcomer and a trespasser, so I stood with my hands at my sides and didn't say anything. What would I have said? You're standing too close to the edge? I didn't say anything. I did, however, notice that one of Julia's twin hair ties had come undone and fallen to the dirt. I picked it up and put it in my pocket. I realized then that I was shivering.

"Stop fidgeting," whispered Julia from behind her hands. "We're almost done."

Only a small part of the skull, about the size of a fist, was visible; the rest of it was buried. The large, curving bones of the torso remained in sight. The open arch of the white ribs was poignant, but the hipbones were terrifying: smooth, blunt knobs that enclosed nothing but ash and dirt. I have never seen anything as empty as those hipbones. The area between them seemed as vast as a steppe. I looked away.

After what seemed a very long time, Julia whispered, "Okay." She sighed, taking her hands from her face and letting them fall heavily to her sides.

I glanced at the charred, busted box. I could feel the energy in the cave. "Julia," I ventured, "ask her about my father. Ask her where he went."

Julia tilted her head. "Do you think this is the carnival, Stranger? I am not a gypsy."

"Please. *Por favor.*" I kneeled in the dirt.

Julia looked down at me. Her hands hung limp and motionless. "I'm tired."

I bent my head. "Please," I whispered.

"Well. Okay." Julia stood next to me, murmuring in Spanish. The only word I recognized was *Dios.* Finally she said firmly, "He's gone."

"What?" I felt a cold iron bar go through me. "Gone? What does that mean?"

"Gone," she repeated. "He is gone."

"Do you mean dead? Or like he went somewhere?"

"No. Not like he went somewhere. Like dead."

"*Like* dead? Or dead? Julia, please concentrate. It's important. Maybe she's thinking of another guy."

Julia stared at me in the gloom, her lip quivering. "I just *told* you. Why do you keep asking me? I shouldn't have brought you here. You have to leave now." Julia clapped her hands together, shook herself, bowed to the busted box, and marched out of the cave. I followed sheepishly. The sudden warmth, humidity, and dense green were almost too much, like waking up from the thickest part of sleep into broad daylight. Julia picked up the rusted bicycle wheel with both hands and flung it into the ferns beyond the clearing. "This is not a junk heap!" she yelled to whatever thoughtless powers or beings had left it there. "Good," she said, wiping her hands on her enormous T-shirt with efficient satisfaction, but to me she looked drained by her crackpot homegrown ceremony. She glanced around the area with a territorial air, hands on her hips, pale in the daylight.

I was shaken. I sat down by the fire pit, fumbling in my knapsack for water, then drinking it down greedily. The water was warm from the day and had the peculiar taste of ash, nutmeg, and limestone that the water here always had, but I couldn't get enough of it. I drank and drank. The striped lizard watched from his outcropping, impassive. The ferns all around us were benevolent and green with life, but there were so many of them, all massed together in every direction, that if Julia hadn't been here I would have had no idea how to get back. It was nothing but succulent shades of green as far as the eye could see. The slight path appeared to have reseamed itself already.

Julia gestured and I followed her out.

• • •

At dinner that night, I sat at the long table next to Jabalí, who was plowing into his rice and beans. Julia was bounding around outside with the dark-eyed boy and three other little girls in party dresses. Like the child she was, and should be. "Listen," I said in a low voice, "I know I'm new here, but I went with Julia to that weird cave today, and I don't think she should be up there. She could get hurt." I knew my tone was scolding, but I didn't care. "She gets way too intense in there. She makes things up."

Jabalí's short, wrinkled forehead shortened further as he frowned. "I got rid of the things that could hurt her. It's what she has left of Marie. She's been going up there all her life, and I'm not going to take it away from her."

I pressed on. "What, you get rid of a few rusty nails and you're a hero? That broken ladder is there, everything is burnt to shit, it's creepy as hell. The fucking *skeleton* is lying there, for fuck's sake. She's a little girl. It's not right."

Jabalí cleaned his plate with a bit of bread. "I meant," he said, "the syringe. I meant the burnt spoon. Marie was trying. She loved Julia." He picked up his plate and walked out of the dining room. He left so abruptly that I didn't have time to ask him how it was that he had used her name. And which name was it, her northern name or her southern one?

I pushed my rice and beans around the plate, worn out by the day and by what I had learned. The ground was always shifting in the ex-convento; the people were masked, but the masks were always slipping, and they weren't that great in the first place. This meant that you were often given a choice about which face to believe: the genius or the convict, the revolutionary or the lost professor, the beautiful one or the junkie, the living or the dying. It wasn't always clear—left eye, right eye—which one was real. Since I had left New York, for instance, my lion had been sleeping soundly. Nothing in my body hurt, not my eyes or my skin or my joints; if I had fevers, they weren't high enough to stand out amid the general sweat and heat of every day; the nodule had grown and hardened, but it never hurt. Malcolm X had taken the pain out of it with her cunt. I was still weaker than I had once been, but not so weak that I couldn't cover it up with a little effort. Now I could heave around big bags of cement. They were real enough. It was as if, with no one here to tell me what my numbers were, those numbers didn't exist. Or did they? I had no way of knowing. Which one was real, the ex-convento or La Hacienda? Did anybody care? Did nothing hurt on me because I was cured, or because I was already dead?

I put my fork down and shoved my plate away, sick of this strange zone of illusions, shades that didn't know they were shades, crackpot cosmologies. A place governed by the dreams of a little girl with no education and an overactive imagination. Why was I here? I was kidding myself. My father was no hippie. He wouldn't have liked it at the ex-convento, and he wouldn't have stayed. He probably went back to Massachusetts, as Julia had hinted before I pushed her so hard; he grew a potbelly and found someone easier to live with than my mother. He had a weak chin. He drank beer in our small living room. He was left-handed. He had been popular in high school. His knees ached when it rained. He probably never went to Mexico at all. Tijuana, maybe. For the day.

The next morning, I packed. It didn't take very long. I carefully counted the money in the knapsack, and it was all there. I folded my few shirts, my pants, my underwear. I latched the suitcase with a solid click. I put my watch on. Leaving my room, I found Malcolm X, Jabalí, and the one who had been in the frog head—the tall, skinny, freckled kid—standing in the courtyard. "I'm leaving," I said. "When are you going to town?"

They regarded me. "Leaving?" asked Malcolm X, giving me her sharp look. "Really leaving? When did you decide this?"

"I've got to go home," I said. "I dreamed it."

Jabalí shrugged. "We're going to town right now. Come on."

Because I was the one who was leaving, I guess, I had to ride in the bed of the truck while the other three rode in the cab. I held tight to the handle of my suitcase and the knapsack strap with one arm, clasped the rusty bed's side with the other arm. The landscape unfurled backward as we jounced down the mountain.

When we got to Ixtlan, I hopped off the truck and gave them all fervent, teary hugs. "I just need to go. You've been great. I'll write."

Malcolm X, her breasts pressing against my chest, stood on her tiptoes to kiss me on the side of the face, like an aunt. Jabalí clasped both my hands in his. "Be well," he said. I watched them climb the steps of the municipal building together, then I crossed the basketball court and headed for the Internet place, to check my e-mail and see if I could book a flight out of Oaxaca. I wanted to walk through the door of my cruddy apartment as soon as possible, experience the miracle of a real shower, sleep in my own lovely, sagging double bed. I would face the music. I would see my numbers. I would *come in*, if that's what it took, all the way to the hospital, all the way through chemo. I would give up my hair. I had been as foolish as the skinny kid with the frog head, who said his name was Xolotl. I would explain everything to everyone.

In the air-conditioned, businesslike environs of the Internet place, I discovered that I finally had an e-mail from Janos. His tone was distant, firm, but not unkind. With the help of a good therapist, he said, he had come to some decisions. He and Caroline had been talking a great deal during these long weeks (weeks? could it have been weeks?); he had the highest admiration for her as a woman and an artist. He enumerated the decisions he had made, with tremendous regret, but what choice did he have? I was an adult, after all. I, wherever

I was, was clearly making choices. He was done with me, as I so clearly seemed to be done with him. He was exhausted. He had to take care of himself. He was responsible, ultimately, for his own happiness. Also, Caroline had given up the lease on the East Seventh Street apartment, and whatever had seemed salvageable from it was now in storage. Janos would be happy to provide me with the key to the storage unit, should I ever come back to New York. If he was out of town, as I knew he often was, his office had been instructed to give me the key. So. He requested that I reply only to indicate that I had received, and understood, his message.

I closed his e-mail and opened the next one, which was from Sarah.

> Gabe—Hey. Look, I know it's been a while, and I totally understand if you don't want to talk to me again, but I've been thinking of you. Peter and I have to bring some of the puppets down to the city in two months for a show, and I would love to see you. If you want to. I'm sorry. Sometimes things happen and it's hard to explain, even to people you really love. I didn't mean to hurt you and, honestly, I'm just the same dumbbell I always was, except now I'm fatter. (too much good cheese!) I found some great people up here, I play the accordion in their band. It feels like Arizona days. Peter and I are renovating a barn. If I don't hear from you, I'll call. I still totally adore you. xoxoxxxx, sarah

I closed her e-mail without sending one back. I replied to Janos: "Yes. I got your e-mail. Thank you." I Googled my father's name, but my father's name was Jeff Collins. There were millions of them, Jeff Collinses everywhere, running companies, playing on ball teams, acting, teaching classes, leading physics seminars in San Luis Obispo, graduating from high school in 1946, 1953, 1988, 2001.

The world abounded in Jeff Collinses. My father could be

hiding anywhere. He could be in prison, like Julia's father had been. I tried the first five listings in Massachusetts: three were disconnected, one who wasn't him told me loudly that he was on the Do Not Call list, and the last was a fifteen-year-old with a private land line for his small business in collectible vinyl records. "Thanks," I said.

I couldn't find any of the people I wanted to find, and the people who wanted to find me had no idea where I was, nor could I explain it to them. Where I was. And where was I, really? No address, no boyfriend, no name, no father. Just a bag full of money and nothing to spend it on, and a borrowed set of flea-ridden wings. I was a bird now, or the shadow of a bird on the ground—a shade, a dark ripple, a random collection of gestures and half-understood inclinations. *Gabriel, in the wind in Mexico, sometime in early spring.*

I walked outside the Internet place. Michael Jordan still gazed soberly over the concrete basketball court. The wind roared across the zócalo, shimmying the leaves. The church lorded it over the valley. I bought a grapefruit soda from the soda machine near the court and drank it. When I was done, I saw Jabalí, Malcolm X, and Xolotl walking down the steps of the municipal building, deep in conversation. I crossed the zócalo, met them at the foot of the steps, and rode back up the mountain in the truck bed, my suitcase banging back and forth against the rusty truck walls.

I remember my nightmares. Every night, I was locked naked in a cage, and lowered into a pit where creatures pecked and bit me. I was shot, or everyone I loved was shot, or I was handed the gun to shoot them with or ordered to shoot myself. My limbs fell off, my face disappeared, I tried to scream and couldn't scream, dark figures mumbled as they plotted my demise, I ran over landscapes that cracked open under my feet, I was caught up in tidal waves, I was trapped in a speeding car with no steering wheel and locked windows. Every night, I woke up in my single nun's bed in a panic. I put my hand on the old, uneven stone floor, listened to the roar of the wind, and gradually quieted down. But the second I fell asleep it started all over again, and by the time I woke up in the morning, I felt as if I had done a week's labors in a night.

During the day, however, I felt necessary, and strong, and sometimes rather happy. I often felt remarkably well. I would forget for hours at a time that I supposedly had cancer, and when the knowledge returned to me, it was like a familiar, bad taste and I would quickly cast around for something to wash it away. Work helped, usually. There was plenty of that. My muscles ached, grew stronger, ached again. My hands and feet grew rough; the skin there thickened. At the end of a good working day at the ex-convento, I couldn't wait to tumble into sleep, nightmares or no. Maybe my lazy lion had somehow changed from a solid to a liquid to a gas, and now it was exiting through the top of my head at night. Or maybe the deal was that I could have my days, but the lion, nocturnal, got to prowl at will through my nights. It seemed like a fair trade.

Malcolm X's room was the same size as mine, but in hers the plaster walls were in far worse shape. The wall across from her bed was pale pink in some spots, gray in others, pitted everywhere, with a major crack that ran diagonally from ceiling to floor and smaller cracks scattered throughout. The wall beside her bed, against which she was reclining, naked, bowed near the top. I had almost gotten used to her body; it looked like a sea creature, made buoyant by her breasts. I was naked as well, stretched across the foot of the bed.

She touched my left calf with her toe. "We call it crossing the third river. It's the dream river. That's where you meet your shadow side."

"Then what?" I closed my eyes, unsure whether I wanted to

fall asleep there or not. I opened them. Malcolm X's charcoal drawings of local flowers, a pear, Javier's dark-eyed face, fluttered on the opposite wall. She had hung a simple, raw cotton curtain along a length of twine across her window. Her colored pencils, her earplugs, her drawing pad, and her reading glasses rested on the nightstand she had made out of wine crates. Her face in the dim light was round and sober; her straight brown hair shone. She had, I thought, nicely shaped ears. I turned on my side, facing her, head propped on my hand.

"Then for about a week you won't dream at all, and you'll feel very light and spacy. Then you'll dream your name."

"Is that what happened to you?"

"Yes."

"And do you never think about going back up top?"

"Less and less. It used to be so painful, but now a lot of that is what seems like the dream. It gets far away. There's so much to do here."

I ran my hand up her short calf, down again. "How long does it take?"

"Less time than you'd think. More time than you might like. Don't move." She reached across me and grabbed a piece of charcoal, her glasses, her drawing pad, and began to draw me.

I remember the library. It felt like my first one, which it was, in a way. It was a wreck, a nightmare. It had roughly half its roof, but even that half was dipping, frayed, its insides perpetually spilling out. The floor had long since returned to dirt. Books were sprawled and stacked and tumbling everywhere, many of them inflated to twice their size from water damage, soaked in mud, splattered with chicken shit, or sloppily mortared together with some sort of groutish stuff to prop up the disastrous cracked and crumbling remains of the adobe walls. Tiered plywood planks toward the back of the structure served as support for nests, and the nests, to the chickens' credit, were generally full of eggs in various colors: blue, green, a rich yellow, speckled brown and white. The chickens were fat, aggressive, and happy. They clucked and flapped and engaged in complex machinations with great energy all day long. The kids loved to feed them, and did so at any opportunity. Chicken feed was an inch thick in places on the ground, which was also sprinkled with old beans, pork rinds, cupcake wrappers, and smears of guava paste. The kids liked to see what the chickens would eat; the results were more unpredictable than you might think.

It had a splendor to it, the ruined library. The broken shelves were mahogany, elaborately scrolled, and ominously empty, split, and unevenly sheared away. Semiroofless, the library was at the mercy of the sky. The books had absorbed decades of sun, sleet, wind, and rain. In addition to the black marks on white paper that composed them, they bore the marks of the weather, the animals, and the people. Teenage couples from the one-road town nearby sneaked off to the library at night to fuck; the younger kids had their fights there after school. The chickens had fattened on their power over this domain of Eros and Thanatos. They were smug, roosting everywhere on half-decomposed volumes, regarding visitors patronizingly.

However, titans though they were, they were no match for the stray dogs, and casualties were high. Across the front of the library was a bent and rusted length of inadequate wire fence, badly anchored by a few moldy two-by-fours. We needed to rebuild the library walls, because we needed the eggs, to eat and to sell, but there was the unstated sense that we also needed the good will of the chickens.

Sweet, the adobe man, tootled up to the church's iron gate one morning in his adobemobile, a truck full of adobe forms, scrapers, and huge buckets of dry clay, and with a globe—made out of adobe?—affixed to the roof. He hopped out of the adobemobile in red-and-white-striped knee-length cargo shorts that exposed the machinery and beige plastic parts of his prosthetic leg. He was a short, lithe man with a clever face, big blue eyes, and a singsongy way of speaking.

"*Hola!*" he called out, opening the back of his truck. "*Estoy aquí!* All right, children, let's go." As I stepped forward from the courtyard with the others to unload the supplies, I noticed that Sweet's hands were scarred as if he'd been in a fire; his hands looked boiled. But he was quite efficient and commanding, and in short order, out by the ruined library/chicken coop, we had become a team: Xolotl trundled a wheelbarrow full of clay and sand to a clear area in the dirt; Helena, who came from the town to do laundry and help us out with various tasks, trundled another, filled with buckets of water; Malcolm X scattered straw on the ground; and I trundled a wheelbarrow filled with trowels, a shovel, adobe forms, scrapers, and hammers. Sweet surveyed the ruined library, squinting. The chickens squawked and clucked inside.

"Holy shit," said Sweet. "You didn't tell me about the roof."

"For the books?" I asked, setting down my heavy wheelbarrow. "For the chickens?"

"You're cute," said Sweet. "Where did they get you? No, *mi amor*, for the adobe. The walls won't last six months without a roof. They'll crack."

"That's how it got like this in the first place," said Malcolm X.

"Where are we going to get a roof?" I asked, thinking: Home Depot.

"We're going to make one," said Sweet. "God help us."

Malcolm X sketched an area about two by two feet in the dirt. She handed me the shovel. "Dig there," she said, and winked. "You know how to dig."

I gave her a swat on the butt, began to dig away, and before long there was a nice square hole about three feet deep. Xolotl, looking dreamy, brought over a large piece of plastic and we arranged it as a liner in the pit, holding it down with books at the corners on the ground above. Sweet, leaning back on his prosthetic leg, tipped in about half a wheelbarrow of clay and sand. Helena waded in, waved her hand. Sweet emptied one of the buckets of water into the pit, and Helena sloshed around, plunging her hands in, rolling up her pant legs, up to her knees in muck the consistency of bread dough. "*Más. Más.* Good, good. *Bastante.*"

Sweet handed Helena an adobe form, and Helena quickly, gracefully filled it with the clay-and-sand mixture, troweled off the excess, and turned the adobe brick onto the straw-covered ground next to the pit. "See?" she said to me. Sweet handed her a double adobe form. Like a magician, with a whirl of her long arms she filled the double form, struck off the excess, and turned two bricks out on the straw. Now there were three new-born bricks drying in the sun, oblong and thick and dull red.

"Like that," said Sweet to me. "Do you get it?"

What was there to get? It was a hunk of clay in a box. "Sure. Okay."

Malcolm X began applying sunscreen to her arms and face. Xolotl sat down cross-legged at one corner of the adobe pit. I sat down at another. Sweet took off his prosthetic leg, leaned it against a wheelbarrow, and sat down at a third corner. He whacked a form and turned a brick onto the straw. The corners of his brick weren't quite as crisp as Helena's. "Here we go, children," he said merrily. "Get comfortable."

"Sweet, how many, do you think?" asked Malcolm X, taking a seat. Helena climbed out of the pit and occupied the fourth corner, shaking adobe off her legs.

He crinkled up his clever face. "I'm thinking, you know, two thousand."

"Two *thousand?*" I looked at the adobe pit. "You can't make two thousand bricks out of that."

"Magic is another word for repetition," opined Xolotl,

slowly trailing the side of his hand along his brick and making swirls in the adobe. Since his sojourn in the sacred tree, his fair skin had deepened to a burnished rose color.

Sweet gestured toward the wheelbarrow. "We will take that technology over there," he said, "and get some more. You can't make too much at a time or it clumps up and begins to dry in the mixing pit." He sighed. "You should have called me two years ago. Oh, well."

Form, adobe, smack of the trowel, a hard shake, brick on the straw. Form, adobe, smack of the trowel, a hard shake, brick on the straw. Form, adobe, smack of the trowel, a hard shake, brick on the straw. I kept trying to crisp my corners, but they came out blunt, ragged, or cracked. Form, adobe, smack of the trowel, a hard shake, brick on the straw. The sun moved inch by inch across the sky.

One day. Two days. Three days. Julia joined us. Then Jabalí. Then the twins from San Luis Obispo, the Episcopal guys, who acted like lovers. Maybe they *were* lovers, who knew? Our nursery of dull red bricks grew next to the library. They had to be spread out so they'd dry. In their uneven rows and scatter-shot groups on the straw, they looked as if they were about to blossom into something else: soldiers, boxers, skyscrapers. We circulated gossip. Sweet produced a few joints from inside his prosthetic leg and we circulated those as well (not to Julia, of course). Form, adobe, smack of the trowel, a hard shake, brick on the straw. I got new calluses, in new places on my hands. My elbows ached. My corners still weren't 90 degrees — 70, maybe. Helena was by far the fastest, best adobe brick maker. She patted each loaf out onto the straw with impersonal speed and accuracy, humming. Her bricks were identifiable by their heft and elegance. Once the wall was built, we'd be able to see who had made it by the differences in the bricks, like different, repeated notes.

Sweet, scooping up adobe, said, "Did you hear what happened at Alma?" Alma was a community like ours about two days' drive away, over the next mountain. Alma was larger than the ex-convento, and the people were shaggier, goofier; they ran a little circus. Their thing was making electricity out of corn, astrology, and orgies. "Raided," said Sweet.

"Jesus," said Xolotl in his delicate voice. "I was at Alma. Raided?"

"Because of the bus strike." Sweet scraped off the excess from his brick. "The *Federales* said they were harboring union organizers. Then the barn burned." He raised an adobe-coated eyebrow.

"Bad days," said Jabalí. "Did they cleanse the ground?"

"Oh, you know them," replied Sweet. "They just panicked. They all ran into the caves up there and took peyote, and four days later they came down and said they were leaving. They're going to Amsterdam." He said "Amsterdam" with a certain amount of disdain.

"Utopians," said Malcolm X with the same disdain.

"Aren't we utopians?" I asked. "I mean, come on. Look at us."

Malcolm X, Jabalí, Xolotl, Sweet, Helena, the Episcopal twins, and Julia, who was playing Twister by herself on ripped-out book pages, looked at me. "No," said Malcolm X firmly. She was covered in adobe. "Utopia is a trap." She gestured at the field of bricks around us, which had grown to be rather large. "You can make adobe out of just about anything. Any dirt, anywhere. Anyone can do it, with a little patience. We're not utopians. We're teachers. We're trying to be what happens after it all falls apart, if there's anything left." The others nodded agreement.

"Oh," I said.

Form, adobe, smack of the trowel, a hard shake, brick on the straw. The sun was hot on my head. Could we do that, adobe brick by adobe brick? Rebuild the world? As our pile of bricks grew, I began to see the shapes of what they might make: a small house, a school, a bench to sit on at the end of the day. The bricks, about as big as shoeboxes, extended in every direction, far outnumbering us. I realized—maybe it was as Malcolm X had said it would be—that I hadn't thought about making one of my boxes in a long time. I hadn't saved any found treasure. I hadn't stolen anything, either, except that feather. It was an odd sensation, not wanting to steal anything, like the idea of never wanting sex again. Though I still did want sex. Though I wanted it with a woman, which was upside down. Was having sex with Malcolm X a form of stealing? Sadly, I had to conclude it really wasn't. She was all too happy to share. A stray dog ambled by and peed on a few bricks. I felt an overwhelming, embarrassing tenderness for the bricks, huddled in irregular reddish lumps in the field, waiting to be born. Form, smack, shake. My corners approached 80 degrees.

"Ah," said Helena, standing up and stretching. "My back."

I glanced over my shoulder at the ruined library. The big rooster, on what remained of a broken bookshelf, crowed. What was left after it all came apart, after the sky had fallen and the world was upside down? If I was a shade now, what was my job?

That evening after dinner, as the singing and drinking were getting started and the Episcopal twins were hooking up their electric violins, I wandered over to the library in a restless mood. I stepped over the busted, rusted chicken fence. Like the adobe bricks, many of the chickens were sleeping, contented balls of feathers in their straw nests. Others scratched at the mix of feed and scraps on the floor. Two pecked a third, who squawked and flapped up awkwardly to roost on an encyclopedia that was listing from missing pages. In the indigo sky, stars were beginning to appear. The chicken smell was acrid, and the half-open space was warm from their presence. I still didn't know how we were ever going to make a roof for the library, and once we did make it, how were we supposed to hoist it up? Some kind of crane made out of palapa with an adobe engine? Cast a spell and sing it up, floating through the air on its own?

I stubbed my toe on a large volume. Kneeling down, I saw that it was called *Música Sacra por Todos los Días,* and that there were the remains of what had once been brightly colored notes on the cover. Inside, smiling children in hair ribbons (girls) and caps (boys) romped with lambs and sat in a circle around a snow-white Jesus in equally snowy robes at the tops of scores of hymns in Spanish that I didn't know even in English. The pages were stained, but the book was intact. Underneath that book, face-down and nearly buried in the dirt, was a little one, hand-bound with strong red string, called *Ma Vida.* Embossed on the front was a gold cross; inside, tiny elegant handwriting in Spanish covered the pages. One page had a line drawing of a heart with rays of light coming out of it. Another had a crown of thorns, looking almost whimsical, unattached to any divine head, floating spikily on the page. The paper was near crumbling and several hunks of pages were missing, but this book, I knew, was truly treasure. It was worth something. Not far from *Ma Vida* was a book called *Historia de las Américas,* coated in chicken shit and a little swollen, but otherwise complete. I put all three books under my arm.

The light was fading fast. I rushed to pick up unruined, or only semiruined, books, the way you rush to pick up pretty shells on the beach as the tide is coming in. I was a nuisance to the chickens who were still awake, pushing them aside to grab large books, small books, slender books, thick books—any book that had most of its pages and at least one of its covers. I stacked them in a neat pile on the other side of one of the ruined walls. I could hear the stray dogs barking, but what could they want with books except maybe to pee on them? Dogs eat chickens, not pages. I clambered over the busted fence, trotted back to the kitchen, and got one of the clunky flashlights, circa 1981. I returned to the library and by the beam of the flashlight rescued book after book, thinking *This is stupid*, but unable to stop myself. What if *Ma Vida* had been written by the little nun with the unfortunate nose whose bed I now slept in? How could I let her book rot away like that, disrespected and unnoticed?

Some of the books were too far gone; I left those to the chickens. But some were half alive. And some were remarkably fit. The stacks against the outside wall grew so high that by the time first light arrived I didn't have to lean over anymore to add to the pile. I dug around in the corners, even checked under the chickens' nests (lots of complaints), until I was satisfied that I'd reclaimed every possible volume. I looked and looked for an edition of Ovid, but there was none. His shape-shifting gods were pagan, forbidden. Adding a book on what seemed to be advanced mathematics to the last stack, I was very pleased with my work. I sat down and closed my eyes, thrilled by the sweetness of the last traces of night air on my face, the library that I'd saved at my back. It smelled musty, also a bit like loam. I felt quite clearly that I understood something, but before I could articulate what it was, I must have fallen asleep.

"Stranger."

I opened my eyes. Early morning. An ache in my neck, the musty books behind me. Scent of coffee. Julia, squatting next to me, drinking from a tin cup. Chickens everywhere, scratching around by the adobe bricks. "Oh, no."

"They were bored. They told me they wanted to go out." Julia offered me the cup. "Wake up." Funny, wild, happy shapes in green felt-tip marker covered her hands and forearms. She threw a stone at one of the chickens and laughed as it squawked and ran away. "*Ai, gordito,*" she called after it.

I sat up. The coffee was weak and sweet. "You shouldn't

have let them out," I managed. "We're going to have to find them all and put them back in."

She settled herself next to me and leaned against my shoulder. Had her legs, in just the time I'd been here, gotten longer? Was her face more defined? Her heavy eyebrows were almost comical, Groucho-like, and, ai, those teeth. She would never be pretty. She would have a different kind of power. I didn't see any auras around the girl, of indigo or any other hue, but Jabalí was right that Julia had a certain quality that was rare in a child. Sorrow, perhaps. I don't know if it was simply the wry cast of her features or something deeper, but even in her liveliest, most knock-kneed moments, she seemed tuned to a pitch children shouldn't be able to hear. She pinched my elbow. "What are you doing out here, Stranger? Coyotes going to get you and eat you."

I gestured at the books. "I found all these. Aren't they amazing?"

She craned her neck. "You gonna sell 'em?"

I looked down at Julia, with green marker all over her arms, the scab on her knee, her unbraided hair, finishing the coffee in the tin cup. "No," I said, "I'm going to make them into a library."

She giggled, wiggling her toes in the dirt. "A library! Why? For the chickens?"

"No," I said. "For you."

She turned around again to look at the books. "My books?" she said, knitting her heavy eyebrows together. "Okay. My books." She took one down from the stack and began turning its pages. It was a medical textbook, with illustrations of livers and gallbladders. Julia peered closely at the illustrations, tapped them with a finger, tried to see what was under the spine. Had anyone taught her to read? She seemed to be palpating the book.

We sat there together in silence as Julia examined it, leaning against the others, watching the chickens wander through the field of adobe bricks in the morning light. After a while, the adobe crew arrived. Sweet took his leg off and leaned it against the wheelbarrow. Helena brought a paper bag of fresh tortillas, a thermos of coffee and another of hot milk. Xolotl did a sun salutation. Julia did it with him, adding improvisatory movements of her own. We took our places by the adobe pit, reached in, and began our workday. I thought my father would be proud of me if he could see me now, covered in dust and building with my strong, calloused hands.

The library is still there, as far as I know, occupying the small, cool stone building, like a catacomb with its low roof, that had at one time been the ice house, then a fallout shelter, then a shed. I like to think that my little nun had sneaked in there on a hot day, chipped off a piece of ice with a nail, and ran the ice illegally inside her collar, took off her wimple and put the ice against the back of her shorn neck, lifted her heavy skirt and held what was left of the bit of ice, already melting, against the back of a knee. I like to think that that was where she began composing *Ma Vida* in her mind, away from the chores and gossip and entanglements of the other nuns, who were always so busy.

Who will ever know about me? she might have thought, and then felt guilty. A workaday nun like herself, in an unimpressive convent in these unimpressive mountains. The town was no more than a few filthy, patched prospectors' tents then. She would have known that it was terribly arrogant, and possibly a sin, to imagine that her life was of any consequence, but she could write, couldn't she, of how she had come to devote her life to Jesus. How she had seen him in a bucket of water and he had transformed her from a poor, ignorant girl into a teacher, a warrior, a bride. She could draw the sacred images she saw in her mind before falling asleep at night.

The little nun would never have, couldn't have, imagined anyone like me, or that I would be the one to find her book so many years later, nearly lost on the floor of a chicken coop. Or maybe she had. In that, the little nun might have been ahead of me, trusting as she did that her book, like her soul, would be found and saved in a world to come that she couldn't have imagined, either. And that I, the unimaginable man from that unimaginable world, would salvage the book of her life, *Ma Vida*, from the convent's destroyed library; that I would cut, plane, and sand what was left of the busted bookshelves, and then anchor them, with considerable trouble and two smashed fingers, into the old stone walls of the ice house; that I would set *Ma Vida* in alphabetical order among its loftier, waterlogged fellows, covered in chicken shit, that had once explained how the sun went around the earth and how homunculi lived inside each drop of sperm. The little nun couldn't have imagined a girl such as Julia, hesitating in the doorway in her torn Communion veil/tablecloth. Or maybe the little nun never existed, because Julia didn't say anything about sensing such a person; she didn't say much at all, gazing around, one end of the veil clutched in her fist. Or maybe the little nun did exist, and she wasn't surprised to see me blow out the lantern and close the door as the dinner bell rang, just the way she had done, heading down the dirt path with Julia to join the others.

The roof of the chicken coop, née convent library, was a sheet of corrugated tin, and after we built the walls, we all attached it in less than a day, with the help of the rest of Helena's family and sixteen borrowed ladders. The chickens flowed into their spot and settled themselves in the shade. Sweet put his leg back on for the last time, buckled it, and tootled away, the adobe globe spinning on the roof of the adobemobile.

I remember the muddy sweat in my eyes, the smell of the dirt, the worn, pocked surface of the long dining table that had grown silky from use, the murmur of talk at dinner, the scratch of chicken feet on what was left of the chicken coop's stone floor, the half inch that the new, splintery latrine door never fully closed. You had to hold the edge of it with one finger as you squatted in the dark. I remember the lesion, like a strange fungus, that welled up around the lump on my thigh, silvering it. I remember the night my nightmares stopped and the week without dreams that ensued. For seven days straight, I felt empty and full at the same time, like the roaring wind of Ixtlan. Then I dreamed my name.

At dinner one night, Jabalí announced that Julia had dreamed that CNN was coming in a few days. The next morning, I slipped the wings back on. They were light and pliable, as if I'd never taken them off, as if they'd actually grown from my shoulders in the time that I'd been at the ex-convento. They seemed that natural. With a subtle movement, I flapped one. It felt spectacular.

Jabalí adjusted the straps for me, smiling. "These are yours now," he said. "You've earned them." Close though he was to me, nearly chest to chest, I couldn't smell him at all. There were a few new pieces in his hair: a bit of painted bark, a fork with bent tines. Julia playfully pulled at a wing tip. I twitched the wing from her grasp.

"You look tall," she observed, coming around to stand in front of me.

"I am tall."

"Not so much," she said. "But now you look it. Let's go." She hopped around impatiently in her little moth wings.

Jabalí stood back, pleased. "Good. *Pájaro.*"

We all hiked out to the sacred tree. When we climbed up, my branch was empty and strong, but now I was able to balance effortlessly. The wings provided ballast, and though we all sat there for the rest of the day, my legs didn't get tired the way they had before. I wasn't bored, either. From my perch,

I could see our humble church, the road that led to the very small town, the mountain road, Ixtlan, and the steeple of the massive church there, inside of which, I knew, was Jesus in a wig and gold lamé hot pants. The local priest, a middle-aged man with a mustache and a confiding way of speaking, was walking slowly down the road toward our church. He was gesturing as he walked, like a man rehearsing a sermon. His hands waved.

"Jabalí." I pointed with my chin.

Jabalí opened his eyes. "*Hola, Padre!*" he called out in a booming voice through his monkey mask, raising his arm and rattling a branch.

The priest on the road glanced up, around. His hat fell off.

Jabalí laughed. "Probably thinks it's the voice of God." He cupped a hand to his ear. "Can you speak up, please?"

Everyone in the tree laughed, lightly shaking the branches. "Ah, we keep his collection box full," said Jabalí. "That's what he cares about."

On the branch above me, Julia, in pink trousers and a yellow dress with ruffles, sang a song in Spanish. We all got dozy in the afternoon, so we swapped jokes, stories, gossip, cures, and unusual events. Alien sightings. Malcolm X told a funny story about seeing the Northern Lights when she'd been doing hallucinatory breathwork for three days. Toward sunset, when everyone had been quiet for an hour or so, listening to the wind, Julia stood up on her branch, grasping the one above her.

"I know my name," she announced, her toes gripping the branch at her feet, just above my head. I looked up. Her long brownish-blackish hair flew out behind her; her expression was grave.

Jabalí stood up on his branch, too. "Child!" He clambered up to where she was and crouched next to her. "This is a great day. When is the ceremony?"

Julia, stretching in her yellow ruffles between the two

branches as if growing taller on the spot, nodded. "I think . . . in one week plus one day. Stranger and I will have our ceremony together."

My heart opened its petals. I began to cry. "Yes," I said, "yes, that's right, that's how it's supposed to be."

Julia gazed gravely down at me. Her thick eyebrows, buckteeth, perfectly oval face, and knotted hair added up to a melancholy beauty. I suddenly saw exactly how she would look when she was eighty-five and we were all gone. "It is," she said. "This is how it's supposed to be." We left the tree quietly that day, walking back to the ex-convento across the field, tails and fins trailing in the dirt.

We continued our vigil, though after a few more days in the sacred tree, I didn't know if we were still waiting for CNN, or if the tree occupation had morphed into some sort of ongoing ritual, or if some of us were, indeed, waiting while others were engaged in a different project altogether. Helena came and sat under the tree for a while, peeling garlic. It didn't matter what we were doing, because I was so glad to have my wings back and so excited that Julia and I were taking names together. I didn't care if CNN never showed up. Now and then, I reached into my pocket to feel the slip of paper on which I'd written my name. On the fourth day, it came to me that I was supposed to wear the wings all the time, except when I was asleep. Malcolm X, laughing as she rolled me over in her narrow single bed, said that was a phase. You're ready, she said, reaching for me.

I wore the wings to dinner.

I wore the wings to breakfast.

I kept them spotless, pulling out any bugs or twigs or other crap and repairing any tiny breaks with glue and thick white thread, sewing in the evening in my nun's cell the way the nun had probably once sewn in the evening, repairing her habit.

I wore them constantly, except at night, when I hung them on two sturdy iron hooks in my room. I fell asleep looking at them. In the morning, I put them on and unfurled them, flapping them, making a great, gorgeous rush of air.

"Leda me," said Malcolm X as we sat by the river watching the water rush over the Burros, and I did.

Xolotl was a pretty fair barber. Almost as good as Sal. He cut my hair for the naming ceremony. In return, I found five perfect sky-blue eggs, pierced them, softly blew out the contents, and gave them to him to use in one of his mobiles. No one knew what was wrong with Xolotl. He had a crack in him where the demons got in sometimes, but the mobiles, which were extremely complex, seemed to help.

The Alma members left us all their power tools on their way to Amsterdam, and though generally we disdained power tools at the ex-convento—and didn't have enough electricity to run more than one or two at a time—Jabalí allowed that they might come in handy. We gave the Alma emigrants a big sendoff dinner. Two of the trapeze guys sat on either side of me at the long table, each one appreciatively stroking a wingtip. I slept between them, drifting from one to the other, being caught and released all night. *Come with us,* the freckled one said in the morning, pressing a piece of paper with an address into my hand. *No, no,* I said as I kissed them goodbye and brushed feathers out of their hair, *it's too cold in Amsterdam.*

Gabriel, thirty-eight, in the cave. Julia, just visible on his right, is turning her head to look at, or maybe listen for, something.

Julia and I sat on the same low branch in the sacred tree, my large wings and her small ones rustling in the breeze. Everyone else had gone in for dinner, but we dawdled in the late afternoon sun.

"...and then we eat," she finished up. "Helena makes chicken mole."

"That's it?"

"It's fun, you know? Like Christmas. We have presents—Papi will give me a present. Malcolm will give you a present." Julia swung her legs. I was surprised she knew about Malcolm X, but then again, the ex-convento was quite small. None of the old doors had locks. Probably everyone knew everything, including the contents of my knapsack and how often I jacked off. I didn't mind, especially. I had become part of them; I didn't need to keep secrets anymore. It was a relief.

I took a deep breath, surveying the land around us, the roads, the roofs, the mountain. The chickens milled around the coop yard, their feathery bodies soft dots of moving color. The new tin roof shone bright as a sword in the day's last light. "It's pretty here," I said. I squinted at the horizon, trying to see over the mountain and all the way back to New York. See who was in Sarah's old house, in my old apartment. See whether Janos was alone in his, or if someone else was there with him, suitably therapeutized and snug, tripping into the atrium to give the Tweeties a special organic treat. I sighed. My lump ached: phantom old life pain.

"He didn't come here," said Julia. "Not here."

"He didn't?"

"No. You did."

"Why?"

"To meet me. To give me my books." She smiled.

"Have you been reading them?"

"Yes. I read all of them. I'm going to start over tomorrow."

"Okay. Where do you think he went?" It was a bittersweet moment, as these things always are—one era ending, and another, which seemed limitless, just beginning. I flapped my wings, proud of my strength in them. Maybe Julia had dreamed them, too.

Julia frowned. "Stranger, don't ask me that."

A silence fell. Left eye, right eye. Which one was more real? It was a choice you made. If I closed my left eye, the massive church in Ixtlan shifted to the right. If I closed my right eye, the massive church shifted to the left. Unseen, unseeable, was the pendulum arc between the two.

I hesitated, then said, "You know, you're not going to be able to call me that much longer."

Julia giggled, putting a hand over her mouth. "I know!" she said between her fingers. "Ha!"

I remember the day before the naming ceremony. It was dry, hot, and the wind was strong. Whenever the wind stopped blowing, the full force of the sun came down on us like a heavy weight. We were all very chatty in the tree, like kids about to be released from school for summer vacation. We bounced on our branches and ate all the cookies before lunch. It was crowded—a few new pilgrims had turned up at the ex-convento and were learning the ropes.

"Tell," teased Malcolm X from her perch near the top of the tree. "Come on. You can trust us."

"No way." I fingered the piece of paper in my pocket. "It's bad luck."

Julia clambered up a few branches past me and sat down. "We're not telling."

I could feel the particularly pointy length of bark that had become so familiar, but also rather dear, poking at the back of my knee. A breeze ruffled my wings, but my balance was unshakable. I tapped Jabalí's shoulder with my foot. "What's Julia's present going to be?"

"Hmmm," he said noncommittally, as if there wasn't one, but I and everyone else in the tree, except Julia, knew that a tortoiseshell kitten was pouncing around in Jabalí's room on the second floor, with a red ribbon around her neck. Just that morning, Helena had been feeding her bits of tuna and purring at her.

One of the new people, a Chinese-American poet who talked as fast as an auctioneer, said, "So when is CNN coming?"

"When the time is right," said Jabalí. "Listen to the wind."

"Oh," said the poet, clearly confused. She turned gingerly to rest her back against the trunk of the tree, looking uncomfortable in her unwieldy papier-mâché tree-frog hands and feet. Green wasn't a good color for her, either.

I laughed, because explaining the logic of it all was so difficult, and somehow beside the point. Malcolm X playfully winged a twig at my head. That roaring wind, as if it were laughing as well, roared around the tree, rustling the branches and shaking the leaves. Above me, Julia, giggling, stood up on her branch and hopped a hopping dance. I had just opened my mouth to say "Sit down," but it was too late.

The wind of Ixtlan had already taken her. She was already falling.

I reached out for her as she fell past me, grabbing for her shoulder, her hair, her ankle, as her body twisted in the air, the wind turning her head-first toward the ground, her small feet toward the sky. I cried out, opened my wings, and with a great push I flew down after her. My shoulders opened. My arms extended, fingers stretched, the air lifting my chest, my neck. I kicked my feet like a swimmer, pushed down as hard as I could with both my arms. The wind pushed back, lifted me, held me. I hovered. I pushed down hard again, nearly cracking my elbows, diving down through the air, so close to Julia as she fell that I could feel her breath on my face, see her smile at me, certain that I would catch her.

I half closed the fan of my wings to plunge ahead of her. I

reached. She grabbed at one of my wings, smile fading, eyes squinched shut. I almost got her elbow, but she was falling too fast for me, and she hit the ground with a terrible sound. A wind gust carried me up again. I had to fight my way down, pressing my shoulder blades tightly together to make my wings flat and still. I hit the ground hard. Kneeling next to her, I knew that she was dead. Her head was tilted at an unnatural angle in the dirt, and her eyes were open, sightless. The polyester moth wings, light as a kite, were broken underneath her. There was a mosquito bite on her small knee, and at the sight of it I began to cry helplessly. I closed her eyes. I brushed a strand of hair off her forehead.

The tree was making a great noise. "Call 911!" I heard the fast-talking poet say. I couldn't look up. I couldn't bear to see Jabalí's face in his monkey mask as he climbed down from the tree, branch by branch by branch.

We gathered sticks. Young and old, large and small, we wandered through the forest by the river. The adults looked for sticks at least five feet long; the children gathered kindling. Javier, the dark-eyed boy who had chased Julia in her Communion veil, ran back and forth like a sheepdog, urging the other kids forward and tossing the useless twigs out of their hands. I walked with Jabalí, who was pushing a wheelbarrow already filled with long sticks. Overnight, all the air had gone out of him. He'd taken everything out of his hair and tied it into a shapeless gray knot. He wore jeans and a faded green T-shirt and he looked old. The wheelbarrow squeaked as it bumped along over the rough earth. Otherwise, it was completely quiet except for the sounds of our footsteps, the crack of a stick now and then as it was broken in half.

Bending down and standing up again, I gathered my share. You had to learn to look at the ground in a certain way, scanning for good ones. A really good one was two inches in diameter, not much more, free of fungus, relatively unbuggy. You stripped the leaves before tossing it in the wheelbarrow; leaves don't burn well, as Caroline had taught me long ago. Malcolm X kept glancing back. I raised my hand to say it was okay, I had the old man with me.

Ahead of us, everyone from the ex-convento, along with a fair number of people from the one-road town, dotted the forest, and they looked like a crowd of people anywhere: in a bus station, at a movie, at a highway rest stop. They roamed forward, bending down here and there. The local butcher had a wheelbarrow. So did Xolotl. And Helena, walking beside her two tall sons in their soccer jerseys. The fast-talking poet had one. Slowly, the wheelbarrows filled with sticks. When they landed on the pile they made a clacking sound.

Jabalí stopped walking, the wheelbarrow handles in his hands. The squeak stilled. He looked confused. I took the handles from him. "Come on," I said, pushing the wheelbarrow forward. "Come with me."

I remember Julia. That isn't her real name, of course.

We took the sticks we had gathered to a clearing, a flat piece of ground upriver. We set the wheelbarrows down. There were perhaps a dozen old piles of ash in the clearing, each one ever so slightly different from the others: a bit taller, or a bit more scattered, or more dense. Tiny pieces of metal gleamed from some of the piles; in one, the thumb of a mitten was visible; in another, what looked like the corner of a photograph. Otherwise, the piles of ash concealed what lay inside. They were mounds, and on top of each mound was a rock.

How furious he must have been with Marie, I thought, not to build her a house like one of these, but to burn her in her own bed. He didn't look furious now; in fact, he had no expression at all. The face beneath his face seemed to have washed away. Once all the sticks were unloaded from the wheelbarrows, a small group huddled around them, talking softly. The kids waded in the river. Malcolm X took out a pocket knife and cut forks into four green, fairly thick branches, cracking the forks open with her hands and cutting the stem of each branch down until it was about a foot tall. Measuring out a rectangular area with her foot, she stuck a forked stick into each of the four corners of the rectangle, plunging it deep into the sandy riverbank. Another group followed with sticks, and I followed them, taking the sticks they gave back and handing them others. Before too long, they had built a narrow platform by weaving the sticks together. The kids rushed back from the river to shove twigs and dry leaves under the platform, filling the space beneath it. The kids weren't crying, but they weren't laughing and talking in their usual way. They were quiet, but sometimes they pushed and jostled irritably, getting in each other's way, as if it mattered who put which leaf where.

We built a very small house around the platform. It was about four and a half feet tall, two layers thick, and it was composed of sticks pushed as close together as possible to make the walls. The roof was a mix of old newspaper and dry palapa, held down with fist-sized stones. The house wouldn't have held up to so much as a rainstorm, but then again it didn't have to. I felt a tightening in my chest.

Jabalí walked all the way around the house, and then he nodded. Malcolm X glanced at the house and nodded as well.

We walked in a long, straggling line back up to the dining hall. A few of the local women were waiting for us. There was cold soup, bread, and water on the long dining table. We ate in silence. After dinner, we all walked into the main church with them and sat in the pews. The local women sang. I watched the candles burn.

Two days passed. Julia lay in the stone library that had once been an ice house, because it still stayed cool there, set far back in shade. For the moment, it didn't just look like a catacomb; it was one. During those two days, we fasted and meditated. Jabalí gathered Julia's things. I lay on my bed. Even now, the nodule on the inside of my left thigh didn't hurt. I wished it would. Malcolm X and I sat together in the courtyard. My wings hung on their hooks, empty. The space between them was enormous. On the second night, I pulled my old laundry bag out from under the bed. It smelled like East Seventh Street. I emptied it onto the bedspread and counted the money.

I dreamed about Julia. I still do. It is always the same dream: she is coming down to meet me at the gate with the blue flowers twined around it. Her feet are bare, but her hair is neatly twisted in little braids all over her head, each one banded with a small white bow. She is holding the burned clay figure of the man in her hand, and she is smiling.

I remember the fire. We carried her down to the riverbank in the middle of the night. The timing wasn't ritual, it was practical: the authorities in the area were willing to look the other way if we had these ceremonies at night, when someone might see a fire from the road, but no tourists would be walking by the river. In three days, Jabalí had shrunk and hardened, like a scar. Xolotl had shorn his hair, leaving an inch of gray stubble. He was exceptionally clean, having scrubbed himself from head to toe. It made my heart ache to look at him. He carried one corner of the shape wrapped in a white sheet; Malcolm X, Javier, and I carried the other three. Javier held his corner tightly with one hand; in his other hand he held a bell. Everyone else walked behind, carrying long, slender lit candles.

When we reached the flat place by the river, we set her down in her house. Gently, Jabalí unfolded the white sheet just to her shoulders. Her young face was regal in repose, like the face of Nefertiti. One by one, people came forward. Helena brought her a tattered doll. Xolotl set a watercolor of the cave near her small hand. In the watercolor, the cave was verdant, with a homey glow inside. Malcolm X brought eggshells and salt. Jabalí ranged many things around his daughter: her dresses and skirts, a book she had liked, the objects he had cut from his hair, driftwood, a picture of a jumping horse from a magazine. The kids from town, arrayed in suits and dresses with scrubbed faces and smooth hair, brought little notes that they had written and rolled into scrolls, carefully tapping each scroll into the interstices of her bier. One little girl whispered something in Julia's perfect, still ear. I came forward. I put the scrap of paper with my name on it near the subtle white shape of her hand. Underneath her, with the dry leaves and the scrolls from the children, I stuffed all the money, working it into the kindling. And very far back, nearly at the edge of the house, deep in a nest of leaves and paper, I tucked my father's radio. At her feet I put one of the books from the library, a lavishly illustrated one about the universe. I stepped back to join the others.

Xolotl and Jabalí came forward with coffee cans half full of gasoline, and they doused the little stick house with it, sparely and precisely. Javier, who was crying, rang the bell. We each came forward and touched our candles to the house. Of all the things I was asked to do there, carrying that candle two feet and touching it to the stick was by far the most arduous. I didn't think I would survive it. Soon the blaze was unimaginably hot, it smelled, and we had to move far away from it. We clustered by the river. Julia changed from what she had been to something else that rose into the air.

No one went back to the tree. If it hadn't been sacred before, it was now. It remained bare, unpeopled. The fast-talking poet and her friends put on their big backpacks and left, stuffing the donation box with money as they went. All the tree-folk costumes went flat, tangled up in a heap in the storeroom: beaks and frog legs and the squirrel tail and my wings, resting folded in the corner.

Any but the most basic tasks of food preparation and trash disposal were suspended. There was no building, no hauling, no digging, no fucking, no washing, no inventing, no sawing, no arguing. Instead, the ex-convento took on a peculiar, desultory air. For the first time, it looked like the poor place that it was. Julia's tortoiseshell kitten pounced unnoticed around the courtyard, fattening on mice, its red ribbon slowly shredding to string.

We drifted through the days. The smell of smoke clung to our clothes, our hair, our skin. Malcolm X sat in the courtyard, drawing charcoal pictures of Julia from memory. Xolotl wandered through the fields with the stray dogs, pulling at his fingers. Jabalí shut himself up in his room on the second floor of the ex-convento. His light stayed on at night; people brought him food, took away the half-empty plates. The mustached priest visited, and stayed for hours. Helena ceaselessly washed dishes and did laundry until every sheet and dish in the place was scoured. The chickens wouldn't lay. On a Thursday afternoon, a CNN truck pulled up to the church's iron gate. Helena, a dishtowel over her shoulder, sent it away. We have no tree like that here, she told them. Try Tlacochahuaya.

After breakfast one morning, I loaded up a knapsack with water and food. Keeping the river on my right, I followed the path past the Burros and up along the ridge until it thinned and tangled, then opened again into the dense terrain of the ferns. I waded in. I closed my eyes. I listened. Far off to my left, the sound of the wind shifted ever so slightly, tuned to an infinitesimally lower pitch. I also heard a faint twitter, a rustle. Keeping my eyes closed, I turned toward those small sounds and walked very slowly, pushing aside the ferns with both hands for what seemed like too long. I must have missed it. Then, suddenly, I stumbled into the clearing.

I opened my eyes. A few yards in front of me was the cave, dull and dark. There was no bicycle wheel today, but several branches had fallen into the clearing. I picked them up and threw them into the ferns. The striped lizard with the long yellow tail watched me from his rock at the mouth of the cave as I sat down by the dead fire pit and drank some water, ate a sandwich. I tried to feel something as I sat there, but all I felt was more or less sated and that the breeze was pleasant on my neck.

Since Julia's death I had become a box with nothing inside. I had one clear thought rattling around like a pebble in that box: it should have been me, and I didn't understand why it wasn't. I had some hazy idea that if I went into the cave, the echoes would talk to me, or a face would appear in the mirror, or the pattern of the bones would be legible as a sign, or I'd have a prophetic dream. Wasn't that what happened to people in caves? And, all right, I was angry. I was furious. Because Julia shouldn't have spent so much time up here. Something terrible was bound to happen. So I was also daring the gods, in my own way. Go ahead. Do your worst.

Squaring my shoulders, I went into the cave. It was just as it had been: the gloom; the foxed, scorched mirror; the burnt figures in their diorama; the bones in the corner; the lantern, which, as usual, had fallen over. I righted it. I didn't like it in there any better than I ever had. But Julia had had duties here, and the least I could do was to carry them out for her.

What was the song she sang? I remembered part of the tune and hummed it as I proceeded around the cave. I knelt down by the diorama and moved the clay figures around the shoebox on the ground in what I hoped approximated what Julia had done, then put them back in their original places. I scuffed dirt over a few animal turds. I stared into the mirror until my features didn't look like my own anymore. The flowers on top of the ashes and bits of bone were dried and brown, so I went outside and gathered an armful of ferns and flowers and scattered them over the traces of the body in the busted box. Since the first time I had been in this place, the bones had receded a bit farther into the dirt; the shape of the figure was blurrier. My anger and bravado drained away. My fury flattened. I put my hands over my face in the way I had seen Julia do it. I lowered my hands. I sang what I could remember of her song, then made up the rest. I stood there, bored, restless, and not a little creeped out. But I stood by the bones of a dead woman I'd never known and didn't like, and did the things we must do for the dead.

I finished the song for Julia's mother. The bones in the box remained exactly the same — mute, smooth, and cold. Water dripped in the back of the cave. I put my hands over my face, concentrating. I lowered my hands. I began, uncertainly, "He was born."

The cave was silent.

"He was born and he was a running man." I found a tune.

The cave was silent.

"He was born and he was a running man and he made a house."

The cave was silent, and it remained silent as I sang the rest, finishing, quaveringly, on "Amen."

The cave was silent. Water dripped in the back. The barely visible figure in the busted box didn't move. And yet. I was held there. It wasn't time to go.

I put my hands over my face and concentrated. I lowered my hands. I didn't want to do it, not at all, but the thing in my chest was immovable. I would be tethered there forever if I didn't, a permanent fixture in the cave's gloom, half shade, half mortal. The nodule inside my left thigh began to ache. That was a sign. So, reluctantly, I began.

"She was born."

Silence.

"She was born and she was a strange child." Even under these circumstances, I refused to say "indigo."

Silence.

I continued. "She was born and she was a strange child and she climbed a tree." I sang, and I went on singing, louder and louder, sweating in the cool of the damp cave, jumping up and down in place a little, inventing a few things here and there that were probably true, even if I didn't know them for a fact. "And she fell," I finished. "And she fell. And she fell. I could not catch her."

I stopped singing.

I listened. The cave was quiet in the way that a natural place is quiet: not dead silent, but inflected with the buzzings and whirrings of bugs, bird noises, the rustle of the ferns, the tap of some creature on wood (a woodpecker?), a drip drip far back in the cave, and the faint murmur of the river in the distance. It was cool where I was. It smelled like old water and older dirt, like nutmeg, like ash.

My left thigh really hurt. I put my hand on it; the silvered lump moved when I touched it, rolling painfully, hard under my skin. Above me, the roof of the cave was dark, and it seemed to extend upward limitlessly and unpredictably. I looked up into the darkness. If the cave was a clock, I was one minute on that clock, but I was every part of that minute, and the shadow of the minute, and the echo of the minute, the anticipation and the memory of the minute. In that minute, I existed. I could feel my blood pounding in my ears, my feet in the dirt. I could feel the breath entering and leaving my lungs. The taste of coffee, of water. The beat of my heart. Arms and legs. Hands and feet. Curve of spine. The powerful ache in my thigh. My empty shoulder blades.

But I was still tethered by the immovable thing. I squatted in the dirt, thinking *lightness lightness lightness*. There was a whirling in my head and then suddenly I was so hot—the heat began at the base of my spine and rose to my ears, the tip of my nose, flamed my eyes. I was growing hard and at the same time I thought I might shit; my heels pushed down into the ground; my bowels twisted. The whirling moved down into my chest, spun my heart. I pulled my shirt off, mopped my sweating face with it. The lump on my thigh was searing, and that pain, or something, was making me harder. But the hardness was strange to me, and I didn't entirely like it. I couldn't see what was arousing me, and I didn't know if that was what this was, or if the wind was having a joke on me, playing with me, pulling at me. I pushed myself down, futilely, then kept my hand there. My ears burned. My left hand burned. I thought of that man, the first one, so many years ago in the bus station in Fort Lauderdale. His exophthalmic eyes, his gold wedding ring flashing, the seam he opened in me that day, letting me out, letting something else in.

I came and my thigh opened. The pain was terrible, but it was also a relief. I made a sound, touched my thigh. The shell was quite thick, bright white, slick with a light smear of blood; I gave my thigh a gentle push, then a firmer one, to release the egg. I caught it, warm and wet, in my other hand. It was about the size of a robin's egg. How can I describe what I felt? A nearly unbearable tenderness suffused me as I held the small egg in my hand, a weeping that began far within me before I began to sob, and then a joy: how fragile it was. How extraordinary. How unspeakable. No one would ever know, and no one would believe me anyway. But there, in that place, I held the miraculous thing in my hands, cradled its delicate warmth. My thigh was bleeding where it had split; with one hand, I pulled my shirt around it and managed to tie a bad knot.

I lay a fingertip on the smooth, slick shell of the little egg. The whirling in my head stopped. The immovable thing, the invisible tether, had released. On the bones of my shoulders were veins and muscles and skin, but nothing else. I knew that there wouldn't be anything else, ever. My left hand was cool; the heat in the rest of my body was gone as well. My dick was soft. The gods were done with me. I had changed back.

I limped over and looked in the half-melted spotty mirror again. There was no one in there but me: an ordinary man standing in the dirt, wingless, a bloody rag around his thigh. *Gabriel, now.* That minute gave way to the next, and the next.

I walked out of the cave into the sunlight, and gently set the egg amid the ferns.

6

The Sunburst and the Moonglow

WHEN DID I FIRST stumble into the wrong grove? Is that even the right question?

My mother shuffled the cards. Arthritis had crimped the ends of her fingers, but she was still fast. Slap, slap, slap. She dealt us each a hand. We were sitting by the pool at the Moonglow, the motel she owned down the road from the Sunburst. Mostly, she lived in the Moonglow now. I liked it there. In addition to the pool, it had a view of the beach. We could watch the waves. On the concrete deck, the air smelled of salt and chlorine together. The tortoiseshell kitten, leggy and nearly grown, sat on the white aluminum table between us, batting frantically at the cards.

"Watch, Gabe," my mother said. "See? That's what we call an echo." She smiled, pleased. In her old age, she didn't waste any movements or play extra cards. She ate one grapefruit for breakfast each morning, smoked one cigarette every day. She was slim and brown. Her gaze was quick.

"Let me see that again."

She slapped down two cards.

"Ma, listen."

She gathered her cards gracefully back to her hand in a small, sharp fan. "What?"

"Dad—"

She made a face. Then her face softened. For just an instant, I could see the woman she had been then: the tender, barefoot one with long, flowing red hair, pouring food coloring over ice and listening to her old Bob Dylan records while her husband spent hours making guitars that no one would ever play. She folded her fan. Her face resettled into its present form. "You know, Gabe, I like to think that he went to sea. Men used to be able to do that. They went to sea, and women waited behind and looked out to sea from the widow's walk. Sometimes the men didn't come back, and the women never knew. Was it a sea monster? A siren? Pirates? Were they kings in other countries, or slaves? It was terrible not to know, but it was also a blessing, because you were free to imagine all sorts of fates for them. So." She gestured in the direction of the ocean. "He's out there somewhere. I think it was a siren, but . . ." She shrugged.

I took my mother's hand and smiled at her. She picked up my hand and kissed it. "My turn, Gabe. You aren't the same. Where have you been, my blue-eyed son?"

I set my cards down. I nodded. I told her the story of all my transformations, beginning with my time in the city and everything that had happened to me there, and the lazy lion that was following me, and the strangers I had met, and the peculiar and magical people of Ixtlan.

She lit up a second, excess cigarette as I talked.

But wait, I said, because I was still her son, after all, remember the house in Bishop, and all of it, and the magnificent City—

My mother sat back. She looked at the sea, then at her small, spotted, slender hands on the aluminum table. Then she told me her story, and she built the City again in the air between us, and it was both the same as and different from the City I thought I knew. She leaned two cards together, balanced a third on top of it. It was like this, she said, protecting the structure from the wind with her hands.

7

The City

You RETURN, CHANGED—yourself, and something else as well.

If you take the F train from the leafy parts of Brooklyn to Manhattan, there are perhaps fifteen or so thrilling minutes when the train runs on elevated tracks, and the city is ranged before you on the other side of the river: gleaming, silver, the buildings tall and close-set. Then you dip down into the tunnel, into black, and when you emerge from the train onto the street, the buildings aren't silver but brown and red and white and many other colors, and they are lower and less compressed and dirtier than they looked from the windows of the train. You can see people going in and out of them. You can see what sorts of businesses are there. You can see the way the light changes as it touches the various surfaces: stone, wood, brick, glass.

I work at the New York Public Library. I am in charge of something: I am turning all the records of the dead in New York City into a vast, illustrated digital archive. Every morning, I walk between the stone lions at the library entrance, ascend the marble staircase, and turn to my chosen labor. I keep my mother's old Ovid, its blue spine nearly crumbled away on a shelf above my desk. Boxes arrive every day, full of yellowing paper records, mysteriously stained and oddly torn; often, years are missing from the boxes. We search for those years. Young people with fanciful hair and inscrutable tattoos feed the yellowed paper into scanners; slightly older, crankier people set up the digital files; I sculpt and tend the immaterial vaults of information that the files become, sorting and moving and arranging the dead, building a city out of light for them, who have also become light. I am making another New York, a weightless New York, for them. In that New York, they are remembered forever. They walk the streets, laugh, quarrel, fall in love. They are my book of changes, a book that never ends.

I am happy. I am going a bit gray. Janos is even grayer. Sarah and I stay in touch. The tortoiseshell cat spends her days sleeping in the window, dreaming of the birds she can sometimes still catch in the garden. My lazy lion hasn't padded away, and from time to time he wakes up and claws me, perhaps to remind me that he's untamed. Like the tortoiseshell cat, the lion likes to prove that he is still in full possession of his prowess. Indeed, we respect it. We can smell the lion, and the lion can smell us, whether we're just waking up, or walking on the Promenade, or eating in a restaurant. You might see two men, nicely dressed, one slightly grayer than the other, one heading toward round, both ordering well. We see the lion, for the moment sleeping at our feet under the table, his mighty head on his paws. My ears don't ring anymore; instead, I constantly hear, though faintly, as if from far away, a tympanic, windy sound.

On that same train from Brooklyn to Manhattan, and on others as well, I often look up to see Miranda, Leah, Natasha, and Anna smiling down at the passengers from their cardboard stars, still aloft, still victorious, fresh from their latest lingerie-tearing ordeal. Sometimes I idly do the math in my head as the train moves under the river, and I know that it's barely possible that Fleur is still alive, even less possible that she's writing the books. And yet there she is, reigning over every train in the city, the constellation of her muses fixed between ads for podiatrists and fragments of great poetry. If those muses were to look back at me, they would see the ordinary, interesting face of a man on the train, not quite old and not quite young, almost handsome, gray at his temples, opening his briefcase to look over the list of names of the dead. We wouldn't recognize one another, though we were all so close once.

If it's a nice day, at lunch I walk over to Grand Central to buy a fancy sandwich from one of the fancy stalls that line the upper concourse, and as I head back across the central hall to Vanderbilt Avenue with my white plastic bag, I look up. High above my head, shining in the deep blue, is the map of the heavens that ornaments the lofty aqua arch of the ceiling, each constellation in its place. And above them somewhere, watching the sky below, are the gods, who had their way with me, and sent me back.

And, as you may know, when the hero comes back from the underworld, he has to bring something with him. Tortoiseshell cats don't count. So I bring you my story. I tell you all my secrets. I show you all my gods and goddesses, shining like paste jewelry in shoeboxes. My City. A house on Pineapple Street with windows like sails, a little girl with brownish-blackish hair standing at one of those windows like a grave captain at the prow of a ship. The silver flowers and rhinestone stars on the street. You've seen me around, maybe on the train, or walking along by the river, or maybe we'll meet when I carefully set you in your place in my city made of light. Or maybe we won't meet at all. Or maybe we're about to brush past each other in

Grand Central, under Orion or Cassiopeia, maybe our sleeves will touch and you'll catch a glimpse of my profile, my ordinary face, the dark shape of the bird in flight on my hand, as I disappear into the crowd. Maybe, for a long or a short time after, you'll remember me.